CRAZY

Woman

CREEK

CRAZY

Woman

CREEK

To Emerald: Dream big. Write from your heart.
Just do it.

and,

To the precious people of Buffalo, Wyoming:
Thank you for letting me wander all over your
charming little town. Thank you for letting me sleep
at the super cool Occidental Hotel where the
cowboys in the saloon downstairs kept me up all
night singing under a bullet-riddled ceiling. I loved
every minute.

ISBN - 978-0-9888739-2-6
E-Book ISBN - 978-0-9888739-3-3
Crazy Woman Creek

Published by Virginia Hull Welch, 2013
www.virginiahullwelch.com

Cover design by Piret Mänd

i

Other books by Virginia Hull Welch:

The Lesson
Inspirational Romantic Comedy
Based on a True Story

What to Do When the Blessings Stop
When God Sends Famine

Contents

Chapter One

Buffalo, Wyoming Territory, March 22, 1880

"James is missing, Sheriff Morris."

Lenora Rose stood primly across from the desk, her grim face belying how flabbergasted she was as she watched Cyrus Morris stop fiddling with his pocket knife, look up and stare a few seconds at the impeccably dressed young woman, and then wordlessly drag his worn leather boots from his desk to the floor with an irreverent thud. With no attempt at discretion, he looked her over from her frilly hat to flounced-topped toe, screwed up the corner of his mouth in disdain, and leaned to one side to direct his comment not to her but to his counterpart across the room.

"Luke, get the lady a chair," he said, still sizing up Lenora.

The deputy nodded and in a moment set a hard-back chair in front of her. "Ma'am," he said, nodding politely.

Lenora registered only a tall blur of denim, leather, and faded cotton before the younger man returned to stand behind his desk.

"Have a seat Mrs. Rose," said Sheriff Morris.

The sheriff's order was bland enough, but his tone of weary resignation, as if he were greatly put upon, having to chase down and drag home runaway husbands several times a week, made Lenora woozy. His contempt for the fairer sex was well known throughout the Territory, but Lenora hadn't expected crass. This was going to be more difficult than she had thought, but she needed his help so she sat down, creating as she did a waterfall of chocolate velvet billows that spilled around the chair and across the floor. Now that two pairs of eyes were trained on her, she was glad she had taken the time to steam press her best winter dress, which had been stored in the oversized trunk she had brought from New York. Her life might be falling apart, but at least she looked presentable. Then again, the clothes-as-confidence tactic that normally sustained her suddenly made her feel terribly conspicuous in this citadel of guns and tobacco. She clutched her matching beaded reticule more tightly to calm her hammering heart.

"Mrs. Rose," said the sheriff, sounding bored and motioning toward the deputy while rummaging noisily in his desk drawer, "this is Deputy Luke

Davies." Sheriff Morris pulled a sheet of paper and a fountain pen from the drawer. "He's new."

Lenora turned toward the deputy. "How do you do?" she said, expecting no reply. She did not recognize the deputy from around the Territory. But she did remember that James had told her months back that Buffalo was preparing to hire a second lawman sometime this year. The sheriff's office had been enlarged for his coming; the sweet fragrance of fresh lumber met Lenora's nose the moment she stepped into the sparsely furnished room. She smiled a half-smile. Deputy Davies nodded politely a second time, made a semblance of a smile, and sat down.

Just then a moisture bubble inside a piece of wood hissed sharply through the door of the wood stove next to the sheriff's desk. Someone had recently put coffee on to boil. The gray speckled graniteware was beginning to make inviting little percolating sounds.

"Now, Mrs. Rose, what do you mean by 'missing'?" Sheriff Morris leaned back in his chair with his arms across his chest.

Lenora was taken aback by the barely veiled skepticism that undergirded the sheriff's inquiry. Missing meant missing. It wasn't as if she was too simple minded to interpret the seriousness of the events of the last forty-eight hours. Bizarrely, as she was thinking this she noted a brass cuspidor to the side of the sheriff's desk. She was glad she was seated at an angle that prevented a view of its odious contents. Her stomach was queasy enough without having to avert her eyes from an open bucket of spit.

"I mean he didn't come home. All night. He left the ranch on Saturday evening on horseback. I thought he'd be back by the time I put out the lamp, or perhaps by morning, but he never arrived."

"So you think something has happened to him, huh?" said the sheriff. He picked up the fountain pen and began making squiggly marks on the sheet of paper.

Lenora glanced at his work. Doodling. The man was doodling. "I think it's possible." Wasn't that a logical conclusion?

"Did you ask around to your neighbors?"

"No. I thought—"

"Was he drunk?" Sheriff Morris leaned forward a bit, elbows on his desk, his large, rough fingers resting under a ragged gray mustache. He stared into Lenora's eyes as if his glare alone would root out the truth.

Lenora shrunk back a little in her chair. "You know James never imbibes." Sheriff Morris' insinuation stung, but Lenora wouldn't allow herself to dissolve into a sloppy mess of nose-blowing, handkerchief-dabbing weeping womanhood. If she did, she surely she would irritate Sheriff Morris more than she already had. He was her only hope. She willed herself to stay calm.

"Where did he say he was going?"

4

"My husband chose not to reveal that information to me." The facts, just the bare facts.

"You mean to tell me that he jumped on his horse and rode away, in the damned dark, without giving you any idea where he was headed?"

Sheriff Morris' irritation fouled the air like an unpleasant body odor at a social gathering, unsettling Lenora despite her rehearsals on the long wagon ride to town meant to help her keep her poise. Hastily she unbuttoned the pearl clasp on her glove and reached into her bag for a handkerchief. She dabbed her eyes quickly and discreetly, hoping to draw little attention to her increasing distress; but of course, it was too late for that now.

And as if her lack of composure were not bad enough, there was the problem of the deputy, whose presence only served to heighten her humiliation. The law office was too cramped to allow privacy. She could not see him, but she could feel him still watching her, his eyes following her as continuously as her own shadow since she had stepped through the door, observing her every movement, absorbing her every tortured word.

Between the two lawmen, Lenora felt as though she were on the witness stand and had just delivered damning testimony about James' disappearance to a jury of her peers. One of them, to be sure, had already cast his vote to throw her in the hoosegow at best or condemn her to the gallows at worst. How the other would vote she was not sure. Nevertheless, she felt an absurd compulsion to trace her fingers around her throat to assure herself that her neck was still free of anything more constricting than her collar. Finding only the familiar ruffle of white lace she had sewn herself, she stiffened her back and continued with renewed spirit.

"A husband is under no obligation to reveal to his wife all his business," she said, searching for a timeworn route to reason the sheriff could understand. "My husband is not just my husband, Sheriff Morris. He's my friend. But even I don't know what he was thinking when he left Saturday night."

"Did he take food and water with him?

"He left in haste. He packed no provisions."

"Was he armed?"

"He left his Sharps behind."

"No rifle? He went out at night unarmed?"

"He may have taken his revolver. I didn't think to check the house for it."

Sheriff Morris glared at Lenora a few seconds. "Sounds like he was in a real bad hurry." Then he halted his questions and stared at Lenora, dissecting her story with his eyes.

The coffee pot rattled. Deputy Davies' chair scraped the wood floor behind her. He walked to the stove and wordlessly grabbed a flour sack towel from where it hung on a nail and used it to push the coffee pot to a cooler part of the stove top. Like nearly all men she'd seen in the Territory, he was fit from a life of physical work, but he was much taller and broader than James. Lenora noted, somewhat absently, that he had lots of wavy brown hair, spare facial whiskers, and wore no wedding ring. Without a doubt a lot of girlish hearts had set to fluttering and swooning around Buffalo when Deputy Davies first rode into town.

She shook herself. How could she notice such things about another man considering the grave business that had brought her to town? The strain of James' disappearance was making her as mad as a March hare.

Deputy Davies returned to his chair, out of Lenora's sight. No one seemed interested in coffee right now.

"Sheriff Morris," she said finally to break the impasse, "It's not like James to run off and leave me for two days."

"Oh? How long is he usually gone for?"

Lenora blanched. "Sir, you misunderstand—"

"No, Mrs. Rose. I understand real well. James got himself worked into a pother over God-knows-what you did or said and took off on his horse."

Lenora fingered her handkerchief trying to find a dry spot to wipe her eyes. She felt attacked. She felt naked, utterly stripped of the cloak that concealed her private thoughts. How could Sheriff Morris so keenly assess the situation she had brought to his door? She felt as if this evil man had peered into the darkest part of her mind; worse, he had put his finger inside and touched her there. She wanted nothing more than to finish this dreadful questioning business, obtain a promise of a search party, and run out of his office to the safety and privacy of the ranch.

"Or else," continued the sheriff, in a wicked tone befitting this twisted seek-and-find, "he's found more comfort at Lydia's place than at home."

Sheriff Morris' reference to the brothel above the Buffalo Belles Saloon was outrageous to be sure, but it confirmed to Lenora that she had lost control of this interrogation; it was useless to spar.

"I'm worried something unfortunate has befallen him." Speaking aloud her fear made it spring to life. Lenora could no longer hold back the sobs. She covered her face with her handkerchief and gulped for air. "Perhaps," she said, gasping for breath, "most husbands withhold parts of their lives from their wives, but my James does not. I trust him, and he trusts me."

Sheriff Morris snorted.

How dare he! Something in Lenora's heart shifted. She must fight for James. He was missing, possibly injured or dead, and this, this infuriating man wasn't taking her seriously. In short order the tears stopped as anger fed by humiliation trumped fear. Rage began to bubble quietly from her core, like a hot spring deep within the earth. If she didn't get away from this vile man soon she would burst forth with a steaming geyser of scalding retorts. She must not let that happen. James' life was at stake. This was about him not her.

"What did you do, Mrs. Rose, to make your husband run off and abandon you?"

Before Lenora could form a response, the deputy moved suddenly in his chair, as if he were about to stand up, thought better of it, and sat down again. She avoided looking in his direction. She felt less visible if she didn't make eye contact. No doubt the deputy was too enthralled with her salacious drama to do anything but listen. Just think of the gossip that would spice up every supper table around Buffalo this evening. The delicious story of James and Lenora Rose would be spooned up just after the onion soup but before the tea and custard. Yes, she was certain that the scandal of her life would be the main dish in every dining room in town. Well, she didn't care. If that's what she must suffer in order to find her missing husband and bring him home again, so be it.

Through the thin office walls the clatter of a team of horses pulling a loaded wagon over frozen mud interrupted the interrogation. "Whoa!" shouted the driver, then the muffled thump of a man jumping to the ground and the snorting and pawing of large animals.

Lenora used the brief interruption to compose herself. "My husband did not run off and leave me," she said, "I didn't do anything." That was true. "It was after supper." Also true. Then what? How to say it? "After we had finished eating, instead of going out to the porch with his pipe, as he always does, he got up and left. That's all. He left and

9

hasn't returned." Lenora had said enough, and though not a fully developed picture of the events of that night, it was all true. She fervently hoped that Sheriff Morris would see she was telling the truth, end his stupid questions, and immediately form a search party.

"Mrs. Rose," the sheriff finally said, standing up, signaling an end to their meeting, "Your husband is a solid citizen, a churchgoing man, and a smart rancher."

Lenora nodded, grateful for the softened tone in the sheriff's voice, though she was guarded. She did not know how to read this man, which badly upset her apple wagon.

"Everyone in this town will speak of his honesty and trustworthiness in business and whatever else he's involved in. James Rose is a good man."

Lenora nodded again and stood up as well. Surely his words of praise meant something positive. Off to the side she heard the deputy politely stand up in anticipation of her exit.

"James Rose," the sheriff continued, leaning forward on the desk with both hands so that Lenora got a better look at his tobacco-stained whiskers, "is also the biggest hothead in all of Wyoming Territory."

Lenora gaped. James had a temper. But that didn't mean he was hateful enough to abandon in a moment of passion his wife, his ranch, and the herd they'd worked so hard to build. James loved her.

Even with his hot temper, he was a faithful husband who took care of his wife. His love was stronger than his anger was hot.

Wasn't it?

"I'd wager a week's pay that your husband is off somewhere, waiting it out, hoping to put the fear of the Almighty in you. Probably thinks you've learned your lesson. Probably headed toward your place right now."

What an outrageous excuse for a sheriff!

"Nevertheless," he said, standing straight again, "if it makes you feel better, I'll get some volunteers together and have them search the area around your ranch."

If it makes me feel better? This man was impossible.

"Thank you again, Sheriff Morris," said Lenora, extending her hand and smiling demurely.

"I'll send one of the men to your ranch if we have any news."

She thanked him again and somehow managed to add, "Good day." She had gotten what she had come for, but ooh she was mad. Now she must flee this upsetting office, she must get outside into the brisk, head-clearing spring air, away from these arrogant lawmen while her eyes were still dry and while she still held the reins on her tongue. She turned to say something polite to the deputy but was so close to tears that all she could manage was a brief nod. Then she turned abruptly toward the street, and with a fetching swish of her voluminous petticoats, was out the door.

#

"Silly woman," muttered the sheriff as the door clicked shut. Having taken no notes for the investigation, he sat down again and returned the paper and fountain pen to the drawer. When he looked up, he saw his deputy, who was still standing motionless behind his desk as he had been when Lenora made her brisk adieu.

Deputy Davies stared, eyes transfixed either by his own imaginings or by whatever captivated his attention on the other side of the windows that flanked the office door—or both.

"Whatcha looking at? I was polite," said the sheriff, his tone brittle with mock defense.

Deputy Davies broke from his concentration then and turned to Sheriff Morris, who was reaching into his shirt pocket for his tobacco pouch.

"Polite?"

"For the lady," said the sheriff, pulling on the pouch string. "It was the nicest thing I could think to say about that struttin' rooster she married. Crowing all the time."

"James Rose is dead," said the deputy. He looked back to the window, choosing to ignore the sheriff's rant. Only two days sharing office quarters with the veteran lawman, and already Luke knew that it was best not to blow more air on the fire when Cyrus got to pumping his bellows.

"What makes you so sure?"

"Not sure, just figuring."

"How's that?"

"No man in his right mind goes off and leaves a woman who looks like that all alone to fend for herself. James Rose is dead."

"If you insist," said the sheriff, fingering a few shreds of tobacco.

"If he isn't dead, he's addle brained beyond redemption or blind. Of the three, I say—dead."

"You haven't seen James Rose blow his mouth to kingdom come when he's convinced some fella from one of the big ranches has rustled one of his steers." Sheriff Morris stuffed a wad of the fragrant chewing tobacco in his cheek, pulled the drawstring closed, and slipped it back into his pocket.

"Don't need to," drawled Deputy Davies in his thoughtful Tennessean way while reaching for his hat and overcoat and starting for the door. "I've seen Mrs. Rose."

"Where ya headed?" said the sheriff.

"Out," said Deputy Davies as he ducked his head to keep from banging his noggin on the door frame. "I have more questions for Mrs. Rose."

Chapter Two

Luke swept his eyes up and down Main Street, searching for the lovely Mrs. Rose while he pulled his gloves from his pocket. Spring ignored the calendar this year, choosing to come on its own schedule. Consequently everyone in Buffalo had rolled into town to purchase necessities before the next blizzard shuttered businesses and scattered shoppers to their isolated ranches. The air glistened as rays of icy sunshine made the day brilliant but still bitterly cold. The heavens overhead were cloudless, endless, and sparkling blue, surveyed only by the Big Horn Mountains to the South.

A cloudless sky, Luke knew, meant the temperature would drop cruelly when the sun started to set; Mrs. Rose would not dawdle in town. She would hurry to finish her other business, if she had any, and rush back to her ranch before sundown. And as sure as he was born and raised a ranching man, Luke knew also that, dolled up as she was in such frippery, Mrs. Rose had not come to town on horseback.

Not finding Lenora on the street, Luke turned right to walk the two blocks to Olathe's Feed and Livery Stable, the logical destination for a visitor who arrived in town by any kind of horse-pulled rig. As his boots clunked along the boardwalk in a southerly direction, his mind worked methodically, sorting Mrs. Rose's responses to Cyrus' rude inquiries.

Cyrus was a bully, but his bullying had gotten the information he wanted from Mrs. Rose. Cyrus was first and foremost a lawman, always rough, aggressively thorough, and even crude at times, but a lawman with a reputation for bringing 'em in.

And a woman's tears didn't always stem from sorrow. Mrs. Rose could be a first-rate actress. It wouldn't be the first time a lawman had been bamboozled by a pretty face. Yet it irked him that Cyrus had been so hard on her. She was so young. Clearly she was upset over her husband's disappearance, and in his gut, Luke doubted that her worry was feigned. But why did she wait two days to come to town with her report? She was hiding something for sure. But what?

Luke's musings over Mrs. Rose were not solely the result of a trained analytical mind unwinding the threads of a tightly wound story. Her hair. His thoughts kept returning to that thick bundle, the color of rich coffee, pulled into a perfect bun at the nape of her neck and festooned, feminine-like, with a gossamer net of crocheted silk under that fashionable, velvety hat. In all his twenty-six years, Luke had never seen a woman dressed so elegantly, except in Ma's Godey's Ladies Book, but that was so long ago his memory of those gauzy fashion plates had dimmed, rendering them more angelic than mortal.

That was Mrs. Rose. A living, breathing illustration stepped out of the pages of Godey's, as foreign to the rough environment of the Territory as an angel. How long was her hair? Surely to her waist or longer. No woman in Buffalo or Fort Laramie dressed or carried herself with the grace of the alluring Mrs. Rose. She was pretty, but Buffalo had its share of pretty women. Mrs. Rose had something more.

He would ponder what that more was later.

#

The air inside Olathe's livery stable was musty with barn odors. Clouds of grain dust swirled lazily where shafts of sunlight sliced through the few high windows and near the wide, double-door entrance. Horses munched noisily in their stalls, oblivious to their visitor. Luke paused inside the doorway to allow his eyes to adjust to the dimness. Olathe was talking to someone at the far end of the stable.

"Deputy Davies," Olathe called out. "Morning. What can I do for you today?" Olathe stood up from where he had been squatting on the barn floor, partially underneath Mrs. Rose's one horse, checking to see if the quarter strap was secure.

Lenora was seated in the buckboard, draped in the emerald-green cloak she had stored in the wagon, her back to Luke. When she heard the deputy's name, she turned around in her seat. Her eyes widened with surprise. What's he doing here?

Luke tipped his hat to Lenora as he approached the wagon, shook hands with Olathe, and inquired about his health. The men exchanged the usual pleasantries. "I'm here to see Mrs. Rose," said Luke, not bothering to look at Lenora. "I'm going to accompany her home."

Lenora's mouth fell open in a mix of surprise and alarm, but realizing that Olathe would overhear if she responded, she closed her mouth, pulled her cloak a little more tightly around her shoulders, turned herself to the front of the buckboard, and stiffened her shoulders in a prim, determined way.

"I see," said Olathe. He glanced between Luke and Lenora as if he hoped for an explanation to this odd arrangement. But Luke wasn't volunteering information and Lenora let her obstinate posture do her talking. The elfish little man, who had to stand on a milking stool to groom his four-footed clients, must have decided to leave well enough alone. "I'm almost done here," he said. "You want me to hitch your horse to the wagon?"

"He's not used to a harness. I'll just tie him to the back," said Luke.

17

"Alright then. I'll be only a second." Olathe brushed a few wayward gray hairs from his forehead and then squatted again to give the strap one last tug. Soon he stood up and motioned with his hand to Luke that he was finished.

While Olathe watched them both with extraordinary interest, Luke finished tying his steed to the iron ring at the rear of the wagon and climbed aboard. Lenora continued to stare straight ahead, as stony as the Great Sphinx of Giza, while Luke sat down on the buckboard seat.

"Thanks, Olathe," he said as the stable owner handed him the reins.

Before Luke seated himself, Lenora scooted to the farthest edge of the buckboard seat and pivoted her legs at an angle to ensure no bodily contact. She scooted so far to the right that half of her thigh hung off the edge; she had to grip it with her right hand for balance. Even so, once Luke sat down there was no empty space between her hips and his.

Fear seized Lenora, with two thoughts crowding out all others. One, in a few minutes all of Buffalo would see her shamelessly parading down Main Street seated next to a man not her husband, and two, Deputy Davies was the manliest man she'd ever seen. She'd hardly noticed him in the sheriff's office, where the distraction of her upsetting report had kept her focus on the sheriff. But now he was smashed against her, their hips closer than a litter of nursing piglets. His bigness overwhelmed her, a bigness exaggerated by his all-male trail overcoat,

18

heavy denim pants, and rough ranch boots. Both
realizations caused her heart to beat a little faster.
She stared straight ahead, hoping stupidly that if she
acted as if everything were perfectly normal,
somehow, magically, to town folk she, the deputy,
and the wagon would be invisible.

In a moment Luke was leading the single horse
in a wide arc to exit through the high barn doorway.
Lenora's heart pounded in her chest. What did this
mean? Why was the deputy pursuing her? How
would she survive the ride through the two blocks
of town?

"You aren't going to pull this thing down the
middle of Main Street?" Lenora sat frozen faced,
only her lips moved. She didn't dare to turn and
look at Luke.

"Do you know a better route?" Luke
responded, calm as a Louisiana swamp on a sultry
August afternoon.

"People will talk!" whispered Lenora, her hand
still one with the buckboard seat.

"Can't disagree with you there," Luke said,
tilting his head a little closer to hers but keeping his
eyes on his task. The wide brim of his hat brushed
the face-framing brim of hers. "But then, I've
learned that people will talk no matter what you do,
good or bad, so you might as well just go on doin'
what you're doin.'"

And he did. As they pulled onto Main Street, a
hundred pairs of eyes, or so it seemed to Lenora,
fastened onto her horse and wagon. Her Morgan

had never clippety-clopped so loudly or moved as funeral slow as it did now while they jostled and creaked over the frozen ruts of Wyoming mud. Lenora kept her eyes fixed on the Morgan's back side as if a big brown pooping behind was the most mesmerizing thing on earth. Though they passed the hardware store, the millinery, the tobacconist, the bank, the town's six saloons, a dentist-barber shop, the doctor's office, and other trading establishments, Lenora never saw anything but the pooper and the people, shoppers and clumps of laughing soldiers from nearby Fort McKinney, all of whom she was sure were taking note of the rolling spectacle. She desperately wished she had chosen a poke bonnet to hide behind today instead of her open-face kiss-me-quick. She refused to look at Luke. Doing so might make the whole scene real, or worse, make it appear to townspeople that she knew him.

She must be dreaming. This was not happening!

They were nearly at the edge of town and approaching French Creek when out of the side of her eye Lenora saw with horror that three elderly lady members of the Johnson Ebenezer Christian Church, her church, had paused from their shopping chores to watch Lenora roll by. Despite her partial vision, Lenora could see the startled looks on all three faces.

Just then, the buckboard slipped into a deep rut, which caused the forward part of the wagon to dip suddenly and lurch to a stop. Lenora slid to the right, grabbing wildly for the front of the wagon with both hands to keep from being thrown off the seat, but failed. Her shiny beaded reticule slid off her lap with a whoosh and her with it. Embarrassed, she picked up her bag and righted herself. With a gloved hand she swiped at dirt from the wagon floor that had soiled her skirt, not so much because it was soiled, but to avoid looking in the direction of the all-too observant church ladies.

"Take my arm," said Luke.

Lenora looked down at the bag on her lap and pretended she had not heard him.

"Take my arm," he repeated, more urgently now. "It will give you some balance."

Hesitantly, and still fixing her eyes on the horse's fascinating rump, Lenora obeyed and slid her arm into his. But she held her arm stiffly, so that her elbow formed a rigid triangle to protect her from jostling against him, as effective as a cattle prod and every bit as friendly.

Finally, blessedly, they were beyond the stares of the curious people of Buffalo. About a half mile beyond the edge of town, Lenora wordlessly removed her arm from Luke's, never leaving the safety of the far edge of the buckboard seat. Then, for the first time, she turned to face him.

"Why did you tell Mr. Olathe you were accompanying me home?" Her tone was fraught with annoyance.

"I wanted to spare you."

21

"Spare me?" said Lenora, so flummoxed she hardly felt the cold.

"Yes, spare you."

"What are you talking about? Do you have any idea of the trouble your foolish act has created for me?"

Luke took his eyes off the horses and looked directly at Lenora. "I told Olathe I was accompanying you home ma'am because, considering your circumstances, it seemed the wisest thing to say."

"I fail to comprehend such wisdom, sir." Lenora was deeply engaged now, emboldened by the privacy afforded by an empty prairie. She returned his eye contact without a trace of self-consciousness. "Your actions have only added to my distress. You have increased my burdens during a very difficult situation."

Luke raised his eyebrows.

"It is incomprehensible to me that you think you have somehow acted wisely on my behalf," she continued.

The clatter and creak of the buckboard rolling over rough ground filled the taut silence. The reins squeaked rhythmically as the horse's shoulders pulled against the leather while the curb chain at its mouth jangled each time he turned his head.

Luke took a while to answer, and when he did, his tone was sober. Again he turned directly toward Lenora, so that their faces were only inches apart.

"It seems, Mrs. Rose, that you are unhappy to be seen by the citizens of Buffalo riding with me through town like a free and law-abiding citizen who has gone to the sheriff for help."

Lenora opened her mouth to object but Luke cut her off.

"So," he said, looking intently into her puzzled green eyes, "if you prefer, I'll turn this wagon around right now, and go back and lock you up for the murder of your husband."

Chapter Three

Lenora shut her eyes and took a deep breath to steady herself. It took her a few seconds to respond. "I didn't kill my husband, Deputy Davies. I love my husband. I would never do anything to harm him. Never." Her voice cracked as she started to cry. She pulled her hands through the slits in her cloak to retrieve her wet hanky from her bag. She fumbled under the cloak a few seconds, found the hanky, and dabbed her eyes.

"That may be true. But there's going to be a lot of people in this town who will have their doubts if your husband doesn't come home soon." Or if we don't find him and his horse rotting at the bottom of some steep ravine. The ragged, flesh-tearing crags of the canyon southwest of town rose in Luke's mind.

24

Lenora nodded in understanding, her eyes fixed on her hands, which now sat motionless on her lap.

"You haven't helped things any by not going to the sheriff sooner," said Luke, more gently now.

Lenora nodded again, too distraught to speak, tears spilling faster down her reddened cheeks. She turned her soiled hanky over and over, trying to find a clean corner to wipe her eyes. The only dry spots left were the pink crocheted roses on the edges.

"Here," said Luke, pulling a faded red handkerchief from his coat pocket. "Use mine. It's clean."

Lenora took his hanky, shook out the folds, and blew her nose. "Thank you," she said, her voice quavering.

"How long you and Mr. Rose been married, Mrs. Rose?"

"Four years."

"You got kin around here?"

"No. We came out here to homestead. Alone. Both of our families are back East, in New York."

"What's your pa do?"

"He manages a mill. A fabric mill. On the side he deals in international fabrics, beautiful imports from all around the world."

Luke nodded. "You happy homesteading?"

"Yes. Very. This is our grand adventure."

"You like living in the Territory? Never wanted to sell the ranch and head back East?"

"No, never. Why do you ask all these questions about our personal lives, Deputy Davies?"

25

"Just trying to get a full picture of your husband. Piece clues together. Motives. He's not here to explain his actions."

"I see."

"Who's watching your little ones today, while you came to town?"

Lenora grimaced silently and then put both hands over her face, tears streaming again. After a few seconds she removed her hands and wiped both eyes.

"I'm sorry to upset you, Mrs. Rose."

"I know you mean no harm," she said, after taking a gulp of air. "The good Lord has not seen fit to give us children." She said this softly, as if confessing to a terrible sin.

Poor woman. No husband, no kinfolk. No children. With this sad revelation hanging in the air between them, Luke decided to delay his interrogation out of respect for her feelings. They rode a few minutes without talking, each looking straight ahead, listening to the rhythmic rattle of the wheels on ragged dirt road.

"Now," he said, turning to face her, "ready to talk?"

She nodded.

"Tell me what happened. After he left the ranch, what did you do?"

Lenora took another deep breath and began. "I waited. It was after dark, like I told you, and drizzling too—it rained all night—so I stayed in the house and waited."

"You didn't search in any of your outbuildings? The barn?"

"No. Not that night. But the next morning when I woke up, Sunday, and he still wasn't home, I looked everywhere. The barn, the pens, the privy. When I realized he wasn't anywhere near the house, I saddled Beast—"

"Beast?"

Lenora pointed toward her Morgan. "That one's Beast. James took Beauty when he left."

Luke gave her a blank look.

"From a fairy tale I read in French class," she explained.

"I see."

"Then, when I didn't find him near the ranch, I saddled Beast and went farther out. Almost to the border of our property. I tried to follow his tracks, but the rain from the night before made it difficult. I was out looking for him for hours."

"Did you get help from any of the neighbors?"

Lenora paused before she answered and looked down at her lap. "I figured I could cover a lot of ground by myself."

Luke nodded to show he was listening, and after he'd heard enough, they rode in silence a while. The wagon wheels turned slowly to the clip clop of the tired horse in front, straining to pull the load by himself, echoed by Luke's horse clip clopping in the rear.

Wheels were slowly turning elsewhere. She didn't go to her neighbors. Luke was certain any

27

rancher in the area would have put aside his Sunday plans to help her, had she asked. She took two days to go to the sheriff. Two whole days. Enough time to hide a body, even for a woman. And what about Beauty? Where was James' horse? Mrs. Rose might find it difficult to bury a horse, though Luke had heard of equally amazing criminal feats accomplished by women.

"Mrs. Rose, I'm sure you've heard the saying, 'There's strength in numbers.' Didn't it occur to you that if more people were searching for your husband than just yourself that he might be found faster?"

"Deputy Davies," Lenora said, straightening her posture, "My husband is no ordinary horseman. James excels at horsemanship. He can take care of himself and Beauty."

"You said he left in the dark."

"He did."

"Even a good rider can stumble in the dark, especially if the moon is hidden by rain clouds."

"But why would I jump to the conclusion that he was injured and in need of a search party? I wouldn't insult my husband's abilities."

"Then you figured he had ridden off on purpose? With no plan to return?"

A flash in her eyes told Luke he had scored.

"How, sir," said Lenora, effecting a more formal tone than she had earlier, "am I to know what my husband was thinking when he left? As I told Sheriff Morris, I am not privy to my husband's

28

thoughts, and if he cares not to share them with me, I am left to deduce what I will."

With that she turned away from Luke and drew her arms through the slits in her cloak for warmth. Luke wished he could harness his horse to the wagon to shorten their time in the elements. He didn't dare snap the reins to urge Beast along. It wouldn't be moral to work an animal like that, even though Luke was hungry, Mrs. Rose probably was too, and surely Beast was tired. Beast. What a name. Luke called his horse, horse.

"Perhaps he said something to you before he left the house." Luke said it like a question. He looked over at Lenora but she refused to face him.

"What were his last words to you before he left?"

While he waited for her answer, Luke could see the cold sun slipping closer to the earth in the western sky. Beast plodded along, slower now, his head hanging a little lower as time passed. Luke's fingers were numb and his backside ached. He wondered whether following a pretty woman to her ranch made him an astute investigator or a slobbering idiot. He wasn't a betting man, but if he were, he'd put all his money on the idiot.

"That's our place," said Lenora, pulling a gloved hand out of her cloak to motion to the East, "over there." She pointed to the silhouette of a large barn, the only structure visible in the bluish purple twilight. As if Beast understood his mistress' words, he threw up his head and whinnied,

29

quickening his pace a little to reach his sheltered stall and a manger full of feed.

"Mrs. Rose, you haven't answered my question."

"I have given you the facts of my husband's disappearance, sir. Twice." This time Lenora looked boldly into Luke's eyes. "I cannot tell you more than I know, Deputy Davies, no matter how many times you and Sheriff Morris insist on inquiring."

"Whoa!" Luke pulled on the reins abruptly to halt the wagon, and then he set the brake. To Luke the sudden quiet after so many miles in the creaking wagon made their aloneness on the empty prairie seem intimate. His heart fluttered at the knowledge.

"Why are you stopping? We're not there yet," said Lenora.

Luke didn't answer. Instead he moved both leather reins to his left hand. With his right he reached for Lenora's wrist, grabbing it tightly and jerking it toward him ever so slightly. Lenora pulled back but she might as well have pulled at the Rock of Gibraltar. Luke held firm.

"Mrs. Rose," he said, his tone rising to match the seriousness in his eyes, "you need to understand. A jury will not let you off that easy. Your husband went missing on Saturday. You didn't report his disappearance till Monday morning, and neither did you seek help from neighbors. That's two days, Mrs. Rose, and I don't think your excuses for delaying a trip to town

30

during those critical two days add up to a hill of beans."

Their faces were close, just inches away. Luke wished it were not like this, that he was not the investigator and she was not the suspect. For the first time the badge he had coveted for so many years felt like a constraint. It took all his concentration to keep his mind focused on his job and off her beauty. He desired her, and he knew he desired her. Luke glanced downward fleetingly, his eyes taking in her thick velvet wrap. Never mind the shapeless cape meant to conceal all. With clarity that would keep him awake at night he remembered how she looked, standing stiff and prim in the sheriff's office, the curvy lines of her bosomy silhouette as cleanly cut as paper snowflakes at Christmas, her female form so different from his, and so very intriguing. Never before had his desire for a woman focused so keenly on any particular one. This time, the object of his male yearnings had a face and a name.

"I wager a jury will see it the same way," he continued, still gripping her wrist. "That's two days when your husband could be exposed to the freezing rain, dying of his injuries, or torn apart by vultures. A reasonable person, especially a man's wife who claims she loves him, doesn't let that happen."

Luke saw anger building in those captivating green eyes, eyes that worked on his insides like a tornado, emotions swirling round and round, his usual calm self beset by howling winds of concern, unease, wonderment, and many questions, not to mention physical desire—leaving him unsettled and prickly. Her presence discomfited him, an upset that had nothing to do with her fishy account of her husband's disappearance. Above all, he hoped the swirling maelstrom that tugged at his heart and his manhood would bypass his head. He was a professional. He would act, at all times, like the disciplined gentleman he was. But this desirable, irascible damsel in distress was making him crazy.

"I came out here today to try and help you. But if you won't be truthful with me, then there's nothing I can do for you. Only God can help you." *And why do I care?*

"Here's what you can do to help me, Mr. Lawman. Unhand me," said Lenora, gritting her teeth. "I didn't ask you to accompany me today. I asked only for help in finding my husband, which, I believe, is what you have sworn to do, is your duty to do, in the course of upholding the laws of Wyoming Territory."

Luke hesitated. He searched her eyes, looking for anything, any path to her heart that he could use as an opening for the truth. It wasn't his way to beat information out of suspects. But he could see in those determined eyes that she had snapped her heart shut, and with it, her mouth. She did not trust him.

"I meant no disrespect, ma'am," he quietly said. He removed his grasp on her wrist and turned back to the reins. He released the wagon brake and commanded Beast to start walking again. *Irritating woman. I would have ridden off into the black night of no return too.*

Neither of them spoke the rest of the way to the Rose ranch. Before they pulled into the yard Luke heard barking, a deep aarwhooof of a large dog, over and over again, growing louder and more frantic as the wagon drew closer. As they pulled around the corner of the house, Luke saw the source of the hullabaloo.

"What's your dog's name?"

"Ulysses," was Lenora's crisp reply.

"Distract him so I can unhitch your horse."

"I'll unhitch my horse myself, thank you. I hitched him up before I went to town. I'll unhitch him now that I've returned. This is my ranch."

"It may be your ranch, ma'am, but it's in my jurisdiction."

Lenora flinched.

"I'm going to take a look around, including the barn. Call off your dog so I can do what I need to. I want to get back to town while there's at least a little bit of light." *And while I'm still in control of my temper.*

Lenora called to Ulysses, an enormous bullmastiff, ordering him to sit, which he did promptly, all except for his tail, which fwumped, fwumped, fwumped on the ground in a noisy display of dog anticipation. Luke jumped down from the wagon and circled to the other side to help

Lenora climb down. Ignoring his extended hand, she wrapped her skirt and layers of petticoats around her legs as best she could and clumsily jumped to the ground, coming close to pitching herself forward into the frozen mud. Luke watched her ridiculously awkward dismount and marveled at her stubbornness.

"I'll check the outbuildings and look for anything out of the ordinary. If I see anything I'll let you know. Otherwise I'll be on my way," said Luke, holding the bit strap to keep Beast from racing toward the barn on his own.

Lenora only nodded.

"I have to get back to town. Sheriff Morris is out with the others by now, looking for Mr. Rose. He'll be wondering what happened to me."

Lenora nodded again, standing several feet away as if the deputy had something catching.

"If I hear any news about your husband," Luke continued, reaching for Beast's lead line, "I'll send word." He tipped his hat and then jerked on the lead line to guide Beast and the wagon into the barn.

"Thank you," she said. Then she looked down at her dog. "Supper, Ulysses." She turned toward the house, Ulysses following close behind, tail wagging excitedly all the way. In a minute, she and Ulysses were inside, the door bolted behind them.

#

As Lenora shut the door behind her, she was instantly struck at how little comfort she felt by standing in her much-longed-for front room. All the

34

way from town she was consumed with a desire to get home where she would feel safe, where everything was familiar and, above all, normal.

The silence startled her. Everything about the cozy ranch house looked normal. It was as she left it. So normal, in fact, that she half expected to see James step out of their bedroom any second, face freshly washed for supper, a smile on his face, a kiss for her forehead.

But James was not here, and nothing was normal. Silence was not normal. Awful and foreboding, it made the little house as unwelcoming as a dank cave. Gruesome images of James, his bloodied, lifeless body fallen somewhere in the wild, clamored to overtake her thoughts no matter how many times she willed them aside. They followed her through the bedroom, the tiny kitchen, and the lean-to as she checked every place to assure herself she was really alone.

Disappointed and deeply disturbed to see no evidence that James had returned, Lenora determined that the only logical thing to do to keep up her courage was to act like everything was fine, like everything was normal. She must not give in to her fears. She would build a fire in the cook stove to warm up the chilly kitchen and prepare something hot for supper. She wouldn't feel so lonely with a crackling fire for company. It would make the atmosphere seem less strange too.

Soon the cook stove was putting out a little heat, making comforting popping sounds as the

metal expanded. As Lenora fed the stove she
listened, taut and nervous, for the sound of Deputy
Davies' horse, anxious to have him ride away from
her property so she could get to the barn and
perform the evening chores without an audience. He
sure was taking his sweet time investigating her
ranch she thought, irritably. Finally she heard the
sound of the barn door bolt sliding into its frame,
then the familiar sound of a horse galloping out of
the yard. Within minutes the sound faded to
nothing.

Once Lenora was certain that Deputy Davies
was gone, she felt more acutely alone than she ever
thought possible. For an instant she almost wished
he had stayed. She had been rude. She should have
offered him something to eat and drink before he
made the long, cold trip back to Buffalo. But that
would have been awkward, her being a married
woman.

Blast that man! Deputy Davies shouldn't have
come here in the first place. Not only was he brash,
commandeering her wagon like that, but his bold
questions had humiliated her enough for a lifetime.
A wave of embarrassment overflowed her afresh as
she recalled how she had blubbered like a newborn
all the way from town. What must he think of her?
No, no, that wasn't right. Why should she care what
he thought? Those two were a pair, that Morris and
Davies. Lawmen indeed!

Lenora shook herself. The milk cow must be
pitiably swollen by now, as it was several hours

past evening chore time. She must check on the chickens and cattle as well. James' twenty expensive Brahman steers were who-knows-where. Now that Deputy Davies was finally gone, she lit the lamp, changed hastily into a set of James' work clothes, and calling to Ulysses, left the house to just as hastily complete the evening barn chores— James' chores—so she could return to the safety and warmth of the ranch kitchen. She was not one to entertain fearful thoughts while alone on the ranch, but James was gone. Nothing was right. All of life had turned upside down. The world, and the ranch too, had become strange and frightening.

After sliding the heavy barn door bolt, Lenora's first thought was that it was awfully quiet in the barn. The cow should be mooing, anxious to be relieved of its load. She hung the lamp on a nail where it couldn't be knocked over and start a fire, and then walked to the cow's stall. She was stunned to see the animal quietly munching fresh hay, standing in fresh, clean straw, its udder flaccid from recent milking. But where was the milk?

She walked next to Beast's stall. Beast was noisily munching from his feed box. He had been rubbed down and was standing in clean straw too. His stall had been thoroughly mucked out and his harness set on its rack in the tack room.

Well, that was nice of him. A Southern gentleman. But he's a rogue Southern gentleman, and with that Confederate twang, probably a cornbread-eating Southern sympathizer to boot.

Though the deputy's meddling discomfited her, Lenora set aside her annoyance and hurried through her final chores, making sure the chickens were secure in the poultry house and that the gate enclosing the Brahmans in their corral was secure. But everything was in order there too. There was nothing for her to do, so calling to Ulysses, she grabbed the lamp and started for the house.

As she approached the porch she saw it, her milk can sitting to the side of the door. She lifted the lid to see the creamy white milk Deputy Davies had left for her. Unmoved, she picked it up and went into the house, fed Ulysses, ate a simple supper of bread and leftover soup, then undressed and shimmied into her flannel nightgown as fast as possible. The bedroom was cold! While she performed her evening routine she contemplated what she would do if James did not come back. She must hire someone, and soon. She could not care for the animals by herself now and the garden and the fields later, when the weather grew warmer and the ground became soft for planting.

But no, she shouldn't be thinking such thoughts. It wasn't right. James would come back, surely he would ride into their yard tomorrow, there would be explanations and tears, and they would be together again. Life would be normal again.

With Lenora's mind heavy laden with doubts, her body exhausted and achy from bouncing on the buckboard to town and back, and Ulysses curled up on the floor beside her, finally, gratefully she slipped into their feather bed, a wedding gift from her parents. She shivered under icy sheets and several layers of quilts. How she missed James' strong arms around her, his sweet kisses, his warm body next to hers!

It didn't take long for the tears to come. *Come back James. Please don't be angry anymore. I'm sorry James. I love you James. Please come back.*

#

Ulysses' throaty growl awoke Lenora from a shallow, troubled sleep. What time was it? It must still be night, for there was not the faintest moon shadow to help her see the corners of the room.

Before Lenora had a chance to light a candle or hush Ulysses she heard it, the unmistakable sound of a man's heavy boot stepping slowly and stealthily to avoid detection outside her bedroom wall, one foot then another, exactly as she had heard it the night before. The sound was heart-stopping close. Every muscle in Lenora's body was taut, waiting for her mind to discern if she was awake or dreaming.

She wasn't dreaming. Lenora slid her hand across the mattress to poke James awake. In a horrific instant she realized he was not there.

Then Ulysses began to bark ferociously, as if he'd seen the devil himself creep into the room.

Chapter Four

"You learn anything more from her?"

With a wet splooth Sheriff Morris spat a stream of tobacco juice onto the ground, leaving a splotch of brownish-yellow spittle to seep slowly into the rich brown dirt of the Great Plains. Pale green grasses, thin and fragile, were beginning to appear on the undulating prairies, the cottonwoods near the creeks sprouting buds so small one had to stand underneath the branches to see them. Yesterday's cold snap had broken and the air was pleasant, almost warm. Spring would not hide its face long.

"Sort of," said Luke, guiding his horse closer to the sheriff's mount so they could talk. The search party moved in twosomes, Sheriff Morris and Luke in front, two volunteers from Buffalo settlement a hundred yards behind. Other mounted volunteers were scattered to the four corners of the Roses' ranch and beyond. "She knows more than she's telling."

"We knew that already," said Sheriff Morris.

"I needed to convince myself."

"Now that you're convinced, any idea what she's hiding, or why?"

Sheriff Morris spat on the ground again and wiped his mouth with his sleeve, adding another faint splotch to his mottled brown cuff.

Luke shifted in his saddle, making the leather squeak. "Not exactly. I've narrowed it down some though." But that was an understatement. Luke had thought of nothing else since he'd left Lenora on her ranch the evening before. He had lots of ideas about Mrs. Rose and her motives, most of them unsettling. He could hardly fall asleep for thoughts of her, alone on the wide prairie. He couldn't get those green eyes out of his mind.

But then, he hadn't tried.

"Well?" said Sheriff Morris.

"What I can't figure is who she's protecting, herself or her husband."

"Her husband," said Sheriff Morris. "We been over this ground before."

"I know. But I can't get her to talk about what happened before he took off. Either he left on his own, with no plan to come back, or he left on his own and something has happened to him and he can't come back."

"I told you he's a hothead."

41

Luke nodded. "Yeah, you told me. But have you thought about this: maybe he never left his house."

"You think she killed him? That little girl? She didn't kill nobody. Rose just ran off and got his fool head broke on some rock. Probably his horse fell in the dark. He's probably lying on the prairie right now, half froze to death with a busted leg and a cracked skull. Stupid kid. No one can tell him nothin'."

"We don't know that," said Luke. "No one knows for sure what happened to James Rose." *Except perhaps his weeping wife.* "And there's the Sioux. Or the Cheyenne."

"Indians don't take prisoners," said the sheriff, sounding disgusted. "And if the Sioux or Cheyenne had him, they would split his head open and run off with his horse."

Luke was embarrassed. He should have come to that obvious conclusion on his own. "Any woman can kill a man. I hear Belle Starr carries two pistols and is never far from her rifle. Even a woman can pull a trigger."

"Lenora Rose ain't no Belle Starr."

"Maybe." said Luke. "But Mrs. Rose is clever enough to weave her story in a way that suits herself."

"Meaning?"

"If he ran off because he wanted to, she doesn't want us to know. And I'm of a mind to believe that's the case," said Luke.

42

"Finally you come around. What made you change your mind?"

"I didn't change it. I'm not sure what I believe, not even about that. But a sane man doesn't risk his neck and his horse by riding into the prairie in the dark unless he's got a good reason."

"Yep." Sheriff Morris spat again.

"He's running to something or he's running away from something."

"I follow you," said Sheriff Morris as they ambled along, eyes to the ground, looking for any sign of the missing rider or his horse. High above them a hawk floated soundlessly on an air current, circling slowly, lazily, as it eyed the thin grass below for a warm-blooded lunch.

"Everything around that ranch had something to say," said Luke, mulling aloud.

"Such as?"

Luke turned around to see how far back the other two members of the search party were. Satisfied that they were still within sight, he turned back to Sheriff Morris. "I went inside everything 'cept the house. The barn, the shed, the chicken house, the smokehouse, even the privy. Everything was good quality and in good order. James Rose is a man who cares about his stuff."

"So?"

"So Rose may have left his ranch on his own power, but he didn't abandon it. He had enough money to stock it right. Keep it repaired. It didn't look to me like he was fixing to leave and not come back."

"Then he left, like I said, and he's injured," said Sheriff Morris.

"Mrs. Rose insists that's not possible. Says her husband is too smart for that."

Sheriff Morris shook his head in disgust and spat on the ground again.

Luke pulled his broad-brimmed hat down a little farther on his forehead. The sun was higher in the sky now, and though its warmth was welcomed by the riders after the cold snap they'd shivered through the last few days, he was sweating under his heavy coat, and they were all thirsty. They'd been scouting for several hours on the far eastern reaches of the Rose ranch and had found no sign of James Rose or his horse. The ground had been soft enough for his horse to make impressions the night he disappeared, but the hours of rain after he had ridden away from his ranch had obliterated any clues to his movements.

"We're not far from the North-East Creek," said Sheriff Morris, halting his horse. "You can see the cottonwoods," he said, pointing to the gray smudge at the eastern border of the Roses' property. "Let's rest a bit, water the horses."

Luke nodded. He halted his horse too, turned around in his saddle, and motioned with his arm to the two other men to catch up with him and the sheriff.

In about twenty minutes the foursome was near enough to the creek to see that another rider had stopped for a drink. A handsome brown Morgan stood just feet from the rushing waters, which flowed icy cold and fast from spring runoff. The horse's lead was looped tightly to a leafless red ash. Its head drooped unnaturally, and it acted as though it was sleeping, because it did not lift its head as the four riders approached. A nearby stand of cottonwoods, naked from the ravages of winter, provided no camouflage for whoever had tied up the Morgan, neither did the low scrub pine that grew along the prairie's edge that led to the drop-off to the creek. Yet the horse's owner was nowhere in sight.

"Hullo!" called Sheriff Morris as he halted his horse some twenty feet away.

Instantly the Morgan became alert, jerking its head and snorting. It yanked at the lead, frantically trying to free itself. It jerked violently, again and again, raising its front legs high into the air for added leverage, all the while whinnying piteously.

"Something's wrong," said Luke, and without waiting for Cyrus' opinion, he goaded his horse closer to the creek bank. Luke's heart beat rapidly as he approached; he dreaded what gruesome thing he might see in or near the rushing water. The drop from the bank was straight down—this part of the creek was no good for wading. But the drop was only about two feet. A man could lie on his belly and easily scoop water into his mouth without fear

45

of falling in. But if he fell, he would be sent on a one-way ride to eternity, especially if he fell at night, when no one was around to hear him yell for help. The shimmering water was swift, deep, and cold enough to squeeze the breath out of a man. Luke looked downstream and wondered if that was what happened to the horse's owner.

"Help us with this animal!" yelled Cyrus.

Luke broke from his morbid reverie, tied his horse securely to a cottonwood, and joined the others as they tried to get control of the Morgan. It took several minutes of false starts and many soothing words, but finally the exhausted Morgan was calm enough to be led to the creek. Its eyes were cloudy and it trembled. Luke filled his hat with the refreshing water to make drinking easier for the horse. It drank like it hadn't put its mouth to water in days.

"It's his, isn't it?" said Luke as he watched, amazed, as Beauty slurped noisily from his hat. He bent down and filled his hat again from the creek and lifted it to the horse's mouth.

"It's his alright. I'd know that Morgan anywhere. James Rose always had to have the best of everything," said Cyrus.

And that's why he had the prettiest wife in the Territory. The memory of Lenora, waiting alone at the ranch for her James to come home, pained him. Someone would have to tell her. "Sad to see such a beautiful animal go three days without water," said

46

Luke, steering the conversation away from his true thoughts.

After the search team's horses had drank all the water they wanted, the four men sat on the ground, their horses and the Morgan tethered nearby, munching quietly what little spring grass they could forage. The men needed to rest a while before handling the depressing tasks ahead of them. Most urgent, James Rose's body must be found and returned to his widow. His horse must be returned too.

"His body is probably mighty far downstream by now," said Sheriff Morris, reaching into his pocket for his tobacco pouch. "We got more searching to do, but at least now we won't waste time looking where he ain't."

"Wherever his body is, it's well preserved," said one of the volunteers with a grin. Ben Slocomb was a slender young man, hardly out of his teens, with sandy hair and eyes that twinkled with mischief. His attempt at humor in this dark circumstance provoked chuckles.

But Luke barely nodded in agreement. He was thinking. "How do you suppose he fell in?" he said.

None of the men answered.

"Even in the dark the creek wouldn't surprise him," Luke surmised aloud. "He'd hear it before he saw it, and it's his land. A man knows his own land."

47

"I was wondering the same thing," said Sheriff Morris, gazing downstream, his chewing tobacco temporarily forgotten.

"And he tied up his horse," said Luke, motioning toward the red ash, "as if he had stopped for a drink. He didn't stumble onto the creek in the dark. He came here on purpose."

"Maybe he leaned over too far." Jed Whitehall, a plainspoken, plain-faced rancher of about thirty, idly tugged at a dry bit of straw still clinging to the soil since fall. He put the clean part of the creamy-white reed in his mouth and started to chew. "Accidents happen. People lose their footing. It happens to the best of us one time or another. It probably happened very fast."

The others nodded in silence, humor forgotten while each searched up and down the water for answers. As he searched Luke imagined the terror of James Rose as he slipped and fell into the icy water, all alone under the cloudy black darkness of a late spring rain. Luke studied every bush, every spindly, leafless sapling that rooted along the bank, but the creek wasn't revealing its secret. James Rose may have called for help, panicked and frightened, but his cries would have been swallowed by the night. The knowledge that a man died on this spot seemed to hallow it for Luke.

"Maybe he killed hisself," said Ben. The other three stopped their search and looked at him.

"Son, you're too young to know how it was with James Rose," said Sheriff Morris. "Suicide is

48

for losers. James Rose wouldn't take his own life. That's not the way winners do. He had too much pride in him to just give up."

The older men nodded in sober agreement.

"Besides, he had everything going for him," said the sheriff. "Best piece of land in the county, prosperous ranch, pretty wife. No, James Rose didn't take his life."

Luke and Jed nodded silently in agreement. Ben looked chastened and said no more.

The men agreed they should notify Mrs. Rose of the loss of her husband as soon as possible, return Beauty to her stall on the Rose ranch, and then go back to town to assemble a new search party for the next day to retrieve the body. This second group of searchers would focus on the banks of the North-East Creek that marked the eastern edge of the Rose property, downstream from where they'd found Beauty.

As the men rested and talked, Luke looked beyond them to the creek bank, imagining again James Rose's last minutes on earth. With difficulty he tried to conjure a picture of Rose slipping and falling from the bank into the dark and frigid water, but he couldn't. It was only a two-foot drop, hardly menacing by daylight or moonlight. The creek was fast and mercilessly cold, but Rose was young and strong, a man who performed by himself all the demanding physical chores of a small but thriving cattle ranch. Something wasn't right. Luke stood up.

49

"I'm going to take a look around," he said. "I'll be back in a few minutes."

Luke banged his hat on his thigh to smack excess water from it and then placed it on his head and approached the creek. He walked slowly up and down the flat bank, stepping on patches of snow interspersed among thickly packed, dry grasses blown nearly supine by unrelenting winter winds. He searched for anything that would put to bed his unease regarding James Rose's accident. If his death had been anything other than accidental, surely some bit of evidence to indicate foul play would be here, where he died. Another set of footprints. A second set of horse tracks. A personal item dropped and left behind, unbeknownst to the owner. In particular he looked for any sign of struggle. He looked for blood.

For a quarter of an hour Luke walked up and down the bank on the side of the creek where they found Beauty, about three hundred feet in both directions, canvassing the ground as he went. Finding nothing, he returned to the others, who were mounted and waiting. Beauty's lead line was tied to Sheriff Morris' saddle horn.

"Seen enough?" said Sheriff Morris as Luke walked up to his horse to untie it.

"Enough," lied Luke. "The Rose Ranch is that way," he said, pointing west.

As the five horses and four riders turned toward the Rose ranch, Luke couldn't shake an unsettling feeling that he had unfinished business here. Could someone have pushed James Rose into the water? Luke had not found a scrap of physical evidence around the death site to indicate homicide. But to voice his unfounded suspicion aloud to Cyrus, who evidently had already decided from the circumstances that James had slipped and fallen to his death, would make Luke look like an amateur. Luke's suspicion was mostly a feeling, and how could he explain a feeling, especially to someone as cynical as Cyrus? To convince him, Luke could only put forth hard evidence, and he certainly had none of that.

But like the scratching of a hairy burdock leaf that has burrowed into his sock, a niggling thought scratched at Luke's mind: Could Mrs. Rose have pushed her husband to his death?

Chapter Five

Ulysses was the first to hear the sad procession, an elegy of four horsemen and a riderless horse. Perhaps it was the scent and not the sound of his master's prized Morgan that the alert pet discerned on the late afternoon breeze, but whatever it was that aroused his canine senses, it triggered a predictable response in the most prominent part of his anatomy. His agitated barking sent Lenora scurrying from the kitchen to the front door to see what so disturbed her dog.

But before she left the house, she surreptitiously peeped through white lace curtains at the front room window into the yard. She saw nothing out of order, no four-legged critters hissing or pawing at Ulysses, no two-legged visitors either, but Ulysses' barking was not to be ignored. Of one thing Lenora was certain: she had not imagined the stealthy steps of an intruder outside her bedroom

window the last two nights. Ulysses hadn't
imagined them either, and she was grateful that his
barking had scared him off.

Had he returned?

With the ominous sound of the trespasser's
boots uppermost in her mind, Lenora was taking no
chances. She wiped the bits of floury biscuit dough
still clinging to her fingers onto her calico apron
and then reached above the front door for James'
Sharps rifle, where it was always stored, ready for
use. But now, for the first time in her married life,
Lenora, not James held the Sharps in defense of
their ranch. The sobering significance of this act did
not escape her, but this was no time to indulge in
self-pity.

Lenora acted quickly. She could tell by the
change in his bark that Ulysses had run to the rear
of the house. She moved to the bedroom where,
from the tiny window, she could see not one but a
group of men on horseback approaching from the
East. She lifted the long arm into position and
cocked the trigger, never taking her eyes off the
riders.

She watched, heart thumping like a drum,
every muscle taut with anxiety, finger on the
trigger, as Ulysses suddenly stopped his frantic
barking and bounded out of the yard toward the
horsemen, who by now were only a few hundred
feet away. But Ulysses' chain stopped his escape
abruptly. After a few minutes Lenora watched as
one of the riders halted his horse, dismounted, and

bent down to greet her dog. The tall man scratched Ulysses behind his ears, rubbed his head, and then reached into his pocket and pulled something out, evidently a treat, because Ulysses began to exhibit all the familiar signs of a tail-wagging sentry just waiting to be bribed.

Then Lenora saw the riderless horse following the mounted riders, and as slowly and silently as the dawn rises in the eastern sky, so was the dawning of truth in her mind. She realized who the tall man was, and more important, what that riderless horse meant.

God oh God, let it not be so.

She stared, transfixed with terror, as the tall man remounted his horse and joined the rest of them as they made their way to her front yard. Finally she saw them round the corner of the house. She unhooked her finger from the trigger and eased the Sharps down to her hips.

#

Lenora did not wait for them to knock. She stepped into the doorway, Sharps still in hand, though she had the presence of mind to remove her apron, check for any stray bits of biscuit dough on her shirtwaister, and smooth her hair. A lady does not greet visitors with an apron on, even when her missing husband's horse returns home without him.

"Good afternoon, Mrs. Rose," said Sheriff Morris, tipping his hat and dismounting from his horse. The others tipped their hats as well, but only Luke dismounted with the sheriff. Once Luke's feet

54

were on the ground, Ulysses walked up next to him and parked on his haunches, panting and slobbering, hoping to be thrown another dainty by the treat man.

Lenora recognized the two men still on horseback. The elder was a local rancher she knew from church. The younger was the son of a neighboring rancher. She tried to be polite and return their greetings, but when she opened her mouth no words came out. Her breaths came in short, shallow puffs; she felt like she would faint. She reached for the door frame to steady herself. The air was fraught with the tension of the unspoken.

"We found this horse tied up by the North-East Creek," Sheriff Morris said, motioning toward Beauty and meeting Lenora's eyes. "We think it's Mr. Rose's. We found no sign of the owner."

"It's James'," said Lenora, still gripping the door frame for support.

"We searched the area where we found her," Luke said. "She was tied a few feet from the creek. It looks as though Mr. Rose stopped there for water."

"And you didn't find any sign of him?" asked Lenora. Hearing her husband's name helped her come back to the moment. She took a few steps toward Beauty, pressed her face against the animal's head, and closed her eyes while she lovingly ran her hand down its smooth coat. The pungent smells of horse sweat and saddle leather sharpened her memory of Beauty's missing owner. Where was James? What happened to him?

"No ma'am. None of his clothing, no hat, no shoes. No tracks either. Saturday night's rain washed away any tracks," said Luke.

Lenora stopped nuzzling Beauty and stepped away to face the lawmen. "Surely he left some evidence somewhere. There must be something out there to explain what happened to him. A man doesn't just disappear like a ghost." She saw the two ranchers exchange furtive glances. Her heart flip flopped in her chest.

"Sheriff Morris, what happened to my husband?" Lenora's voice took on a tinge of shrillness.

"Mrs. Rose, we believe that—"

"Wait," said Luke. "Jed, will you and Ben take the horses to the barn? Beauty shouldn't wait any longer. There's fodder, the water pump's around the side of the house, and you can let your own horses rest a bit for the ride back to town. I'm sure Mrs. Rose here will be happy to get you something to eat too before we leave."

Jed and Ben didn't need to be asked twice. They tipped their hats to Lenora while Sheriff Morris and Deputy Davies handed their reins to them.

Sheriff Morris and Luke watched Jed and Ben walk to the barn, and once they were inside it, both lawmen, almost in unison, removed their hats. Lenora recognized the gesture and what it meant.

Her heart pounded wildly. She could hear the blood rushing past her ears.

Sheriff Morris opened his mouth to speak. "Mrs. Rose—"

"Just tell me! Tell me what happened to my husband!"

"No one can be sure, ma'am," said the sheriff, flinching at her outburst, "but it looks like your husband fell into the North-East Creek. We believe he's dead, probably downstream a good ways. We're planning to send a search party downstream tomorrow, first thing."

"You think my husband drowned?" Lenora's face contorted with disbelief.

"The evidence looks that way, ma'am," said Luke.

"Evidence? What evidence? You said you had nothing! You have no evidence at all that my husband drowned." Lenora was starting to flush red. She punctuated her angry words with her hands.

"What kind of evidence do you expect from a drowning, Mrs. Rose?" said Sheriff Morris. "He fell in three days ago. His body is long gone downstream. Finding the body is the only evidence we can hope for."

"Sheriff Morris," said Lenora, finding her feisty self once again, "You don't know James Rose. My husband would never, NEVER, be so clumsy as to slip and fall into a rushing stream."

"We searched the entire creek bank, Mrs. Rose. All four of us," said Sheriff Morris, exaggerating the facts. "Nothing else makes sense. Your husband drowned."

Lenora trembled with anger. "Your investigation, sir, if you may flatter yourself by calling it that, has resulted in a conclusion that is not only faulty, it's preposterous."

"Listen here," said Sheriff Morris, stepping closer and growing redder in the face than Lenora. "We've been all over that area, where we found her, his horse." Sheriff Morris wagged his finger angrily toward the eastern border of the Rose ranch. "There's no evidence that anything happened to your husband other than a drowning. You can wish it away, ma'am, but James Rose drowned in the North-East Creek."

"That's impossible." Lenora's eyes flashed wickedly with anger to match the sheriff's. These idiotic men. She'd had all she could take. Intimidation. Accusation. Exhaustion. She knew she wasn't acting ladylike, but she didn't care.

"What makes you so sure his body ain't in that creek? You know more about this than you been telling?" sneered the sheriff.

With that, Lenora's temper went from simmering hot springs to volcanic eruption. "You haven't conducted an investigation! You've made an assumption, that's all. An assumption based on nothing. What can you possibly deduce from a tied-up horse and no rider? It can mean anything."

Lenora banged the butt of her Sharps on the ground for emphasis.

"Mrs. Rose," said Luke, stepping a little closer to her. His tone was far more entreating than the sheriff's. "I walked all over the area where we found Beauty. There's nothing to be found. No sign of him at all. The only logical place the body can be is in the creek."

"I'll thank you to cease referring to my husband as a 'body.'"

"Please calm yourself ma'am. We're trying to help," said Luke.

"I will not calm myself! You call yourselves lawmen? What kind of lawmen find a horse and nothing else, and then concoct a wild story about a drowning that no one witnessed? If you would do your job and conduct a *real* investigation, my husband would be here right now."

A little voice in the back of Lenora's mind was telling her she was out of control. She ignored it.

"Looky here young lady, we don't have to put up with your mouth. We done our best. We rode all day, got others searching too. You couldn't have done any better," said Sheriff Morris.

"You mean you're not going to search anymore?" said Lenora. *Stupid, puffed up lawmen. They think they know everything because they wear those tinhorn badges. They don't know James.*

"Only down the creek. For a *body*," said Sheriff Morris, leaning into Lenora's face.

"You're wasting your time, Sheriff," said Lenora, leaning right back into the sheriff's face, returning his glare. She was way beyond intimidation now. "You'll never find my husband in the creek. And since it's quite apparent that your investigation, if you want to call it that, is complete, you leave me no choice but to find my husband myself."

With one hand Lenora started to lift her Sharps to her waist from the ground where it had rested, determined to end the standoff with the last word followed by a huffy retreat to her biscuit baking. But before she could grip the Sharps with both hands, Luke threw his hat to the ground and reflexively lunged for the Sharps. He jerked the weapon out of her hand with one of his and with his other he grabbed her upper arm and started to drag her away from Sheriff Morris. The sheriff shouted something nasty, but Lenora was so startled by Luke's action and Ulysses was barking so fiercely she heard only the sheriff's angry tone and not the words. Luke didn't release his painful grip on her arm until they had rounded the corner of the house, where he turned her about, face to face.

"What do you think you're doing?" he said, breathily, his voice low, his forehead creased with concern. "You want to get arrested for threatening an officer of the law?"

"I didn't threaten anyone," Lenora fairly hissed in his face. She rubbed her arm where Luke's fingers had pressed into her flesh.

"Looked that way to me. To Sheriff Morris too."

"I hate him! He doesn't listen to me. He had his mind made up from the day I gave my report. He doesn't know James."

"You have to be patient with Sheriff Morris," Luke said, his tone conciliatory. "He's old school."

"You mean old fool."

"Mrs. Rose, you must accept the truth—"

"Do *you* know the truth? Do *you* know what happened to my husband?" Lenora drew herself up in a defiant stance.

Deputy Davies' face softened into a look of genuine kindness. "Mrs. Rose, I know this is hard for you, and I'm sorry to upset you like this. I wish it were different. I wish your husband were alive and I could bring him home to you. But ma'am, he drowned."

"In a pig's eye."

Luke squeezed his eyes shut briefly as if to think, or perhaps compose himself. Lenora wasn't sure, though she noted that he never released his grip on her Sharps. When he opened his eyes again they stood staring at one another a few awkward seconds. Lenora looked into his eyes and was surprised to see ... pity? Compassion? His intense gaze reached to her very soul. She felt exposed.

And then, wordlessly and gently, Luke put his free hand on Lenora's shoulder. "Mrs. Rose, I want you to think about hiring some help as soon as you can."

"I've already thought about it. I'm not the simpleton you lawmen think I am." Lenora angrily jerked herself, shaking his hand from her shoulder. She saw a flash of hurt rise in his eyes, which, strangely, made her regret her lack of grace. Deputy Davies, it appeared, had a touch of tenderness in his heart, unlike his spittle-stained windbag of a partner.

"Did Mr. Rose have a will? Did he leave you enough money to get someone out here to help you with the chores?"

"I asked you not to talk about my husband as if he were dead and buried."

"Fine," said Luke, with a sigh. He started again. "Mrs. Rose, do you have the means to hire a ranch hand until your husband returns?"

"What does it matter to you?"

"I'm ... I'm ... just looking out for a citizen of Buffalo," he stumbled. "Mr. Rose, I mean. I'm looking out for Mr. Rose."

Lenora screwed up her face a little, puzzled.

"Mrs. Rose, if you were my wife, left here all alone on this ranch, and I was missing, I would hope someone would look out for the welfare of what's mine till I returned."

Lenora did not respond other than to stare.

"Good neighbors do that," Luke added, as if he needed to clarify himself.

Lenora's heart softened a little. Perhaps Deputy Davies wasn't cut from the same cloth as the crusty old coot.

"I don't mean to belittle your abilities, ma'am. You and your husband have done a fine job of running this ranch. But you can't take care of this place all by yourself."

Deputy Davies was right about the urgency to hire a ranch hand. She had been putting off the hiring decision. How difficult it was, how weighed down this decision made her feel. How bizarre to even think of hiring someone to replace her James. Such a notion was sacrilegious. But James' horse was now in the barn, and her beloved had not returned with it. She could procrastinate no longer.

But that wasn't all that bothered Lenora about Deputy Davies' summary of her situation. The way he framed his explanation, portraying himself as her husband, if only to illustrate his thought, embarrassed her down to the tips of her toes. Deputy Davies was a nice looking man. He had kind eyes, a well-balanced face, and a charming way of speaking that made people trust him. But until he spoke about the two of them, together as man and wife as he had just done, she had not thought of him as anything but the big, slow talking deputy who asked lots of probing questions. But he was an eligible man, an attractive man. So flustered was she at the mental picture his words had created of them together that, for once, she found herself speechless.

Then, before she could untie her tongue, with icy clarity a new thought rose unbidden in her mind: Could it be that men from around the county

63

would hear of her husband's "drowning" and consider her ... available?

"I have a little money in the house, but James keeps our accounts. I don't know what we have. I'll go into town tomorrow and inquire at the bank."

"Good."

"Deputy Davies," said Lenora.

"Ma'am?"

"My Sharps, please."

Chapter Six

"Come in, Mrs. Rose. How lovely you look today."

Bank Manager Edwin Morehouse stood aside as Lenora stepped into his office and sat down on the closest of two visitors' chairs. She hoped her awkwardness did not show. Banking was James' purview. She had never before ventured into a bank, not even shiny new Wells Fargo Bank of Buffalo, a bonus for the West after the merger of the banking and overland mail systems years earlier. James had explained to her the significance of the merger to western ranchers, but she had not thought it important at the time. She arranged her navy blue barracan skirting evenly around the chair as she seated herself. The toes of her red silk, high-button shoes, the ones with the side bows, peeped daintily from underneath her hem.

"I thought you might be in to see me," said the portly gentleman, seating himself behind a mammoth polished desk. "I asked the window clerk to inform me when you arrived."

"Thank you," said Lenora, embarrassed at the attention. She folded her gloved hands—red, to match her shoes—in her lap and sat rigid in the chair. Even though she had requested this meeting, she felt like a little girl again, called into her father's office for her bad behavior. Mr. Morehouse was old enough to be her father. His perfectly groomed English mustache was entirely white.

"I'm sorry about your husband's accident, Mrs. Rose. James was a good man. I'll miss his visits to our establishment."

So that's how it was. Why did everyone assume James was dead? With a pang of guilt, Lenora knew why. She had not been exactly forthcoming when she was interrogated by the sheriff and Deputy Davies about the events that occurred immediately before James' disappearance. James had good reason to leave her. She wondered if the weight of that secret would squeeze her chest with regret the rest of her life. If James decided to stay away forever, how would she survive each day without him?

"I appreciate your concern, Mr. Morehouse. But my husband is missing, not dead. I see no reason to believe the worst until I have factual evidence to support that morbid conclusion."

Mr. Morehouse blinked and looked stunned, but quickly recovered. "I understand that Sheriff Morris has a search party underway as we speak," he said.

"That is true."

"Then let us hope that Providence intervenes, for your sake."

"That is how I pray, Mr. Morehouse."

With the courtesies taken care of, Mr. Morehouse shifted in his chair and reached for a thick black ledger on his desk. Lenora expected him to open it and tell her how much money James had deposited into their savings account, but instead the imposing man leaned forward over the ledger and rested his folded hands on it. Through Mr. Morehouse's open office door Lenora heard the sound of a newborn crying in the waiting area. Evidently its mother put something in its mouth to soothe it, likely a sugar-teat. The cries stopped with suddenness.

"I imagine, Mrs. Rose, that you came in today to learn about your account here with Wells Fargo."

"Yes, I did. James normally handles these affairs."

"Did your husband ever discuss your account with you, Mrs. Rose?"

"No, there has never been a need for that. James takes care of everything."

"I see."

Mr. Morehouse leaned back in his black leather chair and toyed with his fountain pen. Lenora wondered why he was needlessly drawing out this conversation. She just wanted a number, that's all, so she could make a wise decision about hiring a ranch hand. But Mr. Morehouse was a powerful man in Buffalo settlement and its surroundings, and she was intimidated by his presence. He and his large family lived in the grandest, most beautifully appointed house in town. Lenora had only seen from the street their lavish flower gardens ablaze with prairie hollyhock, wild yellow roses, pink peonies, and peach gaillardia. She had admired also their extra-large horse stable. She had heard that the Morehouses had dedicated an entire room of their home for use as a water closet. Even her family in New York, as comfortable as they were, didn't enjoy such extravagance, though Lenora knew there were fine city homes nearby that did. Here in the untamed Territory a posh potty was unheard of. As she sat across the desk from this important man, especially without her husband to do the talking, Lenora felt very small indeed.

"Did James ever tell you how much money he deposited in your account?"

"No sir."

"Have you thought about your future, Mrs. Rose, if the worst comes to pass?"

"I have thought about it." Why was this man so inquisitive? Lenora was starting to get annoyed. She needed information, and she needed to get back to her ranch. Chores were waiting and the ride was long. She didn't need a fatherly chat. She needed a number.

"Can your family help you in the interim?"

"They can, yes. But I have no interest in returning East, Mr. Morehouse. Wyoming Territory is my home now." Unthinkable. Going back to New York without James, leaving their land behind. Abandoning their dream. God forbid.

"What are your plans if your husband does not return?"

"I can't make plans until I know how much money is in our account, Mr. Morehouse."

"Of course." That seemed to wake up the banker. He opened the ledger and flipped through the pages. He ran his finger down a column and then stopped. "Your savings account shows a balance of just over three hundred dollars, Mrs. Rose. Three hundred twenty-two dollars and fifteen cents."

Lenora's heart sank. Three hundred twenty-two dollars. She had land. She was not poor. But three hundred dollars wouldn't last long if she had to pay a ranch hand. Perhaps this is why James was dead set against hiring Sam Wright, the day laborer who was always pestering local ranchers for work. Lenora had asked James, begged him many times to hire someone to help him with the grinding chores of a growing cattle ranch. He resisted every time.

"We have just the one account, Mr. Morehouse?"

"Just the one." Mr. Morehouse shut the ledger. "Of course, you're not without options, Mrs. Rose."

Options? Lenora felt a brief flutter of hope.

The banker stood up and walked around the corner of his desk. He dragged the remaining visitor's chair closer to Lenora and sat down, easing his generous behind between the two arms, which creaked slightly as he moved. Through his large office window flanked by burgundy velour drapes fastened with gold cord, Lenora saw the twice weekly Wells Fargo stagecoach pull up noisily and stop in front of the bank. Idly she wondered if Mr. Morehouse's office was situated where it was for that very view.

"Options such as what?"

Mr. Morehouse leaned forward a bit as if he had a secret to share. Lenora picked up the spicy scent of after-shave mingled with stale cigar.

"You can always sell your land. You own it free and clear. Or at least you will in less than two years, when you've fulfilled your homestead obligations."

Lenora nodded sullenly. She may have been hazy about their financial accounts, but she knew very well the details of how they acquired their ranch. Free land had so excited her and James before they left New York, it was all they had talked about during their betrothal. It was all any young, adventurous eastern couple talked about in those long ago, carefree days.

"Your husband was a smart homesteader, Mrs. Rose. He chose one of the best parcels before they got all gobbled up by the big ranches. Having that North-East Creek run across your whole eastern edge—might as well be liquid gold flowing across your property."

"You are right, Mr. Morehouse. My husband is a smart homesteader," said Lenora, correcting his tense. "Too smart to sell."

Mr. Morehouse flinched as if she'd spat on him. "I don't mean to insult, Mrs. Rose."

"Of course not."

"But you will have to make some difficult choices by and by, if your husband does not return."

Well that was true. But selling their homestead was not one of them.

"All of your wealth is tied up in that land. How else will you manage if you don't sell?"

I have no idea. Right now all she could think of was how much more bulbous Mr. Morehouse's fleshy nose looked now that he was sitting directly across from her instead of behind his desk. And how tired she was of men in this town second-guessing her. And how she needed money to hire a ranch hand.

"We'll see what the future brings," she said, unsmiling. She stood up to leave.

Mr. Morehouse stood up too. "In the meanwhile, Mrs. Rose, if there's anything I can do, or the bank can do, to assist you during this difficult time, I hope you will contact me immediately. We are here to help."

"What I would like, Mr. Morehouse, is to withdraw fifty dollars from our account."

#

Lenora clutched her navy silk reticule a little more tightly than usual as she walked along the boardwalk on Main Street on her way to the general store. Fifty dollars was a lot of money. Her parents had spent that much on clothing and shoes for her in one shopping trip in the past, but never had she been personally responsible for so much cash. Certainly she had never carried such a large sum on her person.

She was still thinking about the treasure in her bag and how to make it last when she heard a ruckus of men's voices. She looked in the direction from where she heard the sound to see a crowd of men clustered in front of one of Buffalo's six saloons.

Nothing good here.

Curiosity propelled her toward the noise nonetheless. On the opposite side of Main Street Lenora saw two men, one heavy set, the other of slight build and unusually short stature, trying to lift a third man onto a horse. All three were dressed like ranch hands with their wide-brimmed hats, oversized neckerchiefs to protect their mouths from trail dust, dungarees, dark shirts that never seemed quite clean, and rough boots. From their clumsy movements and slurred speech, Lenora deduced that they had spent a good part of the morning in one of the saloons.

But what fascinated Lenora was that the heavy man had the third man over his shoulder, his arms about his friend's legs and, absurdly, was trying to throw the poor pickled soul across the saddle. The little man was doing his part by valiantly pushing on the third man's backside.

"One, two, three!" said the heavy set man. On three the two men gave all they had into a united umphf! hoisting their friend onto the horse in one quick but sloppy movement, whereupon he slid to the other side of the beleaguered animal, landing head first on the ground, flopping limply onto his back in the dirt with a sickening thud. His overly large black hat fell off and rolled a few feet away in the dust. The crowd went crazy, whooping and laughing, cheering on the drunks, urging them to repeat the stunt.

"You blashted jackass. Get up!" yelled the big man to his friend on the ground, as if the intoxicated man laying supine in the dirt had the capacity to do anything other than bask in the sun on a fine spring day. The heavy set man uttered a few cuss words Lenora had heard before along with a few particularly purple ones that surely no dictionary on earth contained. Inexplicably he aimed most of his ire at the little man, who defended his manhood with equally purple prose and obscene finger gestures. Lenora was embarrassed to be watching and listening to such a ribald performance, but the three men were so funny she found herself laughing right along with the crowd.

After cursing the prone man and vainly ordering him to stand several times, the heavy set man motioned to the little man to help him, once again, to push their friend onto his horse. Lenora watched as the heavy set man repeated his routine, picking up the third man and throwing him over his shoulder.

"Heave! Heave!" cried the heavy set man.

"I'm heaving, I'm heaving," complained the little man.

Just then the third man, half on, half off his horse obediently and heartily heaved his breakfast, fouling himself, the heavy set man, and the horse tack. The crowd guffawed.

Useless.

Lenora couldn't take her eyes off the spectacle. She chuckled with the crowd as she watched the heavy set man ungraciously dump his smelly friend on the ground like a discarded old coat, and then, while filling the spring sunshine with ever more colorful English, proceeded to swat the sticky filth off his shirt with his hat.

"A merry heart is as good as medicine."

With heart-stopping alarm, Lenora instantly recognized the owner of that masculine timbre and knew he was close. She spun around and was mortified to realize she had been observed by the handsome deputy as she laughed at the antics of drunkards.

"Deputy Davies." Lenora could feel a full-blown crimson rush rising to her eyebrows. How long had he been standing behind her?

"Good afternoon, Mrs. Rose," said Luke, tipping his hat.

"I do believe you speak that verse out of context," she said, trying to paint a religious gloss on her profligate behavior.

"I doubt if the good Lord begrudges us a chuckle now and then, though some people might call their condition sad," he said, nodding toward the drunken ranch hands.

"I thought you'd be searching the North-East Creek for a ghost today with the others," said Lenora, deftly changing the subject.

"Sheriff Morris didn't think he'd need many men, seeing how they've narrowed it down to just the creek. He took a couple of volunteers with him. He asked me to stay behind and keep an eye on things in town."

"It must be a handy character quirk to always be so sure of oneself, like Sheriff Morris," said Lenora.

"Folks might say the same thing about you." Deputy Davies gave her one of his look-into-her-soul gazes again.

What did this man want from her? She bristled. "Well, if you'll excuse me, Deputy Davies, I have an errand to finish before I get back to my ranch."

"I'll accompany you."

"Oh that's quite alright. I've managed quite well by myself up till now."

"I'm sure that's true, ma'am. But I've been thinking about some things that might help with our investigation. We need to talk."

Chapter Seven

"Time is insufficient for questions, Deputy Davies. I have a ranch to run." Lenora busied herself as she spoke, fiddling with her gloves as if his investigation was not worth her full attention.

"I understand about ranching. I'll just walk with you while you finish your errand."

"Deputy Davies," she said, meeting his eyes, her dander fluffed like a duck about to take flight, "if you intend to put me through another interrogation, you might as well know right now that I have every intention of withholding my cooperation. I have told you everything I know. I will not suffer another inquisition." She lifted her chin defiantly.

"For a rancher's wife you sure use a lot of big words."

"I should hope so. My parents paid a princely sum for me to learn those big words."

Deputy Davies cocked his head, prepared to listen in his patient way.

"I attended private school in New York," she explained, "Mrs. Bindleton's School for Young Ladies. Diction was prized, as was deportment, along with the classics, of course."

"Your parents must have been mighty disappointed when you flunked deportment."

"I beg your pardon?"

"You know what I'm talking about." Luke's humorless declaration seemed to make Mrs. Rose even more perturbed. He could see it in the flash of her eyes. Luke saw something else there that he itched to uncover. What did she know that she would not reveal? Cyrus was right about one thing. The odds were that Mrs. Lenora Rose wasn't inclined to harm another human being, especially her husband. But she had maintained from the beginning that her husband was not dead, or at least, that he had not drowned. If she was right, where was he?

"I must repair to my ranch now." Lenora started to step around him.

"You said you had an errand." Luke took a quick step toward her, blocking her passage with his body. That was a mistake. Her nearness caused a warm wave of desire to flow over him. He clenched his fists at his sides in a foolish effort to stop a heightened sense of arousal from reaching his brain, as if tensing hand muscles could give him control of the rest of himself. "Where shall I escort you first?" he said, his voice husky and flat as he strived to cool the flaming effect she had on him.

Lenora sighed. "I'm trying to locate a hired hand named Sam Wright. I hear he does odd jobs for several ranches in the area, and quite economically."

"That's your Sam right there." Luke turned a half-turn and pointed toward the three-ring entertainment in the street. The ranch hands were still fussing with the horse, but the crowd around them was a little thinner now.

"Right where?"

"There, passed out by his horse."

Lenora turned back to look at the street. As she did, a bouquet of her exquisite cologne, as sweet as a basket of Georgia peaches, wafted into Luke's nostrils. *I bet she perfumes her hair. A woman who smells this good could make a man give it all away for just one night.* Luke shook himself. He must keep his mind on his work. If he was not careful, his investigation of Mrs. Rose would become as dubious as the fox's guard duty over the henhouse.

At times he worried it already had.

"The big one is his friend, Buck Jennings. He's the mean one of the three. The little one is Mitchell Pendergrass, also known as Pea-Pod Pendergrass. All part-time itinerant ranch hands, part-time jail birds."

"Oh," she said. "I guess I'd better wait till he's sober." Then Lenora turned again and stared at the drunken man a moment, as if the knowledge of who he really was had trouble sinking its way into her mind.

"Good idea."

"The general store," she said, still staring at Sam Wright, "then home."

Together they walked the few doors down Main Street to Aeschelman's Mercantile. A bell tinkled over the door as they stepped into the cool and dusty retail shop. After a few seconds its proprietor, Mr. Faustus Aeschelman, appeared from behind a rough brown curtain that separated the rear storage area from the shelves heavy laden with sundry foodstuffs and dry goods.

Aeschelman's was a feast for the eyes, a dazzling cornucopia of material delights for adults and children alike. Every surface—even the ceiling where Mr. Aeschelman had suspended odd-shaped items too difficult to crate—called to the shopper to handle, taste, or smell. Barrels, boxes, and tins of foodstuffs, farm and household tools, bolts of cloth and boxes of sewing notions, toys and dolls, and colorful glass jars of various candies, hard and soft, were crowded into this marvelous emporium. All those sweet and savory smells mingled together to create a shopping sensation that could only be described as musty goodness.

After the duo had exchanged the usual greetings with the storekeeper, Lenora ordered what she came for and waited while Mr. Aeschelman assembled her purchases on the scuffed oak counter and rang up the sale. Luke stood by silently, watching and waiting like a body guard hovering around his assignment. Mr. Aeschelman glanced at him occasionally, as if he were searching for a clue as to why they were shopping together, but Luke's eyes gave nothing away. He kept his eyes on Lenora most of the time.

"I'm so very sorry about your wife, Mr. Aeschelman. Aleida was a saint." Lenora accepted her change from Mr. Aeschelman and dropped the coins with a muffled clink into her bag.

"She angel now," said the plump German proprietor as he pointed toward Heaven. The forlorn widower smiled behind his frothy white beard, but his smile did not reach his eyes. He said no more as his sausage-like fingers assembled Lenora's purchases into a tight bundle: coffee, sugar, ten yards of lustrous daffodil taffeta and thread to match. She watched him cut a length of stiff brown paper, place her purchases in the center, and then expertly fold and refold the edges into a neat package. He secured it with firmly twine.

"You gave her a beautiful farewell, Mr. Aeschelman. Aleida liked pretty things. She wouldn't have been disappointed."

Mr. Aeschelman looked stricken, nodded silently, and pushed the package toward Lenora. Luke picked it up before she could reach for it, nodded to the storekeeper, and he and Lenora left the store, the bell over the door tinkling as they exited.

After the shadowy interior of the mercantile the noon sunshine seemed very bright. Few shoppers were in the street because it was time for the noon meal for most folks. Luke pulled his hat down a little lower in front of his face. Lenora pulled her frilly blue bonnet from behind her back and tied it with a bow under her chin.

"What happened to his wife?" said Luke, taking Lenora's arm and guiding them toward Olathe's.

"She died of sepsis about two weeks ago. Sad. They have six children, five boys and a girl, Anneke, who is the youngest. She's nine."

"That is sad."

"The funeral was sadder. James and I attended. All those big boys crying, the little girl inconsolable, and Mr. Aeschelman looked so lost. He still looks lost."

"I know that sorrow."

"You do?" Lenora stopped walking and faced him.

"My ma died when I was little."

"I'm very sorry to hear that, Deputy Davies."

Luke nodded a thank-you and started walking again. "I'm long over it. I remember only a few things about her."

"How old were you when she passed?"

Luke intentionally slowed his pace to have more time with Mrs. Rose. He was torn between speeding up his investigation, because she must get back to the ranch before sunset, or slowing it down to draw out his precious minutes with her. He dawdled also because he didn't like the thought of her riding alone in her wagon the nine miles back to her ranch. The Territory was a wild place, dangerous for everyone but particularly for isolated ranchers whose spreads were far from town. Bands of Cheyenne and Sioux still troubled settlers in the area despite the fact that the U.S. government had established a military presence nearby, Fort McKinney, a year earlier to deal with the threat. Lonely and often intoxicated soldiers from the fort were problem enough when it came to a beautiful woman making her way about town without an escort. Luke winced when he thought of what a Sioux or Cheyenne warrior might do to an unprotected woman alone on an isolated ranch.

"I was six."

"Deputy Davies, you speak with a touch of southern. Where do your people hail from?"

"I was born in Tennessee. My ma's folks lived there. Pa and Ma had a sheep and cattle ranch."

They stepped off the boardwalk onto Main Street, and Luke took Lenora's arm as he guided them across. He helped her step up onto the opposite boardwalk, tipping his hat to fellow shoppers they passed.

"How did you come to be in Wyoming Territory?" said Lenora.

"Pa was lonesome a long while after Ma died. One day he decided it would be better for all of us to be near his folks, just outside Fort Laramie. Eight years ago he sold the ranch and moved us seven boys back here."

"Seven boys? Your father never had to hire help."

"Nope."

"Why didn't you stay on the ranch?"

"Good question." Luke paused to think before answering. "I guess I was looking for excitement, a change."

"I remember feeling that way about coming here," said Lenora.

"I bet your folks had a hard time letting you go," said Luke.

"My mother took it the worst. I have no siblings, and Mother had a whole life planned for me. I assure you, Mother's castles in the air didn't include a cattle ranch in Wyoming Territory."

Luke glanced at the delicate woman on his arm and wondered how young she was. From the smoothness of her cheeks and her elaborate way of dress, she couldn't have been much out of her teens. It must have been very difficult indeed for her parents to put her on a wagon bound for the many dangers of the untamed West, so far from civilization.

"Have you written them about your husband's disappearance?"

Lenora took a deep breath and pursed her lips. "I have not."

Luke gave her a studied look. "You're alone here Mrs. Rose."

"Yes, that is true. But I see no reason to distress them so early in the search."

"I understand your thinking, but the earlier you contact them, the earlier they can help you. I could arrange for a message to reach them. Fort McKinney has telegraph."

"I appreciate your concern, Deputy Davies, but that won't be necessary. My husband will be found. And depending on his condition, at that time I will decide whether my folks—and Mr. Rose's—should be notified. If I contact them now it will only give credence to their fears about my going west."

"Are you concerned about alarming them, or are you worried they'll hightail it to the Territory and insist you go back to New York?"

Lenora stopped walking, removed her arm from the deputy's, and turned to face him. Her eyes flashed with annoyance. "You, sir, are scandalously intrepid in your approach to this investigation."

Luke stopped walking as well. "I don't know what intrepid means, but I can read the look on your face."

"Oh?"

"You don't want your folks to know you've been left alone to run your ranch."

"I'm not a mule, Deputy Davies. If my situation becomes dire, I shall not hesitate to seek help from family. But up to this point, I have things well in hand."

"No one would ever compare you to a mule, Mrs. Rose." *A purebred filly, perhaps, but never a mule.*

"And you, Deputy," said Lenora, starting to walk again and changing the subject, but this time keeping her arm to herself, "Did your parents dissuade you from leaving the family ranch at Fort Laramie?"

"I waited till Pa didn't need me anymore. Matthew and Mark, my older brothers, are still bachelors, and they seemed happy to stay on. My younger brothers were around to help too, so Pa was taken care of."

"Matthew and Mark? Don't tell me: the brother born after you is John." Lenora chuckled. "What about the other three?"

"When my ma ran out of gospel books, she turned to the Old Testament. Amos and Aaron, the twins. Then Seth, the youngest."

"Your mother was religious."

"I don't rightly remember much about my ma. I suppose so. The only book we had was the Bible. And Ma's ladies' magazines."

"Those were the only forms of literature your family had in the house?"

"It was enough."

"What did you discuss at meal times if you had no books?"

Luke thought about the question a few seconds before answering. "Our day. The livestock. Pa would read the scriptures. Of course, for a few years there our minds were taken up with the war. Supper talk was filled with troop movements. Battles and the like."

"At our house the war took our focus away from pretty much everything else the entire four years. But I was quite little then," added Lenora, "I didn't understand most of the conversations about battles or why they mattered."

"Well, most of our battle conversations," said Luke, in a slow drawl, "were along the lines of, 'Paaaaw, Luke ate all the taters again!'"

They both laughed.

"Your father never remarried?"

Luke shook his head, remembering sadly how his pa struggled to keep an air of civility about the homestead after Ma died. The dirty house, the scruffy way he and his brothers looked all the time without a woman to supervise the care of their hair and clothes. "Seven wild Indians make a tribe. Pa never met a woman desperate enough."

Olathe's was a hundred feet away. Luke dreaded having to end the light conversation and perform the unpleasant and historically rancorous chore of questioning Mrs. Rose. Though he had to get on with his duty, he didn't care to embarrass her in front of Mr. Olathe. He lightly touched her arm. "We can stop here." He turned and faced her.

"Why?"

"Mrs. Rose, I have to ask you a few more questions. I'm thinking you'd prefer to talk here than at Olathe's."

Lenora's face fell.

Luke sighed gustily and forced himself to continue. "You seem certain Mr. Rose did not drown."

Lenora stared at the ground and nodded dejectedly.

"You speak of him like he's still alive."

"I've told you, I have no evidence otherwise."

"Mrs. Rose," said Luke, waiting for her to lift her head and look at him. When she didn't respond, he gently touched her chin and tilted it upward to force her to meet his eyes. "Why, Mrs. Rose," he repeated, looking into her eyes, his finger still at her chin, "Why is his horse, left tied to a tree for three days without food or water, exposed to the rain and cold, why is that not enough evidence for you that your husband died out there, that night, in the storm?" Luke let his hand fall to his side and waited.

Lenora met his eyes but did not speak. Luke saw there something other than the anger and resentment he'd seen before. He saw terror. Uncharacteristically, she said nothing.

"Do you really think that your husband would abandon his horse, an exceptional horse, one he prized, to die on the banks of the North-East Creek?"

Lenora bowed her head again and looked at the ground. Again she did not answer.

"I can't believe that James Rose was such a man."

"Then what do you believe, Deputy Davies?"

"You're the one under investigation, Mrs. Rose. I ask the questions."

Her head shot up. "You think I killed my husband," she said, backing away from him a step. Her eyes flashed with outrage and her whole body stiffened.

"I didn't say that."

"But that's what you think, isn't it?"

"If a body isn't found soon floating in the North-East Creek, a lot of people around here will think that." Luke's tone was deliberately slow and calm as he tried to defuse the situation.

"You think I killed him and hid his body somewhere." Lenora's voice rose slightly.

"Mrs. Rose, no one said that. I'm just trying to fill all these holes to protect you from the wrath of a vengeful jury."

"Really?"

"You were the last person to see your husband alive. People think what they think." Luke hadn't wanted the conversation to go like this. He wished they could have stuck to ranches and family and books. But for her sake, he had to be blunt.

"I have not asked for your protection, Deputy Davies, nor do I require it."

Luke grimaced inwardly. He had overstepped the professional boundaries of his position. He had failed to be discreet in his dealings with Mrs. Rose. He would guard against this in the future. But she was wrong about one thing: She *did* need

89

protection, though it was futile to argue with her about it. This woman had a huge need to prove her independence.

"There's holes in your story, ma'am," said Luke, striving mightily to keep his voice calm so that she wouldn't take off in a huff. He needed answers, and he didn't care to end their time together as before in another angry exchange.

"Are you finished with your questions?" Lenora's tone was terse now, her torso trembling with anger.

"No, I—"

"Alright. I'll tell you what I did with my husband's body."

Luke's eyebrows shot up. He hoped from the bottom of his soul that this was not a confession, that he misunderstood what she had just said. He did not want to arrest Mrs. Rose.

"May I have my package, Deputy Davies?" she said, her hand extended toward her purchases.

Luke handed her the bundle, pushing down an anxious thought as he did that she might be planning to whack him over the head with it. But she didn't. Instead, she stood opposite him, a strange look of determination mixed with rage etched into her flawless face. She paused before speaking and drew a deep breath.

"I murdered my husband."

Luke was speechless, unbelieving what he was hearing, though Lenora looked sufficiently serious to merit a valid confession. She continued, her eyes flashing with anger and contempt.

"I smashed his brains with an anvil while he slept. Then, when I was certain he was dead, I skinned him and cut him up into a thousand pieces. Most of those I canned and stored down cellar. The rest I baked into a double-crust pie and ate for supper."

That scallywag of a woman.

"He was delicious."

Then Lenora turned, and with not so much as a by-your-leave, made a few large and angry strides, and in a moment was through the wide open door of Olathe's Feed and Livery.

Chapter Eight

White rays of sunshine streaming through Lenora's bedroom window were more demanding than any alarm clock. In response she pulled the quilts over her head in a recalcitrant snit.

She would stay in bed until she died.

Why get up? James had not returned, and Sheriff Morris had brought her no good news. No news at all, in fact, though the sheriff had said he would send word. She had anxiously awaited the sound of approaching horse hooves while she slogged through her daily chores in the house and around the barn. But none came.

How futile ranching seemed without James. What was the point? Together they had built something worthwhile, they were growing a dream. A livelihood. A legacy. A life. But now the onerous and dirty chores that fell to her alone were only motions to be performed, meaningless tasks she must do to fill the time, to keep the animals fed and milked and safe. Even the thought of breaking soil for her annual vegetable garden gave her no joy as it usually did. Her daffodil silk lay untouched. She would lay out the pattern and cut out her new dress—someday.

She was tired all the time. She hardly slept at night and food had no taste. Her appetite had disappeared with James. Her corset was growing loose.

Blackness settled over Lenora's soul. She felt cursed. Maybe James was so angry at her that he had deserted her once and for all. Maybe God was angry with her for the things she'd said to James the night he vanished. Maybe He had killed her husband to teach her a lesson.

Or was James injured somewhere on the vast prairie, waiting for help that did not come? Was he alive? Was he dead? Maybe she would never learn what happened to him or where he went on that tragic and rainy night after he left Beauty tied to a tree on the banks of the North-East Creek. Maybe she would spend the rest of her life on this torture rack of the unknown, her mind pulled in every direction until she thought she would scream from the strain.

Maybe she had already lost her mind. She certainly was not acting herself lately, telling Deputy Davies that cockamamie cannibal story. What evil spirit had possessed her to speak such outrage?

Well who cared anyway? She was sick of the deputy's repetitive questions and Mr. Morehouse's assumptions and Sheriff Morris' accusations. She was sick of all of them, and she was angry at the frustrating black hole of oblivion she had fallen into. If James was lost then all was lost, and what she said or did made no difference. Without James, she could fall no farther.

Or perhaps not. With burning shame she remembered how she had let Deputy Davies touch his fingers to her chin without protest. And worse than worse, in a moment of truth, she acknowledged to herself that she had liked it, the feeling of his gentle caress, the warm look of concern she saw in his eyes.

Perhaps his concern was genuine?

But how could she deny the memory of her dear James by exhibiting such brazen behavior? She was no trollop. Until James stepped through the front door of their ranch house by his own power or until his body was returned to her, she was still a married woman. She should not notice another man's good looks, and she certainly should not take wanton pleasure in another man's touch, no matter how dire her marital circumstances appeared, no matter how innocent the contact.

The mooing of a milk cow waiting to be relieved of its burden interrupted Lenora's sad reverie and served as another reminder that James was not here. She must get up. Now.

Hellfire and damnation, she did not want to endure another day of this entombment!

Angrily Lenora yanked at the bedding. As she did, James' rifle fell with a clatter to the bare wood floor, waking Ulysses, whose frenzied barking filled the little room before he was on all fours. She had forgotten her new nightly routine of moving the rifle from its place above the door to her bed, insurance against another visit from the faceless trespasser in heavy boots.

"Stop it, Ulysses!" *Dumb dog.* "Stop it!"

Reluctantly Ulysses stopped barking, but not before Lenora grabbed James' leather belt from a drawer and whacked the panicked animal across his snout. Ulysses yelped in pain, which made Lenora wince. The bullmastiff look stricken, whimpering while settling himself at the foot of the bed—a safe distance from his mistress—where he cowered while eyeing Lenora, who had slumped down onto the edge of the bed, bare feet on the floor, the belt still in her hand, utterly dejected.

At first she had failed to tell Deputy Davies about the footsteps outside her bedroom wall because she didn't want him snooping around her ranch more than necessary to conduct his investigation. But now she was resolute in her plan to keep silent about the incident and deal with it herself lest another encounter with the handsome deputy create needless temptation. As for the irksome sheriff, she would do everything in her power to avoid ever talking to him again.

Besides, the intruder had not returned. Perhaps there had never been an intruder. Perhaps, in her overly distraught, sleep deprived mind, she had imagined the entire scenario. Or, God forbid, perhaps she was haunted by an evil specter in her own particular valley of the shadow of death.

Lenora sat on the edge of the bed, breathing hard, appalled at her cussing and black thoughts and feeling profoundly guilty for her wicked treatment of her loyal pet. She was falling apart, and she did not want to go on. She must unburden her secret to someone, soon.

"I'm sorry, Ulysses," she said, looking at the timid, soulful eyes of her dog. "Forgive me?"

Ulysses whimpered but stayed where he was. Finally Lenora got up from the bed and walked over to him, sat down on the floor and wrapped her arms around the trembling animal.

"I'm sorry, Ulysses," she said. "I'm so sorry." She held onto the dog for several minutes, until the animal stopped trembling and started licking her face. After she knew Ulysses was calm, she released her hold and leaned back against the cool, hard bedroom wall. For a long time she sat there staring at the ceiling, stroking Ulysses' back and half listening to the animals in the barn hollering to be fed, unable to find it within herself to get up off the bedroom floor to face another meaningless day.

After a long while she pushed herself up and stood, but not before she promised herself that,

James or no James, she would be in church next Sunday.

#

Luke tried to be discreet as he kept one eye on his hymnal and the other on the church's narrow entryway, waiting for Mrs. Rose to appear. Service had begun, the pump organ was in motion, and though it was unseasonably warm, all voices were raised with fervor to sing "The All-Seeing God" from *Divine and Moral Songs.* Still there was no sign of Mrs. Rose.

> *Almighty God, thy piercing eye*
> *Strikes through the shades of night,*
> *And our most secret actions lie*
> *All open to thy sight.*

Luke swept his eyes around the whitewashed sanctuary again, convinced that he must have missed the thick bun of coffee-colored hair that so captivated him. Mrs. Rose did not strike him as the type who would stay home from service without good reason. As he turned his head slightly over one shoulder, his eyes locked with those of a girl about sixteen standing with her mother in the pew behind his, her face framed prettily by a beribboned rose bonnet. She blushed coquettishly, eyes smiling over the top of her hymnal. Luke snapped his head back to his own hymnal and returned to singing.

> *There's not a sin that we commit,*

97

Nor wicked word we say,
But in thy dreadful book 'tis writ
Against the judgment day.

Then a flash through an open window, a woman on a buckboard pulled by a familiar brown Morgan. Above the singing Luke could not hear Mrs. Rose setting the brake or tethering Beast to graze during the two-hour service, but he imagined it clearly in his mind's eye.

And must the crimes that I have done
Be read and publish'd there;
Be all exposed before the sun,
While men and angels hear?

After a few minutes every head in the room turned to watch Lenora walk down a side aisle, alone, on Luke's side of the sanctuary as she searched for an empty seat. A married couple a few rows in front of him scooted down the pew to make room for her.

Mrs. Rose looked charming today, distinguishing herself from the somber flock of black crows on the front row by appearing in a modest, long-sleeve, pale yellow bustled dress with three layers of frills on the overskirt and a matching bonnet. But then, Mrs. Rose looked charming in everything she wore, though Luke wondered how a woman survived frivolous layers of heat-capturing petticoats in a stuffy building like this one.

Although service had hardly started, already he'd been tempted more than once to loosen the collar of his stiff white Sunday shirt. The sanctuary was crowded, and the numerous warm bodies made the heat more oppressive. All the Gothic-style windows on both sides of the sanctuary were pushed open for ventilation, but no breeze cooperated to provide a respite from the heat.

They sang several hymns. Then Reverend Thomas took the pulpit, instructed everyone to open their bibles, and began to preach about eternity. Luke tried and failed to follow the message, which became a low buzz in the back of his head. His mind was on Mrs. Rose. She was beautiful even from the back.

Not long into the Reverend's message, women began pulling fans from their reticules, snapping them open and wagging them back and forth to create personal breezes in distinctly feminine style. Luke wiped his forehead with a handkerchief. Other men did the same. Somewhere in the rear of the sanctuary a small child fussed, whining on and off in an irritating way. Finally Luke heard the sound of someone carrying the child through the entryway. A door opened and closed but was stingy about leaving a breeze. The muffled whines of the child grew fainter then disappeared. Luke quit listening to the Reverend Thomas altogether. It was too hot to think about Hell.

Then he saw Lenora slump sideways, languidly fall forward, and with a soft thump and a swish of petticoats, hit the floor. Reverend Thomas' extravagantly long beard stopped bobbing and the sanctuary suddenly hushed. Luke was on his feet in an instant, rushing to Lenora's pew, clearing the crowd around her. He crouched on the floor near her body and felt her wrist for a pulse.

"She's not breathing. She needs air," he said, urging worshippers to step aside. "Mrs. Rose!" he said, softly fingering her cheek. "Mrs. Rose!" She didn't respond. "We have to get her outside," Luke said to the gawking crowd that surrounded them, "where it's cooler."

Luke quickly untied the bow under Lenora's chin and pulled her bonnet away from her head. He put his right arm under her knees and with his left he cradled her head and shoulders. With the entire assembly looking on, he carried her through the entryway and out the front door of the little white church. He paused at the top of the steps, unwilling to lay her on the dirty ground. She was dressed too fine. The yard around the church was trampled, more dried mud than grass. Lenora remained unconscious in Luke's arms while he cast about, trying to decide where to set her down.

"I'll get a blanket from my buggy," offered Dr. Biggerstaff, who had followed Luke through the door and recognized Luke's dilemma at once. Buffalo's only physician, Dr. Cornelius Biggerstaff was an average-size, middle-aged man with a bald spot surrounded by salt-and-pepper hair. He pushed his wire spectacles up his nose as he spoke to Luke.

100

Luke nodded.

"And water," the doctor added, as he hurried down the wood steps and around the corner of the clapboard church building to the stables where worshippers parked their conveyances and provided shelter for their horses.

Luke gazed down at Lenora's face, which had turned an unworldly, bluish white like fine porcelain. Her lips were exquisitely fashioned, supple and kissable. Her bosoms strained against the form-fitting fabric of her bodice. Her body, limp as it was, felt sensual and soft against his. His thoughts wandered to places they ought never to go—on the church steps, no less. Luke groaned.

Lord, you promised not to give us more temptation than we can bear, but I got a bear of a temptation threatening my salvation right here.

Reverend Thomas ended service early due to the heat and the general disturbance, and now churchgoers were spilling out the door past Luke and Lenora. Most of the men used the opportunity to visit and smoke. But older female members of Johnson Ebenezer, motherly types, buzzed about Lenora like bees at a picnic. Two in particular, Eleanor Graves and Ada Mendelssohn, in their bombazine dresses and lamp-shade style hats reminiscent of earlier decades, tied in overly large bows beneath their wrinkled chins, joined Luke on the narrow threshold, fanning Lenora and tut-tutting over the poor girl and "wasn't it a pity" and "they still haven't found his body" and "only twenty-two" and "all alone on that ranch so far from town."

Luke was still holding Lenora on the church steps and the two women were still fanning and waiting for Dr. Biggerstaff when Lenora's eyes fluttered slightly. She began to loll her head slowly and make low moaning sounds.

"Mrs. Rose," said Luke quietly, bending his face down close to hers. The faint fragrance of flowers, redolent of magnolia, filled his nose. Everything about this woman was quintessentially feminine; that was her allure. Luke tried to memorize this moment and its gifts, her fragrance and the feel of her, to carry them back with him to his lonely room at the boarding house.

Low moaning.

"Mrs. Rose."

At the sound of the steady, masculine voice, Lenora drew up her right arm around Luke's neck, nuzzled her face into his shoulder, and purred, eyes still closed.

"Hold me," she said, breathily.

Now it was Luke's turn to stop breathing. "Mrs. Rose, I'm not—"

"I'm so sorry, darling. Never again."

Never again?

"Hold me. Please don't leave me."

Mrs. Graves and Mrs. Mendelssohn stopped fanning and looked at each other, speechless, eyes wide with shock. Then they looked at Luke, who remained stoic, sobered by the knowledge that Mrs.

Rose surely imagined she was in the arms of another, missing man, the one to whom she truly belonged. The one she waited for.

Luke's ears burned with embarrassment, not because of Lenora's murmurings but because he couldn't remove her arm from around his neck. Both of his were occupied holding her. More churchgoers stepped through the doorway. Luke met their startled looks impassively. He had done nothing wrong.

Dr. Biggerstaff arrived with a lap blanket accompanied by a small boy toting a bucket of well water. Luke carried Lenora down the steps and laid her gently down, straightening her skirt for modesty. Lenora started to come around after the doctor dipped a borrowed hanky into the water and pressed it to her face, though she was still groggy from being out so long.

"Mrs. Rose. Mrs. Rose," the doctor said urgently. Lenora had been unconscious for at least a minute and a half.

Luke withdrew from the scene on the ground to let others take over. He stood nearby, watching, sensing that he had been involved enough today with the lovely Mrs. Rose to set tongues wagging until long past harvest time. How could he possibly foresee that she would mistake him for her husband in her confused state of mind? He only meant to move her to the open air. And what did she mean by "never again?"

"What happened?" said Lenora, as she began to come around. She blinked her eyes repeatedly.

"You fainted," said Dr. Biggerstaff. The doctor kneeled on the ground beside Lenora, holding her hand and pressing the damp cloth about her face.

Lenora said nothing, just stared, wide eyed, at the doctor and the halo of faces crowded around above her head. She seemed to have trouble comprehending.

"You think it was the heat, doctor?" asked a female onlooker.

Mrs. Marietta Nolan crouched next to Dr. Biggerstaff, using her cane to steady herself, ignoring the mess the dried mud made of the hem of her dress. She was that kind of woman. Good-hearted beneficence overflowing from zaftig dark blue georgette with a halo of parted angel hair pulled loosely into a small bun pinned at her nape.

"Probably, though she's under a lot of strain right now."

"Shame on me. I should have looked in on her before this." Mrs. Nolan shook her head.

"You still can. They haven't found the body," said Dr. Biggerstaff. "Her hardest days are ahead."

"When was the last time you ate, Mrs. Rose?" asked Dr. Biggerstaff, turning back to Lenora.

It took Lenora several seconds to answer. "I don't ... remember." Lenora's eyes were completely open, but it was evident by the puzzled look on her face that she was still having trouble grasping what had happened to her.

"When she's back on her feet, Doctor, will you tell her I'll be by to see her?" asked Mrs. Nolan.

"I'll tell her," he said, and then, as Mrs. Nolan struggled to stand, he offered his arm. "Here, Etta, let me help you up." Dr. Biggerstaff took Mrs. Nolan's free arm while she used her other, gripping her cane to awkwardly pull herself to a standing position.

"Tell her I'll be by soon," she said, batting at the front of her skirt to loosen the mud dust.

"I'll do that," said the doctor, still standing over Lenora.

"Thank you," said Mrs. Nolan. She took a last, pitying look at Lenora. "Poor thing," she said, shaking her head again, and then she walked away.

Dr. Biggerstaff crouched down next to Lenora again. "Are you getting enough rest?" he said.

Lenora looked at the doctor blankly.

"Emmaline and I are going to take you home," said Dr. Biggerstaff, not waiting for Lenora's answer. "And I want you to come to my office in the morning. Do you understand me?"

Chapter Nine

Lenora paused outside the sheriff's office, bracing to lock horns with the cantankerous Sheriff Morris. She deduced from his absence at her ranch door that James' body had not been found by the second search party. If they had succeeded in their grim mission, they would have delivered it to her by now. This meant that, after all these agonizing days of waiting and wondering, she still did not know with certainty whether she was a widow, an abandoned wife, or the unlucky spouse of a vindictive husband bent on maintaining the upper hand in the most cruel manner, as the sheriff had so indelicately suggested at their first meeting. Inwardly Lenora raged at the injustice of having been thrust into this wretched purgatory of being.

She took a deep breath and, steeled by her rage, turned the doorknob and crossed the threshold.

Lenora shut the door behind her and stood, shoulders erect, holding her parasol and matching silk bag, her appearance today in this clutch of masculinity exceeding in contrast her former lush attire. From her straw filly to her pointed leather high-tops, she was adorned in creamy white barege, her lavish polonaise and feminine bustle draped over yards of silken tussah, which had been drawn up into innumerous rows of ruffles. The bow that tied the filly under her slender chin was the identical root beer foam color of the tussah, rendering her visage equally frothy.

"Mrs. Rose," said Luke, smiling as he politely pushed back his chair to stand and greet her.

Lenora blushed and returned the smile. After Dr. Biggerstaff and his wife Emmaline had escorted her home from church on Sunday, Emmaline had taken her aside and explained to her—overly melodramatically and in blistering detail, in Lenora's opinion—who it was that had carried her unconscious self from the floor of Johnson Ebenezer Christian Church to their buggy blanket spread on the ground outside the sanctuary in full view of the entire assembly. Thankfully, Lenora had virtually no memory of her dreadful humiliation. But seeing Deputy Davies again, and in such close proximity, kindled her imagination keenly. She blushed again. He was so tall and handsome. Why couldn't she have been rescued by some ugly, flat-footed farm hand and been spared all the drama and gossip associated with the so very attractive, so very eligible deputy?

Deputy Davies' desk was spread with official-looking documents, as if he had been reading before Lenora entered. In the center was his lunch from the boarding house, slabs of roast beef, overcooked and dry but nesting on thick slices of freshly baked white bread. The sandwich sat untouched in the middle of a piece of waxed paper. In the small, enclosed office the tang of dill pickle was sharp.

Sheriff Morris sat at his desk, bent over a coffee cup and nothing else. Steam from the cup twirled silently upward. Sheriff Morris did not stand up.

"It's been several days," said Lenora, not moving away from the door, "I thought it appropriate that I should enquire."

"Have a seat, Mrs. Rose," said Sheriff Morris.

Luke brought a visitor's chair and set it by the sheriff's desk as before. Lenora thanked him. He nodded and returned to his desk.

"I'm sure you realize by now, Mrs. Rose, that we did not find your husband's body in the creek," said Sheriff Morris, cupping his hands around his coffee.

It took every ounce of Lenora's strength to hold back a saucy I-told-you-so. She snapped her lips together to keep her tongue from escaping. If sprung from its cage it would mate with the monster

108

of injustice now loosed in her soul and produce offspring meaner and more feral than a herd of wild boars. She simply nodded.

"I sent four good men downstream. They searched clean up to Clearmont. Day and a half of riding each way. Found nothing."

"Please do provide me their identities that I might properly extend my gratitude," said Lenora.

"Deputy Davies will see to that," said Sheriff Morris, gesturing absently toward Luke's desk.

Lenora glanced toward Deputy Davies. Their eyes met and he nodded in agreement. Lenora felt a little zing within, as if her heart were a taut, vibrating string, and an unseen hand had just plucked it. For the first time she saw that Deputy Davies had beautiful eyes, gentle brown and full of kindness. His skin was an earthy tone, probably from hours in the saddle. He was handsome of form, but it was beauty from within that—

What kind of a trollop thinks such thoughts in grave circumstances such as these? Horrified at her heathen inclination to lasciviousness, Lenora abruptly turned back to the sheriff.

"And the next step of your strategy is, sir?"

"My deputy is preparing a message. We'll send someone to all the towns downstream of the North-East."

"What kind of schedule do you foresee for this endeavor?" asked Lenora.

"You mean how long?"

"Yes."

"Depends."

Sheriff Morris stood up and walked to the wood stove. He poured himself another cup of coffee and returned to his desk, but not before attacking a pesky itch in a singularly masculine section of his anatomy. Lenora held her breath, expecting that any second the crotchety old fart would, with equal grace, deposit something warm and wet into the cuspidor parked near his desk. She noted, wryly, that he failed to offer any liquid refreshment to his guest. After the raunchy exercise she had just observed at the wood stove, she deemed his oversight a blessing.

"Depends on what, sir?" asked Lenora.

"On the others."

"Please explain your reasoning, Sheriff Morris." *Heaven help us. Drawing information from this insufferable man is like milking a farrow cow.*

"I can't know how long before the other offices report back," said Sheriff Morris, becoming testy. "Depends on numbers."

"Numbers, Sheriff Morris?"

"Most of the towns up North only have one man." He slurped a mouthful of coffee. "This ain't New York. We're too far north and west for railroad. Fort McKinney's got telegraph, but every little wide spot in the trail anywhere near here depends on the stagecoach. That includes any settlement downstream from where your husband drowned."

Lenora stiffened. The lout, he obviously enjoyed provoking her, and she knew all these railroad-telegraph-stagecoach details already. Telegraph lines followed railway routes. Yet somehow, illogically, she had hoped this frustrating reality would not affect her situation.

"Sheriff Morris, is it not true that Clearmont is twenty-nine miles northeast from Buffalo?"

"That's about right."

"Sir, do you really believe it likely that my husband's body floated unhindered all those miles and miles," Lenora gave a little wave of her hand, "that it somehow bypassed every fallen tree, every overhanging bush, every protruding embankment?"

Sheriff Morris banged down his coffee cup. Coffee sloshed onto the desk and his shirt. He ignored it.

"Someone needs to educate you on who's the sheriff in this town and who's the widow of a missing rancher." Sheriff Morris leaned over his desk, eyes flashing with anger at Lenora.

"Cyrus," admonished Luke with hushed restraint. He didn't say it as if he expected a response.

Sheriff Morris looked at Luke, back again at Lenora, and then screwed up his face in disgust. Then he leaned back in his chair while his angry words hung in the air, filling the cramped office with tension and ill will.

"I only meant," said Lenora, choosing her words slowly and carefully, "that if your men, after a careful search, did not find James' body between here and Clearmont, a distance of nearly thirty miles, then you would have me believe that you have concluded—in your professional opinion, of course—that his body floated *beyond* thirty miles in a matter of only days?"

Sheriff Morris jumped to a standing position. "Girlie, someone didn't raise you right," he said, banging on his desk again, this time with a fist.

"Cyrus!" Now Luke stood up, smacking the back of his chair against the wall in his haste, though he stayed respectfully behind his desk in deference to his boss.

Lenora glanced at Luke in surprise. She had not before seen this side of the man. Briefly their eyes met, and that connection, fleeting though it was, strengthened and calmed her. She turned back to the sheriff and more quietly said, "Sheriff Morris, my husband *alive* couldn't have swum thirty miles in such a short time. The only way a cadaver could make the trip on your schedule is in a steamboat!"

Lenora stood up, locked angry eyes with Luke's grave ones, then turned about and, without another word, walked out the door. Somehow she mustered sufficient grace not to slam it, though on the inside she slammed it quite violently indeed.

#

The door had hardly clicked shut before Luke left his desk and stepped angrily to the sheriff's desk, his mouth set in grim determination.

"Why?" asked Luke rhetorically, both his hands on Cyrus' desk, leaning in to put his face close to his boss. "The woman is mourning her husband!" He said this slowly and evenly, carefully enunciating each word as if the sheriff was too dense to comprehend the big picture and needed to have things S-P-E-L-L-E-D O-U-T.

"Uppity bluestocking is what she is," snapped the sheriff, though he looked shocked at his deputy's uncharacteristic outburst. Sheriff Morris reached into his shirt pocket for his tobacco pouch. "Wish James Rose would come back from the grave so she'd stay the hell out of my office," he growled. He sat down and began pinching shreds of tobacco from the pouch with his thumb and index finger, not bothering to make eye contact with Luke.

"Why blame the woman? She just wants to find her husband."

"Hogwash. She doesn't have him to henpeck anymore so she henpecks me."

Luke rolled his eyes. "She has reason to be upset," he said, striving for self-control. It would serve no purpose to advertise his feelings for the grieving widow. And her bluestocking ways were just one of her abundant charms. He stood up and walked to the window and remained there, hands on his hips, gazing down the street. "Every day we don't find that body it looks worse."

"We'll find it."

"Beyond the thirty miles to Clearmont?" Luke stayed at the window, arms folded across his chest now, but turned his head to speak directly to the sheriff.

Sheriff Morris stopped pulling the string on his tobacco pouch and looked at Luke. "How do I know?" he said, irritation building in his voice. "I don't got any more clues than you."

"I don't like this whole thing."

"What's to like about a dead body and a nagging widow?" said Sheriff Morris as he used two fingers to put a pinch of tobacco in his cheek.

Luke glared at his boss. "We don't *have* a body." They had a widow for sure, but Mrs. Lenora Rose was no nag. Luke kept that thought to himself. Cyrus was riled enough.

"For God's sake, Luke," said the sheriff, raising his voice several levels, "the woman doesn't even have enough sense to put on widow's weeds." Sheriff Morris leaned back in his chair and lifted mud-caked boots onto the edge of his desk. A small chunk of dried mud broke off and fell onto the desk. With his heel he shoved it to the floor, scraping the desk as he did.

"She doesn't believe she's a widow. She thinks he's still alive."

"Lunatic female," muttered the sheriff between noisy chaws of tobacco. "All of 'em, loony."

Luke stared pensively at the sheriff a few seconds. Then abruptly he left the window, rounded his desk, and pulled his hat from the rack in the corner of his small office area. He scooped up the

114

loose papers on his desk, folded them over twice, and shoved them in his shirt pocket.

"I'll be back in a while," he said, moving toward the door.

"Where you going?"

"Aeschelman's," he said, smashing his hat onto his head, "to send these letters."

"Hmpf," grunted Sheriff Morris. Then, pointing to Luke's lunch, "You goin' to eat that?"

Luke turned back to his sandwich and pickle. "Help yourself," he said with disgust. Then he strode out the door, not refraining from indulging, as Lenora had, in the type of deliciously loud and satisfying exit that perfectly suits a heated farewell.

#

A bell tinkled over the door at Aeschelman's General Store. Lenora looked up from the rear corner of the mercantile toward the street and at once recognized the tall silhouette of Deputy Davies darkening the doorway. Not desiring to be grilled again about James' disappearance, her first inclination was to hide. But that was silly. There was no reason to fear more questions; she had harmed no one. A furtive glance around the compact store told her that she had no place to hide anyway. She squared her shoulders, preparing to engage with the deputy. She knew he'd have something to say to her, likely probing and insulting. He always did.

Mr. Aeschelman heard the bell too, walked through the rough brown curtains, and stood at the counter waiting expectantly.

"Morning, Faustus," said Luke. But instead of stopping at the counter he proceeded directly to the rear of the store where Lenora had her eyes fixed on a display of mouse traps. His boots clunked on the bare wood floor in a thoroughly masculine fashion, commanding the attention of both the storekeeper and Lenora.

"Ma'am," said Luke, tipping his hat as he approached.

Luke stopped a few feet away from Lenora. Even without looking at him his very nearness made her chest tighten and her stomach flutter. The weather was warmer now so he wasn't bundled as usual in his thick corduroy coat. His shiny deputy star was pinned to his cream-colored shirt, which like everything he wore had served him many years but was clean and complemented a muscular physique. He had a sturdiness about him, like a well-built house, a place that never changes, a place you can always come back to. Lenora set the mouse trap back on the shelf and turned to respond, but he spoke again before she had a chance.

"You look lovelier than usual today, Mrs. Rose." He smiled, his eyes taking her in, head to toe, appreciatively.

"Thank you," she said. Her voice may have been stiff but the rest of her quivered like jelly. She was self-conscious under his gaze and annoyed at

116

herself for enjoying his compliment so much. She shouldn't be noticing the deputy and his fine points at such a time as this. The man was tall, handsome, and, when he wasn't accusing her of murder, decent and likable. But he always seemed to be hanging around, wanting something from her. She wondered when the vexing questions would start.

"Dressed like that, it's hard for me to imagine you in your barn, feeding farm stock and mucking stalls." Luke smiled again and pushed his hat back.

Lenora chuckled at the absurdity, which broke the ice at least temporarily. She returned the smile.

"I borrow James' work clothes for chores."

Luke's smile disappeared. "I have to ask you something," he said, straightening up.

Lenora looked up at him, but for the first time the thought of being interrogated didn't make her defensive. Perhaps it was nothing more than his obvious efforts to make her feel at ease, but something surely had changed in their tenuous relationship. She no longer felt like Luke was on the opposing side.

"Why do you burn your bridges behind you?"

Lenora sighed audibly. "Sheriff Morris doesn't take me seriously. Never has. It's all I can do to keep from screaming when he starts into it."

"I tried to tell you before. He's old fashioned. He treats all women with a certain ... gruffness."

"The word is condescension. And knowing that he treats all women badly is supposed to kindle a flame of charity in my heart for the man?"

117

Luke grimaced. "I know he's a leathery old boot, but you could at least try to be patient with him."

"I will try, Deputy Davies, I promise. Because you ask. But before I take on such a herculean task, don't you think I should master something easy, like walking on water?"

Ignoring her sarcasm, Luke pulled the letters from his pocket and waved them in front of her. "Sheriff Morris instructed me to contact every town downstream from where we found your husband's horse," he said. "He really is making a sincere effort to find your husband."

Lenora's conscious was smitten. At some deep level she knew that both Deputy Davies and Sheriff Morris were doing the best they knew how to find James. They'd been handed a difficult and frustrating task, made all the more difficult by a prickly wife who was angry at her loss and fearful of her future. She also knew, upon reflection, that her criticism of Sheriff Morris' investigation was a criticism of his deputy as well. She felt very ashamed of her caustic words.

"I apologize, Deputy Davies. I must learn to tame my tongue."

Luke nodded in appreciation.

"Truly, I am grateful for all you and the sheriff are doing on my behalf. It can't be pleasant for you." Lenora moved her shopping basket to her other arm and began removing her day gloves. It gave her something to do. It was an awkward moment.

It must have been awkward for Luke also, because he changed the subject. "You hired Sam Wright yet?"

"No, not yet. Some of the neighboring ranchers have been by in the evenings, taking turns at helping. Such nice people."

"All good people," agreed Luke.

"But then Ben Slocomb came over recently and offered to help every day until James returns," she said. "I offered to pay him, even if it was just a little, but he refused."

"That's neighborly of him."

"Indeed. I hope his parents aren't behind it. They need his help as much as I do."

"I'm sure they don't mind lending him to you for a while. He has brothers who can help. Ben's young and strong. Ranch chores won't hurt him."

"I'm sure they won't. But I can't be taking advantage. I don't know how long this trial will last."

Lenora's reference to her missing husband sobered their pleasant encounter instantly, like a swiftly passing cloud darkens the sun. Lenora needed to remind herself why it was that she had engaged Deputy Davies in the first place, lest her newfound interest in the all-too-available deputy cause her to forget who she was, the very-much-married Mrs. James Rose.

It appeared to Lenora that their business was finished, but nevertheless Luke leaned idly against a wood column as if he were reluctant to end the conversation. But before either of them could say another word, the bell over the entry door tinkled loudly, momentarily pausing their conversation while they both turned to see who entered. Lenora's guard went up when she recognized the shopper— the biggest gossipmonger in Buffalo. Luke stood up straight as well.

"Mrs. Biggerstaff," he said, deferentially putting his fingers to his hat.

"Why Deputy Davies, how nice to see you," cooed the bosomy older woman, grabbing Luke's arm. Her face lit up like saloon gas lights on payday. "I just saw Mrs. Mendelssohn down by the bank and I was telling her how chivalrous it was of you to carry poor Mrs. Rose out of the service last Sunday the way you did the poor thing so alone now and her husband drowned and all and that ranch to take care of and having to care for all those smelly animals and—"

Lenora stepped from behind Luke, her face flushed with embarrassment and annoyance.

"Lenora," gasped Mrs. Biggerstaff, clasping her hand to her chest. "I didn't realize you were with the deputy," she said, a little too tartly for Lenora's liking.

Reluctantly, it seemed to Lenora, the older woman released her hold on Luke's arm. "I'm not with the deputy," she said, trying to modulate her

120

voice in such a way as not to sound defensive. She hoped her face didn't reveal how hard her heart was pounding.

"Oh," said Mrs. Biggerstaff.

Lenora heard a lot in that oh—none of it good. "I was just leaving," she said. Then, remembering her manners, "Thank you again, Mrs. Biggerstaff, for accompanying me home on Sunday. It was very nice of you and the doctor."

"It's what Good Samaritans do, dear. Nothing more."

"Nevertheless, I appreciate it. Please give my regards to Dr. Biggerstaff."

"You haven't come to see him, dear. He's worried about you. You promised." Mrs. Biggerstaff shook her finger at Lenora in a teasing way.

Yes, she had promised. But doctors cost money, something that had become very dear of late. Besides, she felt fine now, and no one ever died from swooning. In fact, in every dime novel Lenora had ever read, it usually led to something good.

"If you would be so kind to relay to him that I'm feeling perfectly fine. If I have any more episodes—which I surely won't—I promise to come to town and see him. And now," she said, wresting the conversation away from the busybody and turning back to Luke, "If you'll excuse me, Mrs. Biggerstaff, I must be about my town business so I can get back to my," she paused here, "animals."

Mrs. Biggerstaff stiffened slightly but smiled sugary-sweet and bid them adieu. She left them and walked, stiff shouldered, to the counter to speak with Mr. Aeschelman.

"Deputy Davies," Lenora said, hotly aware that Mrs. Biggerstaff was listening to every word, "You were going to tell me where I might locate Sam Wright."

Luke seemed to know his lines without benefit of a script. "Ah yes," he said. He gave her the directions to find Sam, told her how much to pay "and no more" for the ranch hand's services, urged her to contact him immediately if Sam gave her any trouble, and then, rather formally, wished her a fine afternoon.

#

"Faustus," said Luke, after the women had exited the store. "I want to send a telegraph. Can you get someone to deliver a message to the operator at Fort McKinney today?"

"I send Joss today," said the eager proprietor, speaking of his teenage son. Mr. Aeschelman bent down and pulled a sheet of paper from under the counter. "Joss ride horse," he said, setting the paper on the counter directly in front of Luke. Then Mr. Aeschelman took the pencil out from behind his ear and handed it to Luke.

"You write," said Mr. Aeschelman, "I work." Luke nodded, and with that the storekeeper excused

122

himself and went behind the brown curtain to the private area of the mercantile.

Luke began to write.

Buffalo, Wyoming Territory, May 12, 1880

Dear Sheriff Clarke,

I trust you are well. I am faring as to be expected.

Sheriff Morris and I are investigating the disappearance of James Rose, a rancher who may have had dealings with an itinerant ranch hand with whom you are acquainted, one Samuel Wright. It would be advantageous to our investigation to receive from you any and all information you may have concerning Mr. Wright. No detail is insignificant.

Cordially,

Deputy Luke Davies

Chapter Ten

The spicy-sweet scent of cinnamon sugar
filled the little kitchen where Lenora pulled a warm
coffee cake from the oven in anticipation of a visit
from Mrs. Nolan. Busyness, Lenora had learned,
was an antidote to worry. And since James had
disappeared, socializing during daytime hours no
longer seemed like sinful idleness. There were days
that Lenora thought she would go insane from the
endless hours of extreme quiet, from loneliness as
sharp as a scythe. She had begun to dread her
morning trips to town, because when she returned at
day's end the rooms in her house seemed gloomier
than when she left. Being around people was a
highly sought after distraction from the accusing
voices in her head. Worse, the empty rooms of her
little house seemed to buzz a constant reminder,
he's not here, he's not here, he's not here. At the
ranch there was no escaping James' absence. At

least when she was in town she felt like she was taking steps toward finding him, and best of all, she was among people. At the ranch she only waited, existing, slogging through interminable days of meaningless sameness, endless chores, and hours of unwelcome solitude.

Lenora filled the coffee pot with well water, put ground coffee in the basket, and set the pot on the rear of the wood stove where it was farthest from the fire. She would start the coffee percolating after Mrs. Nolan arrived so that it would be fresh with their cake. She sniffed the cooling pan, pleased with its fine appearance. She removed her apron and smoothed her hair. Despite the present evil circumstances, she was so anxious for someone to talk to that in a quirky way having a guest over almost seemed like a celebration.

Almost on cue Ulysses started barking loudly in the yard, heralding the sound of horses' hooves. Lenora peered through the front room window and saw her guest about a quarter of a mile away. She went outside to greet her. Spring had been late this year, but hyacinth bulbs blooming thickly on each side of the front porch were worth the wait. Their delicate purple glory provided a cheery welcome, belying the heaviness that permeated the little ranch house.

The sound of the horse and wagon grew louder, as did Ulysses' barking. In a few minutes Lenora's smiling visitor was pulling to a stop in front of the house.

125

"Etta," said Lenora, smiling up at the wagon after it came to a stop, "so good to see you." She meant it sincerely. She craved the fellowship of this understanding woman more than ever right now.

"Lenora, dear," said Mrs. Nolan, smiling broadly. "I should have come sooner. Here, help me down." The woman handed her cane to Lenora, who held it in one hand and offered her other one to support her guest as she alighted.

"You go on in the house and move the coffee pot to a hot spot on the stove," said Lenora, handing the cane to the older woman. "I'll tether the horses."

Once the horses were tied securely in a grassy area for grazing, Lenora returned to the house, anxious to indulge in a few hours of unburdening herself to a dear friend.

"My, that cake smells good," said Mrs. Nolan, seating her herself on a wooden chair and leaning her cane against the kitchen table. She leaned over the cake that Lenora had set in the center of the table and inhaled. Yards of navy cotton skirting spread around her like a tent. She wore a crisp white blouse with a black cameo at her throat. Her white hair was parted in the middle and pulled into a loose bun at the nape of her neck. For a woman in her sixties, she had an unusually flawless complexion and a wisp of natural pink in her smooth cheeks.

"Have you had many visitors?" asked Mrs. Nolan as she watched Lenora pull cups and plates from the wall cupboard.

"Yes, several. Womenfolk from the neighborhood. One or two from church."

"Good. You shouldn't be alone out here day after day."

"True. But when they come I almost feel more sorry for them than I do for myself," said Lenora, pulling silverware from a box behind a curtain beneath the dry sink.

Mrs. Nolan gave her a puzzled look.

"They think I'm a widow. It's more awkward for them than for me."

"Hmm," said Mrs. Nolan, not taking her eyes off Lenora.

After a while the coffee began to percolate, letting off little bursts of steam. When they were both settled at the table, coffee in their cups, crumbly coffee cake on plain white china plates, Mrs. Nolan reached across the table and took Lenora's hand.

"Tell me dear, how are you faring? You alright?"

The pure compassion Lenora saw in those ancient eyes undid her. She started to speak, but so many thoughts bubbled to the front of her mind all at once that her mouth became like a crammed funnel, and nothing came out. She felt the hot sting of tears forming at the back of her eyes. Mrs. Nolan waited patiently for Lenora to sort her thoughts.

127

"Where do I begin?" said Lenora, setting her fork onto her plate. "You ask how I'm doing," she said. Lenora closed her eyes briefly to compose herself, knowing that speaking aloud the worst of it—hearing it with her ears—would likely cause her to fall apart. "It's a nightmare," she finally said, "It's Hell. I don't know where he is or what has happened to him. Or if anything has happened to him at all!" She started to sob, reaching for a cloth napkin to muffle the sound.

Mrs. Nolan held Lenora's hand and let her cry. When the sobbing grew quieter, she released her hand. "What do you mean you don't know if anything has happened to him? They found his horse." Mrs. Nolan spoke the words tenderly and quietly, as if trying to soften their impact.

"But they didn't find *him*."

The older woman pondered Lenora a moment. "Lenora dear, what is it? Do you fear the condition of the body? Sheriff Morris and his men are doing their best to find it before it's, it's … destroyed."

"No, not that." Lenora looked down at her lap where she folded and refolded her napkin. After a few seconds of weighty silence, she lifted her head to meet the kind eyes of her friend. "They're looking for a body, Etta. But I'm not sure there is a body." Lenora took a deep breath to steady herself, pausing before speaking. "I think it's very possible that James left me." With these nearly whispered words, the most painful of revelations, tears started to stream nonstop down her face, spilling onto her white calico work dress. She opened the napkin and covered her face, quietly sobbing. Her torso shook with grief.

"Lenora," soothed the older woman, "James would never do that. He would never leave you." Mrs. Nolan pushed her half-eaten coffee cake aside and scooted her chair closer to Lenora's. She wrapped one arm around the heaving younger woman. "Lenora, what happened? You must tell me what is going on. What you know."

Lenora's sobs were louder now, despite the napkin she used to muffle them.

"Do you want to talk?"

After a minute Lenora removed the napkin from her face and nodded her head in assent. Her face and eyes were red and puffy from crying. "I need water," she said. Mrs. Nolan removed her arm so that Lenora could get up from her chair. She walked to the bucket she kept on her work table, dipped the napkin into the water she had left there for cooking, and refreshed her face with it. The startling effect of cold water helped to stem the sobs. "I'm going to have another cup of coffee," said Lenora shakily, as if to fortify herself for what was ahead. "And you?"

"Yes, to the top," said Mrs. Nolan, perhaps sensing the same need.

Lenora poured for them both and then sat down and faced her guest. She put her hands on her lap and straightened her back, prepared at last for this dreaded moment. She knew without doubt that it was time. Time to confess. And strangely, she felt ready, even eager, to release the weight of her awful burden. "On the night James left, we had a terrible fight."

Mrs. Nolan's pupils widened with surprise, but the rest of her face was placid.

"I said evil things to him, Etta. Unforgivable things."

"What happened, Lenora? What made you so upset?"

"We had argued before. Many times. The same thing. He was killing himself, Etta. He was buying more Brahmans, enlarging the pasture. Working. Always working. Many times I asked to help him but he wouldn't let me. He said I wasn't brought up to do barn chores. I would have gladly helped, Etta. I wanted this ranch as much as he did."

"I know you would have helped, dear."

"And I watched him work often, so I wasn't entirely useless. I couldn't do most jobs as well as he could, but I could have at least helped."

"Yes."

"I told him, 'James, you have to hire someone to help you.' But he wouldn't. He kept saying we couldn't afford it and that he'd be fine."

Lenora spooned cream into her coffee, stirred it a bit, and took a sip. The sound of Ulysses' chain dragging across the yard interrupted the momentary silence. Lenora had taken to chaining Ulysses during the day to ensure that he stayed on the property. She needed him to alert her when someone was approaching. Not only that, the sound of the dog's chain dragging back and forth, back and forth, during the long, lonely days since James left comforted her. Likely now Ulysses had spotted some small field animal and was preparing to pursue it.

"But it wasn't *fine*." Anger rose in Lenora's voice. "That Saturday night, I asked him to please set out the bathing tub for me. We had church service next day."

Mrs. Nolan nodded, set down her coffee cup, and listened.

"James always brought in the tub for me on Saturday night, and emptied it again too. But when I asked him to set out the tub, he went crazy, Etta. He started yelling at me, saying awful things. Horrible things." Lenora put her hand to her mouth and shut her eyes tight at the memory. "He terrified me. All I could think was that he was working so hard, always so hard. He was so tired. It was too much for him. He must have been exhausted beyond measure."

"I'm sure he was."

"But instead of waiting for him to calm down, I got mad."

"What did you say?" asked Mrs. Nolan, timidly, as if she were afraid of the answer.

"I told him that first thing Monday I was going to go town and hire Sam Wright myself, whether he agreed or not."

"Oh my." Mrs. Nolan put her hand over her heart. "That must have riled him something awful."

"Oh Etta! I had asked him so many times to hire Sam, but every time he said no. Money. It was always the money."

"Hired hands do cost."

"I know that. But it wasn't only the money. He didn't like Sam. He never really said why. He just didn't like him. I knew it would make him furious if I brought up Sam's name, but I was so tired myself after being on my feet cooking and cleaning all day that I didn't care."

"Sam drinks."

"They all drink! Do you know of a ranch hand around who doesn't drink?"

Mrs. Nolan didn't have time to answer.

"I wanted to make him mad, Etta. I wanted him to see how his exhaustion was turning him into a wild man. I wanted to have a big fight to end all fights, to deal with our problem instead of each of us going our separate ways all the time, me sulking in one room and him brooding in another. Nothing ever changed," said Lenora, exasperation evident in her voice.

Mrs. Nolan put her elbow on the table and rested her chin in her hand, taking it all in. "What happened next? To make him leave, I mean," she asked.

"I was screaming at him. I don't remember ... I don't even remember what I was saying. I was out of my mind with anger at him, and then…" Lenora

132

started to breathe heavily and noisily, clutching her middle, gasping for breath. "Then his hands were around my neck, and he was choking me." She let out a little sob.

"Dear Lord have mercy," whispered Mrs. Nolan.

"Then he looked stricken, and he let go. He didn't hold my neck very long, Etta. Only for a few seconds. He didn't mean to harm me. He just ... he lost control and I—"

"Oh Lenora."

"He left me then—we were in the kitchen— and he went to the bedroom and got his coat and hat. I said, 'Where are you going?' And he said, 'Out.' And I saw his gold pocket watch on the table. Oh Etta, James loves that watch. His father gave it to him when he turned eighteen—it was his grandfather's—and it is so precious to him. He wears it everywhere. And I picked it up and I *threw* it at him. And I screamed, *screamed,* Etta, 'You forgot your watch!' It struck his back. Then he reached down and picked it up and he looked at me, and he looked so, so broken. I'd never seen a look like that on his face before. He didn't say anything. Not good-bye. Nothing. He slipped the watch into his coat pocket and left. When he shut the door I started screaming at him all over again. I was like a mad woman, Etta. I screamed and screamed. I told him I hoped he died out on the prairie. I told him to never come back."

133

Lenora laid her head down on the table, convulsing with grief. Mrs. Nolan put one hand on Lenora's head, smoothed her hair and prayed, speaking unintelligible, soothing words. After a few minutes Lenora quieted herself, sat up, and waited for Mrs. Nolan's response. The woman tenderly reached for Lenora's hand.

"Lenora, I know you feel terrible about the things you said, and James is guilty too, but not for one minute do I believe that he left you because of what you said or did."

Lenora did not meet her eyes. She only nodded, keeping her eyes on her lap.

"Did James ever hit you, Lenora?"

"No! Never!" Lenora lifted her head up to say this, as if for emphasis. "He gets in a lather easy enough. Everybody knows that. But he's not a wife beater."

"James cares about you, Lenora. He loves you."

Lenora nodded again, speechless and spent.

"Don't let the enemy bury you alive in guilt and condemnation. You're listening to lies."

"If James could have returned to you after he left that night, he would have. He would not abandon you, Lenora." Mrs. Nolan's tone was of utmost confidence. "Something happened to him out there by the North-East Creek. If not, he would have jumped right back on that fine horse of his and ridden straight to this ranch as soon as he had cooled off."

"How can you be so sure?" said Lenora.

"James would never leave his horse to starve or freeze to death in a surprise spring squall. Everyone knows James Rose took good care of his animals. And Lenora," she added, "If James wouldn't abandon his horse, do you think he would abandon you?"

Lenora shook her head and screwed up her face in pain. Etta's assessment made sense, but Lenora was too distraught to speak, her mind assailed by doubts. She caused James a lot more grief than Beauty ever had.

"If they hadn't found his horse, Lenora, I might believe differently. Then maybe, maybe I'd believe that he left you of his own power. But that's not what happened."

"He didn't drown!" said Lenora, finding her voice.

"Maybe not. But likely, he is dead. There's no other plausible reason for him not to be here with you now. Only the Great Divide would keep him away from you and this ranch."

Lenora leaned over the table, her head in her hands.

"Do you believe that, Lenora?"

A long pause. Lenora sat up again and looked directly at her guest. "James wouldn't intentionally leave Beauty to die. That's unthinkable," said Lenora.

"Of course."

135

"But I'll *never* believe that my husband stupidly fell into the North-East Creek and drowned."

Mrs. Nolan nodded.

"As for what *did* happen to him, why he hasn't returned ... I honestly don't know what I believe, Etta," Lenora shook her head. "I'm tormented day and night by that question. I think about one scenario then another. I never come to a logical answer. And when I don't find an answer, I go over all the facts again. It's all I ever think about. Not knowing is making me crazy."

The women sat silently a few moments, overwhelmed by the awfulness of the story Lenora had just shared and the frustration of the unknown. The disappearance of James Rose loomed before them like a mighty, unscalable wall. There was nothing to do but wait. They'd said everything there was to be said.

"How long will you wait, Lenora?"

"Wait?" Lenora looked eye to eye at Mrs. Nolan. "Forever. I'll wait forever, Etta, if that's how long it takes."

"You mean until you have his body?"

"Yes, until I have his body."

In the heavy silence that followed, Lenora pushed back her chair and reached for her dirty plate and silver. She carried them to the bucket of sudsy water by the dry sink where they landed at the bottom with a muffled clunk.

"And if they don't find a body, will you sell?"

"Give up the ranch? Never." Her words were resolute but her heart was quavering. When James was there the long hours of arduous ranch work were meaningful; they were building a dream. The ranch had purpose, and working it together gave them power. Without James the ranch was lifeless and dull, mere equipment, buildings, and dirt. Until now Lenora had not realized how very much more important relationships were than possessions. She hid this thought from her friend. She may have already lost James. If she lost the ranch she would have lost it all. She had to keep believing that James would return. Any other scenario was too painful to contemplate. She wouldn't put flesh on the bones of her fear by voicing them aloud.

"Body or no body, people are already talking," said Mrs. Nolan. She folded her napkin and placed it on the table.

"Oh I'm sure they are. And what do they say about the wacky woman who refuses to play the grieving widow?" Lenora already had a good idea of the nature of the gossip circulating around town, but it wouldn't hurt to hear specifics. "Whatever wild tales you've heard, I just hope they won't lead to a dunking."

Mrs. Nolan chuckled at Lenora's reference to a colonial witch test. "It's not that grave. Some just think that the juices of grief have pickled your brain," she said, making a circular motion with her finger near her head to indicate insanity.

Lenora rolled her eyes and shrugged. Mrs. Nolan laughed at her histrionics.

"Others are offended that you're not wearing black."

Lenora stopped drying the dish in her hand. "I'll shroud myself in mourning clothes when I have a reason to!"

"Of course you will, dear. You always do the right thing."

"Meddlesome busybodies," muttered Lenora, drying the dish distractedly.

"Then there's the scuttlebutt about you and Deputy Davies."

This time Lenora put down the dish and rag and turned full around to face her friend. Oh dear. "And what blather is that?" She tried to sound casual, as if she hadn't a clue, but the knowing look she saw in the older woman's eyes told Lenora this was no casual moment.

"People can be cruel, Lenora."

"What have you heard?" Lenora almost stopped breathing from the strain. She walked to her chair at the table and sat down.

"Some are making a big to-do out of the coincidences."

"Coincidences?" Lenora was truly puzzled.

"Deputy Davies seems to be around you or your place a lot."

"Hmpf," said Lenora. "That much is true. But I'm under investigation for murder, so he tells me. Naturally he watches what I do and searches for opportunities to question me." She said this matter-of-factly, but her heart was pounding like a drum. She had worried from the start that the handsome deputy's many public appearances with her would start the rumor mill grinding. Now that she found herself attracted to the man, she feared her feelings were etched across her forehead for all to see, like that hapless Esther Prynne and her scarlet letter. Only Lenora hadn't indulged in anything more scandalous than looking and admiring. Life was not fair.

And were the deputy's intentions entirely grounded in a legitimate need to perform investigative tasks? Lately Lenora had taken to wondering.

Mrs. Nolan observed Lenora's emotional response but said nothing.

"Murder *and* adultery. Well, I can't sink much lower, can I?" said Lenora, bluffing. "I have no children to beat or starve, and it's been so long since I robbed a bank that I've quite forgotten how, so I guess I have truly hit bottom."

Lenora hoped to deflect the seriousness of the gossip she'd just heard with humor. It worked. Both women laughed out loud, though Lenora was shaking within.

"I'm glad you haven't lost your sense of humor," said Mrs. Nolan, still laughing.

"No, only my mind. But that's no big loss, is it?" said Lenora, wiping the tears—this time from laughing—from her eyes with the dish rag. "Sufficient to the day is the evil thereof."

"True."

Laughing released the tension in the kitchen. Then Mrs. Nolan sobered a bit and turned to Lenora.

"Besides the worries, how are you feeling otherwise?"

"Tired, all the time tired. I go to bed early enough but when I wake up it's like I never slept."

"The strain of waiting and not knowing takes a lot out of a body."

Lenora nodded in agreement.

"Mrs. Slocomb tells me Ben's helping out with the chores," said Mrs. Nolan.

"Yes, God bless him. I don't know how I'd manage without him. I can't keep accepting his favors, though. I have to hire Sam as soon as I can find him."

"Favors?"

"I'm not paying Ben. He refuses money."

"Oh," said Mrs. Nolan. "I see your dilemma." That seemed to put her in an odd state of consternation. She tapped her fingers on the table, thinking. "Perhaps he just wants to be a good neighbor in a practical sort of way."

"Perhaps. But for how long?"

"Don't let pride provoke you into something rash, Lenora. James must have had good reason to dislike Sam Wright. Perhaps he knew something about him that you didn't. Men talk." Mrs. Nolan dragged her cake plate toward her again and took a bite, daintily wiping her mouth with her napkin.

"I can't keep leaning on neighbors, Etta."

"They don't seem to mind. Only you mind."

Lenora sighed. "The one piece of information I really need is not whom to hire but how long to hire. If I thought James would show up at the door tomorrow or next week I'd say fine, Ben can keep coming over without pay. But I can't take advantage of the boy. He could be working for nothing for a very long time. Only God knows how long. I have to hire someone."

"Hmm," said Mrs. Nolan, putting down her fork. "Maybe you should talk to Deputy Davies about that."

"Deputy Davies?" Lenora stiffened in her seat like a hound dog on alert. "What does he have to do with this?"

"He might have some thoughts on hired hands and who's reliable and such. It's his job to know what people are up to. Perhaps he can give you some names."

Lenora eyed her friend. "You know something?"

"Nothing in particular. I do know that Sam Wright and Deputy Davies both spent time near Fort Laramie. Perhaps the deputy knows something about Sam's background."

"I see."

"What are you going to do, dear?" asked Mrs. Nolan.

141

"I don't know. I'm too tired to make all these decisions, Etta. I'll sleep on it one more day."

The friends chatted a while longer and then said their good-byes with much hugging and well wishes. Mrs. Nolan promised to return soon and made Lenora promise to call on her if she needed anything. Lenora watched wistfully as her friend's buckboard rode away in a thin cloud of dust. As the dust diminished to a tiny gray dot on the prairie, Lenora felt more sad and lonely than she ever had in her life.

#

Lenora's eyes popped open for no apparent reason. In the soft and silvery moon glow she saw the fuzzy shape of Ulysses, fully abandoned to secret doggy dreams, lying on his side on the floor next to her bed. Though she could not see anything distinctly in the dimness, she imagined his chest rising and falling in rhythmic cadence. She imagined him sleeping deeply, as he should, without a care in the world.

Before she had enough time to start missing James' warm body next to hers, the door latch jiggled in the front room. Lenora's heart jumped to her throat. With one seamless motion her hand was on James' rifle, the bed quilt was flung into the air, her feet were on the chilly wooden floor, and Ulysses was out the bedroom door and in the front room, jumping madly, front paws on the door, barking with all his might. Over the hullabaloo from her dog, Lenora heard the sound of someone's feet sprinting through the yard. She peered through the front window, but even with the faint moonlight, she saw nothing but ghostly silhouettes of her out buildings and a few trees.

Chapter Eleven

Luke sat astride his horse, scanning the horizon a few miles outside town. It was too early for the purple lupine of summer to shoot their arrowheads upward to the sun, too early for Indian paintbrush to wash the landscape with bold strokes of yellow, persimmon, and scarlet. But even in their absence the beauty of the Wyoming prairie in spring was an immeasurable bounty for lovers of all things created. Where grass was sparse, delicate sand lilies, their waxy-white star points set on tufts of dark green, were interspersed with nosegays of Alpine wallflowers, cheery yellow bursts of blooms as welcome as a pot of gold at the end of a treasure hunter's trail.

The temperature was moderate, and a soft breeze gave Luke some relief from the ravages of hours in the saddle, unprotected from an endless sun. It was a good day to return to the North-East

144

Creek to look for more clues to the disappearance
of James Rose, which is what drew Luke out of his
dreary office in town this fine morning.

As he rode Luke wondered at his motivation.
Was it curiosity, an innate zeal to unravel a mystery
that kept him on the trail of the missing rancher? At
one time, when Luke was young and starry-eyed
about the work of a lawman, this might have been
the case. He'd learned since that most criminal
investigations contained disappointingly little of the
mysterious. If someone went missing there were
logical reasons: they were hurt, guilty, or dead—
rarely kidnapped. He wasn't sure which applied to
James Rose. But he knew from the start that the
unlucky Mr. Rose had not willingly abandoned his
wife. And every day that passed, Luke became
more certain that Mrs. Rose had not murdered her
husband.

Well then, was it curiosity about the life of
James Rose that kept Luke on the hunt, curiosity
about what he could have been involved in,
criminal or otherwise, that could have led to his
death? Luke was curious. But not curious enough
for the search for James Rose to crowd out all other
thoughts twenty-four hours a day, as it had since the
plucky, the prickly, the exquisite Mrs. Rose had
first stepped into his office.

Then there was the matter of Christian charity.
Mrs. Rose was surely a widow. And we ought to
look out for widows and orphans. Luke knew this to
be true because his ma had taught him that and

other moral principles from the Good Book. Of
course, Mrs. Rose didn't think she was a widow.
But in everything that mattered, she was widowed.
Her husband had been gone some time and showed
no signs of returning. She didn't have children to
care for, but she had a ranch and animals—almost
as much responsibility as a house full of children.
The only problem with Luke showing Christian
charity to Mrs. Rose is that if he, being single,
demonstrated even a hint of brotherly love in Mrs.
Rose's hour of need, he would only complicate
things for her in a most embarrassing way.

Which is why Luke had made Mr. and Mrs.
Slocomb promise not to divulge that the chore
money they gave their son for helping Mrs. Rose
came from the deputy's pocket.

And then there was Mrs. Rose. If Luke were
honest, he would admit that in all the hours of
searching and in all the tasks he'd completed in
town related to the investigation, it was Mrs. Rose's
pretty face and womanly form, not a certain
rancher's watery fate, that anchored his thoughts to
the search. He searched for Mr. Rose, but his search
hours—and his off hours—were filled with
thoughts of Mrs. Rose. Did Luke even care for the
welfare of the man? It was a difficult question.

Well, he certainly didn't wish him any harm.

But what Luke felt about the luckless James
Rose didn't matter. The man was dead. Luke knew
it in his bones, had known it from the day his
widow had first come to town with her report just as

146

surely as the big sky of Wyoming hung over his head, just as surely as if an angel had whispered in his ear. It was more than just a lawman's sixth sense, honed by years in the saddle, tracking criminals and missing people. And the sooner Luke found his body, the sooner his widow would mourn him and get on with the business of living.

And perhaps, just perhaps, Luke would be part of her business. Luke would make it his business to see that he was. To that end he was boldly honest with himself. As he urged his horse toward the North-East Creek, he realized with shameful clarity his true motivation. As long as Mrs. Rose thought of herself as a married woman, Luke would respect her feelings and the law of God and behave himself. But when James Rose's body was finally brought home, wrapped in a blanket and slung over the back of a horse—as it surely would be—Luke would be the first in line to court his widow.

He must do everything in his power to find that body.

Luke was halfway to the creek when he saw the dust cloud of a buckboard and two Morgans interrupting the horizon to the East. He halted his horse and pulled his hat down to shade his eyes. The team was a great ways off, but it was evident from the light color fabric the driver wore—which appeared as just a smudge to Luke—that a woman drove the team. She was alone. Luke's concentrated hard on the rider. Coming from that direction and riding alone, the driver could only be Mrs. Rose. He sincerely hoped it was her.

Slowly the wagon came into view. Luke saw a look of recognition and then surprise on Lenora's face. She shouted at her team to stop them, pulling on the reins with both of her dainty gloved hands. Once she had set the brake and wrapped the reins securely around a metal hook installed for that purpose, the only sounds on the wide prairie were the jingle of the reins as the horses got settled, pawing and snorting as they did.

"Deputy Davies, good morning. What brings you out this way?"

Luke tipped his hat. "I'm headed toward the creek to take another look around. And you?"

Luke tried to keep his eyes on her face, but everything about this woman intrigued him, including all the lovely details below her neck. She wore unusually simple clothes for a trip to town, that is, unusually simple for her, as if she had dressed in haste. A pale green lawn skirt with matching shirtwaist sprigged with tiny pink rosebuds. But no frills today, though her exaggerated poke bonnet was made of the same feminine lawn. The bow under her chin was the exact pink shade as the rosebuds. She complemented the panorama of spring flowers all around, though she surely was the fairest flower of them all.

"Actually, Deputy Davies, I was coming to see you."

"Ma'am?" Luke noted that she did not say she was coming to see Sheriff Morris. The thought gave him pleasure, but then he realized that she would never willingly come to the office to see Cyrus; she would cross the road to avoid him. Luke was merely the only lawman left to come to for help. His pleasure faded fast.

"Someone was on my property last night. Whoever it was tried the latch."

"Did you see him?"

"No. Even with the moon it was too dark to see well. I heard him run across the yard after Ulysses started barking." Lenora pulled a pink, lace trimmed handkerchief from her reticule and gently dabbed the perspiration from her face.

"You have any idea who it was?" Luke's mind was already casting about, bringing up any number of ne'er-do-wells about the Territory, particularly in Buffalo. No one face stood out.

"None at all."

"Did he take anything? Leave footprints?"

"Nothing is missing. The animals are all accounted for. I didn't think to look for prints."

Luke nodded, thinking.

"Deputy Davies, this is not the first time. It's happened several times before."

"You never said anything before."

"No," she said, grimacing a little with embarrassment, "I was reluctant to involve the sheriff's office." She patted her throat and the back of her neck with her handkerchief.

149

Luke had no difficulty figuring out why that would be.

"It started ... not the night that James disappeared." She paused, thinking. "The night after that. Sunday. I distinctly heard the sound of a man walking outside the house in the middle of the night. Maybe very early morning. Under my window. He stepped very stealthily, as though he didn't want to be heard. At first I thought I had imagined the sound, but that time too Ulysses went crazy with barking and the man ran off."

"I wish you had come to me sooner," Luke said, shifting in his saddle.

"I failed to use wisdom," admitted Lenora, looking down at her hands.

"Any evidence the man left behind the first time is long gone."

"I suppose that's true."

"Let's hope there's something to learn out there now," said Luke, gripping the reins tighter. His horse was getting antsy, flicking his head back and forth.

"I hope you can find something that leads you to the man. I've been sleeping with James' Sharps, but even with the rifle at my side I don't sleep well."

Luke thought she looked a little pale. Doubtless her sleeping troubles were partly related to the fact that she was not used to sleeping alone. That thought led to another thought; he was ashamed about the pictures that rose unbidden in his mind. He too had trouble sleeping at night since he had met the fetching Mrs. Rose. She shouldn't be alone at her ranch so far from town. She needed a man. Luke felt a wave of desire come over him, but he willed his face to show nothing but professional concern. God forbid she look into his eyes and catch a glimpse of his thoughts. He wished he could have met Mrs. Rose in other, better circumstances.

"I have other urgent business in town, Deputy Davies, so I must not dally," said Lenora as she unwrapped the reins from the metal hook. "I'll be on my way."

"That reminds me, Mrs. Rose. One more question."

"Yes?" Lenora stopped what she was doing and looked back to Luke.

"Did you ever determine if your husband left unarmed? Did you find his revolver?"

"I apologize, Deputy Davies. It slipped my mind. Yes, I found his Colt. It was right where he left it in the bedroom."

Luke silently shook his head, thinking about the ramifications of that fact. "Shall I escort you to town?"

"No, that's quite alright, Deputy Davies," said Lenora. "Under the circumstances I think it would be more fitting if I continued alone."

"I understand," said Luke. "If I see anything suspicious at your place I'll send word. Keep me posted if you see or hear anything yourself."

"I will, Deputy Davies."

Luke made like he would snap the reins to urge his horse, but then he stopped and turned back to Lenora.

"Mrs. Rose, do you want me to send someone out to check on you?"

"You are very kind, Deputy Davies, but the neighbors have been coming by quite regularly. I'll be fine." She shouted to the Morgans and snapped the reins before he could object, and in a minute she was rolling noisily down the worn wagon ruts to town in a cloud of prairie dust and clomping horses' hooves.

#

Lenora knocked briskly on the dark green door of the Biggerstaff's home in town, hoping anxiously that Dr. Biggerstaff had not been called away to a birth or farm accident that would keep him away for hours. She urgently needed to talk to him. After the scare she'd had this morning, paying his fee was the least of her concerns. In a few seconds she heard the sound of feet approaching. The handle on the door opened, and the next moment she was eye to eye with Mrs. Biggerstaff.

"Lenora, good morning. What brings you here today, dear?"

Lenora made a slight smile and stepped into the Biggerstaffs' front room, chafing as usual at the oozy sweetness in Mrs. Biggerstaff's tone. Lenora knew she'd have to go through the irksome wife to get to Dr. Biggerstaff, but the woman's presence never failed to rankle. Lenora always felt like she

152

had to be on her guard around her. Anything she said in her presence was bound to be around town by midafternoon, but not in the bland state it was in when it left Lenora's lips. By the time Emmaline Biggerstaff was through with it, it would be hashed, seasoned, and fried into a savory tidbit designed to whet the appetites of the most discerning palate.

"I need to see Dr. Biggerstaff."

"Yes?"

Lenora set her mouth in a line and entered into a brief stare down with Mrs. Biggerstaff, determined not to volunteer information that the woman obviously hoped Lenora would divulge. In the tense but silent interlude an enormous tabby, waddling from years of culinary indulgence, slinked into the foyer and made its way to Mrs. Biggerstaff, curling its portly body around her ankles and purring loud enough to be heard from several feet away. Mrs. Biggerstaff bent over heavily, picked up the fat feline, and cradled it under her protruding bosoms. Lenora was relieved for the momentary distraction, though she wished Mrs. Biggerstaff would dispense with the questions and fetch the doctor. As Lenora waited Mrs. Biggerstaff scratched the cat's neck and cooed nonsense sounds into its ear. Lenora was convinced the woman dawdled just to provoke her. Finally she could stand to wait no longer.

"Is the doctor in?" said Lenora, tempering her voice to hide her irritation.

Mrs. Biggerstaff kissed the top of her pet's head, seeming in no hurry to give any quarter to Lenora. Finally the woman stopped fawning over her cat and met Lenora's eyes. "He's in," she said. "Please wait in the parlor." Mrs. Biggerstaff nodded her head toward the small waiting room off the foyer.

Lenora watched her sashay out of the room, noting the attitude of contempt in the woman's shoulders. Lenora was glad she had kept her mouth shut about why she had come today.

Once Mrs. Biggerstaff was out of sight, Lenora stepped into the parlor and sat down on the deep ruby moire settee. Despite the irritating ways of the woman who had decorated this little room, the charming details of its appointments reflected talent. The curtains, pulled aside by silky gold rope, were made of the same red moire. A white, cut glass lamp graced a mahogany side table. Bas-relief nymphs danced around its clear red glass base. The floral carpet was thick and lavish in its complex, woven design of multiple colors. The room overlooked Main Street, and one could sit on the floral side chair near the window and peer unnoticed through lace privacy curtains at the goings-on of Buffalo citizens in the street below. Lenora wondered how often Mrs. Biggerstaff did exactly that.

"Lenora." Dr. Biggerstaff appeared at the entrance to the parlor.

"Dr. Biggerstaff, how good to see you," said Lenora, standing to greet him.

"Come in, dear," he said, pointing toward the hall that led to his office. "This way."

Lenora followed the doctor down the narrow hallway, half expecting to see Mrs. Biggerstaff at the end, hanging around like a hungry dog at a barbeque, hoping for someone to drop a scrap. Lenora was relieved when she got to the door of the doctor's office to see that his wife was nowhere in sight.

"Have a seat," said the doctor, motioning to a chair across from his desk while he shut his office door. After a little small talk, mainly inquiries about the sheriff's investigation and the doings on the ranch, Dr. Biggerstaff got down to business. "What brings you in today, Lenora?"

Lenora sat straight up, bracing herself to hear aloud the horrible words that she had been able to speak only silently to herself ever since she had awakened this awful, awful morning.

"I'm bleeding."

Chapter Twelve

"Ghosts, is it? Next she'll be hearing voices calling to her from the bottom of her well."

Sheriff Morris scratched idly at his jaw, leaned back in his chair, and noisily lifted his worn boots to his desk. A small fire burned in the office wood stove this warm late spring day, just small enough to keep the coffee at a drinkable temperature. He directed his gaze at his deputy, who was sitting at his own desk, absorbed in recording the observations he'd made at the Rose ranch. When the sheriff mentioned ghosts, Luke stopped writing and looked up, meeting the sheriff's eyes straight on.

"Ghosts don't make footprints," said Luke, his voice taut. "Someone wrapped in real flesh and blood has been creeping around her property. I saw the prints myself. I think someone's watching her comings and goings."

"It's a ranch for Christ's sake. Ranch owner. Ranch hands. Ranch visitors. Prints could belong to any old yahoo." Sheriff Morris put his hands behind his head and closed his eyes.

"Only a trespasser would leave tracks right beneath her bedroom window."

"It's convenient, ain't it? Ghosts only haunt the widow when she's alone. No one else has seen 'em. And James Rose ain't here to tell us why his own boot prints are on his property, near his own house," replied the sheriff.

Luke set his mouth in a straight line. Lately he had little patience with Cyrus' smugness, and his sarcasm was worse. Three months had passed since they'd found James Rose's horse abandoned on the banks of the North-East Creek. His young wife was left to care for a busy ranch alone, and all indications were that she had done nothing to bring this evil on herself. The Buffalo sheriff's office had an obligation to find the rancher's remains, determine his cause of death, and assist his widow. So far they'd failed at all three. But it seemed to Luke that Cyrus was not in the least perturbed at their lack of success. Mrs. Rose was right: the sheriff had made up his mind from day one to discount her testimony. Consequently he also discounted any evidence that might be useful to their investigation. Luke was frustrated with the slow pace of the search for the dead rancher and daily grew more annoyed with Cyrus' laissez faire

157

approach. He bit back a sharp retort. Sparring with Cyrus would get him nowhere.

"All the downstream towns reported back yet?" asked Luke, changing the subject.

"Every last one." Sheriff Morris sat up again in his chair and, using a rusty nail he'd pulled from his pocket, began scraping the grunge beneath his fingernails.

Luke knew there was no need to ask for elaboration. If any of the downstream towns near the creek had reported finding a body or personal effects thereof, Cyrus would have told him by now.

"No one's seen hide nor hair of James Rose," said Luke, stating the obvious. Lost in thought, he looked beyond the sheriff to the street, though his mind was far from the sights and sounds on the other side of the grimy window. A lumber wagon rumbled slowly down Main Street and stopped in front of the sheriff's office to let some shoppers on foot cross from one boardwalk to the other. "And he left his house without a weapon."

"I told you he was in a hurry when he left. How long it been now? I don't keep track."

"Twelve weeks last Saturday," said Luke. Then, as if realizing for the first time the full import of what that meant, he said, "Doesn't it bother you that after three months his body hasn't been found floating downstream from where we found his horse?"

"Obviously it bothers you." Sheriff Morris didn't look up as he said this, just kept his eyes on his fingernails, scraping away.

"His body, or what's left of it, should have surfaced by now," said Luke, thinking aloud.

"S'pose so."

"Even if a wolf or coyote got him, there'd be bones."

"Uh huh," mumbled the sheriff. The corner of his mouth lifted slightly in a smirk. Slowly he said, "Which reminds me: Some folk around this town think the Roses got a wolf problem of another sort."

Luke became rigid in his chair. "What do you mean?" But Luke suspected he knew. His heart beat a little faster and his breathing quickened. Instantly his deal with the Slocombs surfaced in his mind. He hoped that the elder Slocombs had kept their promise not to speak to anyone about his payments to Ben. But to deflect any interest the sheriff might show in his reaction to the bait he'd thrown his way, Luke made a pretense of reviewing the notes he'd just made, keeping his eyes trained on his paperwork to avoid eye contact with Cyrus.

Sheriff Morris slipped the rusty nail back into his pocket and sat up a little straighter. "Finding a dead James Rose would make things easier for you."

The sheriff's statement was so replete with innuendo that it took Luke off guard. Frantically he cast about trying to form a safe response. "Finding James Rose would make things easier for

159

everyone," he said, this time turning toward the sheriff to show he wouldn't be intimidated, "most of all, his wife."

The sheriff gave Luke a skeptical look.

"And it would free us to move on to other tasks," added Luke, knowing how lame he sounded and hoping his face didn't give him away. His heart beat so hard he feared that Cyrus could hear it from where he sat across the room.

A stagecoach pulled by four brindled horses flashed past the window just then. The dust they kicked up was so thick that even through the closed door Luke imagined the taste of it in his mouth.

"Other tasks?" asked the sheriff in an oily tone. The smirk was back. "And what task would you move on then?"

"If you got a pebble too big for your gizzard," said Luke, annoyed, "spit it out." He knew where this was going, but he deemed himself man enough to defend himself from Cyrus' insinuations or whatever silly gossip was going around town. Not only that, he had a clear conscience. No mud could stick on him.

"Buffalo has a number of ugly widows that need assistance," said the sheriff, coyly, "but you picked the prettiest one in the Territory to investigate."

"I didn't pick her. *She* picked *us*. She came to us, remember? None of the ugly ones have come looking for our help in finding a missing husband.

And Cyrus, if they do," Luke said, drawing out his words for effect, "they're all yours."

Sheriff Morris laughed and Luke smiled, mostly from relief that the interrogation had lightened up.

"Well," said the sheriff, getting up to pour a third cup of coffee, "you realize you showed up here in town the same time Rose went missing. People love a good story. Some are making hay of the coincidence."

"They're connecting me to his disappearance?" Luke was stunned at this news. Heretofore he'd worried that others might link him to Mrs. Rose in a romantic way. Such a notion had been front and center in his thinking of late. But he had never had an inkling that someone might think he had anything to do with the disappearance of her husband. It was an absurd notion, unfounded, outrageous in the extreme. How could anyone suggest such a tenuous connection between dots located so far apart? One man comes to town and another goes missing. If anyone saw a relationship between these two events it was because they wanted to.

Sheriff Morris sat down with his cup of coffee. He took a long, noisy slurp. "Like I said, people are always hungry for a good story. Pretty young woman. Handsome young deputy. Kidnap. Murder. Missing body. Now all we need is a murder weapon and a bag full of gold coins to make a happy ever after."

161

Luke was incredulous. "That's ridiculous."

"I know," said the sheriff. "But it keeps the womenfolk busy." He chuckled to himself. For a moment neither lawman spoke. Sheriff Morris took another noisy slurp of coffee. "You're new in town Luke. People don't know you real well. You make a good target for gossip."

Luke's heart skipped a beat. Did Cyrus know him well enough not to be suspicious? Was this a fishing expedition? Is that why Cyrus threw out the bit about a wolf?

"*You* know me," said Luke, trying not to sound defensive. "You got my credentials from Sheriff Clarke before you hired me."

"Yeah," said Sheriff Morris, eyeing Luke over the top of his cup. "I know what he told me."

It seemed to Luke that his boss enjoyed this charade, toying with Luke like a soul on a string suspended over the flames of Dante's Inferno.

In that instant the office door handle turned and through the doorway ran a boy about eight years old. His faded, too small, cotton shirt was open at the neck, his hole-y pants were held up with rope, his hair needed a good shampoo, he was barefoot, and he was out of breath. He shut the office door with a whack, making every window in the room rattle, not just the window on the door.

"Hey, what's the ruckus?" growled Sheriff Morris.

"I gotta talk to the deputy," said the boy, unmoved by the adult's obvious displeasure. His

162

sweaty chest heaved from running. "I got a telegraph message for him," he said, panting, "from my pa."

"I'm Deputy Davies," said Luke, standing up. "Who's your pa?"

"Mr. Aeschelman."

Luke walked to where the messenger boy stood by the sheriff's desk. The boy pulled a grubby envelope from the pocket of his pants. It had been folded several times over. Luke pulled a penny from his pocket and handed it to the boy.

"Thank you," he said, breathless. He handed Luke the telegraph message and ran out the door as fast as he had come in, slamming it just as bone jarringly as he had when he entered.

Luke stood in front of the sheriff's desk and looked at the envelope.

"What?" said the sheriff. "Who's it from?"

"It's from Fort Laramie."

"Yeah?"

"I telegraphed Sheriff Clarke about Sam Wright a while back."

"What for?"

"Because Mrs. Rose is looking to hire him to help on her ranch till her husband returns." Luke regretted the last four words the minute they left his lips. "I want to know if he has more vices than just liquor."

Sheriff Morris shook his head in disgust. "That's not the kind of help she came to us for."

Luke gave the sheriff a determined look that made it clear he would not incriminate himself. He pulled a knife from his pocket and used it to slit the envelope. He removed the single sheet of paper inside, unfolded it, and began to read silently.

"Well?" demanded the sheriff.

Luke began to read aloud:

Fort Laramie, Wyoming Territory, June 25, 1880

Deputy Davies:
I apologize for the delay in responding to your inquiry. I have been overtaken by pressing concerns related to the current flurry of exercises at Fort Laramie.

Samuel Theodore Wright born Richmond, Virginia 1838. Implicated in the beating death of a Leesburg, Virginia woman, 1859. Insufficient evidence to convict. Implicated in suspicious death of his wife, Amelia Flora Wright, Alexandria, 1861. Insufficient evidence to convict. Known to have a vile temper. As you are already aware, he has been arrested multiple times for public drunkenness at the settlement here by Fort Laramie.

I trust you have settled in comfortably in Buffalo. I am sure you are of great assistance to Sheriff Morris. Let us know how you are faring.

Cordially,
Sheriff Hiram Clarke

Chapter Thirteen

"A baby? That's not possible!" Lenora trembled with the shock of Dr. Biggerstaff's diagnosis. "I've been married four years. I'm not able to conceive."

Across his desk Dr. Biggerstaff raised his eyebrows. His hands were clasped, resting in the center of sloppy mounds of paperwork along with his churchwarden pipe, his stethoscope, and various other medical oddments. His glasses slipped down his nose. With an absent shove of an index finger he pushed them up again.

"Well, you can and you have," he said gently, smiling a small, guarded smile. "However, I wish you had come in sooner, like I asked. This could have been avoided. You're not well." His smile disappeared.

Lenora sat across from him flushing with embarrassment, mostly because the doctor had asked so many personal questions. Perhaps she should have come to see him after she had fainted in church, but financial matters were such a sticky wicket, and she had had no reason to believe she was in a family way.

But above all else she was in a panic, her thoughts running in every direction like wild horses out the barn door of her mind. How would she care for the ranch *and* a baby without James? How would she meet all the financial obligations that came with a new mouth to feed? Being in a family way meant she must no longer dawdle. She must hire Sam Wright immediately if she had any hope of keeping the ranch. Then again, when it came to the ranch, was she being bone headed? Was it wise to waste her limited energy and dwindling bank account trying to hang onto the ranch? Should she ask her family in New York for help? Should she lease the ranch and move into town? Maybe she should consider taking in boarders. Or should she sell the ranch and move back East? Why oh why had James run off and left her with all these difficult decisions?

Lenora bent her head and covered her eyes with her hand to think. She felt very small. But mostly she felt alone, acutely alone, like a speck of driftwood in a vast sea, tossed to and fro, no power of its own to dictate its course. Things just happened to her, outside her control and without reason. Life was grinding her to powder. Where was God? What had she done to deserve so much loss and sorrow? Did God hate her? Surely He was punishing her for her sins.

She felt a rush of heat behind her ears. She began to weave in her chair. It was difficult to sit up straight. Blackness encroached upon the area behind her eyes.

"Lenora! Here, put your head between your legs." Dr. Biggerstaff jumped up from his chair and rushed around his desk to her aid.

Lenora found it easy to obey, letting herself fall forward in her chair. The doctor leaned over her, both hands on her shoulders.

"You're staying in town tonight. I'm going to get you a room at the Occidental," he said.

"No!" Lenora jerked her head sideways to speak. Intuitively she knew that if she stayed away from her ranch even for a short time, slowly she would lose her hold on it altogether and with it, James' dream and hers. "I have to get back to my ranch."

"You're not fit to travel. You need to be in bed at least a week to stop the bleeding. And you are so thin. I can feel nothing but bones in these shoulders. Now put your head back down and be still before you end up on the floor." Dr. Biggerstaff's tone was firm but not unkind.

After a bit the doctor left Lenora's side and busied himself, opening and closing a cabinet somewhere in the back of his small office. In a few seconds he returned, wafting an exceedingly sharp, foul smelling rag under her nose, redolent of ammonia, which caused her to wince and shrink back. Whatever was on the rag cleared her mind at once. Still woozy, she forced herself to sit up. She let her reticule float on her lap while she gripped the edge of the chair with both hands to steady herself. She was embarrassed to be so incapacitated in the doctor's presence. Through the door the mantle clock in the parlor chimed twelve times to mark noon.

"I'll be fine," she said, looking up at the doctor. "I have Ben Slocomb in the evenings to do chores. And I'll hire Sam Wright. Today. I'll hire him today. He can come in the mornings."

"You're not going anywhere or hiring anyone. You're going to do nothing but rest today. Do you want to lose this baby?"

Baby. Was there *really* a baby? Lenora struggled to grasp this new, frightening yet exciting idea. When she had missed her monthlies it had given her no cause for alarm. She had never been regular. And she had heard from other women that seasons of mourning or great stress could cause the monthly flow to cease altogether. But in her case did it really mean a baby? It didn't seem real. She must be dreaming.

"When? When is the baby coming, Dr. Biggerstaff?"

Dr. Biggerstaff pushed his glasses up his nose and creased his forehead in thought. With his other hand he held onto one of Lenora's shoulders to ensure that she didn't fall off the chair.

"By my calculations, you're about twelve to fourteen weeks along. I reckon you'll be rocking a little bundle right about Christmastime."

Twelve to fourteen weeks. That meant she conceived right about the time James went missing. The awesome timing of the two events was exquisitely painful yet exquisitely sweet. She might not ever see the face of her beloved James again, yet forever she would be reminded of his image when she gazed into the face of their son or daughter. With a stabbing pain that brought tears to her eyes, it occurred to her that James might not ever see or hold his own child. What robbery! She alone would savor that joy. How strange that so much pain could mingle simultaneously in her heart with so much comfort. She opened her bag and pulled out a hanky to absorb the tears before they ran down her face and embarrassed her even more.

"I feel better now, Dr. Biggerstaff. I must return to my ranch."

"You're staying here."

"I can't!" Lenora stopped dabbing and bolted upright in her chair, turning around to face the doctor, who had returned to standing over her, gripping her shoulder to make sure she didn't hit the floor.

"Jostling in a wagon is dangerous," he warned. "You risk more hemorrhaging. You should be in bed. Bleeding at this early stage is not a good sign."

169

"If I can just get back to my ranch, I promise to stay abed a whole week."

"Uh uh," said the doctor, shaking his head. "Too risky. You'll need someone to be there with you during the day. Otherwise you'll be on your feet trying to take care of yourself the minute you get home. You move about too much and you will lose that baby."

Dr. Biggerstaff sounded unusually stern. Lenora knew he was only doing his best to perform his duty as a caring physician, but right now she felt like a little girl again, trying to wrest approval from her papa for a bigger, faster pony. But somewhere in the bottom of her consciousness, like a prairie dog peeping out from its hidden dark hole, a little thought raised its head. She didn't have to ask anyone's permission to return to her ranch. She was a woman on her own now. No one had the authority to make her stay or go. It frightened her. She could easily make a wrong decision and suffer for it. Her baby might suffer too. Now there was a sobering thought. But she wasn't going to lose her ranch. Likely she had already lost James. And even if she stayed in town a week to rest, she still might lose this baby. If she had any say in the matter, any power at all, she was not going to lose the ranch that she and James had worked so hard to build.

"Dr. Biggerstaff, I know you mean well. But I *am* going back to my ranch." She turned and looked him directly in the eye, intent on making her point very clear.

170

Dr. Biggerstaff looked stunned at her bold declaration but had no time to respond.

"Today," said Lenora, not removing her gaze. Then, plaintively, "Will you help me?"

Dr. Biggerstaff removed his hand from her shoulder, walked around his desk, and sat down in his high-backed oak chair. For a minute he regarded Lenora, his lips pursed, annoyance evident in his eyes. Then the tautness in his face softened. He pushed his glasses up his nose and leaned forward over the desk. His shoulders sagged in resignation. His mouth was set in a straight line.

"I'll help you, yes, if you insist on going home."

"I insist."

Dr. Biggerstaff sighed. "Fine. But you have to get other help besides a ranch hand. Immediately. You'll need a driver for your wagon. You can't drive yourself back to your ranch. You need to lay down—and stay down! I can't emphasize how serious this is. You need to lay down in the wagon all the way to your ranch. And your driver needs to go slowly so you're not bounced around the prairie like tumbleweed. Once you get home you need to stay in bed till the bleeding stops and for several days thereafter."

Lenora nodded.

"You have to have a woman in to help you, too."

"I can ask the Widow Nolan. She might come."

171

"Good. I'll arrange for someone to get her a message right away. Meanwhile I'll ask around town to see who's available to drive you home."

"Please start by asking Reverend and Mrs. Thomas. They'll probably be willing." Betsy had been out to the ranch twice already to encourage Lenora. It would be good to see her again, if only briefly.

"Yes, of course."

"And Sam Wright? Can you get a message to him to come out tomorrow morning?" said Lenora.

"Yes, that too."

"Thank you, Dr. Biggerstaff. This means a lot to me."

Dr. Biggerstaff shook his head, his mouth drawn up in a doubtful frown. "You know this is crazy, don't you? I don't agree at all with what you're doing. You're not thinking about your baby. You should spend at least a week in town convalescing at the hotel. Two weeks would be better." Dr. Biggerstaff slapped his desk to emphasize his words.

Lenora was unmoved. "It is imperative that I return to my ranch, Doctor Biggerstaff." She had his word that he would help, and that's all that mattered. That little bit of encouragement strengthened her to stand her ground. She would stay on her property. Deep down, however, she hoped she wasn't being foolish when it came to her baby's welfare. She didn't feel foolish. She felt desperate.

"Why? Why is it so important to be on your ranch? I would think you'd be lonely out there."

"I am at times."

"Then why won't you stay in town? There's good people here. They'll help you."

Lenora knew why, but it was hard to find the words to explain. Her world was upside down and inside out. Not only did she fear she'd lose the ranch if she vacated it, even temporarily, but being on the ranch was her only remaining semblance of normal living. If she woke up tomorrow to spend the day, and the next and the next, staring at four gray walls in a strange hotel instead of the familiar surroundings of her tidy ranch bedroom, then life truly would be too bizarre to cope. She had to hang on to the routine of the ranch. She had to eat, sleep, and think at home—while she still could. Doctor Biggerstaff genuinely cared about her and the baby, and she was grateful for his concern. But she didn't care to share with him her poignant need for normalcy, for the comfort of routine. She feared it would sound like she was running from the truth, as if she were striving to create a dream world for herself because the real world she lived in was too painful. She knew that wasn't true. When the evening shadows crept upon the close of another day on the ranch without James, her doubts of seeing him alive again were strengthened, cord upon cord. She knew the odds. James was probably dead. She wasn't creating an imaginary world into which her lost husband would inexplicably, miraculously ride. She was trying to preserve a small portion of a real world without him.

"I'm more comfortable at the ranch," she said. At least it was the truth.

"This goes against my better judgment," groused the doctor, "but let's not dally." He rose from his chair. "There's much to be done before we get you home."

Out of habit Lenora started to stand up.

"*You* stay right there!"

She sat down quickly.

"I'll get Emmaline to get you comfortable in the spare bedroom while I get everything in order."

Just then a soft scurrying sound erupted from behind the door to the doctor's office, where Emmaline Biggerstaff had spent a goodly amount of time eavesdropping. Doctor and patient turned toward the sound.

"That gluttonous cat," said Doctor Biggerstaff, grimacing in disgust. "Won't touch mice," he added, reaching for the doorknob. "Not rich enough for her majesty's rarefied appetite."

#

"You doing alright back there?" asked Betsy, turning herself around on the buckboard seat to check on Lenora. The slightly rounded, thirtyish parson's wife was well shaded from the sun in a plain tan poke bonnet and a long-sleeve, faded gray dress. "I can have the Reverend stop the wagon for a while if you need a rest from all the bouncing."

"It's no problem, Mrs. Rose. I can stop now if you want," chimed Reverend Thomas, continuing to face forward, raising his voice above the racket of the wagon wheels and hooves.

"No, I'm fine. Please don't stop. I want to get home. The sooner I'm in my own bed the better."

"True," said Betsy. She tucked a stray wisp of light brown hair under her bonnet. "Doctor Biggerstaff made me promise we'd take it easy."

"You've kept your promise," said Lenora, trying to sound cheerful to hide her discomfort and dismay. The Thomas' sacrifice brought another topic to mind. "Who's minding the children?" she wondered aloud. The Thomases had five, the oldest, Elizabeth, was just fourteen.

"Lizzie's capable of keeping them out of trouble for one night. Though if I smell smoke around suppertime I'll be on one of your horses in a minute and galloping back home," laughed Betsy.

"I am truly beholden to you and the Reverend."

"You're a light load," said Betsy. "You don't need diapering, burping, or rocking. And I trust you sleep through the night without demanding to be fed. You are easy."

Lenora smiled at Betsy's effort to make her feel better about being a bother. Town folk—even people whom Lenora had never met—had been more than kind when Dr. Biggerstaff sent the word out that Mrs. James Rose was "ill" and needed tending. Various volunteers had prepared her

wagon box to resemble a down-lined nest awaiting
a clutch of eggs, with layers of borrowed quilts
underneath her and several pillows besides.
Reverend Thomas' lone dappled gray followed
behind, tethered to the back of the wagon. The
Reverend would return to town after seeing Lenora
safely home, leaving Betsy behind until Mrs. Nolan
arrived.

From Lenora's prone position on the wagon
floor, she could see the large head of the
Reverend's horse bobbing ludicrously over the rear
wall of the buckboard, seemingly supported only by
thin air. Occasionally she would make eye contact
with the animal, which seemed to be staring at her
as though she were a circus freak. She laughed to
herself. Her predicament was absurd.

But she laughed between groans. Regardless
of the efforts of the well-meaning town folk, in the
bouncing, creaking, mercilessly hard wagon bed
Lenora felt less like an invalid and more like that
little piggy that went wee wee all the way home.
Her hips and back discerned every rock, every rut,
every bump in the worn path from Buffalo to the
outreaches of the Territory. She was terribly
uncomfortable, and she couldn't wait to slide
between the sheets in her own feather bed.

Not only was she physically uncomfortable,
her limited view from the bottom of the wagon box
cut her off from geographical markers, which made
the trip endless. All she could see was the wide blue
sky of Wyoming directly above the wagon and any

bird or flock of birds that had the courtesy to fly directly over the wagon for her personal viewing. Once she saw a horned grebe, its haunting red eyes and black-and-cream striped face clearly identifiable against the pale blue panorama. And then in a rush of whooping wings, a crèche of tundra swans drew near. Lenora heard them before she saw them. And then there they were, directly over the wagon, their long, graceful white bodies soaring majestically, their jet black beaks sharp against the clear sky.

"I feel like a sow being hauled to market," said Lenora, chuckling. "I've never ridden in the wagon bed before." *And I never thought that I'd do it like this. If only James were here. What would he think of his well-turned out, city born and bred wife being conveyed like stinking farm stock in the back of his buckboard?* The notion was so funny that she forgot to feel sad at the thought of him.

"Well you don't look like a sow ... yet," teased Betsy.

Lenora had confided to her pastor's wife the true nature of her condition. Both women laughed. Might as well laugh. A moment of merriment was all to be gained from her ridiculous situation.

"And we're not taking you anywhere but back to your comfy pigpen," Betsy said, laughing. "Now try to relax. We're not far."

Betsy leaned in to her husband and said something, but Lenora couldn't hear. Sleep was out of the question, so she resigned herself to waiting

177

for another bird to fly over the wagon, congratulating herself each time she identified one. After a while she sensed from her many trips to town that they must be nearing her property.

"Do you see our barn, Betsy?" she said.

"I think so. Another ten minutes or so. Hold on, dear."

Ulysses would be sniffing the air by now, thought Lenora. The house, the barn, the out buildings, her dog. Knowing that she came so close to being separated from the sweet and simple trappings of home for a season made her appreciate them all the more. But as the minutes passed, it seemed awfully quiet to Lenora.

"Do you see Ulysses?"

"No, Mrs. Rose," replied Reverend Thomas, raising his voice and turning his head slightly toward the rear of the wagon. He yelled over his shoulder. "He's probably distracted with some critter more interesting than a couple of old folk on a buckboard."

"He barks to raise the dead when a visitor approaches," said Lenora, raising her voice also. "He can't leave the property. He's chained. You sure you don't see him? He usually runs toward the road when he hears a wagon."

"Perhaps he escaped from his chain," said Betsy, couching her musings as a question. "Probably he saw a playmate to romp with and jerked himself free. He'll be back soon," she added cheerfully.

178

"I don't see him anywhere," said Reverend Thomas. "We're almost there. I'll search the property once I get you settled in the house"

"Thank you, Reverend Thomas."

Lenora could tell from the slackened pace of the buckboard wheels that they were approaching her house. Ulysses should have been dancing all around the front yard, barking his fool head off, begging for his evening meal of kitchen scraps. But there was no sound except the occasional mooing from the barn. It was a contented mooing, not a distress call, which told Lenora that Ben had already milked her cow. The sun was low in the sky, another clue to Lenora that Ben had come and gone. It was late. Ulysses should be hungry. Why couldn't she hear her lovable, slobbering dog calling to be fed?

The wagon cleared the corner of the house. Reverend Thomas halted Beauty and Beast, set the brake and secured the reins, settling the wagon about fifty feet from the covered porch.

"There's Ulysses, at your front door. Some guard dog he is, sleeping on his watch," said Reverend Thomas, jumping down from the wagon to the ground.

Lenora's heart caught in her throat. Ulysses never slept through a visit by a horse or wagon, especially at suppertime. "Are you sure, Reverend Thomas?" she called from the floor of the wagon box. Instinctively she went rigid, breathing shallowly to better hear any little sound of her dog.

179

But all she heard was the sound of Reverend Thomas' feet hitting the ground as he jumped from the wagon.

Then the crunch of the Reverend's boots on dry earth as he approached the house. Lenora waited tensely. Two bats flew over the wagon, their jerky wing movements clearly identifiable against the backdrop of the dusky blue and purple sky.

"What is it, Thaddeus?" called Betsy from the wagon. Her tone, too, was taut with tension.

Lenora recognized the breath of alarm in Betsy's voice. And when Reverend Thomas didn't answer his wife, Lenora's heart beat faster. She didn't move and hardly breathed, trying to discern with anxious ears what was happening at her front door. Finally she heard the Reverend's footfall as he returned to the women. His grim face appeared at the side of the wagon box.

"He's not asleep, Mrs. Rose. He's dead. Someone…" The Reverend swallowed and, grimacing, reached for his wife's hand, "someone cut off his head."

Chapter Fourteen

Plans changed. Reverend Thomas was so shaken by the grisly carnage and the evil message it conveyed, he wouldn't think of leaving the women alone overnight.

Ulysses' head was missing. His body lay, lifeless and grotesque, in a lurid splotch of tacky, partially dried blood. Hideous fingers of red-brown liquid ran down the sides of the porch, dripping into Lenora's flower garden in a gruesome montage of the pure and the vile. Bluebottle flies flit about the carcass, their glistening metallic abdomens and brilliant red eyes creating an unearthly contrast to the drying brownish blood and matted hair of the victim, laying their eggs in utter oblivion of the ghastly events that preceded their call to dine.

An angry thwack of an axe—the bloody murder weapon had been flung into the garden—had killed the animal. This single brutal act should

181

have been adequate to satisfy the most insatiable bloodlust. But who could explain the scorching hatred evidenced in the macabre detail that Reverend Thomas refused to speak of?

Ulysses' paws had been hacked off as well.

#

No one slept deeply that night. Betsy shared the one bed with Lenora. Reverend Thomas made what sleeping arrangements he could, tossing and turning uncomfortably on old quilts spread on the floor of the front room. Before he turned in he carried Lenora into the house, cleaned up the front porch with rags and water, dug a shallow grave for the remains, and told himself he would search for the missing body parts in the morning, lest Mrs. Rose find them by chance as she walked about her property after she convalesced. Likely scavengers would finish them off before she stumbled on them, but the Reverend was taking no chances. Mrs. Rose had been traumatized enough in the last few months.

Next morning, like a malevolent specter that refuses to vacate its haunt, a sense of the killer's presence clung to the rooms of the ranch house, greeting Lenora with her first conscious thought of the new day. Someone had snuck onto her property while she was in town. Someone had performed a bloody, evil act upon her innocent pet.

Why? Was it an act of vindication against her? Against James? Certainly not against Ulysses. He was chained most days. What possible harm

182

could he have caused another rancher's herd or flock? And why kill him in such a gruesome way? What kind of person would do such a despicable thing? What did it mean? Hatred? Anger? Resentment? Jealousy? Someone, Lenora thought with horror, had actually been pleased to inflict a violent, bloody death upon a guileless animal, knowing that Lenora would return home to find the aftermath. It was all so intentional, so calculated, so designed to shock and upset.

If that is what the killer had intended, he had been eminently successful. The weight of the bloody, evil deed pressed heavy on her chest, her mind absorbed with the significance of it. She wondered as she lay there—growing uncomfortably warm under the heavy cotton quilt while hazy streams of light shone through her bedroom window indicating it was past morning chore time—if she would ever feel peaceful and safe again while alone on her ranch.

"Lenora," said Betsy, opening the bedroom door tentatively to see if the invalid was still sleeping, "Good morning."

"Good morning to you," said Lenora brightly. It was way past her usual rising time. She was wide awake.

"I thought you'd be coming around by now. Your breakfast is ready," she said, her head peering around the edge of the door.

"Come in, Betsy," said Lenora, pushing aside disturbing images of her decapitated dog and the evil thwacks that had severed his head so violently.

"We thought it best to let you sleep in," said Betsy. She walked toward the bed with a plate of biscuits and jelly in one hand, a cup of coffee in the other. A plain linen napkin lay across her arm. Steam rose deliciously from the heavy cream-colored mug. "It seemed the best plan under the circumstances."

Lenora knew intuitively that her pastor's wife wasn't speaking about her delicate condition, but rather the bloody scene that had shocked them all when they arrived at the ranch early yesterday evening. Betsy's face was somber, her normally jovial aspect subdued by the gravity of the find. She too must feel the presence of the specter. She spoke in hushed tones, as if she were afraid the unseen visitor was still around and might hear.

"Thank you," said Lenora, pushing herself into a sitting position. She smoothed her hair. She wasn't accustomed to being seen by anyone first thing in the morning, other than James, without first performing an elaborate toilette.

"Here," said Betsy, leaning over to put the biscuits and coffee down, "I'll leave these on the nightstand. I've already put some warm water in the pitcher," she motioned toward the wash stand at the far end of the room, "for you to clean up."

"Thank you."

"And remember what Dr. Biggerstaff said about staying off your feet," she said, pointing to the bordeloue next to Lenora's bed, "no privy." She moved toward the door. "I'll leave you for a few minutes so you can freshen up, then I'll come back and we can chat while you eat your breakfast."

"Good idea," said Lenora, pulling back the too-warm bedclothes and swinging her bare feet over to the edge of the bed. "Just give me five minutes."

Lenora took care of her necessities, enjoying the freshness the wash water rendered to her face. But she was distressed at the thought that she was too frail to walk to the privy behind the house. Even that small privilege had been stripped from her. Well the antidote to that was easy enough. She must get back on her feet as soon as possible. But Dr. Biggerstaff had said she must stay in bed at least a week. She sighed as she climbed back into bed, wondering where she would find the strength to make herself stay there seven days or longer. There was so much to do and so much happening. Besides, other than being tired more than usual, she felt fine, despite the physical evidence to the contrary. The good doctor might as well have sentenced her to seven years.

A soft knock at the door.

"Come in, Betsy."

Betsy sat down gently on the side of the bed.

"Where's your plate?" said Lenora, reaching for hers.

"The Reverend and I already ate." Betsy folded her hands on the lap of her gray dress, the same frock she had worn from town the day before. She sat silent and stiff, observing Lenora as if she had something heavy on her mind.

"My chokecherry jelly must have not set well on your stomach," Lenora said, wryly. "Tastes pretty good to me, though." She smeared a red blob of jelly onto the remaining half of one biscuit.

"Your jelly is delicious. Better than mine."

"Etta Nolan taught me to how to make it. But you didn't come in here to talk about my jelly," said Lenora, noting Betsy's somber demeanor. "Is something wrong?" Her mind flitted to James' Brahman steers and the other stock in the barn. *Oh no! Surely not—*

"No, nothing," said Betsy, somewhat hastily. "All your Brahmans are just fine. Chickens too."

Lenora sighed gustily.

"Everything on your property is just fine. Reverend Thomas made a thorough inspection before breakfast."

Betsy kept silent, however, about what he had found that wasn't fine as he walked abroad the ranch. Two of Ulysses' paws had been flung willy-nilly into high grass behind the barn. The other two paws and the animal's head remained missing. Likely they would be found, he had said, after the vultures started circling.

Lenora's heart dropped back into its place in her chest. For now, all was well. All she had to deal with was the murder of her dog, which, compared to the potential loss of James' beloved herd and all the farm stock, seemed comparatively manageable, though acutely painful. Truly, each day had enough trouble of its own.

"You're obviously disturbed, Betsy. What is it then?" Lenora placed her empty plate onto the nightstand, picked up her coffee cup, and took a sip, waiting.

"Reverend Thomas and I have been talking. We think you should move into town."

Lenora pursed her lips into a thin line. She had an idea this was coming. She set her coffee cup down on the nightstand and intertwined her fingers over the quilt.

"I appreciate your concern, Betsy, but I won't abandon my ranch. I owe it to James to keep on keeping on until he comes home or until ..." Until when? She didn't know. She wouldn't allow herself to think that far into the future. It seemed unfaithful on her part to plan a future without him.

"You wouldn't be abandoning the ranch, Lenora. It would just be for a season."

"I'm going to have a baby, Betsy. I have to preserve this ranch for him. For her."

"All the more reason to move to town. It's safer there. For you and the baby." Betsy's tone was turning to pleading.

Lenora reached out her hand and placed it over her friend's. "The ranch is perfectly safe, Betsy. I have James' rifle. Ben Slocomb comes every afternoon. Soon Sam Wright will come in the mornings. It's not like I'm alone. And," Lenora took a breath to steady herself, "I'll get another dog." Her chin quavered. She never would have thought she would grieve so over Ulysses. Stinging tears formed her eyes. She wiped them with the sleeve of her nightgown.

"Something's not right," said Betsy, trembling. "I feel it," she tapped on her chest over her heart. "This is not the end of it," she said, shaking her head.

"It?" Lenora knew what "it" meant. But she wondered why the pastor's wife seemed so very upset, so convinced of impending doom. Tears ran unchecked down the dear woman's face. "Please don't cry," said Lenora, "I'll be fine out here."

"Oh Lenora," said Betsy. She grasped Lenora's hand in both of hers, squeezed her eyes shut tight, and took a large, noisy breath. "You know so little, out here by yourself all the time. You don't hear."

"Hear what?" Lenora was truly confused.

"Talk."

"Oh, that," said Lenora, off-handedly. "I'm not worried about that."

Suddenly Betsy grabbed both of Lenora's wrists and held them, almost vice like, against the bed covers. Lenora had never seen such a serious look on her face.

"Lenora, listen to me," said Betsy. "I don't cotton to gossip mongering, and I do everything I can to not be the vessel that pours it out all over town. But you need to know what's happening, because mark my words, it will affect you—your baby too—and not for any good, either."

Lenora started to open her mouth to object. She paid little heed to rumors. In her parents' social circle in New York, rumors came and rumors went. It was what people did for entertainment. But Betsy's words were so alarming and the look on her face so serious that they stopped her retort as crisply as a curling iron.

"What I'm about to tell you could harm your baby too, Lenora, might cause people to think you're unfit to be a mother. Might make them feel justified in taking that baby away from you once it's drawn its first breath."

Betsy had Lenora's undivided attention.

"There was talk, at the beginning I mean, when James went missing, that you were touched in the head."

Lenora gave a little gasp, her mouth opening wide with shock. Betsy released her grip on her wrists, sat up a little straighter, and waited, letting that arrow strike its target neatly.

"Some days I've worried about that myself," quipped Lenora, trying to turn the tense moment into a joke. Her friend did not return the smile, which was unusual for Betsy, always the clown. Lenora sobered quickly.

"With grief. Touched with grief. Some people thought you were insane to believe that he was still alive."

"I had—have—no reason to believe otherwise!" Why did she always have to explain this to people, over and over again?

"Be that as it may, some people still think that, Lenora."

Lenora was dumbstruck. How could people reach such a morbid conclusion about James with so little evidence? No, with no evidence at all!

"But I—"

"There's more, Lenora. Please let me finish."

Lenora nodded mutely.

"The deputy."

Lenora cast her eyes downward at the bed clothes, bracing for what she knew was coming. She felt a rush of blood to her face.

"I don't know what the nature of your relationship with the young deputy is, Lenora, but I'm sure it's pure."

Lenora looked up and met Betsy's eyes. She hoped her friend spoke honestly. She hated to think that secretly Betsy judged her. She had done nothing wrong. However, when it came to the deputy, recently her mind had wandered to places she never thought it would go, but no one but herself and God knew about that. Being that James had chosen a quarter-section for its proximity to the creek and not its nearness to town, Lenora had few enough friends in Wyoming Territory, and Betsy

190

was one of the dearest. If she cut herself off from Lenora because of a silly story, it would be a tragedy, a lonely state of affairs indeed.

"Thank you," said Lenora, quietly.

"But people love a salty story, Lenora." She stopped and let her words sink in.

Lenora's breath caught in her throat and her heart beat loudly in her chest. She swallowed, a big I'm-almost-afraid-to-ask swallow. She asked anyway. "What, exactly, have you heard?"

"Some seem to think that the handsome deputy is involved in the disappearance of your husband."

Lenora shook her head and rolled her eyes. "That's ridiculous," she said, a hint of anger in her voice.

As if on cue, a milk cow in the barn let out a belligerent moo, protesting in sympathy with Lenora.

"He arrived in town the same time James went missing," said Betsy, as if that explained everything.

"That's a fact," said Lenora, becoming agitated. "But it's a fact that has absolutely nothing to do with James' disappearance. Pumpkins turn orange in autumn, but that doesn't mean that orange pumpkins cause squirrels to hide acorns or geese to fly south."

"I'm just telling you what I've heard. Please try not to get upset, Lenora. You know none of it is true." Then, as if to soothe, she said, "I know none of it is true."

God bless the dear woman.

"What's all this got to do with my baby?" asked Lenora. But before the words were out of her mouth, the answer exploded in her head like a sizzling bolt of lightning. How could she be so dim witted? So slow to grasp the obvious? Once word got around town that she was expecting, because of the timing of both men's movements, some would be convinced that the baby was Deputy Davies' and not James', and she would have no way to prove them wrong. Unless James returned alive, able to speak for them both, she would live under a cloud of suspicion the rest of her life. And her baby would be shunned as a bastard, the fruit of an adulterous relationship.

"They'll think the baby is the deputy's," said Lenora, putting her hand to her mouth, awestruck, the horror of that truth sinking in. But no, that was too wild, too unbelievable to grasp. "Surely you exaggerate, Betsy," said Lenora, "It can't be all that bad."

Betsy somberly nodded.

"I don't know what to say," said Lenora. "What's to say?" she continued, stupidly.

"You know what else?" Betsy's eyes lit up suddenly then, as if she had a juicy story.

"You've already told me the worst, so surely anything else you have to say is good news," said Lenora, morosely. "However, your eyes tell me it's

192

going to be funny." But secretly Lenora worried that it could be worse. A seed of despair had been sown in her soul. It would be hard to believe any good news after what she'd just heard from Betsy.

"Perhaps a little funny," she said, "A little mirth is good for the soul," She gave Lenora a cagey grin.

"Go ahead," said Lenora, "Don't keep me waiting. I'm in desperate need of whatever amusement I can glean from this nightmare." She leaned her head back against the wooden headboard, closed her eyes dramatically, bracing herself against more outrageous gossip.

"They're now referring to the creek that borders your property as 'Crazy Woman Creek.'"

That did it. Lenora clutched her stomach and broke into laughter, long peals of wonderfully satisfying, tension busting howls, accompanied by much shaking and streams of salty tears. Betsy joined in then, falling back on the bed, howling right along with Lenora. They were still making a ruckus, shaking and wiping their eyes on their sleeves when Reverend Thomas appeared at the bedroom door. Lenora saw him before his wife did.

"Reverend Thomas?" she managed to choke out, at once ashamed that she was carrying on like a maniac so close on the heels of the death of her beloved Ulysses. How could she help it? She was a hopeless loon. Ask anyone in Buffalo.

"If you ladies can collect yourselves a moment," drawled the minister, "a Sam Wright is

193

on the porch. Says Mrs. Rose summoned him about a job."

Chapter Fifteen

Luke's shooting hand slid silently, automatically to the butt of his sidearm, assuring himself that it was in position, ready to defend. He was used to seeing farmers and ranchers with their teams and wagons making their way from their land to town, often accompanied by bonneted wives and a passel of excited children. But a lone rider on a horse, coming from the direction of the Rose ranch, put him on alert. He stiffened his posture in the saddle and squinted to bring the horse and rider into focus, but they were still too far away to identify.

He cast about in his mind, trying to think of a logical scenario to explain why a solitary gentleman would be visiting Mrs. Rose. The sight of the offender and his horse irritated Luke. He was doing his best to act and think with moral rectitude, a conscious response to his growing fondness for the Widow Rose. It irked him to think that some yokel was breaking the rules, jumping into the contest before him. To his obsessed state of mind, the interloper had to be a competing suitor. Whoever the lout was, it was too late in the morning for him to be a Good Samaritan come to help with the chores; and it was too early in the day to be Ben Slocomb. No man had any business visiting Mrs. Rose, except perhaps Reverend Thomas or Dr. Biggerstaff. But out of a sense of propriety, neither of those two gentlemen would come calling absent the company of his wife.

Between Luke and the unknown rider lay a quarter of a mile of treeless prairie scrub, splotchy tufts of green-gray brush grass clinging to the dry red earth, rimmed by low, pointed hills. The day was clear, the sky cloudless, making visibility good but still not good enough for Luke to make out the identity of the man or his horse. Luke's jaw was set, stiff with tension. He kept his horse moving rather than halting it to get a better look. He preferred to create the impression of dispassionate interest. After all, he reminded himself, he was the deputy. Even outside town limits, he was in charge. It was the other rider who should be nervous.

The stranger's horse seemed to be in no hurry, and after a few minutes, Luke saw why. As it drew closer, he recognized the ancient dappled gray gelding as the same one that kept losing its besotted rider in town weeks back. After a space, Luke halted his horse to meet up with Sam Wright. The ranch hand pulled on his reins to slow his steed,

196

then he pushed his too-large black hat—likely a cast off, gauging from its faulty fit and decrepit appearance—back on his head.

"Morning, Deputy."

Sam grinned broadly, exposing an upper mouthful of crowded, overlapping, yellow teeth. His tongue darted in and out of a wide hole where four lower front teeth had long ago abandoned ship, giving his mouth a look of busyness that drew attention toward his lips and teeth and away from his bloodshot eyes. His grizzled face reflected a certain aversion for the blade, and his stained shirt and pants he had surely slept in, likely every night for the last month.

Only ten seconds in the ranch hand's unkempt presence made Luke feel foolish for letting his thoughts be led in circles by a thread of jealousy. It was hard to imagine that this sorry looking ranch hand was ever accused of any crime that stemmed from a relationship with a woman. Luke would bet a month's pay that no female in her right mind either side of the Mississippi would willingly take an interest in Sam Wright, drunk or sober. Perhaps, thought Luke, trying to be charitable, the mangy mossback had been easier on the eyes before he took to liquor. Or perhaps it was a case of misidentification—the wrong Samuel Wright. The message from Fort Laramie detailed a Sam Wright in his early forties. From the sallow color, gray stubble, and crows' feet this Sam looked more like sixty.

197

"Morning, Sam. You're far from town. Must have heard that Mrs. Rose is looking for help."

"Yeah, she in a bad way back there," said Sam, gesturing with his hand toward the Rose ranch, which was only a feint gray smudge in the distance.

"I heard she was under the weather."

"I never seen her," said Sam. "They tell me she in bed. Resting."

"Who's they?"

"Parson." Sam thought a minute, knitting his eyebrows as if it were difficult to dredge up events that occurred less than thirty minutes prior. "And his wife."

"Reverend Thomas?"

"Eh?" said Sam, his tongue hanging, dog like, out the space between his lower teeth. He seemed to have missed the train of thought, which was now chugging down the tracks without him.

Luke looked at the unshaven, trail-worn, sun-weathered ranch hand, his mouth hanging open stupidly, and marveled that anyone anywhere could actually think Sam Wright clever enough to slither his way out of a murder investigation. The man was as dumb as a stump and only slightly more useful. Ranchers used him for chores because he was reliable—when he was sober, about one hour out of every twenty-four—but mostly they hired him because he was cheap.

Sam seemed to wake up suddenly. "Yeah, them. Parson and his wife. They looking after Miz Rose a spell."

"You going to be helping out Mrs. Rose then? With morning chores?"

"A while."

"Did the Thomases say how long they are going to be staying with Mrs. Rose?" As harmless as he seemed to be in his current state of befuddlement, it bothered Luke to think that Sam would soon be spending even a brief amount of time on the ranch every day, alone with Mrs. Rose. He was a man who had been suspected of deadly violence on more than one occasion. Luke was too experienced in dealing with dangerous criminals to be deceived by appearances to the contrary.

"Eh," Sam paused to think, the question apparently falling on the near side of difficulty. "Parson and his wife are helping her out."

"Yes, Sam, I heard you. But do you know for how long?"

Sam hung his head and put a tobacco stained finger to his mouth, deep in thought. Finally he looked up, his face bright with an idea. "You got a smoke you can spare for a hard-working man, deputy? I'm clean out of tobacco." Sam patted his empty shirt pocket dramatically and made a ridiculous, sad face.

"No, no tobacco," said Luke, sighing to himself.

199

Sam looked genuinely crestfallen. In the silence that followed, Luke glanced downward, taking in the size and style of the ranch hand's costly boots. They were newish, the toffee leather still smooth, not scuffed from rocks and prairie brush, the tooling and stitching exquisite.

"Those your boots?" Luke asked, cocking his head toward Sam's feet.

Sam looked at his feet as though he needed to remind himself of what item, exactly, was attached to the lower part of his legs. He studied them a few seconds and then looked up. "I'm wearing 'em, ain't I?"

"That doesn't necessarily mean they're yours," said Luke, evenly.

"I didn't steal 'em, if that's what you mean."

"No one's accusing you of theft, Sam. I just want to know where you picked up the fancy foot gear. In those you're mighty overdressed for mucking stalls."

"I earned 'em," said Sam, stiffening with indignation. "Fellow couldn't pay me. I been looking out for his stock a few weeks, so he give me these boots. I earned 'em fair and square."

"I see." Luke studied the boots long enough to commit their general appearance to memory, then shifted in his saddle, took off his hat, and ran his fingers through his damp hair, hoping for a breeze, even a warm one, to cool his sweaty scalp. Summer was full upon the land. He tried to ignore the burning sensation the unyielding sun projected on his exposed skin. His backside hurt, his mouth was sticky with thirst, and his canteen was dry. Only a few birds cut through the sky during this warm period of the day. Prairie critters had the sense to seek what shade they could or crawl below ground till the cool evening breezes came up to make things bearable. It was uncomfortable interrogating Sam under the unrepentant sun, but the elusive Sam Wright was here, and at least for the moment, he was sober. Luke regarded the ranch hand's words, and then decided to change the direction of his questioning.

"You ever work for James Rose?"

Sam blinked. Luke saw his pupils grow wide in a flash of recognition as ephemeral as a campfire spark. Luke knew he had put his finger on something that caused an emotional response inside Sam, and he wondered what it was. He put on his poker face so as not to give away his thoughts.

"He ever hire you to work at his ranch?" Luke repeated when Sam did not answer.

As if he had just awakened from a short nap, Sam snorted disdainfully, shook his head, and chuckled quietly to himself. As he did another warm breeze picked up a powerful scent and delivered it to Luke, a sour whiff of toxic morning breath, the worst he had ever experienced. He held his own breath a moment, unwilling to inhale.

"You're new, deputy," sputtered Sam, still chuckling. "You didn't know James Rose."

"No, I didn't," said Luke, striving mightily to keep impatience out of his tone. "Educate me."

Sam shook his ahead again. "Big city boy." He spat the words. "Thought he was better than the rest of us. Fancy clothes. Always swinging his gold watch in your face." Sam waved his leathery hand back and forth to demonstrate. "Even his steers had to be better than everyone else's. Wouldn't buy from locals. Not Mister Biggety Britches. He sent to Chicago for those Brah, Brah ..." Sam searched for the word.

"Brahman."

"Yeah, the Brahman. Nothing but a bunch of flapdoodle. Poppycock and flapdoodle, all of it." Sam's mouth drooled as he worked himself into a palaver. He swiped at his mouth with his sleeve.

"What do you mean?"

"He was a macaroni! Fool macaroni! Didn't know nothing about raising steer. If it hadn't been for the neighbors helpin' out he would have lost his fancy ranch first winter out here."

"He came all the way from New York and didn't know how to ranch?" asked Luke.

"Hell no! Just showed up in Buffalo one day, flashing his wad of greenbacks all over town, buying himself the nicest piece of dirt in the Territory. Showing off that pretty wife of his too, in her clicky-clack shoes and frilly dresses. Ain't another woman in these parts that dresses as pretty as Miz Rose."

202

Luke only nodded, all too conscious that some were already talking about him and Mrs. Rose. Better to say nothing about the way she dressed.

"Good riddance. To him, I mean. Not her. Where he is now he ain't impressing nobody, no how."

Luke pondered Sam's last comment. What, exactly, did he mean? Did Sam know where James Rose was now? Did he mean in this life or the next? How could he speak of the whereabouts of a missing man with such certainty? Luke was tempted to push for answers but decided to let the questions rest and come back to them later. He didn't have sufficient evidence to lock up Sam, and right now the man was talking. If Luke pushed too far Sam might clam up, or worse, flee the Territory.

"So you knew him? You worked for him?" said Luke.

"Nah. Never worked for him."

"Why's that?"

"The fool didn't want no help."

"You tried to get work on the Rose ranch?"

"I knocked on his door couple times. Asked for work. But he always shooed me away. Not friendly like, either. Treated everybody worse than a chicken-thieving wolf. It wasn't like I was no beggar. I wanted work. I ain't never asked for no hand-out."

"What about Jennings and Pendergrass? They ever try to get work on the Rose ranch?"

Sam swore vehemently and jerked in his saddle. "Peapod? Maybe. Not sure."

"What about Jennings?"

Sam swore again. Luke noted his agitation but gave nothing away while he waited for an answer. Sam had clammed up again.

"What about Jennings?" Luke finally demanded.

"I don't know nothing about Jennings. What he does with his time is his business."

Luke regarded Sam coolly as he debated how hard to press for an answer. He had little to pin on these three clowns, and being free men, they could ride out of town whenever they wanted, taking their guilt with them undetected. The lack of hard evidence in this case frustrated him.

"People didn't like Rose much, huh?" said Luke.

"If you can find a soul in town will talk good of James Rose," said Sam, laughing again, "I'll buy us both a drink."

Laughter caused Sam to cough, a wet, phlegmy eruption that originated deep in his chest. He fished in his pants pocket and pulled out a grimy hanky, wiped his mouth, and stuffed the hanky back into his pocket. Luke waited for him to finish. He seemed to want to talk. Best let him.

"What do you know of his wife?"

"Miz Rose?" Sam shook his head. "Nothing like her husband. Sweet woman. Once, when Mr. Rose chased me off the property, when he ain't

204

lookin', she brung me a plate of biscuits and gravy. Hot coffee too." Sam smiled at the memory.

"Can you think of anyone who is angry enough at James Rose to want him dead?"

"Eh?" Sam's tongue was hanging out his mouth again.

Luke tried not to stare.

"Dead," repeated Sam. He paused to think, scratching his jaw as if doing so would warm up frozen brain juices, get them flowing.

Why was this clown having difficulty understanding a four-letter word? Certain topics, Luke noted wryly, greased the old coot's flapper, while others gave him lockjaw. But Luke had the good sense to wait. Perhaps eventually he would pull some useful information out of this inscrutable prairie dog.

"No, not dead, exactly," said Sam.

"Then what, exactly?"

Sam screwed up his face as if thinking was painful. "I'm thinkin' most folk is just jealous of his stuff."

Luke remembered the impeccably maintained house and barn, the many well-built, useful out buildings, the prize livestock, the abundant grazing land, all bordered by the widest, longest flowing creek in the north-east section of the Territory. Even more vividly he remembered the fetching face and shapely form of the unlucky rancher's young widow. Longing rose within him. He wished he could be the one to treasure her now, to protect her.

Now that she was feeling poorly, the temptation to sell the ranch and return to her kin in the East would be overwhelming for her. It was his biggest fear.

"Jealous enough to kill?" asked Luke.

"You're the deputy," said Sam, turning petulant. "That's for you to chew on." He pulled the reins sharply to the right, indicating his desire to end the questions and get moving. "I gotta get to town, Deputy Davies. It's hot as Hades out here." He took off his floppy hat to reveal thinning gray hair plastered to his head with sweat. Histrionically he began fanning himself with the hat, as if Luke wasn't aware of how hot it was seated on horseback under a Wyoming summer sun.

Luke figured he'd gotten all he could from Sam anyway, and he was determined to check on Mrs. Rose and ride back to town before nightfall. He nodded and pulled at his own reins.

"Deputy," said Sam, slapping his hat down on his head before they parted. He pointed to Luke's canteen. "You got anything more medicinal than creek water in there?"

Luke shook his head. "Sorry, Sam. Dry as a Quaker picnic."

"Me too," said Sam, poignantly. "Me too."

#

The sound of an approaching rider sent the Reverend Thomas outside to investigate. Luke tipped his hat in greeting and dismounted, relieved to be out of the saddle and to see someone

206

trustworthy looking out for Mrs. Rose and her ranch. He noted Ulysses' absence. Probably pushing his cold snout down a rabbit hole somewhere, thought Luke. The men shook hands.

"What brings you out this way, Deputy?" said Reverend Thomas, a warm smile on his face.

"Just checking on things," said Luke, intentionally vague about what or who those things were.

"Glad you're here, Deputy. Your timing couldn't be better."

Luke gave the Reverend a quizzical look.

"We'll talk after your horse is looked after," said the Reverend, lowering his voice, "in the house."

"Mrs. Rose alright?" Luke wondered at the conspiratorial tone the Reverend used. Luke had heard she'd taken sick, but he had no idea what was ailing her and was too polite to inquire of the people most likely to know. He had learned only that it was serious enough to require the nursing services of another woman.

"Mrs. Rose is going to be fine. Just needs to rest. But I'd prefer to include her in our conversation."

Luke nodded. His interest was always piqued when it came to Mrs. Rose's affairs, but he was patient.

"Why don't you get your horse some water and feed in the barn, then come into the house for a bite yourself. I'll tell Betsy you'll be joining us for dinner."

Luke was agreeable. Reverend Thomas returned to the house while Luke led his horse to the barn. After his animal was well watered and munching contentedly on fresh hay, Luke made a once over of the barn's gloomy interior, his eyes sweeping dark corners and the section of the hay loft visible from the ground. Everything was in order, tack hanging on the wall where it always was, stalls cleaned of debris, Beauty and Beast well groomed and in good health. Ben Slocomb was doing a good job.

But there was a haunting, sepulchral feel about the place that made Luke edgy. Something wasn't right. A strange prescience made the hair on the back of his neck prickle, a sense that something invisible but very real and very evil hovered in the barn. No, not necessarily the barn, he realized with sudden clarity. He had sensed it when he first rode onto the Rose property. Luke stood statue still a moment, muscles taut, ears and eyes on high alert, listening and looking for anything unusual. A thought came to him that it might be a good idea to climb the ladder leading to the hay loft to survey the entire barn from the height of the loft instead of the limited vantage point of the barn floor. It had not occurred to him to do this the day before when he checked the property. But yesterday he hadn't had the willies.

He walked to the ladder and began to climb. He stopped halfway up and listened. Nothing. He continued to climb until his eyes were even with the floor of the loft. Just then a barn swallow, startled by Luke's intrusion, flapped noisily, swooped from his perch high above the hay loft, and flew directly over Luke's head into the broad light of the open barn door.

Luke watched the swallow until it was beyond the edge of the barn door and then he paused a second to listen again. No sound. He climbed two more rungs of the ladder until his chest was even with the loft floor. It was even darker in the loft than on the barn floor, and it took a few seconds for his eyes to adjust. He scanned all about, looking for anything out of the ordinary. Everything seemed as he expected: the loft was dark and musty with grain dust, but there was an unusually large number of dung flies and an odd, sickish smell hung in the air.

Then he saw a low depression at the far end of the loft, like an eddy created by water slipping quickly down a funnel. Above the depression was an indeterminate dark blotch on the barn wall, its color and content obscured by the gloom. He climbed a few more rungs, hoisted himself into the loft, and walked the few steps to the depression to investigate, rustling dry hay as he stepped.

About two feet from the wall Luke jumped back, repulsed by what he saw. Ulysses' lifeless head lay in the depression in the hay, his teeth still bared in death. As Luke's eyes grew accustomed to the dimness, it became obvious that the long, dark streaks on the wall were dried blood. A spray of blood formed a rough ring in the hay around the animal's head. Clearly someone had stood on the barn floor and flung the head upward into the loft, where it had struck the barn wall with force and then fallen back into the hay, fouling it and leaving a gruesome find for an unsuspecting visitor. Flies buzzed about the head.

Doubtless this was what Reverend Thomas wanted to speak with him about. Luke made another quick scan of the loft but, other than the area near the discarded head, the hay had not been disturbed since it had been stored there many months earlier. Seeing nothing that would help him unravel the mystery of the missing James Rose or the murder of his dog, Luke determined to clean up the mess in the loft after dinner.

He climbed back down the ladder. Shaken by the brutality he'd seen inflicted on an innocent animal, he felt compelled to check on the welfare of all the horses again, his own as well as Mrs. Rose's and Reverend Thomas', even though he had checked on them only minutes earlier. Once he had assured himself that they were unharmed, he stepped outside the barn into the bright noonday sun and looked around in every direction to make sure there was no one watching the property. Seeing nothing but prairie grass and low hills shimmering in the heat, he washed up at the pump, more thoroughly than usual, and walked to the house.

#

Before the clomping of Luke's boot heels could be heard on the front porch, Reverend Thomas and Betsy had informed Lenora that he would be sharing dinner with them. Nevertheless her eyes grew wide when the tall and handsome deputy stepped through her front door, hat in hand. She tried to act normally, but there was nothing normal about Deputy Davies stopping by to check on her. There was nothing normal either about hostessing from a daybed, which the kind Reverend Thomas had fashioned out of clean straw, blankets, and pillows so that Lenora could spend daylight hours propped up in a sitting position in the front room instead of languishing all alone in her real bed, cut off from visitors.

And there was nothing normal about the heightened awareness she felt when Luke's tall frame darkened the doorway. Her heart yearned in her chest when Luke's eyes went straight to hers, and for a moment it was as if they were the only two in the room. Lenora caught a stricken look that flashed across his face lightning fast, and just as fast she saw it disappear behind a mask of professionalism.

"Sorry to see you ailing, ma'am," he said, his eyes tender with compassion.

"Thank you, Deputy Davies. Forgive me for not getting up, but Dr. Biggerstaff insisted I remain prone for a good while."

Luke stood by the door, still holding his hat, saying nothing and looking like he didn't know what to do with himself. Betsy walked out of the kitchen then, wiping her hands on one of Lenora's aprons. She walked directly to Luke and extended her hand in greeting.

"Don't worry, Deputy," she deadpanned, "Lenora isn't contagious."

Lenora swallowed hard to force down a chuckle. Betsy turned to her and winked.

"Deputy Davies, come and help me move this table closer to the fireplace," said Reverend Thomas, gesturing to the table visible through the kitchen door. "That way Mrs. Rose won't feel like she's eating alone."

"Or would you rather we all join you on the floor?" quipped Betsy to Lenora. "I don't see any reason why you should be the only one who gets to have a picnic."

Both men laughed, which greatly reduced the awkwardness of this unusual seating arrangement, while they picked up the table and carried it easily to the front room and set it down near Lenora. They went back to the kitchen, retrieved three chairs, and set them by the table. Betsy returned to the kitchen to finish dinner preparations.

In short order the two men and one woman at the table and Lenora in her daybed had finished a hot meal of fried ham, fried potatoes, and hot tea. By the time Betsy was clearing the dirty dishes, however, the mild joviality that had played across

212

the room had been replaced by somberness. When Betsy had cleared away the dishes and set a pot of coffee to boil, she sat back down and made eye contact with her husband. Reverend Thomas leaned forward over the table, his long salt-and-pepper beard brushing his clasped hands, and looked directly at Luke. His face was serious, his voice lower than usual.

"Deputy Davies, when we returned from town yesterday evening, I found Mrs. Rose's dog, dead. Someone killed him and left his body on the porch." He swallowed. "Whoever did it removed the animal's head."

"I knew he was dead," said Luke, looking equally grim. "I found his head in the barn."

The women gasped. Reverend Thomas leaned his elbows on the table and rested his head in his intertwined fingers.

"I had a bad feeling in there," Luke continued, "while I was tending my horse, so I decided to take a look around. I found the head in the hay loft. Someone threw it up there. It hit the wall and fell into the hay. There was a lot of blood."

Lenora let her head fall back on a pillow for support and closed her eyes, imagining in the most acute way the vivid act just described. She saw Ulysses' head flying through the air, heard the muffled, wet smack of it hitting the barn wall, saw it land with a swoosh in the hay. Her breathing became shallow, which caused her face to turn pale. What did it all mean? Why was she being stalked,

213

her dog murdered, her husband missing? There had to be some sense to this agonizing series of tragedies. Most of all, when would it all end?

"Mrs. Rose," said Luke, his voice gentle but direct, "I need to ask you some questions. Are you well enough to help me?"

Lenora opened her eyes. "Yes, I'm fine. It's just all so unbelievable."

All three at the table stared at Lenora. As if she didn't feel foolish enough already, dining on the floor in her own home with the Reverend, his wife, and the deputy seated nearby. And entertaining in her nightgown yet! What was the world coming to?

"Don't worry," she said, noting the concern on all three faces, "I'm fine. And even if I weren't, I'm already in a good position for fainting." She smiled wanly at her weak joke. At least she hadn't lost her sense of humor. It wasn't all that difficult to crack jokes since they had found Ulysses' remains. She was too numb with the shock of recent events to mourn her myriad losses anymore.

"Do you have any idea who did this, Mrs. Rose?" asked Luke.

No, she didn't. But it was evident from the footprints on her ranch, the repeated attempts by some unnamed person to enter her home uninvited, and from the brutal murder of her dog, that she was a target. But why? And who? Her mind was blank.

"I have no idea."

"Did James owe money to anyone?"

"I don't think so. But he never told me about our debts, whether we have any. I don't know."

"Do you know of anyone that James was having any disagreements with?"

She thought again. She was embarrassed that she couldn't give Deputy Davies any hard information. She tried to dredge up logical answers to illogical events. But there weren't any. And she was so very, very tired. She leaned farther back into the makeshift daybed so that the pillow and not her neck supported her head.

"I can't think of any. No."

"Do you suppose someone's just trying to frighten her, Deputy Davies?" said Reverend Thomas.

"It's possible. James Rose owns the nicest parcel in this part of the Territory. Since he's been gone so long, it could be that someone wants to give his wife a good reason to hightail to New York City."

Lenora's head popped back up. Frighten her? "Who would want to do that?" she said, aghast at the thought of abandoning her ranch out of fear.

"Anyone who badly wants the ranch and herd and has the money to buy them," said Luke. "Know anyone like that?"

"Any number of large ranches around these parts would welcome the opportunity to annex yours," said Reverend Thomas, looking at Lenora. "You've got water all year round, not just during the wet spells."

"Of course," said Lenora, embarrassed. Why hadn't this scenario occurred to her already? A few local ranchers had approached James in the last four years, offering to buy them out. But James would not be tempted. He had purchased a dream, and so had Lenora. There wasn't enough cash in all of Wyoming Territory for them to give that up.

"We've had offers for the property," said Lenora, "but James turned them down promptly. And those came from our neighbors," she said. "They're our friends."

Reverend Thomas and Luke exchanged a look.

"Has anyone approached you lately about buying?" asked Luke.

"No."

"If someone wanted to buy her out," said Betsy, "and planned to use fear as a motive, they might be smart enough not to tip their hand."

"True," said Luke.

The room was quiet several seconds. In the silence Lenora felt Ulysses' absence more keenly. Until now she had not realized what a comfort the daily sounds of her pet's movements outside the house had been for her since James left. She even missed his bone-rattling barking.

"Mrs. Rose," Luke said, "has Buck Jennings or Pea-Pod Pendergrass ever come 'round asking for work?"

"I don't recall ever seeing either of them out this way." Lenora debated volunteering her next thought, because she didn't want the conversation to veer anywhere near her argument with James. But a decapitated dog was serious business, so she forged ahead. "And if they had ever spoken to James in town, he would not have told me. We didn't always agree on the subject of hiring help."

Luke looked intently at Lenora, but if he had an opinion on the Roses' disagreements, he kept it hidden behind an impassive face.

"Who was on the property yesterday besides myself?" he asked.

"Ben Slocomb was here in the afternoon, like every afternoon. After that, there was no one but you. I was in town most of the day. I didn't arrive back with the Thomases until suppertime."

"What did you see when you arrived?" asked Reverend Thomas, directing his question to Luke.

"Nothing. I arrived before Ben did. I looked over everything—house, barn, out buildings. Everything was in order. Ulysses was happy to see me. He was on his chain. I fed him some jerky."

Lenora winced at the thought of Ulysses' last few hours alive. She could easily picture Ulysses' slobbering happiness at receiving a treat from the deputy. How could anyone butcher an innocent animal? Why would anyone take pleasure from such an act?

"I'll ride out to the Slocombs after I leave here and see if Ben saw anything suspicious," said Luke. "I'll ask at your other neighbors too," he said, speaking to Lenora.

Lenora's eyes met his. She saw nothing but kindness, so much so that she temporarily forgot her embarrassment over her current condition and their awkward dinner arrangements. Appearance didn't matter so much anymore. Having people that cared, she had learned, took the sting out of a lot of life's difficulties.

"Deputy," said Reverend Thomas, "You don't suppose Ben had anything to do with this?" Reverend Thomas absently ran his hand over his long beard.

Luke paused to think, shook his head. "I've thought about that some. But I've no good reason to suspect Ben. He's a good boy. Runs off at the mouth sometimes, but he's never given his folks any trouble that I've heard of. Also, this doesn't look like the work of someone so young."

"No, I suppose not," said Reverend Thomas.

"Probably a good idea if I stop in and question him, though, his parents, too," said Luke.

"Looks more like the act of someone who's angry," said Betsy.

"I agree," said Luke.

"I don't know of anyone who'd be angry at me," said Lenora, thinking aloud.

"Not you, Mrs. Rose, your husband," said Luke, looking grim.

Just then the hiss and rattle of a madly percolating coffee pot caused them all to look toward the kitchen.

218

"I forgot the coffee!" Betsy jumped up from the table and walked briskly toward the kitchen. While they waited for her to return with the coffee service, Luke turned again to Lenora.

"Did Sam Wright come around before today?"

"You saw Sam on the way in?" interrupted Reverend Thomas. He leaned in to Luke a bit, looking stunned. Betsy entered the room then with cream and sugar and clean spoons.

"I passed him about a half mile down the road."

"Did he tell you anything?" asked Reverend Thomas.

Luke looked confused. "He said he'd been by to see about helping Mrs. Rose with morning chores until she's on her feet again."

Reverend Thomas and his wife looked at each other, eyes wide with knowing. Lenora looked stunned too.

"Deputy Davies," said the Reverend, "Before Sam rode out of here this morning, I told him what happened to Ulysses. He said he was going to town today, and he volunteered to tell you everything when he got there to save me the trip. You're telling me he said nothing to you about the dog?"

"Not a word," said Luke.

Chapter Sixteen

"Having you at the ranch these last few weeks has made me think about a lot of things, Etta. And I've realized something important."

The hot spell had broken, and the mild temperatures of early summer had returned, making the wide open prairie a welcoming place again. Even the small prairie animals seemed unusually frisky in the cooler temperatures. Blacktail prairie dogs with their creamy white throats and dark almond eyes skittered excitedly, poking their noses from their holes, sniffing and twitching, entire families of them staring at Lenora and Etta as they rolled by, as if the buckboard were part of a funeral train. In the distance a small herd of pronghorn antelope stopped grazing long enough to stare as well, their black faces all as one, observing the women in the buckboard dispassionately. After a minute the bored creatures returned to their grassy meal, ignoring the wagon altogether.

And this morning, after so many dreary hours of lying in a makeshift bed, riding in the buckboard with Etta Nolan was positively glorious for Lenora. She exulted in the simple acts of taking a hot soak in a deliciously deep tub of water instead of making do with a sponge bath, wearing a pretty fitted dress instead of a shapeless nightgown, holding onto the reins, and sitting upright on the buckboard seat like a human passenger instead of a farm animal dozing in the wagon box. After a trying season of inactivity, she appreciated the smallest routines of living as never before. She couldn't stop smiling this morning. Soon, she thought to herself, she must make a new frock of the daffodil silk, something unusually special, with lots of hidden tucks that she could let out as she grew bigger in front.

"And what is that, dear?" said Etta, gripping the buckboard bench to keep from sliding off. But before Lenora answered, Etta said, "I know you're excited about getting out of the house, but can you slow your horses down just a little? Buffalo will still be there if we take it at a trot instead of a stampede."

Lenora laughed. "Yes, of course. I'm sorry." Deftly she pulled on the reins to slow Beauty and Beast. "I'm just so happy to be going to town." She let go of the reins with one hand and patted her still-flat abdomen. "And I'm so happy about the baby."

"The baby will be a comfort to you," said Etta, raising her voice a little over the noise of the wagon wheels.

Mrs. Nolan didn't say it, but Lenora's mind easily finished the thought. *In the loss of your husband.* But the unspoken words dampened Lenora's spirit only a little. The sudden pang of grief she felt when she realized that James might not ever hold their long-awaited child gripped her heart so fiercely she felt she couldn't breathe. But already she was learning to push the pain to the back of her mind as quickly as possible. She felt too good, the day was too beautiful, the baby too healthy and too *real* to allow her thoughts to become veiled in a shroud of mourning. James still had not come home and might not ever again. But she had to go on living. She had the baby growing within her to think of now.

"Now what were you going to tell me?" said Mrs. Nolan.

"I've made a decision."

"Oh?"

"I can't live alone, Etta. Having you with me these past few weeks, after being alone so long, makes the thought of spending another night by myself on the ranch without James—or you—most unpleasant."

"Of course, dear. Anybody would feel the way you do."

"Not only that, when James first went missing, I was determined to hang on to the ranch at

222

any cost. But after all the things that have happened since then, now holding onto the ranch all by myself seems naive."

The elderly widow nodded, listening intently over the racket of the wagon wheels and the clip clop of the horse team.

"But I'm not a quitter, Etta. And now that Sam Wright is behind bars, I have even more reason to stick it out until I've fulfilled the five years. I have nothing to fear anymore. With that episode behind me, I have every reason to give it one more year. James would want that."

"Are you sure, Lenora?"

"If I can stick it out another year, the ranch will be one hundred percent mine. The baby's too." Lenora patted her abdomen again. "If James isn't back with us by then, I'll sell and move back East with my folks."

"Do you really think you can handle the ranch and a little one by yourself Lenora? Even for a short time? You've never had a baby. You don't know how much work is involved."

"I didn't say it would be easy." *Nothing has been easy yet.* "To tell the truth, I expect it to be difficult. But neither is it impossible. I have to at least try to hang on until I get full ownership."

"A year is a long time, Lenora."

"A year and a half to be exact."

Etta shook her head slowly side to side and made a straight line of her mouth.

"Don't look so glum, Etta. I didn't say I'd do it entirely by myself. I plan to ask Mr. Morehouse at Wells Fargo for a loan this morning. If I can get an advance against the sale of the ranch, I'll have enough to hire a foreman full-time. If James doesn't come back before the ranch is ours, once the property is in my name I'll sell it and pay off the mortgage with the proceeds."

"And if James comes back before then?"

"Then the mortgage will be his problem to solve."

"Ooh," said Mrs. Nolan, drawing out her 'o' a little bit longer than necessary.

"What do you mean, 'Ooh'?"

"You'll hire a foreman to live on your ranch?"

"Room and board plus a pittance wage is the only way I can afford to hire someone. The ranch isn't big enough to pay cash wages."

"True," said Mrs. Nolan with a sigh.

"And I can't keep accepting favors from the Slocombs. I must start paying Ben for his services. To do otherwise would be taking advantage."

Etta nodded again but said nothing. Lenora shifted the reins in her hands. They were growing numb from gripping hard for so long.

"Sam Wright is locked up where he belongs, thank God, so hiring him is out of the question. Betsy Thomas tells me it won't be long before I won't be able to lift the harness to hitch and unhitch my horses. I have to find someone. As soon as possible too."

"I suppose it wouldn't do to overexert yourself and end up in bed again."

"Never!" If there was anything Lenora dreaded it was the mind-numbing effect of forced inactivity. She had to keep busy, keep moving, and keep her mind occupied to stay sane.

The ladies rode in silence a while, enjoying the fresh morning air and wild sense of freedom that comes from traversing through wide open spaces. Before long the weathered storefronts of Buffalo appeared as a gray spot on the prairie.

"You sure you don't want me to wait with you until your son shows up?" asked Lenora.

"No dear, you've plenty of errands in town to take up your time. Malcolm knows to meet me at Aeschelman's. He'll be right on schedule. And if he's late, I can always wait in the milliner's shop and visit with Ellen. I haven't been in to see her in a while. Besides, I need a new hat."

"Like you need another head."

Both women laughed. Mrs. Nolan was known about town for, among other things, the endless parade of distinctive bonnets she sported.

"How can I thank you for all you've done for me, Etta? If you hadn't sacrificed to come stay with me, I would have ended up languishing at the Occidental." Lenora shuddered at the thought of the toll that would have taken on her bank account, not to mention the loneliness inherent in staying so long in a strange place, bereft of family and the comfort of familiar surroundings.

225

"Think nothing of it. I was glad to do it. I'll come and stay with you when the baby arrives too. Now there's something to look forward to!" Mrs. Nolan smiled broadly, her laugh lines framing her eyes under her bonnet.

"I would like that very much, Etta," said Lenora, reaching for the elderly woman's hand and giving it a squeeze.

#

As Lenora pulled onto Main Street, it seemed to her that the presence of two women, one young, one old, riding on a common buckboard was of greater interest than usual to shoppers and other pedestrians. Two men occupied in carrying a corn harvester out the front door of Aeschelman's actually stopped, grunting under their load, to watch them roll by. Others pointed and whispered, staring and putting their heads together to share some dark secret, and not all that discreetly, either. And though Lenora saw a few passersby who knew her from church, oddly, no one waved a greeting. Then, as they slowed the wagon for a pedestrian in front of Wells Fargo, Lenora saw Mrs. Graves walk out of the bank. She too stopped to watch the movement of the buckboard. Lenora saw Mrs. Graves look in her direction. Lenora smiled, but instead of returning the smile, Mrs. Graves blanched, turned her head, and proceeded to walk down the street.

A niggling sense of alarm arose in Lenora's mind. How bad was the gossip, really? Perhaps

Betsy had not exaggerated after all. Lenora leaned over and spoke closely in Mrs. Nolan's ear.

"Etta, something doesn't feel right. People are staring."

"Yes dear, I see that."

"I hope I'm not embarrassing you."

"Not at all." Mrs. Nolan smoothed her skirt, tucked a stray wisp of white hair into her frilly bonnet, and sat up a little straighter in the buckboard seat. "Just keep guiding the horses and smile when you see their faces. There's nothing you can do about the dark thoughts on the other side of those eyes."

"Yes," said Lenora, her voice tremulous. But for the most part she found it easier to avoid their faces altogether. She shook inside when she saw the open displeasure staring back at her from people she knew about town. It made her all the more panicked and anxious to get her buckboard and horses behind the dark walls of Olathe's Livery. She stared straight ahead and guided the horses, which seemed anxious as well to reach the creature comforts at the stables.

Not soon enough Lenora was pulling on the reins to slowly guide Beauty and Beast through the wide open door of Olathe's. She brought the big animals to a stop, set the brake, and held the reins, waiting for Olathe to appear. The old man heard the jingle of the harness and the creaking of the wagon and came from the back of the stable to greet them. Out of habit Lenora smiled at him. She was taken aback when the little man rudely refused to return the courtesy.

"Ma'am," he said, with minimum politeness. His jaw taut, he met Lenora's eyes for the briefest instant, enough to be civil and no more, and then walked around the wagon to the other side to help Mrs. Nolan down. Naturally the elderly woman would be assisted first in disembarking, but Lenora felt the rebuff acutely just the same.

So this is how it is. The heretofore likable and friendly little man suspected her of damnable things. If someone she thought of as a friend was inclined to believe the wild tales circulating about the lunatic adulteress at Crazy Woman Creek, then Lenora realized, with a feeling of doom, that her troubles with gossip would only get worse. As she sat stiff and prim on the buckboard bench waiting for Olathe to help her down, resplendent in her creamy white barege and silken tussah, she wished she had worn something to town today a little more reserved.

At least, she thought with wry humor, she hadn't worn her blazing red kidskin boots and matching gloves.

Olathe finished with Mrs. Nolan and then, instead of returning to Lenora's side of the wagon to help her down, he ignored her and walked over to Beauty and took hold of the reins attached to the horse's harness.

"You going to be long in town, Mrs. Rose?" he said.

228

Lenora's mouth parted slightly with shock. Never had a man treated her with such disrespect in all her life. By this time Mrs. Nolan, using her cane, had thumped her way around the wagon to Lenora's side.

"Bennett Olathe," she said, leaning heavily on her cane with both hands after the long, bone-jarring ride to town. "Act hospitably and help Mrs. Rose down."

Olathe didn't move, just stood there, tight lipped.

"This is my livery," he finally said, a look of steel determination in his eyes.

"Fiddlesticks!" snapped Mrs. Nolan. She turned abruptly away from Olathe and took a step toward the wagon, where Lenora sat, speechless and incredulous. Mrs. Nolan leaned on her cane with one hand and extended her other to Lenora. "Here, let me help you," she said, loudly enough to make it clear the words were more for Olathe than Lenora, "Shameful thing when we have to suffer such a shortage of gentlemen in this town."

"That's alright, Etta, I can manage," said Lenora, shaking inside but doing her best to lower her yards of barege skirting over the side of the wagon without catching the flounces on anything sharp. Once she was safely standing on two feet, she turned to Olathe.

"I'll be several hours in town," she said stiffly. "Thank you for looking after my horses."

Olathe only nodded.

229

Lenora turned to Mrs. Nolan. "One minute, Etta, and I'll get my basket." Lenora stepped close to the wagon and on tiptoes reached over the side for her shopping basket, grabbed it, and then took Etta's arm. "Let's go."

Once they were outside the barn and out of Olathe's hearing, Lenora turned to Etta. "My, after all that I'm glad he didn't turn my horses and wagon away too."

"He needs the money you pay him to feed and water them."

"I know, but still ..."

"Try not to let it ruin your day, dear."

"It pretty much already has." Lenora turned back toward the barn to see if Olathe was staring after them. He wasn't, yet she could still feel his ugly glare on her back.

"Maybe they're right about the widow's weeds," Lenora said quietly, half to herself.

"What do you mean by that?" said Mrs. Nolan, guiding them toward the center of town.

"Maybe I should be wearing mourning clothes. Some around here are offended that I don't. But honestly Etta, I don't feel like a widow. I still don't have any proof." Lenora's voice began to crack, shaken more by Olathe's cold reception than the issue of when to wear mourning black. One thought merely fanned the flames of the other.

"And what if you wore black? What would they say then?"

Lenora thought a moment. What *would* they say? Her mind had never trod that path. If she wore black, like some thought appropriate, wouldn't they stop talking about her altogether? The two women stepped gingerly onto the planks of the stepping bridge that crossed narrow Clear Creek, being careful not to catch their heels in the wide spaces between the planks. They stepped onto the boardwalk, clutching their skirts with one hand to keep them from dragging on the edge of the step up.

"That I was mourning my husband." Wasn't that the logical answer?

"Maybe." Mrs. Nolan clasped Lenora's hand in hers. "Or maybe they'd say, 'Scandalous, isn't it? Look at that shameless Mrs. Rose. Husband missing only a few months and already she's wearing black." Mrs. Nolan rolled her eyes in exaggerated shock, throwing her head back for dramatic effect. "Why is she in such a hurry to start the one-year mourning period? Couldn't she wait till they've found his body? Probably has set her cap for some other fellow already. Outrageous! The wanton woman, her husband not even buried yet.'"

Lenora's heart nearly skipped a beat and her pulse quickened. Mrs. Nolan hadn't directly spoken of her growing interest in Deputy Davies, but her oblique reference had touched a nerve. She stopped walking and turned to face her friend.

"Etta, I haven't set my cap on anyone. You believe me, don't you?"

"Of course I believe you."

Lenora let out an enormous, shoulder heaving sigh.

"But I also believe that Deputy Davies is smitten with you."

Lenora clasped her hands together and cast her eyes to the ground. Was it so obvious? Had she encouraged him by allowing him to interrogate her in public? Was she deceiving herself that the attraction was only on his part? She hoped she wasn't guilty of playing fast and loose with his heart—and her own reputation—out of loneliness and fear.

"Pretty much the whole town thinks that way," added Mrs. Nolan.

Lenora had an idea this was so, but hearing it from Etta left no doubt. "What will I do?" Lenora almost whispered the question.

"Do? There's nothing to do. The cat is already out of the bag. No use tying it with string now."

The two women started walking down the boardwalk again, and then suddenly Mrs. Nolan stopped. "No," she said, putting her hand to her chin in thought, "that's not right, either."

Lenora stopped too and looked into the very dear, very kind eyes of her friend.

"Lenora, can't you see how unwise it is to dance to their tune?"

"What do you mean?"

The stagecoach went past just then, clattering briskly through the center of town, trying to stay on schedule while it sent up small storms of fine, choking dust. Lenora reached into her reticule for one of her lace-edged hankies to cover her mouth. Mrs. Nolan waved the dust away with her hand.

"It's like that story in the Bible. Luke, I think. Jesus talked about the naysayers. 'We have piped unto you, and ye have not danced; we have mourned to you, and ye have not wept.'"

"I don't hear any music," said Lenora morosely, a single tear beginning to roll down her face. She wiped it away with her now-dusty hanky.

"No matter what our Lord did, the unbelieving criticized Him. And when John the Baptist came, foregoing bread and wine, they said he had a devil. But when Jesus ate and drank with publicans and sinners, they called Him a glutton and a drunkard. So you see, there was no pleasing those people."

Mrs. Nolan waited while Lenora composed herself. When her tears had stopped, Mrs. Nolan took her hands in hers.

"Do you understand what I'm trying to tell you?"

"I think so. Nothing I do will be acceptable if they don't approve of me."

"Hmm," said Mrs. Nolan. "You do understand."

"This is not about widow's weeds, is it Etta? It doesn't matter whether I wear black or not."

"Exactly."

Lenora nodded silently, her face screwing up into a deep grimace of grief. Then the dam burst. "I am so *confused*," she said, speaking in a fevered whisper and shaking with sobs. "I don't know whether to act like a patient wife, waiting for his return, or like a widow, accepting that he's dead. This really is making me crazy! I don't even know how to dress when I come to town! What do I do Etta? What do I do?"

"Here, Lenora, come with me," said Mrs. Nolan quietly, guiding Lenora off the boardwalk and into a secluded spot, shaded but weedy, between the tobacconist shop and the barber's. Mrs. Nolan took care to keep her back to the street, shielding Lenora from onlookers. The old woman opened her reticule and fished around for a handkerchief while Lenora hugged her middle, gasping for air and trying to muffle her sobs.

"What do you do? You keep standing on the truth," said Mrs. Nolan, finally finding the hanky and handing it to Lenora. "That's all we're called to do anyway. Walk in the truth. People will believe whatever they want about us. We just keep standing on the truth until He makes our righteousness shine forth as the noonday sun."

After a few tense minutes Lenora managed to calm herself. When she was able to breathe again, she said, "Thank you, Etta, I'll remember what you said." Her voice quavered a little, and her face, she knew, looked wretched, pink and puffy. Oh well.

Mrs. Nolan threw her arms around Lenora and hugged her. How good her embrace felt.

"One more thing," said Mrs. Nolan, releasing her hold. "Take one day at a time. As much truth as you have for today, walk in that. Try not to worry about tomorrow. Each day has enough problems of its own, remember? Don't worry about tomorrow's problems today."

"I will," mumbled Lenora, "I mean I won't," she corrected herself, smiling weakly, though she wondered how she managed to do even that.

"Lenora," said Mrs. Nolan, more quietly, "Do you like him? The deputy?"

Lenora's first instinct was to flame up in embarrassment and hold her tongue. She hadn't expected the conversation to turn this direction and was unprepared. There was, it seemed, no hiding her true feelings or anything else from this intuitive woman. And after releasing so much tension by sharing her confusion with Etta, it seemed that sharing her angst about Deputy Davies would not be unwise. She paused to allow her herself to sort her thoughts. Searching for her true feelings about the deputy was like plunging into deep waters for a gold coin. The truth was buried somewhere, but she would have to swim blindly through the murk and feel around in the mud to find it. Reflexively she looked around to see if anyone was nearby enough to hear them. Seeing no one about, she answered, keeping her voice very low.

"I didn't at first. But I *think* I do now. He's ... kind. And he's been very helpful since James left." She thought of Sheriff Morris and how the deputy had begun to ally himself with her against a common foe, but there was no good reason to explain the details to Mrs. Nolan. Her heart burned within. Yes, she *was* fond of Deputy Davies, but it seemed unholy to say so directly.

"He has a good reputation in Fort Laramie."

"How do you know that?" Lenora's eyes were sufficiently dry, and her hanky was too damp and dirty to use, so she slipped it back into her reticule and pulled the drawstring tight. She felt sturdier now.

Mrs. Nolan made a fluttering motion with her free hand. "A birdie," she said, smiling.

Now that Lenora's face was dry, Mrs. Nolan led her back onto the boardwalk, and in a minute they arrived at the door of Wells Fargo. They hugged again, promised to stay in touch, and then Mrs. Nolan went on her way to the mercantile. Lenora pushed open the heavy, oversized door of the bank, and taking a deep breath, walked in.

Chapter Seventeen

All eyes in the room swiveled toward the young woman in the flouncy cream dress with the elaborate bustle. Lenora tried to pretend that she wasn't the focus of their rude stares, but the pounding in her chest and the blood rushing loudly behind her ears threatened to give away her pretense of calm. She hoped the fear in her eyes did not betray her. Everyone stopped talking at once as time stood still. Lenora felt the burn of all those eyes on her and regretted the obscenely loud clack of her hard heel, high top boots as she walked across the shiny oak floor of the cavernous bank lobby.

Dear God, Am I always going to create a scene wherever I go? How shall I ever survive this?

In a moment a tall brown blur appeared over her right shoulder. She turned her head, and

237

there was Deputy Davies, smiling and tipping his hat.

"Mrs. Rose," he said, as cool as you please, "in that white dress you're prettier than a bouquet of Pearly Everlasting."

Lenora was too surprised by his presence and too aware of the big-eared audience to speak. Yet her only conscious thought was that her dress wasn't white. It was the color of freshly skimmed cream. Snow was white. But fashionable women forgave mere men such ignorance. She said nothing, cognizant that everyone in the room had stopped what they were doing to listen. But deep within, her heart was talking. How comforting it was to find a warm and friendly face in this chilly sea of criticism. Luke's presence strengthened her, and when she looked into his soulful, chocolate eyes she saw the same compassion and caring she'd seen when he had come to the ranch to check on her weeks before. She felt herself grasping for his lifeline of friendship.

"I'm glad to see you today," he said, removing his hat. "I need to speak to you about the investigation."

Luke's voice was the only sound to be heard in the bank. Even the flies seemed to stop their buzzing to eavesdrop. Surely he was aware that all eyes and ears were strained to catch any crumb of gossip he might toss. She might have been happy to see the deputy's smiling face, but she cringed at the thought of speaking to him in public. It could only make matters worse. But if he had news about James' disappearance, she needed to hear what he had to say. And seeing the cold reception from so many already this morning, she was reluctant to cut the thin thread of human warmth he dangled in front of her.

"Deputy Davies," she whispered, leaning in to him slightly, "this is hardly an appropriate venue for a tête-à-tête."

A hint of a smile lifted the side of his mouth. "If you mean this isn't a good place to be whispering, I agree with you," he whispered back. His eyes twinkled as if the two shared a delicious secret.

Lenora straightened herself. "I have important business I must attend to here at the bank, Deputy Davies," she said, choosing her words carefully knowing the whole room was weighing them.

"I'll wait for you."

Lenora's first instinct was to object. People were watching. But she and Luke were already creating a scene just by speaking calmly of ordinary things in broad daylight; arguing here in the bank would only add grist to the gossip mill. Above all she didn't want to meet him at the sheriff's office. Sheriff Morris might be at his desk, a thought that heightened her anxiety before she had spoken a word. But there was worse. If Sheriff Morris was not at his desk, she'd create an even more salacious scandal by conducting business with the deputy, alone, behind his closed office door. Finally, she didn't care to be anywhere near Sam Wright, who had been locked up at the sheriff's office, awaiting trial, since Ulysses' bloody murder. Considering all these pitfalls, having Deputy Davies wait outside the bank so that they could speak on the street after her business with Mr. Morehouse seemed the least gossip-worthy scenario.

Lord have mercy. What a sticky twist of taffy she was entangled in! Considering the gossip swirling around her, her baby, and the two men suspected of being the father, she was hardly in a position to refuse to discuss the investigation of her husband's disappearance with local law enforcement. But a local law officer was one of the men some suspected had fathered her unborn child! Whether she said yes or no to his request, she walked straight into a storm cloud of suspicion.

But in that moment, when she recognized that she faced two impossible choices, it was as if her very insides were a deep well of water, and somehow she managed to reach down and draw up a bucket of courage. Mrs. Nolan was right. All she could do was also the best thing to do: she must walk in the truth that she had. She knew whose baby was growing in her womb. It didn't matter what these ignorant people thought about the identity of the father. She would keep walking in the knowledge of that truth even if she had to fight dog killers, cattle rustlers, a shrinking bank account, lonely nights, fatigue, widowhood, depression, the hiss of serpentine tongues, and yes, even the loss of her ranch. She would walk into Mr. Morehouse's office on the strength of the truth, and she would get the money she needed.

Today.

Not only that, one other person in town knew for sure that Deputy Davies was not the father of her child—Deputy Davies. Perhaps that explained his calm demeanor.

"I might be a while," said Lenora, glancing at the line at the teller's window. "But if you would like to wait, that would be serendipitous for the moment. And I would be grateful."

"I'll wait." Luke replaced his hat on his head, tipped it respectfully, turned himself, and walked back to his place at the clerk's window.

Knowing that everyone in the room was watching her, Lenora quickly averted her eyes from the deputy and stepped to the end of the line. Before long everyone returned to their business and Lenora was being ushered into Mr. Morehouse's lavish office.

#

As before, Mr. Morehouse invited Lenora to sit down in one of the large, comfortable visitors' chairs. Nothing about the room had changed, but Mr. Morehouse had taken to waxing the slender tips of his English mustache. Such an idiosyncrasy would have lent a rakish air to another man. But because rakish was a word Lenora would never have strung together in the same sentence with Mr. Morehouse, the effect of the two yellowish-gray daggers pointing east and west like the weather vanes on her barn roof only added to the many distractions about his person she had to consciously ignore. She found this difficult. How far beyond his face would the daggers protrude by their next meeting? She caught herself staring and, embarrassed, forced herself to focus on his eyes.

"How are things at the ranch, Mrs. Rose?" Mr. Morehouse leaned back in his black leather chair as if settling in for a long chat.

Oh no, he wants to socialize again. Due to her long confinement, Lenora had much shopping to do after her meeting with the deputy. She sighed.

"The ranch is doing very well." Not wanting to draw out this useless discussion, she was about to end the thought on that note, but because she didn't want to appear disrespectful to James, she added, "Considering that my husband is away, that is."

Mr. Morehouse nodded and kept his eyes fixed on her, scrutinizing her almost to the point of rudeness. She felt uncomfortable, suddenly aware of how extravagant she must appear to this country banker in her multiple ringlets and frilly clothes, her gloved hands and well-turned out toes. She tucked her expensive leather high tops under her skirt and practiced meeting his gaze with all the aplomb she could muster.

"How many new Brahman your herd drop this spring?"

Calves? Surely Ben must have spoken to her about the birthing and how it affected the size of their small herd. Why hadn't she bothered to listen carefully? Because she was distracted by the disappearance of her husband, that's why. She hated to make excuses to Mr. Morehouse. But if she was going to pass herself off as a serious woman rancher, she should be able to rattle off a number. Around spring in the Territory it was all about the numbers. How many born, how many sold, how many rustled was nearly all the obsessed cattlemen ever talked about. Lenora usually got up and left the room when James and the neighbors started jaw boning ad nauseam about the numbers.

"Several," she said.

Mr. Morehouse nodded, stuck out his lower lip like he was thinking deep, bankerly thoughts.

Oh fiddle faddle. I know more about Brahman than this overstuffed plutocrat.

"Sorry to hear about your dog." Mr. Morehouse leaned forward over the desk and clasped his hands together.

Wonders! One of the weather vanes was longer than the other.

243

"Thank you kindly, Mr. Morehouse.
Ulysses is sorely missed on the ranch." He
sounded sincere, and Lenora read nothing sinister
in his eyes. Instantly she regretted being irritated
with the man and his irksome ways. She
shouldn't judge.

"Too bad you hired that saddle tramp
Wright. Wish you had come to me for help.
Could have saved your dog."

Lenora suddenly felt very small again, like
she had when she had first come to Mr.
Morehouse for help. It was bad enough that she'd
stupidly hired the very man her husband would
have nothing to do with. But her failure to honor
her husband's wishes had cost the life of her
loyal and trusting friend. Her heart felt as heavy
as stone in her chest. But she wouldn't get what
she came for if she didn't present herself as
anything other than a competent, confident, and
capable ranch woman. Above all, she must stay
calm and not let Mr. Morehouse's words, no
matter how provocative, pique her in such a way
that she lost control of her tongue. Without a
loan from Buffalo's only bank, she would lose
her ranch.

"Heretofore many local ranchers have taken
advantage of Sam Wright's services without
incident, Mr. Morehouse. I don't know how I
could have foreseen this untoward and tragic
outcome."

Mr. Morehouse nodded, never taking his

eyes off her. Lenora grew increasingly uncomfortable under his unyielding gaze. It occurred to her that she should take control of the conversation before it led her downstream and over a waterfall.

"Mr. Morehouse," she said, taking a large, steadying breath, "I came in today to make a loan against the ranch. I am asking Wells Fargo Bank to lend me one hundred dollars. Today, if possible."

"One hundred dollars? That's quite a sum. Now what would you do with that kind of money, my dear?"

Lenora flinched at his patronizing use of an endearment. Heavens to Betsy! She was running a sizable ranch. What did he think she would do with the money? But she had no choice. She slogged on.

"I plan to hire a full-time foreman to run the ranch until James returns."

"I see. And do you have any idea when that will be? His return?"

Lenora's jaw went rigid with anger. The man full well knew the answer to that question. "No sir. I do not. But even if he never returns, Mr. Morehouse, ownership of the homestead passes to me as his widow." She knew that much about the Homestead Act. James had told her.

"You are right, Mrs. Rose. If your husband dies, you do indeed become the owner of your ranch. But for the alienation of your property to take effect, another event must come to pass."

Alienation? She would look that up in her dictionary when she got home. She would not grovel to this man even more than she was already by asking him to explain.

"And that event is?"

"You must present to the local land office a legitimate certificate of death, issued by a judge, for your husband."

Instantly Lenora saw where this conversation was leading. James was missing, possibly dead. But no one could be certain of his demise, at least not right now. But what if his remains were never found? What if his body was rotting away this very moment, hidden in some cave, out of sight forever? Lenora pushed down a rising sense of panic. She must make Mr. Morehouse think that she was in control of the situation. She must look like a person who could handle the many obstacles to running a profitable ranch as well as any man.

"I'm sure that if I received notice of my husband's death, I could reasonably produce a certificate," said Lenora, hoping her doubts weren't flashing from her eyes like a field of lightning bugs.

"And if they don't find his body?" Mr. Morehouse leaned back in his chair, swiveling idly, back and forth, back and forth.

Lenora got the feeling that the banker was enjoying seeing the cloak of confidence being yanked from her. It made him feel powerful to make her feel small and weak. She felt vulnerable, exposed for the frightened young wife she was.

"I don't know…" She hesitated, grasping for the right words. She didn't want to say that she didn't know what she would do.

"Mrs. Rose," he interjected during her pause, "let me explain how the Act works." The tone he used was one of a condescending albeit patient teacher who's been tasked with staying after school to grudgingly tutor a slow-witted child. "If a man files for the one hundred sixty acres, takes possession, then changes his place of residence or abandons his land for more than six months, the land automatically reverts to the government."

Lenora felt a tight, squeezing sensation in her chest. She forgot to breathe. She felt herself sinking, sinking into a pit of darkness, as if she was falling through a narrow, bottomless barrel. Change his place of residence … abandon the land … six months. Then a disembodied voice penetrated the darkness.

"Therefore, as much as I'd like to help you in your hour of need, Mrs. Rose, I'm sure you can understand how it is not in the best interest of the bank to loan money against land that could soon be alienated to the government."

"Pardon me?" Could she have heard right?

"It is not in the best interest of the bank to

make a mortgage on land subject to seizure."

"But Mr. Morehouse, my husband has not abandoned our ranch. You know that as well as I."

Mr. Morehouse's eyebrows shot up. Without a word he got up from his chair and walked to the window, his back to Lenora, just a few feet from where she sat. He stood there pensively looking out at Main Street. Lenora grew more nervous in the silence. She sensed that he was preparing a speech.

She was right.

"Mrs. Rose, you came in here several months ago certain, in your own mind, at least, that your husband was alive. So I ask you: Is he alive or is he dead?" He turned around then, waiting to observe her response.

Lenora said nothing, just looked at his steely eyes, her hands on her lap, shocked and speechless, wondering what steep cliff this conversation would push her over now. She had an unsettling feeling that all her questionable attempts to be vague about the events surrounding James' flight from their ranch that awful night were about to trap her in a web of her own spinning. Mr. Morehouse towered over her, an elephantine silhouette against the noonday sun. Unconsciously she shrank back in her chair.

"Perhaps you were right," he continued while she squirmed. "We have no way of knowing. But let us presume for the moment that

248

you were wrong. If that is the case, and your husband is dead, the wisest thing for you to do at this juncture is seek to have him declared legally deceased. Death in absentia."

"But it's only been a matter of months." *Four months. I have only eight weeks before the government can take my property.* "It wouldn't be proper to seek a declaration so early in the investigation."

"As a business woman, a ranch owner," he said, drawing out his statement, "propriety should not be your first concern, Mrs. Rose. You have a decision to make that will permanently alter your fortune for good or for evil." He hesitated. "And that of your unborn child."

Mercy. Was there no one in this town who was not privy to her condition? Who spread the word? Surely not Dr. Biggerstaff. He would never breach a trust. Lenora blushed in total mortification. Mr. Morehouse glanced at her but seemed unmoved.

"The alternative is to seek a divorce, citing abandonment. You'd lose the ranch, but no judge in the land would withhold any other part of Mr. Rose's estate from you and your child under such circumstances."

"But I can't lose the ranch!" Lenora could hear her voice rising but felt powerless to get control. She wasn't following the script she had written for herself. But losing the ranch wasn't written into the script! This couldn't be happening to her. James would never just walk away and risk everything they had worked for. And James didn't own anything else. The ranch was their entire estate.

"Oh yes you can lose the ranch, Mrs. Rose. Unless, of course, you have evidence that your husband was taken against his will—kidnapped—that you can bring to the sheriff and the judge to prove coercion."

Lenora sank back against the chair for support, putting her hand to her forehead and closing her eyes to think. The moment seemed surreal. She was aware of only the blackness behind her eyelids and a hellish terror. Her future in the Territory and that of her child loomed before her like an inhospitable, howling wasteland of crushing loss and poverty. But to return to her parents' home would be to revert to the status of a child with all the strictures and humiliation associated with dependency. Since she left New York she had grown into an independent woman and enjoyed the dignity attendant thereto. She couldn't go back to her old life as a grown child in her parents' home.

"Shall I ask the clerk to bring you some water, Mrs. Rose?"

"No. I'm fine. I'm just thinking." She sat up straight and opened her eyes, somewhat renewed, making a conscious effort to look more possessed of her emotions than she felt.

"I understand." Mr. Morehouse walked

around his desk, sat down again, and waited for her to fully recover.

"Mr. Morehouse, a loan would at least buy me some time."

"No, Mrs. Rose. It wouldn't."

"Why wouldn't it?"

"More money in this case would create the illusion that you have more time. In reality you have eight weeks. More money won't extend the government's deadline."

Mr. Morehouse paused, and in the silence the realization of how little time she had to save her ranch sunk down in Lenora's mind with an ominous thud, like the clank of a heavy prison door slamming shut on the damned.

"Do you want my advice, Mrs. Rose?"

She was about to lose everything. Might as well listen to whatever he had to say. Things couldn't get any worse than they were right now.

Or so she hoped.

"Yes, Mr. Morehouse."

"Make a decision today. Whether your husband is alive or dead at this point is irrelevant."

Lenora blanched.

"I didn't mean it to sound so callous, Mrs. Rose. I apologize for distressing you."

Lenora nodded glumly in acknowledgment.

"What I mean is, having your husband legally declared dead has no bearing on his welfare. This is about saving your ranch, not Mr.

Rose. A judicial declaration of death is merely
the only path available to you to stop the
government from repossessing your land. Once
you have the death certificate, the land will pass
to you as his widow. If he returns—may God
bring it to pass—the land will still belong to both
of you. In that happy event, you can take the
death certificate and toss it into your kitchen
stove for kindling."

"And if I did obtain a death certificate, how
long can I last, Mr. Morehouse, without financial
assistance from the bank?"

"Mrs. Rose, it's not a matter of lasting until
Mr. Rose returns. He may never return. And if he
doesn't, you can't possibly run your ranch alone.
You'll have a child to raise and a foreman whose
wages will gobble up every penny you earn."

"But I would be in charge of the ranch for
only a short time until I've fulfilled the
homestead obligation. I only have to manage it
another eighteen months. After that it would be
mine and I could sell for a profit."

"Eighteen months, young lady, is more than
enough time for you to run it into bankruptcy.
What you need, Mrs. Rose, is a husband.
Obviously you're not suited to running a ranch,
especially in your delicate condition."

Lenora began to tremble with anger. It was
hopeless to continue to beg for a loan. This bank
would lend her money when pigs flew. She stood
up to signal the end of this outrage, gripping the

cords of her drawstring bag with such fury that the bag began to sway at her waist.

"I *have* a husband, Mr. Morehouse," she said, reaching angrily for her shopping basket. "What I *need* is money."

"Mrs. Rose, if you foolishly insist on holding onto your ranch, you must learn to make it profitable without plunging yourself into debt you can't pay. That's what other ranchers do in your position."

Maybe, she thought bitterly, she should ask him to lend her a husband. The return would be better and the application process less grueling.

"Thank you, Mr. Morehouse, for all your time and for taking the trouble to explain the fine points of the Act," she said, her eyes flashing with anger. "And thank you for sharing all your pearls of wisdom about ranching."

With that she turned with a flounce, opened his office door without waiting for assistance, and walked out of his office and into the bank lobby. She was struck at once by how much cooler the spacious lobby was compared to the stuffy confines of Mr. Morehouse's office. The coolness helped to clear her mind. If other bank customers and employees were still staring at the scandal-ridden Mrs. Rose as she entered the lobby, she didn't notice. She walked straight to the exit door of the bank and reached for the handle.

Funny thing, she thought as she turned the knob. She hadn't gotten what she had come for, but she was leaving with something perhaps more useful nonetheless.

Chapter Eighteen

A bright midday sun reflecting on the hard surfaces of treeless Main Street caused Lenora to blink rapidly after stepping out of the dim bank lobby. She hoped Deputy Davies would exercise discretion and not wait directly outside the bank door for her. It would be better if their meeting appeared more casual to onlookers.

Lenora stood on the boardwalk, clutching her shopping basket in one hand and reticule in the other, waiting for her eyes to adjust. When she could see clearly she looked up and down the street, expecting to see Deputy Davies hovering nearby. When she didn't see him in either direction she felt self-conscious about searching for him. It didn't seem fitting. So with little ado she started down the street for Aeschelman's alone, thrown off balance by the deputy's disappearance. Her disappointment

255

surprised her. Was she disappointed because she didn't want to brave critical stares alone? She hoped she wasn't that cowardly. Or was she disappointed at not being able to visit with the handsome, attentive deputy a little longer? The latter was a disturbing thought. She quickly dismissed it.

Lenora had walked about fifty feet when she saw a woman she knew only by name emerge from the millinery two stores ahead of her and begin to walk in her direction. The woman, about thirty, clutched the hand of a little girl about five years old who was dressed in a crisply starched pinafore with matching bonnet. The child's mother was dressed equally stylishly in a modest but perfectly tailored shirtwaist dress and complementary bonnet. Lenora smiled in greeting as their eyes met, preparing to pass them. The woman looked shocked and abruptly jerked the child's hand, nearly causing the little girl to fall off the edge of the boardwalk. Lenora watched in horror as the mother dragged the child into the street, scurried to the boardwalk on the other side of Main, and continued in the same direction.

Lenora felt as if she had been slapped. Surely she was being too sensitive. She was imagining things. The woman hardly knew her. She would not intentionally cross the street to avoid passing her, would she?

Shaken to the core and feeling as desirable as last week's haddock, Lenora continued down the nearly empty boardwalk on her way to

Aeschelman's Mercantile. She was relieved to see
few shoppers out and about, though the few she
passed looked so uncomfortable in her presence that
she felt like she was running a gauntlet. Then there
was the problem of the people she couldn't see, the
ones she imagined watching her behind every
storefront window, whispering and pointing and
clucking judgmentally. She could see nothing in the
wavy storefront glass except her reflection, but she
knew that inside the shady interiors shoppers and
shopkeepers had a clear view of her. Again she
wished Deputy Davies had not abandoned her. So
much damage had been done already, so many evil
stories had been told about her—and them—that a
gentlemanly escort down Main Street would make
no difference now. She walked hurriedly to the
mercantile to hide behind closed doors away from
critical stares. Thankfully she arrived in front of
Aeschelman's with no more ugly scenes. Bracing
for whomever and whatever she might face inside,
she took a deep breath, turned the knob, and pushed
open the door.

   The loud jingle of the bell over the door
caused Faustus Aeschelman to look up from the
counter where he was chatting with Luke. A quick
sweep of the store's interior told Lenora that there
were no other shoppers about. Relieved, she walked
to the counter, trying her best to appear nonchalant.
Luke stopped talking and watched her approach.
Mr. Aeschelman spoke first.

   "Mrs. Rose," he said, smiling wide and

nodding good morning.

Luke acknowledged her as well, removing his hat and smiling, looking at ease. It dawned on Lenora then that he had been waiting for her all along, just as he had said, only he had done so at the mercantile to avoid more gossip. It also occurred to her that Mr. Aeschelman's natural, open smile meant he wasn't privy to the stories about her and the deputy. Likely his weak English kept him from wading into the gossip stream. Lenora felt grateful for that lone smile. It felt like a large, leafy oak tree under which one takes shelter from a driving rain. It was just one tree, but one was enough.

"Good afternoon, Mr. Aeschelman," said Lenora. She acknowledged Luke with a brief nod, circumspectly keeping her attention on the retailer. "I've brought a list." She pulled a piece of paper from her reticule and handed it to the shopkeeper. As she did she noticed that Luke and Mr. Aeschelman had been sharing coffee. Two cups were sitting on the counter, half full. They'd been chatting a while. No steam emerged from the cups. Mr. Aeschelman looked over the list.

"You look. I shop list," he said, glancing back at the neatly penned list of grocery and household items. "Ten minutes." Mr. Aeschelman smiled again.

"Thank you," said Lenora, pulling the drawstring tight on her reticule.

Mr. Aeschelman stepped away from the counter to begin collecting Lenora's purchases.

Luke's eyes followed Mr. Aeschelman, waiting for the shopkeeper to move out of hearing range to speak. When the man was far enough to afford them a little privacy, Luke spoke.

"I thought it best to wait for you here."

"How'd you know I was coming to Aeschelman's?"

"Your basket was empty," said Luke, glancing toward the basket on her arm.

"Oh."

Lenora was keenly aware of Luke's nearness, his clean shaven face and intense brown eyes. Most of all she was aware that he was looking at her with more than passing interest, which secretly pleased her. He looked at her in the way a man looks at a woman when he appreciates her femaleness, not any particular part of her, just the look an attractive woman expects to receive when she walks into a room full of men—as if they've never seen a woman before. She felt self-conscious and at the same time very flattered. His eyes upon her made her aware of her hair, her clothes, and her shoes. She hoped nothing was out of place or less than spotless.

"How's everything at the ranch?" he said.

"Fine. Everything's been quiet since you arrested Mr. Wright. I can't thank you enough, Deputy Davies, for getting to the bottom of it." Even the oblique mention of her recent troubles brought an unbidden image of Ulysses, butchered and bleeding. She longed for the day when the

259

disturbing image would fade and she'd remember him only as the slobbering, lovable companion he had been.

"That's what we're here for," he said.

"Deputy Davies, you said you wanted to speak with me about the investigation. Do you have news from the other law offices? Downstream?"

"No, haven't heard anything in a while."

"Did you ever speak with Ben Slocomb's folks?"

"Yes. Ben didn't harm your dog, Mrs. Rose. You needn't worry yourself about that."

"I didn't think so." The deputy didn't seem forthcoming this morning. More like he was content to gaze into her eyes, enjoying the moment. Or at least that's how it seemed to Lenora.

"Then your news is...?"

"It's a question."

Lenora waited.

"Mrs. Rose, what is your husband's middle name?"

"Surely you are not thinking of contacting my husband's family on my behalf, Deputy Davies," said Lenora, taken aback. "That is my purview, and I see no need to alarm them." After the scene in Mr. Morehouse's office, Lenora was in no mood for paternalism. God help the man who thought otherwise.

"You needn't worry, Mrs. Rose. Notifying kin is your business. I was just thinking that knowing all I can about Mr. Rose can only help our investigation."

"I see," said Lenora, softening a little. "I apologize for taking exception, Deputy Davies. I'm afraid I've had an upsetting morning. I'm still on edge."

"May I be of service in some way?"

"No hope of that. In fact, no hope at all," she said, her voice heavy with dejection. Lenora glanced to both sides, worrying unreasonably that someone besides the two of them and the oblivious store owner had entered the mercantile without her knowledge and was observing Luke and her together. Seeing no one she returned her attention to Luke.

"Sounds pretty bad," said Luke.

"It is bad."

"Perhaps if you tell me what the problem is, we can work on a solution together."

Why should he care? Lenora debated baring her soul to the deputy. It did seem that he meant well. He had stood up against the bullying she'd endured from Sheriff Morris. He'd ridden all the way out to her ranch, nine miles from Buffalo, to check on her welfare. Etta Nolan had said that the deputy enjoyed a good reputation in Fort Laramie. And James would have approved of a man who looked after the welfare of a woman whose husband was missing.

Now that incongruous thought gave her a moment of confusion. But not knowing what to make of it, she quickly filed it for later analysis—

probably much later, at night, when she had trouble sleeping.

And Ulysses had liked the deputy.

"The bank refused me a loan," she blurted, amazed to hear herself revealing her personal problems to a man other than James. "Mr. Morehouse thinks I am incapable of running the ranch myself."

"He's right. You can't." Luke's face was placid, giving away nothing, not even a hint of a smile.

Lenora's mouth fell open. "I take it then, Deputy Davies," she continued, recovering her wit, "with a judgment as to the capabilities of the female sex, you are of the persuasion that women should be denied suffrage as well?" Lenora could hardly disguise her annoyance.

"I didn't think we were talking voting rights, ma'am. I thought we were talking ranching." Luke spoke at his usual, unperturbed pitch, which annoyed her even more.

"The premise is the same." Lenora blanched as the words came out. Her failure to sound composed irked her. Then from the side of her eye she saw Mr. Aeschelman stop working to listen from the top of a ladder where he was perched, arm outstretched above his head, reaching for a large box of castile soap. Likely he didn't understand everything they were saying, but Lenora was determined to stay calm and avoid a scene nonetheless. She assumed it was the rising pitch of her voice, not the words themselves, that had caused him to look in their direction.

"It's the same," she repeated more quietly. "Ranching or voting. If a woman wants to do either one she shouldn't be denied the opportunity merely because she's a woman."

"Some people think like you," said Luke, noncommittally.

"And your opinion, sir?"

"I don't know that my opinion matters. I'm not running for office."

"You sidestep the issue, Deputy Davies."

Luke rubbed his chin as if in deep thought. "I suppose when it comes to ranching a woman deserves equal rights like a man."

Well that's better.

"Man or woman," he continued in his unique drawl, "if a person plans to knock on the pearly gates a little earlier than God intends by running a one hundred and sixty-acre ranch all alone, probably best no one get in the way. Can't imagine why anyone would choose such a frustratingly slow and hungry death, though."

Lenora's foot began to tap automatically with nervous tension. "I believe you mock me," she said, her mouth set in a straight line. Instantly another thought struck terror in her heart: Did he know about her family condition but chose the path of discretion by hiding behind the "female" argument to dissuade her from holding onto her ranch? For some unexplainable reason it mortified Lenora to

263

the tips of her toes to think that the eminently
eligible and disarmingly handsome deputy knew
she was expecting a baby. That meant he knew that
she and James ... oh my. She glanced quickly at her
midsection. Nothing showing.

Oh don't be a silly goose. Babies are born into
the world every day and they all get here the same
way. What is, is what is. Men don't think about that
when they see a woman who's expecting.

Do they?

Luke shook his head and drew himself up
straighter, as if he sensed her perturbation and
needed to emphasize his seriousness. "No ma'am. I
don't mean to poke fun. I was just thinking about
specifics, that's all."

He crossed his arms and leaned against the
counter, his tall frame looming over her, making her
feel small and conspicuous. So he was big and
manly and represented the law. So what? In that
moment Lenora reminded herself that she was a
ranch woman, a homesteader. She might have to
work at it, but she wouldn't be intimidated by this
man or any other. Truly, things—and she—had
changed since James disappeared. She pulled her
back up a little straighter.

"Such as?"

"You ever pulled a stuck calf, Mrs. Rose?"

Lenora grimaced at the thought. She was
embarrassed to be speaking of such indelicacies
with a man. Birthing calves was ... disgusting.
James' purview, not hers. "Of course not. That's

264

what ranch hands are for."

"Do you know how to treat steer infected with blackleg?"

Blackleg? She knew it was a cow disease, but what she knew beyond that wouldn't cover the tip of her pearl-encrusted hatpin.

"It's a bovine ailment. One employs the services of a veterinarian for such afflictions."

"What's the best feed to produce a good milker?"

"Deputy Davies," said Lenora, sidestepping the issue, her feathers ruffled, "no rancher alone, not even a man, is capable of doing all those things and knowing all those things. Ranchers depend on the experience and knowledge of others."

Luke remained silent, allowing her words to hang in the air, indicting her. Finally he spoke. "Maybe that was Mr. Morehouse's conclusion too."

Lenora looked stricken. She had debated herself into a corner. Now how to get out of it? "If Mr. Morehouse thinks I can't run my ranch alone, then he should have done his job and lent me the money to hire the expertise I need to succeed."

"Mr. Morehouse doesn't work for you, no matter what he says about wanting to help. He works for Wells Fargo. His job is to look out after the bank's business. Your job is to look out after yours."

"Which is exactly why I need a loan."

"Borrowing money isn't always the answer. Debt is an attractive trap."

"It would only be for a short time."

"Another trap. Everyone thinks tomorrow will be rosier."

Lenora sighed a deep sigh of frustration. "Too many naysayers in this town," she said. "You sound like Mr. Morehouse. I'll bet men don't have to jump over all these fences when they need a loan." Her voice dripped with petulance.

"Maybe not, but a door that shuts in your face isn't always a bad thing. Sometimes it forces you to take another, better road. You just don't know it's better till you arrive at where you're supposed to be."

Lenora only nodded, her eyes cast down to the floor. Suddenly the tips of Luke's fingers were brushing her shoulder, gentle and kind. Startled by his forwardness, she looked up and their eyes met. At once she was bathed in a warm feeling of intimate affection. Something very good stirred deep within her. Something exciting.

"It could even be providential," he said.

His fingers had barely touched her, but it was long enough to set Lenora's heart fluttering and make her breathing rapid and shallow. He had touched her, and there was no denying that his touch, however light and brief, thrilled her.

His touch and kind words had fanned another flame inside her heart. Since she had stepped out of Mr. Morehouse's office, a hopeful thought more wispy than smoke from a match had floated silently up the back of her mind, and now Luke's words were like a breath of oxygen to that near-dying ember. Perhaps, just perhaps, some good would come from the bank's refusal to lend her money. Perhaps her circumstances were not beyond redemption. Things were not always as they seemed. In science class years earlier Lenora had picked up an ugly gray rock covered with wart-like bumps, a homely specimen in a world of precious stones and pretty gems. But when her instructor arranged to have it cut in half, on the inside was the most beautiful fractal of glittering lavender crystals she had ever seen. Perhaps, if she were patient, the end of her current predicament would prove to be as delightful as the inside of that humble geode.

But for now she had to figure out the best way to deal with the warty bumps.

"Yes, it could be, Deputy Davies." For only the second time since she had walked into Aeschelman's, she smiled at him.

Luke looked at her warmly and then glanced toward the area of the mercantile where Mr. Aeschelman was occupied pulling sewing notions from yellow cardboard boxes. Luke lowered his voice. "Are you sure there is nothing I can do to help?"

"Do you know how to get someone declared dead? I mean, legally dead? Mr. Morehouse told me that if I can get a death certificate for James, then our ranch passes to me. Without that piece of paper the government will declare the ranch abandoned—by James I mean—and they will take the land away from me."

"I know how to get a death certificate. And I know about homestead law. But it never occurred to me that you would want to petition for legal declaration." Luke's faced took on an unmerited somberness.

"Until now I would have thought that too. But it's only a formality. If James comes back after the property transfers to me, it would be just as much his as mine."

"I see."

"I have only eight weeks, Deputy Davies," said Lenora, becoming animated, almost pleading. "James has been missing four months. The law allows a man to be away from his homestead only six months before he jeopardizes his ownership rights."

"I am aware of how the Act reads."

"Can you help me?"

Luke glanced again at Mr. Aeschelman before responding. "I'd be pleased to help you, ma'am" he said, lowering his voice to a whisper. "But that's just another reason why you should give me your husband's full name. I'll need it to petition the judge."

"Oh," said Lenora, looking startled, "of course. James is actually his middle name. He was named for his grandfather, Sterling James Rose."

#

Luke's face revealed nothing and he said nothing, just nodded slightly to show that he had heard. But bells were clanging a five-alarm fire in his mind. As if he needed to reassure himself that it was still there, he pushed a hand to the bottom of his pant pocket to touch the expensive gold pocket watch that had been turned over to the sheriff's office just this morning. A child had found it on the steps of Johnson Ebenezer Christian Church. Luke ran his index finger over the lavishly scrolled engraving that embellished its cover, felt the spring-loaded finial at its base, and balled the heavy chain into the palm of his hand. With an uncomfortable mixture of guilt and apprehension, he remembered the owner's initials that had been memorialized in large ornate letters in the center of the flowing scrollwork:

$$sR_J$$

James Rose's pocket watch seemed bigger and harder than it had been when Luke entered Aeschelman's to wait for Mrs. Rose. As he walked along Main Street's boardwalk it slapped against his thigh uncomfortably with every step, a tactile testimony that a man was missing and the lawman responsible to find him was keeping quiet about evidence that could possibly lead to his whereabouts.

Why hadn't he pulled the watch out of his pocket and showed it to Mrs. Rose at Aeschelman's? After he heard the dead man's full name from his grieving widow's enticing lips, there was no doubt in Luke's mind that Mrs. Nolan's account—shared with Luke in confidence—of the events that had taken place at the Rose ranch the night the man had disappeared had been accurate. The feckless Mr. Rose, to refrain from venting his spleen on his beloved wife and assisted by her unusually good pitching arm, had ridden away carrying on his person this very pocket watch. Somehow the man had managed to abandon his tied-up horse at North-East Creek and lose his time piece on the church steps not far from the edge of town, miles from where he tied his horse. If the child had found a skull or one of the cadaver's bones, Luke would have ascribed the distance between the two finds to the foraging of carnivorous animals, which are known to scatter bones. But no wild animal Luke could think of would take such an interest in a gold pocket watch. And he couldn't figure out why the watch hadn't been found before this. There were no flower boxes or any other movable objects on the church steps behind which it could have dropped. Someone must have found the watch elsewhere and laid it on the steps with intent. Someone wanted it to be found.

But all that didn't explain Luke's omission. He had intentionally kept his mouth shut about the pocket watch. Would Mrs. Rose's identification of the watch have led to the discovery of her husband's whereabouts? Maybe, though Luke figured that was unlikely. Even if she had claimed it to be her husband's, what happened four months ago on the banks of a swift-moving creek on a black and stormy night was done, and her claims about the watch one way or another wouldn't alter those events.

So why not show her the watch? If her identification of it would make no difference to the investigation and couldn't change what had happened to her husband to cause him to go missing, why not show it to her? He should show her the watch. He would show her the watch. But he couldn't bring himself to do it right now. It was wrong to procrastinate. He knew it. But James Rose was easier to deal with as a dead man, out of sight though not out of mind. If Luke had pulled that watch out of his pocket for her to identify, he would have seen a look of shock and then grief in those beautiful green eyes, then the tears would stream, resurrecting what Luke had observed at the start of the search and rattled him now when he thought of it: a heart-jerking display of Mrs. Rose's enduring affection for her dead husband. But by all accounts James Rose wasn't the saint she thought he was, and thank God she seemed to be pulling out of her abysmal grief. Better for her, thought Luke, if he left things the way they were. No, resurrecting James Rose and all the emotions the irksome man stirred up in his widow wasn't convenient for anyone right now.

Nevertheless Luke promised himself that when the time was right in the investigation, he

271

would question Mrs. Rose about the pocket watch. But right now he had no idea when that would be.

Chapter Nineteen

Sheriff Morris was sitting at his desk reading a sophisticate—a magazine of interest to only men—when a click of the door handle signaled a visitor. Hurriedly he shut the publication, pulled open the bottom drawer of his desk, stashed the magazine at the back of it, and neatly shut it, taking care not to slam.

His deputy stepped over the threshold looking disturbed. Luke noticed the hasty movements of his boss but was too distracted to contemplate them.

"Howdy," said Sheriff Morris.

Luke uncharacteristically saluted a silent hello with a jerk of two fingers, shut the door, took off his hat, walked to his desk, and hung up his jacket on the coat rack behind it. But instead of sitting down or walking to the wood stove to start the day's second pot of coffee as he usually did at this hour, he walked to the sheriff's desk and stopped, pulled the pocket watch from his pocket, and dangled it in the sheriff's face.

"It's his, isn't it?" said Luke.

"Let me see that," said the sheriff, sitting up straight and reaching for the chain.

Luke released his hold on the chain as the sheriff took the time piece into his large hand. Sheriff Morris turned it over several times, looking at every part. His eyes rested on the monogram

"S-R-J? Whose is this?"

"Sterling James Rose," said Luke, slowly and evenly. Saying the name aloud made him light headed. "I need coffee," he said, heading toward the wood stove, his stomach growling. He had forgotten to ask Mrs. Byrne, the boardinghouse owner, to pack him a sandwich. "Any fresh?"

"There will be when you make some," said the sheriff, his eyes still on the time piece. "How'd you get Rose's pocket watch?" Sheriff Morris pulled on the finial and the cover popped open, but only partially because something had gunked up the hinge. A spattering of dust, like dry earth, sprinkled onto his desk.

"Town kid brought it in this morning. Said he found it on the front steps of the church."

"What kid?" Sheriff Morris pulled a clean white handkerchief from his pants pocket, snapped it open with a flick of his wrist, and began wiping the dirt from the hinge. Red-brown dust transferred to his hanky

274

"Dunn's kid. You know, Octavius. Owns the tobacco shop down the way." Luke stopped talking a moment while he poured water noisily from a covered bucket into the coffee pot. "Octavius came with him. Dragged him in here by his collar while you were having lunch at the Occidental. Made the kid hand it over. Felt sorry for the boy. He only gave it up because of his pa."

"Can't say I blame him. He's not the only one around Buffalo who coveted whatever it was Rose had."

Luke felt a pang of guilt strike his core as sharp as a bee sting. "Then it is his?" He turned back toward Sheriff Morris and contemplated the pocket watch anew, trying to picture the ghostly Mr. Rose riding off into the night, the gleaming watch tucked into his breast pocket. The picture came easily, as did the picture of the handsome but exhausted Morgan tied to a tree near North-East Creek, wild eyed and dying of thirst. After that, there was only a black hole of mystery in his Luke's mind. Night after night for four months as he had lain in bed, waiting for sleep—when he wasn't contemplating the many charms of Mrs. Rose—he'd stood at the precipice of that black canyon, peering into the bottomless darkness, searching for a clue. James Rose had fallen into a black pit, and every time Luke searched for him, he fell into a black pit as well. After a minute he turned back to the stove and drew a match to light the fire. For a few seconds a burst of acrid sulfur salted the air. He bent down and put the match to a pile of tinder in the fire box. Soon a thin wisp of smoke was twirling upward and the small fire began to crackle.

"It's his," said Sheriff Morris, "or it looks just like it."

"Dunn's boy is going to be disappointed. I told him I'd return it to him if we couldn't track down the owner."

Sheriff Morris' eyebrows shot up.

"I know, I know. It belongs to someone around here. Buffalo is a small place. I shouldn't have given him false hope. But the kid was so brokenhearted."

"What's all this dirt?" said Sheriff Morris, peering at the watch. Without waiting for comment from Luke, the sheriff pulled out his pocket knife, snapped open its smallest steel blade, and began trying to pry open the back of the time piece. Luke walked over to watch. In no time the sheriff and Luke were looking at the rusted interior workings of James Rose's pocket watch. Sheriff Morris tapped the watch lightly on the surface of his desk. A shower of fine, red-brown particles fell onto the desk.

"Look at this rust," said the sheriff. "Rose wouldn't let his fine piece ever get like this."

"Is it rust or dirt?"

Sheriff Morris used his index finger and thumb to pinch a bit of the dust on his desk. He rubbed it between his fingers. "Both, I think."

"That explains why it won't keep time."

276

"Where'd Dunn's kid say he find this?"

"Church steps."

"Hmm. He may have found it on the church steps but that's not where it's been for the last four months." Sheriff Morris tapped the time piece lightly on his desk. Another shower of red-brown dust.

"That's what I thought when I first opened it. Someone must have recently set it there. I'm in church every Sunday, and half the town attends Ebenezer. Someone would have seen it before now if Rose had dropped it there."

"What do you make of it then?" asked the sheriff.

"A red herring

"A red what?"

"A smelly red fish that stinks so bad it takes you off the scent of your trail."

"You think someone put it on the church steps to throw us off?" Sheriff Morris snapped the watch shut and held it up in front of him by its chain, where it revolved slowly, turning from one side to the other. Across the room the coffee pot started to rattle. Luke walked over to the wood stove and pushed the pot a little farther from the heat.

"It's possible. I can't believe that someone found a valuable piece like that near the church then left it on the steps hoping the owner would retrieve it again on Sunday," said Luke. "And there's no blood on it. I checked. It was clean all over when the kid brought it in. Only the bits of dirt when you open it

"You think someone wanted us to find it?" asked the sheriff, handing the gleaming fob back to Luke.

"Someone wanted it found alright, but not necessarily by us."

"Maybe they wanted the parson to find it."

"I thought about that, but what's Reverend Thomas got to do with this?" Luke didn't wait for the sheriff to answer. "I don't know why everything in this case has to be so cotton pickin' mysterious. It's not like we're trailing Frank and Jesse James. James Rose was just a dumb rancher who didn't have enough sense not to ride after dark. Finding his carcass should be easy."

"You sound frustrated."

"I am frustrated," said Luke, "And disgusted. We should have found it by now. Dead or alive, without his horse he couldn't have gotten very far."

"Maybe someone knows something about the Reverend we don't."

A look of shock fell over Luke's face. He stared at Sheriff Morris. "I hadn't thought of that."

"The only angels around here are fallen ones. Everybody's got secret sins, Luke. Even the good parson."

Luke disagreed with Cyrus' cynical theology, but it would be unprofessional to dismiss Reverend Thomas as a suspect. Someone was trying to tell them something about the church or the Reverend or both. Someone had intentionally placed the gold watch where it was certain to be found. To dismiss the clue without further investigation because of its proximity to a man of the cloth would be a mistake.

After a while the coffee pot stopped perking, and the two little adjoining offices smelled deliciously of strong fresh coffee. Luke poured a cup for both of them and then dragged one of the visitor's chairs over to the sheriff's desk. It was quiet in the law office. The noisiest part of the day—when the afternoon stage arrived to unload passengers, cargo, and mail, and pick up more of the same—had come and gone and most shoppers had finished their business, loaded their wagons or saddle bags, and returned to their ranches. The men silently enjoyed their coffee a few minutes, thinking about the watch that sat on the sheriff's desk while they sipped little sips to avoid being burned by the scalding black brew.

"Well, Sam Wright didn't leave it there," observed Sheriff Morris, looking at the watch and stating the obvious. "He's been locked up since before last Sunday. If it had been on the church steps before or after service, someone would have seen it."

"You getting anything from him?" said Luke.

"No. Sleeps all day. Can't get much when he's awake, neither. I think that boy was born with something missing," said the sheriff, tapping the side of his head.

279

"What about the boots? He explained yet where he got 'em?"

"He's still sticking to his story about getting 'em in exchange for helping some fellow west of here."

"You get the rancher's name?"

"No. Says he doesn't remember," said the sheriff.

Luke shook his head in disbelief.

Sheriff Morris blew on his coffee and took a noisy slurp. "He gave me a description of the ranch, though, and some landmarks to find it."

"Good," said Luke, though what he really felt was surprise. "Next thing I do is ride out there and talk to him—if he exists. Then I have to get those boots in front of Mrs. Rose." He certainly would not ask Mrs. Rose to come to the jailhouse to determine if the boots Buffalo's most dangerous man wore were the same ones Mr. Rose was wearing when he disappeared. That would upset her. But taking an inmate's only shoes right off his feet had a distasteful quality. Then again, carrying a boot to Mrs. Rose's ranch for her to identify gave Luke another excuse to see her. He resolved to make the trip as soon as he returned from interrogating the unnamed former owner of the boots. "Do you think Sam had anything to do with Rose's disappearance?"

Sheriff Morris shrugged.

"Someone was sneaking around her property before she came to town to report him missing,"

Luke explained. "Could very well be that Sam killed Rose that Saturday night. If he had killed Rose, he knew Rose wouldn't return to his ranch, and he knew Mrs. Rose would be alone. She told me someone was on the property the next night, the Sunday night after Rose went missing. She came to see us the day after that, a Monday."

"Sam's only dangerous when he's sober," said the sheriff. "That doesn't leave him much time for murder."

"You saw the letter from Sheriff Clarke," said Luke.

"I saw it."

"Well?"

"The last time Sam was accused of hurting someone was six years ago."

"What if he's been at it since then but hasn't been caught?" said Luke.

"That's possible," said Sheriff Morris. "But I'm of a mind to think that hooch is running his life now. I don't think he's capable of anything more violent than uncorking a bottle of cheap whiskey."

Luke wasn't so sure, but he didn't want to argue. "The prowling has stopped," he said.

"You seen Mrs. Rose?"

"Talked to her at Aeschelman's this morning. She's doing fine now that Sam's locked up and can't harass her anymore."

"That crazy woman still lighting a candle in the window for her husband?"

Luke pursed his lips and silently prayed for grace. "She's expecting his baby, Cyrus. Don't you think her mind is on her husband more than ever? Hoping he'll come home to be a father to their child?"

Sheriff Morris screwed up his face.

The truth of Luke's own question left him with a hollow feeling. How did he get cast in the center of this drama anyway? He was just doing his job, yet he felt like he was eavesdropping on the private lives of others. At times like these he almost wished James Rose would show up alive, though he winced inwardly when the thought surfaced. The strain of not knowing if he was falling in love with a married woman or a widow was taking its toll. He needed to find Rose's body soon or at least some hard evidence that the man was dead. He would wager that Rose was dead—he had believed him to be dead from the start. But the lack of a body always made room for doubt. It was this singular doubt that stole away Luke's rest at night. He hated living in a netherworld. At times it seemed that fate was toying with his desires, dangling the lovely and vulnerable Mrs. Rose in front of him like a bone in front of a starving stray dog. He could look but not touch, want but not have. These frustrating circumstances made him angry, though at no one in particular. But his failure to find the body made him angry at himself.

All at once it dawned on Luke that Mrs. Rose must feel the agony of that in-between place far more than he did. Neither married nor widowed and expecting a child; she was the one who was suffering the most. Luke felt ashamed for thinking only of his own frustration and not her pain, which must be far more acute.

"She's going to petition the judge at Fort McKinney to have her husband declared dead. She asked me to help her with the paperwork," said Luke.

Sheriff Morris looked stunned. Luke saw the surprise in his face and felt compelled to explain.

"It doesn't mean she believes he's dead. She's trying to save her ranch."

"By killing him off?"

Luke pursed his lips and shot a threatening look at the sheriff. "It's the Homestead Act," explained Luke, striving for control. "The law recognizes only two reasons for not fulfilling your five-year commitment, death or abandonment. He's been missing four months. Another two months and the government can claim he abandoned his land."

"I see."

"If that happens, his land passes to the government. But if a judge declares him dead, even without his body the land becomes hers. She has to live on it another eighteen months though to fulfill the five-year requirement."

Sheriff Morris shook his head back and forth slowly. "Boy, you just jump into trouble with both feet, don't you?"

Luke didn't answer. He'd been thinking the very same thing since he had left Aeschelman's, but Cyrus didn't need to know that. The second the words had left his mouth, when he had agreed to help Mrs. Rose petition the judge, Luke had known he was stepping into very deep, very dark water. He felt uneasy about pursuing the very document that would put James Rose out of Mrs. Rose's life and leave her free to remarry. Had he secretly desired this? The thought that he was guilty of such abject covetousness squeezed the breath out of him. She had asked him to help her; was he wrong to do so? Then again, he had offered his services to her more than once since her husband went missing—who else would she ask now that the help she needed was of a legal nature? Certainly not Cyrus.

Truthfully, he yearned to care for her, to pull her to himself and hold her, to comfort her, and deep inside he knew that no matter what people thought or said about his motives, he would help in any way he could. Tongues would wag. It might even threaten his position as deputy. But Mrs. Rose was alone in this town, she was expecting a child, and she was close to being put out of her home. Saying no was not an option.

Sheriff Morris leaned back in his chair and absently pulled on his mustache. "Let's see," he said, "the husband of the prettiest woman in town, childless but the owner of the choicest spread in the Territory, goes missing. His wife of four years is now expecting her first child. Brat is due exactly nine months after she first visits the town's law office to tell her sad tale to the new, young, very attentive bachelor deputy ... a Confederate."

Luke's jaw froze with outrage, though almost everything the sheriff said was true, even the part about him being attentive. He wished he had been more discreet in his dealings with Mrs. Rose, but it was too late to worry about it now. As for being a southerner, Luke and the sheriff had gone over this ground before and Luke didn't care to spar again. His mother was southern, his father was a Unionist. Luke just wanted to live in peace. Sheriff Morris continued.

"Four months pass and the rancher doesn't come home. Body isn't found. Now that same deputy is rushing off to Fort McKinney to have the missing husband of the very pretty, very available young wife declared dead."

Luke, furious and frustrated, could only stare at his boss.

"Did I mention that the whole eastern edge of the woman's ranch runs along Crazy Woman Creek?" Sheriff Morris' eyes were full of mirth. "You make those trashy dime novels that women fill their heads with look like a McGuffey Reader." Sheriff Morris chuckled to himself.

"You know full well I'm not rushing to have him declared dead," said Luke, coming to his own defense. "As it is, there's hardly time to file the petition and bring in witnesses or collect written testimony before the six-month statute expires. We have to have that much. We have no physical evidence to put in front of Judge Stillman." Luke seethed but managed a veneer of control. "And we don't even know if Judge Stillman is in Fort Laramie. I don't know where his circuit puts him when he's not in Buffalo. I only know he's not scheduled to be here in town till the end of next month."

"I can find out from Sheriff Clarke. He's familiar with Stillman's circuit."

Luke was so worked up it didn't dawn on him that Cyrus had just offered his assistance. "And she asked me to help," he said. "It's the least I can do to see that she doesn't lose her ranch. She's already lost her husband, Cyrus. You know it as well as I do. The declaration won't bring him back from the dead. It just gives her the legal right to stay on her property. That's all this is about."

Sheriff Morris grunted.

"Look, Cyrus," said Luke, his voice rising, "if you're looking for a burlesque show, go to Belles'. I'm just doing my job, and I'm doing it as professionally as I know how. I don't know what happened to James Rose, if he's alive or dead. I suspect he's dead, but I don't know where his body is. If I could release the poor woman from the torment of not knowing by bringing his body back to her I would, and I'll keep trying to do that." Luke leaned forward over Sheriff Morris' desk and bored into him with eyes of fury. "And as for her condition, I haven't so much as touched his

286

grieving widow's pinky finger with a straw broom."

Sheriff Morris looked taken aback at his deputy's hard words. "I suppose she has the kid's welfare to consider," he conceded, though to Luke's ears the way he said it didn't make him sound any more gracious.

Their accusatory exchange smoldered in the atmosphere of the small office long after the heated words were uttered. Luke needed to get out outside to diffuse his anger. Riding always helped. "Let's ride out to the church when we finish our coffee. Take a look. There's several hours of sunlight yet. Maybe we'll find something," he said. "And when we're done there, we probably should visit the parsonage and arrange an interview with Reverend Thomas." Luke dreaded the thought of questioning a Christian brother about the disappearance of James Rose, but he had to do his job.

Sheriff Morris sighed gustily and grimaced. Luke recognized the skepticism in the sigh and the disapproval in the grimace but ignored them. When it came to finding James Rose, Cyrus was skeptical and disapproving of every effort. Luke couldn't bother reacting anymore. He banged down his cup suddenly, stood up, crossed the room, and grabbed his hat.

"I'm going whether you go or not," he said, energized by the thought of renewing the search for Rose's body. "No one will be able to say I didn't look under every rock for James Rose," he muttered, more for his own hearing than the sheriff's. "But first I gotta get something to eat. It's late, but maybe the Occidental is still serving lunch. I forgot to have Mrs. Byrne pack me something this morning. I won't be at the hotel long."

"Get something for Wright, too. I forgot to get a plate for him," said the sheriff, reaching into his pocket for his tobacco pouch.

It wasn't the first time Cyrus had forgotten to bring a ration to their prisoner, who was housed in the cramped and dreary hoosegow, a separate building behind the sheriff's office just big enough for one occupant. Alarmed at Cyrus' confession, Luke wondered how long it had been since Sam had eaten or drunk anything. It was summer. The man needed water several times a day, and it fell to the lawman in the office at mealtimes to tend to his physical needs. In Buffalo that meant Cyrus was nearly always in charge of that chore. Luke felt bad that he hadn't followed behind Cyrus this morning, that he hadn't looked in on Sam to make sure he had a meal and something to drink. Buffalo was too small to have a regular inmate population, so it didn't have established policies about such things, but that only made it all the more inexcusable to fail to feed the one and only inmate they had. It wasn't like they had too many jailbirds to keep track of.

"I will," said Luke, reaching for his hat.

As soon as Luke had shut the door, Sheriff Morris opened his bottom desk drawer and pulled out his magazine.

#

Lenora had spent too much time in town. She had other shopping to do beside her business at Aeschelman's, and she was hungry too, but both would have to wait. With her basket clutched tightly against her body and her reticule swinging against one hip, she hurried to Olathe's to fetch her horses and wagon and return to the ranch before nightfall. She knew why James had chosen the parcel he had, with its enviable access to the North-East Creek and lush pasture land, but now that it was she and not him having to make the run to town regularly for supplies, she rued his decision to settle them so far from town. In their youthful zeal for a ranch of their own, they had never entertained even a shadow of a thought that tragedy could strike so soon, even before the ranch was legally theirs. Her present distress was not James' fault; nevertheless she pushed down an unreasonable sense of irritation with him. He may have not meant to abandon her, but she was, in fact, abandoned.

Main Street was quiet. The only people Lenora saw were three little girls playing in the yard of a house near the end of Main Street close by Olathe's Livery. They were town children, and Lenora did not recognize any of them, not even from church. The girls were jumping rope as she approached, two girls holding each end of the rope while the third girl, clutching her skirts to her body, her long braids swinging up and down, jumped to a bouncy tune they all sang. As she drew closer to them Lenora was horrified to hear their words:

289

Old Man Rose went out one night.
With his wife had a terrible fight.
Found his body face down in the creek.
Horse tied up and feeling weak.

Who killed Old Man Rose?
Oh who killed Old Man Rose?

Town can't tell but deputy knows
Why she went to town to buy new clothes.
Rose is dead and his wife won't speak.
Gonna have a baby at Crazy Woman Creek.

Who killed Old Man Rose?
Oh who killed Old Man Rose?

Lenora felt panic roll over her with the cold, destructive power of a tidal wave. Should she stop and ask them where they'd heard such hideous lyrics? Did she really want to know? What mean-spirited person wrote those awful words? From the mouths of children, but surely inspired by who-knows-who, some wicked, gossiping adult in this unfriendly town.

Once she was directly in front of the girls, she couldn't bring herself to keep walking. She stood frozen on the dirt path in front of the house, watching and listening to make sure she'd heard right. Seeing they were being observed by an adult, the two girls holding the rope smiled politely,

utterly without guile, and one of them waved hello.
All three kept on singing their ugly song.

They don't know who I am! And James' body
hasn't been found! But rather than get involved in a
conversation that could lead to the discovery of her
identity, Lenora smiled back and continued to
Olathe's as if she hadn't a care in the world.

Chapter Twenty

Luke ate a hot lunch of beef stew and yeast rolls and butter. If he hadn't been so diligently banking his paltry deputy's wages, he'd have eaten at the hotel every day. The boardinghouse served plain fare, but it was cheap. When he finished eating and had paid for his meal, he ordered a plate of the same for Sam Wright and charged it to the sheriff's account.

He left the Occidental Hotel carrying in one hand the tray of still-warm food covered with a white cloth napkin and in the other a tin cup filled with cool water. He walked behind the sheriff's office to the single-cell, single-window jailhouse. After balancing the cup on the edge of the plate while fumbling with the key ring with his one available hand, he finally managed to open the

heavy door and enter the dark, overly warm room—
hardly more than a box—that the city fathers had
built to house the accused. As he did the noxious
odor of unwashed body hit his nostrils.

Sam was awake in the cell, lying listlessly on
a dirty bunk, his knees curled up like a child,
shirtless, his eyes vacant. He was dirty and
unshaven. The skin on his thin, wrinkled torso was
glistening with sweat, which trickled between
sparse gray chest hairs. On his feet were the fancy
tooled boots, which looked even more incongruous
on the half-dressed old man than they had when
Luke met him, fully clothed, on the way to Mrs.
Rose's ranch weeks earlier.

Seeing Sam's declining physical state, no
matter what bloody crime he was accused of, made
Luke ashamed that a fellow human being in his care
had gone without, especially someone so pathetic.
Soul to soul, Sam was a man just as much as he
was, made in His image. It was hard not to look at
Sam, though, and wonder again what had brought
him to such decrepit condition. Luke promised
himself that from now on he would check on Sam
several times a day, even though that was Cyrus'
responsibility. It was the only decent thing to do.

"About time," said Sam, rising from his bunk
at the sight of the plate and cup in Luke's hands.
Luke bent low and pushed the food and water
through a shallow opening at the bottom of the cell
door. Despite his weak state, Sam didn't hesitate to
bend down to retrieve them. Luke could smell the

rot in Sam's teeth as he neared the bars. Sam wobbled as he stood up again, grabbed a cell bar to steady himself, and then fell back on his bunk and started eating.

"There's laws against starving an inmate!" he groused between bites of buttered roll. "I ain't drunk nothin' neither, not since yesterday morning! And I don't mean liquor, deputy."

"Sorry, Sam," said Luke, who was standing upright again. "I'll look in on you more regularly from here on out."

"Hmpfh!" grunted Sam, his mouth full of stew. "You'd like me dead. Make you a hero in the eyes of that pretty Rose woman."

"Shut up, Sam," said Luke, quickly forgetting any pity he'd managed to dredge up for the smelly sot. A muscle in Luke's jaw started to twitch. "I brought you the grub. I'll bring you more water before dinnertime."

"I didn't kill her dog!" Sam shoved another spoonful of stew into his mouth and swallowed it without chewing.

"A jury will decide that."

"You got no proof."

Luke didn't answer. No use arguing with an old man who'd lost half a brain to the pickling effects of alcohol; the other half was likely defective from birth. Luke turned and started to leave. It was unprofessional for a law enforcement officer to fraternize with an inmate, and this inmate in particular unnerved him.

"You were on her property too!" shouted Sam, standing up now in his agitation and leaning on the cell bars for support. "What will the jury think of that, deputy? No one can prove that you didn't chop up that dog, just like they can't prove I did it. Maybe you wanted to scare the hell out of her so she'd come running back to your office for protection. Big, powerful Deputy Davies, savior of buxom widows!"

Luke was so annoyed at what he was hearing he wanted to slam Sam's ugly head against the bars. He turned back to him, contemplating how to answer his outrageous charges while somehow managing to strive for control, to try and blunt the sharp spears of his anger. It would be so easy to put this disgusting human being to death. What good had he ever done for anyone? He'd terrified a young widow and murdered her only remaining companion, an innocent, trusting dog. Probably wanted to ingratiate himself with Mrs. Rose to convince her to hire him as a live-in foreman. Then he'd have his way with her. Worthless bag of bones. Hard to understand why God allowed him to take up space on his green earth.

"You got more reason to kill that dog than I do," spat Sam, growing bold after seeing that he had the deputy's attention. His tone was a tat softer than it had been at first though, likely a defensive reflex brought on by the murderous look in Luke's eyes.

"I didn't have any reason to kill Ulysses. He

295

was an innocent animal. But you," Luke said, breathing heavily and clenching his fists to keep them from doing something unforgivable, "are a different matter. Now eat your dinner and pray to God I didn't poison it."

Sam glanced suspiciously at the plate in his hand. Luke turned then and left the jailhouse, taking care to lock the outer door behind him securely. He strode to the front of the sheriff's office, poked his head in the door, and abruptly told Cyrus he was ready to go. Then he and Sheriff Morris saddled their horses and started toward Ebenezer Church on the outskirts of Buffalo.

Chapter Twenty-One

Nothing struck the lawmen as unusual as their horses stepped onto the hard packed, well-trodden earth that surrounded Ebenezer Johnson Christian Church. Luke and Sheriff Morris rode their horses to the church steps first, because that was their ultimate destination. But they saw only bare and weathered gray wood planks, nothing worth their ride from town, so they decided to search the entire area on horseback. If that didn't net them a clue, they would dismount and investigate on foot.

All was as quiet as expected for midweek; services were held only on Sundays. The horse stables behind the church were empty. The only sign of life in the vicinity was a family of sandy brown Mountain Plover that had built a nest in short, brown grasses behind the stables. The small, black-beaked birds with the skinny black legs and white breasts had set up housekeeping in that particular area of the church property because it was dry and sheltered, but mostly they were drawn by the dainties served in the dining hall—flies and other insects hovered around the stables. When the lawmen rounded the corner of the building, the family of five ground birds scattered as one into the clear, late afternoon sky.

Still on horseback, the men slowly wandered to the picnic area where they rode between the rows of wooden benches and tables, looking for any evidence, no matter how small, on the ground or furniture that would lead them to Rose's body. Finding nothing out of the ordinary there, they rode up and down the sparse rows of Ebenezer's little fenced cemetery. Few trees in either area gave them relief from the sun, and in both places they found everything tidy and in order. Aleida Aeschelman's burial mound had settled some since her internment in the spring. Someone, probably her grieving husband Faustus, had recently laid flowers at the base of her modest tombstone. The flowers were wilted but still held the blush of their original poppy yellow coloring.

"Cemetery looks alright," said Luke, looking around from atop his stationary horse.

"Yeah, quiet as a graveyard."

"Let's take a look at the outhouses," Luke said, ignoring Cyrus' sarcasm.

Sheriff Morris rolled his eyes and exhaled noisily through his nose. Luke regretted his decision to invite Cyrus along. Nevertheless the two men sauntered to the extreme rear of the church property. Because he was the younger of the two and lowest in rank, it fell to Luke to dismount and peer down into the two-seaters, which he had done in the spring as well in his initial search for James Rose's body. Luke didn't expect to see anything other than he'd seen before. His expectations proved correct.

It was a small church on a small piece of property. There was no place else to look for evidence of James Rose's remains, so it was time to return to the church steps and begin their search on foot. They dismounted, tied their horses to a stout branch of a tree that shaded the picnic yard, and headed for the front of the building.

"Feel foolish out here, searching for a ghost," said Sheriff Morris when they cleared the front corner of the church. He spat on the ground. "We're wasting time. James Rose's body went down that creek, I tell you. Some wolf got what the fish didn't want. There's nothing left of the bragging bastard."

Luke looked at the oozy blotch of spittle Cyrus had deposited on the ground. "Cyrus, have some reverence. This is the Lord's property."

"This is dirt," said the sheriff, kicking the ground with the toe of his boot. They stopped at the church steps. "And it's all his dirt, as I see it."

Luke decided to drop it. It wasn't just the constant spitting. Like an old married couple, lately it seemed that all the sheriff's personal habits

299

irritated him. Most of all, it rankled him to no end that his boss never made anything but derisive comments about Mrs. Rose. Luke's outburst in the office earlier today was mere venting, a chance to let out a little of the steam that had built up like a pressure cooker inside him. But he hadn't let it all out. He pursed his lips and bit back the blistering retort that rose to his mind. It was useless to argue with Cyrus. He saw things his way and that was that. Besides, they had important work to do.

They stopped in front of the weathered wood steps that led up to the side-by-side sanctuary doors, where they'd begun their search, and stood there, staring.

"Nothing here," said Sheriff Morris, casting his eyes about the church steps, his disgust evident by his tone.

"How about those bushes," said Luke, pointing to large hydrangeas thick with foliage and snowball blooms on either side of the steps. "You take that one and I'll search the other."

"Alright," said Sheriff Morris.

They used their arms to pull back upper branches and squatted and looked under the lowest branches of the leafy white hydrangea. They dropped to a prone position to look deep inside the bushes, their center stalks obscured by broad leaves and enormous blooms. After scarcely a minute Sheriff Morris grunted and lifted himself to a standing position. Luke was still squatting on the ground, peering through branches.

"This is harebrained," said the sheriff as he swiped dirt and sweat from his forehead with his sleeve. "Rose left his horse at North-East Creek. If you insist on continuing this goose chase, we should do it over there. We're wasting time here."

"Dunn's kid found his watch right here," said Luke, pointing to the steps and standing up from where he had been pawing the bush. "And we still don't have the body. This is the most logical place to keep looking for other evidence that could lead us to him. Maybe that's why someone left the watch here, to point us to something else."

"It's suppertime. I'm going back to the Occidental."

"We haven't searched inside yet," said Luke, looking at the sanctuary doors. He took off his hat and started to swat at the dirt on his shirt and pants.

"If James Rose's body is in there," said the sheriff, jerking his bare head toward the doors, "he'd be singing in the choir by now."

Luke took a deep breath and put his hands on his hips. "We're obliged to conduct a thorough investigation, Cyrus. We'd be negligent if we didn't search the sanctuary."

"Fine, go on in. When you see James Rose floating around the ceiling, throw a rope on him and drag him back to town. I got business with him."

"Two sets of eyes are better than one," said Luke, barely managing an even tone. He was determined to not get into it with Cyrus, though his ire was rising like mercury in August, clear to the

301

back of his neck.

"That's true, ain't it?" said Sheriff Morris. "But extra eyeballs only help with things you can see. We're talking about ghosts, and they're invisible, so having me with you won't help your odds, will it deputy?"

Luke huffed noisily, gave his pant leg one last swat with his hat, smashed it onto his head, and started up the steps of the church. At the top step he put his hand to the weathered brass door handle and turned it. Strangely, the door was locked.

"Well, well," said Sheriff Morris, smarmy as ever. "Old Man Rose locked us out. Must have heard us crawling around out here looking for his goddamn carcass. Poor damned soul. Can't abide the thought of being resurrected only to be condemned to living with that overdressed, whiny female. Hell is better."

"That's enough!" shouted Luke, descending the steps in one quick movement. "Enough!" He stopped directly across from his boss, fists raised, ready to knock the lights out of those smart aleck eyes. The thought was most appealing.

"Hmpf," grunted the sheriff. Ignoring the imminent threat to his life, he bent over to pick up his hat, which had fallen off his head when he was on his belly under the bush. He slapped the hat against his thighs to shake off the dust as Luke had done. Then, still clutching his hat, he stood up straight and faced Luke, unfazed by the outburst from his deputy, who was at least a head taller.

Finally he said, "Appears that all the stories I hear around town about you and the Widow Rose are true."

"Not...one...word," said Luke through clenched teeth. He still had his fists raised, ready to strike. "Whatever you've heard is a lie." He realized he was acting crazy—crazy enough to add fuel to the gossip fires burning around town. He was wearing his heart on his sleeve, and dumb as Sheriff Morris was, he was smart enough to read Luke's sleeve. But Luke didn't care. He was sick of Cyrus' mouth. "I don't care what you say about me, Cyrus, but I won't listen to another dirty word from you about Mrs. Rose, you hear?"

Luke had a sudden vision of himself, on his horse, out of work, every worldly thing he owned in his saddle bags, headed out of town southward to Fort Laramie. He liked being a law enforcement officer. He didn't necessarily want to go back and live with his brothers and pa, though he didn't mind the ranching life. But he had had all he could take of Cyrus Morris. If he must go back to ranching tomorrow to get away from Cyrus' daily spew of verbal filth, he was ready. It would not be difficult. What would be difficult would be to leave Mrs. Rose behind, all alone and helpless, on her ranch so very far from town. The thought pained him.

"Put your fists down, you stupid love-struck fool," said the sheriff, returning his hat to his head. "I won't say any more about Mrs. Rose, but you keep her out of my office. She gives me dyspepsia."

Slowly Luke's hands dropped to his sides. He knew at that moment he would have no more trouble with his boss. He also knew that he had just received all the apology he would ever hear from Sheriff Cyrus Morris. He felt spent but relieved, the fight fizzling out of him like a leak in a soft balloon. After a few charged moments of silence, and not knowing what else to say, Luke pointed to the four-foot-high wooden steps.

"I'd take apart these boards to look for his body, but we would have smelled it by now if it were stuffed in there."

"True," said Sheriff Morris, turning back to the church steps. They both stood staring at the steps a few seconds. Sheriff Morris shook his head. "What did his widow say when you showed her the watch?"

Luke hesitated, took a deep breath, and kept his eyes on the steps. The churning in his soul began again. He should have showed Mrs. Rose the watch when he had the opportunity at Aeschelman's, but he couldn't bring himself to do it. Not yet. But he must. But not yet. But he must ...

"I haven't showed it to her yet."

"Why not?"

"I didn't want to upset her. I was hoping to find something over here, some kind of evidence to prove he was really dead, before I rode out to her ranch with it."

Sheriff Morris regarded him skeptically, but to avoid more scrutiny Luke intentionally stared at the steps, as if he were waiting for James Rose to come oozing out of them like a genie escaping from a lamp. Luke knew anything he said would sound defensive, but he plunged right ahead, feeling he had no choice but to elaborate.

"And I wasn't sure if it was his when Dunn's kid brought it in." While that was technically true, all Luke's doubts about the owner had been dispelled once Mrs. Rose had provided her husband's full name. Sheriff Morris, Sam Wright, and Etta Nolan had described it as an expensive gold watch. Luke couldn't think of a man he knew in town who owned a time piece of such fine workmanship as the one that burned a hole in his pocket right now, except for Edwin Morehouse. And Luke had already inquired: Morehouse wasn't missing a time piece.

"It's his." Sheriff Morris spat on the ground.

"We're done here. Let's go," said Luke, hoping to head off any more uncomfortable questions. He was frustrated at finding nothing near the church that pointed to James Rose, yet he was relieved at finally airing the bad feelings that had been bubbling under the surface for some time between himself and Cyrus. In the morning he would question Reverend Thomas and ask for the key to the sanctuary door so that he could look around the inside by himself. He wouldn't bother to ask Cyrus to accompany him. Cyrus was convinced that James Rose had perished in the North-East

305

Creek. The sheriff was entitled to his opinion. Luke was convinced of nothing.

Chapter Twenty-Two

Luke woke up in his cramped, dark room at the boardinghouse with a sense of heaviness, and he couldn't figure out why. Then he remembered the unpleasant business he must tend to this morning. He must question Reverend Thomas and search Ebenezer Christian for clues. Reluctantly he got out of bed, performed his morning ablutions, and then descended the narrow staircase to the boardinghouse kitchen. After breakfast he grabbed the sandwich he had asked Mrs. Byrne to pack for him the night before and headed for the sheriff's office.

It was a beautiful, early August morning in Wyoming Territory. Puffy white clouds, wispy around the edges and thin in some places, fat in other places, floated peacefully across a deep blue sky. The temperature was moderate, and soft northerly breezes promised to keep pedestrians from becoming too hot toward noon. Main Street bustled with shoppers and teamsters. Merchants kept their doors open to catch the fresh air and, hopefully, the interest of passersby.

Luke looked down the street wistfully. A pristine morning like this wasn't fit for questioning his pastor about evidence found on church property of a crime in which the minister could possibly be implicated. No, a morning like this was the perfect backdrop for a buggy ride into the country and a picnic with a pretty lady. His thoughts and eyes turned eastward to Mrs. Rose, alone on her ranch nine miles from town. He wondered what she was doing at that moment. He wondered what she was wearing. He wondered if her hair was loose, hanging down her back, shimmering in the sun, or if she had it pulled back into a soft knot as she often did. Her motherly condition would be evident soon. It occurred to Luke that being in a family way— even with another man's child—could not detract from Mrs. Rose's beauty. Pregnancy accentuated her womanliness.

Luke shook himself. It was not only vain, it was wrong to woolgather about Mrs. James Rose. She was still married to that phantom rancher, that ghost, wherever he was. Irritated, Luke silently cursed his lot. James Rose's stupidity had caused problems for a lot of people in this town, most of all his innocent wife. Why did the foolhardy rancher have to go and get himself killed or lost or killed and lost and create this blasted daily temptation for

Luke? The strain, mentally and physically, of having Mrs. Rose so close but out of reach was killing him.

Sam Wright needed checking on. Luke resolved to stop torturing himself with thoughts of Lenora Rose and keep his mind on his work. In a few minutes he was turning the handle of the door to the sheriff's office.

"You're in early," said Luke as he shut the door behind him with a click.

"I wanted to be here when you got in," said Sheriff Morris from his desk, "to catch you before you went out to pester Reverend Thomas." Sheriff Morris chewed mindlessly on a piece of straw, the exposed end dancing up and down as he spoke.

The day was too pretty to take up Cyrus' insult. Besides, Luke smelled fresh coffee—the real stuff, unlike the dishwater Mrs. Byrne served. Now that was odd. Cyrus had made the first pot of the day. Customarily he left women's work to his deputy. Luke hung his hat on the rack behind his desk and walked to the stove to pour a cup.

"Why?" said Luke.

"Sheriff Clarke sent word. A rider came in last night from Fort Laramie. Clarke asked me to loan you to him for a spell. They're still having trouble with Indians along the Trail. The garrison is moving out and his new deputy hasn't shown up."

"What do you mean moving out?"

"The Army has ordered the bulk of the soldiers at Laramie to expeditions along the Trail.

309

They can't afford to leave many behind to keep an eye on civilians."

Luke stopped pouring and stared at the sheriff. Luke's pa and brothers were members of the civilian settlement at Laramie. "How bad is it?"

"Cheyenne are still kicking up dust down there. Sioux and Lakota too. A few settlers have been killed in the last month."

Luke knew that settlers in the Laramie area had grown accustomed to the Army's presence. Since 1849 farmers, ranchers, and townsmen had lain their heads down at night in peace because of the security afforded by the presence of American soldiers. At first the fort was manned by U.S. Army recruits. But during the War of the Rebellion, Laramie's Union soldiers had been called upon to fight the Confederates, so state volunteer regiments were posted to Fort Laramie. Now, once again, the Army would be sending men in and out of the fort to deal with Indians. It unnerved Luke to think of his pa and brothers fending for themselves on the wide open prairie. Indians were stealthy, ruthless, and bitter, especially the Sioux, who had suffered many losses under Red Cloud a few years earlier.

"That leaves little protection for the settlers around Laramie," said Luke, thinking aloud.

"Which is why Clarke asked me to send you. We've got plenty of volunteers in this town who are accustomed to helping when there's trouble. The settlement outside Fort Laramie has been depending on the Army for protection for years. Clarke needs someone to help him train civilian volunteers."

"What happened to that fellow Clarke hired?"

"His new deputy? He was scheduled to arrive two weeks ago, a recruit from someplace near Fort Collins. He never made it. No one's heard from him." Sheriff Morris pushed himself away from his desk and stood.

Luke still hadn't taken a sip of his coffee. He stared at his cup, eyes fixed but seeing nothing, his innermost thoughts paralyzed by this news. He couldn't leave now. He hadn't found James Rose's body. And Mrs. Rose was depending on him to obtain a death certificate. Above all else, every eligible man in and around Buffalo would rush to court Mrs. Rose if and when she made the decision to declare her widowhood by donning mourning attire. He couldn't be stuck at Fort Laramie when that happened. He just couldn't.

"You look like someone smacked you over the head with a cutthroat trout," said the sheriff. "Snap out of it, boy."

Coming to himself, Luke stepped away from the stove so that the sheriff could reach the coffee pot. "Didn't anyone from Laramie telegraph Fort Collins to find out what happened to him?" asked Luke.

"Of course they did," said Cyrus. "The Fort Collins telegraph operator confirmed that the kid set off for Laramie a few weeks ago. That's all they know."

311

"I can't leave now. I'm close to finding out what happened to James Rose."

Sheriff Morris rolled his eyes and contorted his face into a look that signaled his patience was being tried, grievously tried. "Luke, why can't you get it through your thick head that James Rose is dead? D-E-D-D." Sheriff Morris nearly spat out the letters. "He drowned the night he rode his sorry ass into a prairie storm to get away from his wife. The fish got him, Luke." His voice rose a few notches. "There's nothing left for you to find. Now pack up your stuff and get your horse ready," the sheriff said, shouting now. "I don't want to hear that bastard's name anymore!"

"I just need another couple of days."

"No! What you need is a slap upside the head, you idiot. You been mooning over the man's widow since the day she first sashayed in here. Getting ordered to Fort Laramie is the best thing for everyone. Her included. And it will be paradise for me!"

Luke was silenced by this turn of events. He should have been angry at Cyrus' dressing down, but shock had subdued his emotions for the moment. Not only that, there was too much truth in Cyrus' assessment of his motives to object, at least not with any credibility.

"What about interviewing Reverend Thomas?" Luke tried again.

"Question him when you get back." Sheriff Morris sat down again at his desk and leaned back in his chair, one hand resting on his desk, fingers wrapped around the cup. He pulled the much-chewed straw from his mouth and shoved it into his shirt pocket, for later.

"When will that be?" Luke still stood by the stove, too stunned to make his way to his desk.

"I don't know."

"Is Judge Stillman at Laramie now?"

"I don't know."

"Has the garrison already left the fort?"

"I don't know."

Luke walked to his desk and sat down. He looked dazed. "I can be ready in two to three days. There's some things I need to tend to first."

"You're leaving in the morning."

"What?"

"I put up Clarke's man at the Occidental. Barthel Hughes. Goes by Bart. He'll accompany you to Laramie. I'd send you today but he told me he has other business in town to take care of. He said be ready to leave at dawn tomorrow."

"You heard from Sheriff Clarke a while back, didn't you?" said Luke, growing disgruntled as the details of a conspiracy began to take shape in his mind. "Seems to me he would have sent you a telegraph weeks ago if he wanted your help." Surely the rider Sheriff Clarke sent from Fort Laramie was not Cyrus' first knowledge of his colleague's need for a deputy. Sheriff Clarke would have telegraphed his request to Fort McKinney, a ten-minute ride from Buffalo. And Clarke wouldn't

313

have needlessly jeopardized one of his men by sending him on a two-week trip through Indian Territory unless he was certain Cyrus would send Luke back with him. Cyrus had been sitting on this information for a while. Why?

Sheriff Morris looked up. "You have too many distractions here to do your job. You can concentrate better in Laramie."

Luke gave Cyrus a forty-five caliber glare.

"Besides, Clarke needs you more than I do."

Competing desires wrangled in Luke's soul. Above all, he wanted to stay in Buffalo and finish his investigation of the disappearance of James Rose. He must find that body! And the thought of being so far from Mrs. Rose was like having a hunk of his flesh torn off. But there were other considerations that complicated his decision. Refusing a direct order from the sheriff to transfer to Fort Laramie might make matters worse for Mrs. Rose. Townsfolk would interpret insubordination as proof that he had put his supposed relationship with the widow above his responsibilities to uphold the law. She would be more scandalized than she already was.

On the other hand, he was a free man. He could tender his resignation today and be quit of all these restrictions and out from under Sheriff Morris' thumb. But that scenario, thought Luke glumly, would only reinforce popular opinion that he prized Mrs. Rose above his duties. And without his badge, he wouldn't have authority to continue his investigation.

Aside from these immediate arguments, it might actually suit his purposes to leave for Fort Laramie now. He might have an earlier audience with Judge Stillman. Mrs. Rose did not have much time left to argue her case. And it would be a good idea to check on the welfare of his family. He hadn't seen or heard from them since March when he first arrived in Buffalo.

"I'll be ready at dawn," said Luke.

"Take the afternoon off," said the sheriff. "Give you time to say good-bye to your lady friend."

Luke refused the bait. He didn't make eye contact with Cyrus or respond one way or the other. Instead he stood and reached for his hat. "I'll be at the boardinghouse taking care of business there. I'll come back later tonight to clean up my desk. Remember to look in on Sam."

"Yeah, yeah," said Sheriff Morris with a dismissive wave of his hand.

#

Lenora stood in her kitchen holding the ten yards of folded daffodil silk in her arms, trying to figure out how to cut out a dress pattern without the benefit of her mother's long dining room table. This would be her first attempt to cut and sew a dress since she had lugged the overstuffed trunk of frilly all-new frocks from New York over four years earlier. It was high time she had something new and

315

pretty to wear, even if she was limited to the few plain silks available at Aeschelman's. She could sew better than most, but cutting out ten yards of fabric on her small kitchen table presented a daunting task. She was eyeing the broad rag rug on the floor of the front room when she heard the sound of horse hooves amble into the yard.

Hastily she laid the still-folded silk on the kitchen table and walked to the front room to peer through the window. At the same moment that she recognized Luke's horse, which he had tied to her porch post, she heard a knock at the front door. She threw off her apron, smoothed her hair, pinched her cheeks to make them pinker, and heart pounding with girlish expectation, walked to the door and opened it.

"Deputy Davies," she said, truly surprised, "What brings you all this way? Do you have news?"

"Good morning, ma'am," said Luke, removing his hat. "Yes, I have news. But before we speak I'd like to clean up at your pump. I'm covered with dust. I only knocked on your door to let you know I was here. I was afraid you'd see my horse and be alarmed."

"Of course. One moment and I'll fetch you a towel."

Lenora shut the door. In a minute she opened it again, and in her hands she held a clean white towel and a bar of heavily perfumed soap. Luke took them from her, thanked her, and headed for the pump by the barn. In a few minutes he returned, face shining, hair damp, carrying his coat and hat, and smelling like a Grecian spa. He stowed his hat and coat on his saddle before laying the damp towel and bar of soap on the edge of the porch. Lenora was seated on the backless porch bench, waiting. With a quick but mirthless smile Luke wordlessly sat down beside her, taking care that a respectable distance of several inches separated their hips. Luke leaned forward and kept his eyes on his clasped hands, resting his elbows on his thighs.

A few seconds of awkward silence followed in which Lenora was keenly aware that she hadn't been so physically close to the deputy since their memorable buckboard ride through town many months ago. Only this time, his nearness was not intimidating. In fact, to Lenora it had a comforting quality.

"Deputy Davies, you said you had news?" Lenora turned to him, wondering. She could tell that something weighed heavily on his mind. Had they found James' body?

Luke finally lifted his head and faced Lenora. At once she saw the distress in eyes.

"I'm being taken off the investigation, Mrs. Rose. I've been ordered to Fort Laramie. Immediately. I leave tomorrow morning."

Lenora's mouth fell slightly open and her breath caught in her throat. "Why? You've been assisting Sheriff Morris only a few months. I thought you were needed here."

317

"I am needed here. But for a season I'm needed more at Fort Laramie. The Army has ordered the soldiers garrisoned there to press up the Trail. They're still having problems with the Indians. A few settlers have been killed."

"But what does that have to do with you?"

"Sheriff Clarke needs someone to help him organize volunteers. The civilian settlement outside Laramie has been protected by the Army since it was established in '49. They don't have a militia or any type of volunteer organization to look after them. Until now they never needed one."

"But why you?" Somewhere in the deep recesses of her brain, Lenora was vaguely aware that she was allowing her dismay at his leaving to show. Instead of modulating her tone as she had been taught at Mrs. Bindleton's, she was allowing herself to be led by her emotions. But after all she'd been through since her days at Bindleton's, acting demure didn't seem to matter much anymore.

"Sheriff Clarke asked the Territory for a deputy to be attached to his office to help him, train volunteers and the like. The Territory granted him one but the man never showed up. He left Fort Collins a few weeks ago and no one's heard from him. Until we find out what happened to him or until Clarke gets a replacement, I'm their man. Clarke sent word to Cyrus asking to use me for a while."

"I see," said Lenora.

"Cyrus didn't hesitate to volunteer my services," said Luke. He gave Lenora a knowing look. "Frankly, I think he wants to be rid of me."

Lenora smiled half-heartedly. "No, I suppose Sheriff Morris thinks you have nothing of importance to do here in quiet Buffalo."

"Mrs. Rose, I told you I'd speak to Judge Stillman about a death certificate when he arrives at Fort McKinney in September. I still mean to do that."

"I am obliged for your assistance."

Luke nodded in acknowledgment. "But I don't know where the judge is right now. If he's not at Laramie when I arrive, I'll have to track his circuit schedule from there."

"I understand." Lenora sounded somber. She clasped both hands on her lap in an unconscious effort to calm herself.

"There's worse, Mrs. Rose."

Lenora blinked. "Worse?"

"I may still be in Laramie when the judge arrives here. I suspect that may be the case."

"Why is that?"

"They're having more troubles south of here with the Indians than we are. If Clarke's new deputy doesn't find his way to Laramie, the Territory can't justify sending me back to Buffalo when settlers are losing their lives down South. Not only that, Buffalo has a full contingent of soldiers for protection."

Lenora's heart sunk down to her toes. In a flash of self-awareness, she realized she didn't know, truly, which caused her more grief: another frustrating detour on the road to discovering the disposition of her husband's remains, or the knowledge that Deputy Davies was going away, possibly for a very long time, maybe even forever. Deputy Davies had told her that his pa and brothers had a ranch at the settlement at Fort Laramie. Once he was surrounded by family and all the comforts of home, he might decide that ranching was more desirable than working with nasty Sheriff Morris. It struck her then quite clearly that she had begun to look forward to her visits with the deputy. After he left she wouldn't have any more conversations with him in town or here on her porch. Her long silent days on the ranch would be longer and more silent. The thought pained her.

"Deputy Davies, you have been very attentive throughout this ordeal, and very kind. I appreciate everything you've done to find my husband. You've left no stone unturned. You are a true professional. Your family will be happy to have you nearby again, but Buffalo will be the less without your presence."

"Thank you for the sentiment, Mrs. Rose. But I wish you would seriously consider taking Reverend and Mrs. Thomas' advice. You should move to town."

Lenora sighed and leaned back against the house. "I might have entertained the notion at one time, Deputy Davies. But I think it's too late to redeem myself. I'm shunned in town. At least out here I know a measure of peace."

Luke shook his head dejectedly. "I'm partly to blame. I didn't always use wisdom when I was investigating you."

"Hogwash. What could you have done differently?" She didn't wait for a response. "You're not to blame. I brought this upon myself."

"I don't know how you see it that way, ma'am."

"Out here on this ranch all day, alone, I've had a lot of time to reflect on my ways."

Luke cocked his head and looked at Lenora, waiting.

"People resent my fancy eastern clothes and our nice spread out here. I should have used more discretion. This trial has taught me a few things about how to get along in western society, or in any society for that matter."

With no effort at concealment, Luke gazed up and down at Lenora's modest cotton striped work dress, white and pink with dainty pink flowers printed on the white striping, complemented by long, full sleeves and a demure, plain white collar. "It's no sin to own a nice piece of land," he said, "and I like the way you dress." He sounded entirely sincere. "You always look like a lady. I wouldn't want you to dress any other way."

Lenora was taken aback at the familiar course their conversation had taken. Was it acceptable to discuss her attire with a gentleman? She decided to change the subject.

"I'm taken care of anyway, Deputy Davies. Ben Slocomb comes twice a day now. He does all the heavy chores. I confine myself to the business of the house for the most part."

Luke looked thoughtfully toward the barn. "You pay him to come twice a day?"

"No. I pay him only for the morning chores. He still insists on doing the evening chores as a favor. Such kindheartedness. I don't know how I'll ever repay him or his parents."

Luke nodded. "Ben's a good kid. I'm glad he's here to help you every day. But I'd feel better leaving you behind if I thought you were in town, among grown folk. You should move in with Marietta Nolan. She'd be happy to have you."

Lenora stiffened. "I will not leave my ranch."

Luke blew out a noisy breath. "What if something happens to you, or your baby, and there's no one around to help?"

How does he know about my condition? Lenora blanched. "I am never more than one milking session away from a visit by Ben. He comes twice a day, seven days a week. If I slip and fall and can't get up, I'll just wait for the cows to moo and know that in short order Ben will be here."

Luke grimaced and shook his head in disgust. "You make light."

"And why not? I've lost everything but my property, Deputy Davies." Lenora threw up her

322

hands. "How can I not feel lighthearted? What worry is left to weigh me down? I have nothing more to lose. I've lost my husband. My reputation has been dragged through the mud—could I be scorned more by the people of Buffalo than I am now? The bank has weighed me in its balance and found me wanting. It won't lend me the money I need to hang onto this ranch. Even if I somehow, by God's grace, manage to keep it, I'll spend the rest of my life under suspicion of adultery until my child is grown. Hopefully by that time every finger-pointer in town will be muted by the fact that the offspring of James and Lenora Rose resembles the father. My only worry now is that their doubts won't be dispelled." Lenora leaned back against the house again, clasped her hands together on her lap, and sighed deeply.

"What do you mean?"

"What will happen if the child resembles me more than James, leaving paternity in question?"

"That is not the worst thing a child can suffer." Luke absent-mindedly ran his hand through his hair and stared into the yard at nothing in particular.

"No? What more?" Lenora sat up straight again, her interest genuinely piqued.

Luke turned back to Lenora. His eyes were dark and sober. "Your child could grow up without a pa, wondering all his days what it's like to live in a house with two parents, what it's like to have both a pa and ma to guide him in the different ways of a man and a woman. That's worse, Mrs. Rose."

Then, wordlessly, Luke moved his large, tanned hand toward hers, gently closing it over her small one. Lenora looked down at his hand covering hers and was stunned. With her eyes fixed on his hand, she didn't see the tremulous cast that came over his face nor discern what it cost him when he said,

"Any man would be honored to be a father to your child."

Lenora looked up then into Luke's eyes and saw intense desire. Every nerve ending in her body flared with awareness of his touch and his nearness. And when she looked into those loving eyes, something in her heart broke loose. He cared for her. She had always known it.

Her heart began to beat rapidly to match the wild herd of thoughts that stampeded across her mind. Was this a proposal? Was Deputy Davies actually offering to shoulder the responsibility of being a father to her unborn child? Why would he take a step that could only fan the flames of scandal that had scorched them both thus far?

But what surprised Lenora most of all was not the questions about Deputy Davies' intention that his tender act evoked. It was her memories of James. Heretofore she had thought she had done a good job of resisting the pull of sadness and self-pity that threatened to undo her during her long hours alone on the ranch. Over time she had learned to set her grief on a shelf— extant, but locked away like a treasured memento that she could take down at will when she was feeling nostalgic and then put away again to fondle another day.

But the tender affection expressed by the unexpectedly gentle touch of this man had unlocked her storehouse of memories of another. With a stab of grief so exquisite it shocked her, Lenora realized that the deputy's fingers embraced not only her hand but the wedding band she had worn in faithfulness nearly four and one-half years. Tears sprung to her eyes at the memory of how James had courted her so long ago, how they had loved each other so feverishly, how hopeful and naive they had been when they had set out for Wyoming Territory. How young they had been! They thought life in the West would be as soft as spring rain and as warm as Indian summer. When the icy winds of suffering had blown in, Lenora had not been prepared.

If this wasn't a proposal, reasoned Lenora, then Deputy Davies was proffering friendship, brotherly affection born of shared experience. His life had been shaped by pain too. But in this moment his kinship and empathy failed to comfort. Luke's efforts at companionship only reminded Lenora of the companion she had lost.

Embarrassed at her unexpected display of emotion, Lenora dabbed the corners of her eyes with the fingers of her free hand to keep the tears from running down her face. So many thoughts jostled at once they choked her words, and in her hesitation to respond, she realized that Luke was leaning into her, closing his eyes. Lenora felt a sudden flush of heat on her torso and neck. He was going to kiss her!

"Ah!" she exclaimed, drawing back.

"What?" Luke drew back as well.

"I felt the baby kick!"

Lenora pulled her hand away from Luke's and placed both her hands on her abdomen. Her eyes were wide with surprise and delight.

"You've never felt the baby before this?"

"No, never. Well, questionable little flutterings, but I was never sure. This was truly the baby! I've been waiting for this moment so long!"

#

I've been waiting for this moment so long. Leave it to James Rose to claim what's his. Cyrus said Rose was at his worst when he felt his stuff was threatened. *This is what you get for dallying with a married woman, Luke. Cyrus is right. You're an idiot.*

"It must comfort you," was the only complimentary thing Luke could think to say, and even that tiny concession exhausted his supply of grace when it came to James Rose. Bested by unwelcome competition from the most infuriating interloper he'd ever known, an invisible one yet, Luke leaned back on the bench and rested his head against the wall. Feeling chastened, he closed his eyes to set his thoughts aright. Professional indeed. Mrs. Rose actually thought of him as a professional.

326

He remembered the watch and chain in his pant pocket and burned inwardly with shame. Here was his golden opportunity, probably the last in a good while to return the final, tangible connection the grieving widow had to her dead husband. Luke ought to pull that damned watch from his pocket this minute and hand it to her. It was hers now. But she would be in shock. She would cry. If he pulled it out of his pocket now, instead of fading into the safe, oblivious haze of eternity where he belonged, the nettlesome James Rose would park his ugly spectral backside right between them, every bit the chaperone from Hell. Why wouldn't the infernal spook just die already?

Luke wrestled mightily within. He should give her the watch. Now. Holding onto it a second longer was selfish. It was evil. The burden of his guilt squeezed his chest like a vise. He took a deep breath and—

"Before I leave in the morning I'm going to ask Mrs. Nolan to move out here from town and stay with you until I return."

"Etta has a son to cook and clean for."

"That son has more than a few gray hairs in his whiskers," said Luke with a tinge of disgust. He stood to his feet. "Malcolm Nolan is a grown man. He should be concerned about his widowed mother's welfare, not the other way around."

Lenora stood as well. "Deputy Davies, you said earlier that you had not used wisdom when you were investigating me. Is it wisdom to take an interest in my welfare in so public a manner as to solicit the Nolans? We still don't have his body."

"Mrs. Nolan would never volunteer to anyone that I asked for her help," said Luke, starting for his horse. "And even if she did, it wouldn't change my plans. While I'm gone I intend to see that someone looks out for you."

Lenora nodded meekly. "I must admit, your offer is not entirely unwelcome. I enjoyed Etta's company when I was confined, though I hate the thought of putting her out again." Lenora used the back of her hand to wipe away a silent tear.

"I'm going to water my horse before I leave," said Luke, donning coat and hat. "I will write you from Fort Laramie after I see the situation there. Good day, Mrs. Rose." And with that, he tipped his hat and goaded his horse to walk to the far side of the barn to the pump.

Chapter Twenty-Three

Fort Laramie, Wyoming Territory, August 18, 1880

Dear Mrs. Rose,

*By the good graces of Providence Mr. Hughes
and I arrived at Fort Laramie August 16 in good
health, though not as early as we had hoped. We
had no trouble with renegade Lakota, which we had
feared, but we were delayed when we reached the
swollen North Platte, and we lost two days of travel
time owing to a damaged ferry. I called upon my
family soon after I arrived and found them also in
good health and the family ranch as I left it in early
March.*
*Regarding your petition to Judge Stillman for
a death certificate for your husband, I am sorry to
tell you that I missed an audience with the judge by
only 48 hours. Sheriff Clarke tells me that the judge*

329

*left for Douglas Settlement August 14. Sheriff
Clarke has kindly offered to assist me by
telegraphing the Settlement ahead of the judge's
arrival. To this end I have begun a letter to Judge
Stillman in which I shall outline persuasive reasons
why he should rule in your favor, lacking the body.
I shall keep you informed of any developments in
this regard.*

*I understand from Sheriff Clarke that Sam
Wright will be brought before Judge Stillman at the
end of September when he arrives in Buffalo.*

*Sheriff Clarke lost no time in pressing me into
service. My days are long, filled with organizing
men into teams and planning strategies based on
each rancher's location, the fort being the center of
everything that matters. My desire is to finish here
what I was drafted to accomplish and be relieved of
my duties within a month, time enough to return to
Buffalo to speak to Judge Stillman on your behalf
face to face.*

*Before I left town I secured from Mrs.
Marietta Nolan her promise that she would keep
company with you until my return. I trust that in her
presence you are comforted in your loss and
enjoying the benefit of help with your burden of
ranch chores.*

*You are in my thoughts and frequent prayers.
I assure you that, as God grants me strength, I will
do all within my power to secure the document you
need to preserve a legacy for you and your child.*

In your service,

Deputy Luke Davies

"Well," said Etta Nolan as she sat beside Lenora on the Rose Ranch front porch bench on a warm August afternoon, embroidering in a small hoop frame, "for a man who doesn't talk much he writes well enough."

"Hmm," murmured Lenora, her mind elsewhere. She sat motionless, the letter in her hands on her lap.

"Despite everything, you have much to be thankful for in the way of the deputy's help."

Lenora nodded.

"Thank you for reading his letter aloud to me."

"You're welcome," said Lenora, breaking her reverie. She folded Luke's letter and returned it to its envelope, set it on her lap, and rested her hands on it as she gazed outward, beyond her barn and property to the dry, sun parched prairie that stretched to the Big Horn Mountains under an unbroken blue sky. In the distance shimmering waves of heat rose from the ground. Only a rare bird dotted the heavenly canopy, and most of the ranch animals lay out of sight, resting quietly in the shade of the barn. The low buzz of crickets and an occasional dance of grasses excited by a hot breeze provided a lullaby to the sleepy afternoon stillness. The two women sat in silence a long while,

331

listening to their private thoughts. Finally Etta Nolan spoke.

"It's not like you to sit so long idle, Lenora. What is on your mind?"

Lenora thought a while before answering. "Lemonade," she finally said, still staring out into the nothingness of the prairie. "With lots and lots of ice."

Mrs. Nolan chuckled. "Lemonade and what else?"

Lenora sighed gustily and returned to the moment. "I'm going to lose this ranch, Etta. I've thought about it from every angle. There is no hope."

"Those are mighty gloomy words from one such as yourself. What makes you speak in such dire terms?" Mrs. Nolan tied a knot on the reverse side of her white-on-white spring bouquet, clipped the excess floss with small brass scissors, pulled a fresh length of embroidery floss from the basket at her feet, wet one end of the floss between her lips, and began to thread her needle once more.

Meanwhile Lenora just sat, motionless, her wide indigo cotton skirt spread around her like a queen. Between her yards of billowing blue and Mrs. Nolan's pool of dove-gray cambric, the narrow wooden bench they sat on was hidden from view.

"I can't help it. Everything I've done or tried to do to hang onto my property has turned to ashes. Sometimes I think I'm fighting an invisible foe.

332

Perhaps it is best if I move back to New York now and spare myself this heartache. I have the baby to think of."

"Deputy Davies is still working on your behalf." Mrs. Nolan placed the hoop on her lap and began winding the embroidery floss around the tip of the needle, round and round, to create a French knot.

"You heard what he said in his letter, Etta. He missed the judge by only forty-eight hours. If the good Lord wanted me to keep this land, He would have arranged to get Deputy Davies to Fort Laramie in time to speak to Judge Stillman." Her tone was more than a little peppered with pique.

Mrs. Nolan waved her hand to disperse one of the flies buzzing around the porch. She didn't take her eyes off her embroidery hoop. "I think you're seeing an awful lot in something that is merely a coincidence."

"I'm tired of believing."

Mrs. Nolan stopped stitching a moment, needle in the air, to look at Lenora straight on. "Things aren't always as they seem."

"No, most times they're worse."

Mrs. Nolan shook her head and returned to stitching. "You were a very little girl during the Great Rebellion, weren't you Lenora? How old?"

Lenora cocked her head, thinking. "I was three when it started."

"Have you ever heard of General Irvin McDowell?"

333

"He's a Union officer. I studied him in school but I don't remember which battle he fought."

"He led the Union Army at the First Battle of Bull Run in Virginia, a battle he lost. Around 3,000 Union men died. That was in 1861, our first major battle of the war. Lenora, we thought that number was horrific. We had no idea how much more bloody it would get. President Lincoln lost faith in General McDowell after that terrible loss and replaced him with General George McClellan, which of course humiliated McDowell."

Lenora listened yet never broke her doleful gaze across the prairie.

"A year later in the Second Battle at Bull Run, General John Pope was put in charge, and General McDowell was put under General Pope. They lost that battle too, and thousands more Union soldiers died in the second battle than had been lost in the first. I'm sure General McDowell felt like you do right now when he looked across the battlefield a second time and saw all those wounded and dying boys of his." Mrs. Nolan removed her spectacles, wiped them briskly with her skirt, put them back on, and resumed stitching.

Lenora continued to stare, eyes fixed, seeing nothing but gloomy images of death and loss behind her eyes.

"And then there was Antietam in September 1862. Neither side could claim victory, and both suffered heavy losses. Twenty-three thousand men died on the battlefield in one day. And Lenora, that bloodiest of battles was fought in Pennsylvania. Northern soil.

"In May '63 we lost at Chancellorsville, also in Virginia. We lost again in '63, in September, at Chickamauga in Georgia. In '64 more than 18,000 Union soldiers died in Spotsylvania, Virginia. The Union lost that battle too. The Union had some wins throughout our long ordeal, but most of the time our cause looked hopeless. Much like yours."

Lenora hardened her jaw. She didn't want to take umbrage with Etta. The woman meant well. She was just sick of sacrifice and tired of waiting for ... what? James to ride up to their front door? His body? A letter from some faraway place telling her he had filed for divorce? She felt frozen in time and place, like that woman in the Bible who had turned into a pillar of salt. A woman and a wife, but not. Lenora looked down at her hands. She couldn't meet Etta's eyes. She was ashamed of her angry, black thoughts, but mostly, she was just angry.

"Not only that, no one in America, North or South, had ever seen such unspeakable bloodshed. You were too little then to understand how devastating it was, but Lenora, our hearts bled for four years."

Lenora nodded glumly to show she was listening.

"You know how it ended. The Union won the war, but for a long time victory looked impossible." Mrs. Nolan stopped stitching. "Lenora," she said in a tone that demanded attention.

335

Lenora broke from her melancholy long enough to turn toward her friend. Her eyes were dulled by the heaviness in her heart.

"Just because we suffer losses doesn't mean we are without hope or that we've been abandoned."

"But I have suffered a great loss," said Lenora, becoming animated, "and I feel cruelly abandoned." Just then a particularly unrelenting fly zoomed in toward her face. She poured out her cup of indignation without reserve, swatting madly at the pest with both hands. "And I don't even know what I'm waiting for!"

"I know how you feel, Lenora," said Mrs. Nolan, placing one hand over Lenora's after she had stopped swiping the air. "I'm a widow too, you know."

"I'm sorry, Etta. I'm thinking only of myself. Please forgive me." Lenora lifted Etta's work roughened hand to her lips and lightly kissed it.

Mrs. Nolan leaned into Lenora, gave her a quick squeeze, and returned to her stitching. "There's no need to apologize. That was long ago. My pain is gone. I just want you to know that I understand how angry and abandoned you feel. You are not alone. I'm here."

Lenora nodded dejectedly.

"But child, just because you've lost some battles doesn't mean you'll lose this war. Circumstances can turn to your favor in a single day."

"True." Lenora didn't sound convinced.

"You will find out what happened to James. The most important thing is to never give up."

"I'll try," she said, though her tone of resignation belied any real commitment.

The ladies sat in silence, Lenora brooding and swatting, Mrs. Nolan absorbed in her embroidery. Finally Lenora had had enough.

"Let's go in, Etta. These dreadful flies. Besides, the beans should be ready. We can have an early dinner and go to bed. I'm tired."

#

"It's called a hard bustle."

The sound of the two ladies' heels clumping on the wood planks of Main Street's boardwalk filled the pause that followed. Lenora clutched Mrs. Nolan's arm for moral support, and each carried a shopping basket on their free arm. The street was dotted with a few late-morning shoppers, though town was predictably quiet today because it was harvest time. Lenora tried to discreetly search the faces of those few who approached before they were close enough to make eye contact. She wanted to determine if she'd be shunned or welcomed and respond accordingly. Despite Etta's encouraging words that morning before they'd left for town, Lenora's chest felt squeezed each time she saw another citizen of Buffalo walking toward her on the boardwalk.

"Is it like it sounds?" asked Mrs. Nolan.

337

"Yes," replied Lenora. "It's not like the soft fabric bustles we've always worn. It holds up more dress folds because it's stiffer. My mother writes that it's *de rigueur* in Paris and only the most fashionable women in New York wear them. I plan to get one as soon as I can."

"With a bustle like that you will look as motherly in the back as you do in the front," teased Mrs. Nolan with a chuckle.

Lenora glanced down at the soft bump in front of her, which she could feel but not see through the all-white calico day dress she wore. She hardly showed. "I'm not that big in front. And you know what I mean," she said, "to wear after the baby is born." Then, remembering her promise to herself to dress more like a ranch wife about town, she added, "For special occasions, of course."

The women embraced and then parted in front of Aeschelman's, each with town errands to attend to before meeting again at Olathe's for the ride back to Lenora's ranch. But before they went to their separate business, Mrs. Nolan reminded Lenora to mail the letters in her basket. At Mrs. Nolan's urging, Lenora had finally put pen to paper, informing her parents of the tragedy that had befallen her and the good news of her impending delivery. After some discussion, Lenora was forced to agree that it was sinful to procrastinate. She had dragged her feet in notifying family back East, hoping a miracle would occur and she wouldn't have to distress them. But five months had passed and she still had no sign of James. Her parents, and especially her in-laws, deserved to know the state of her and James' affairs. Her shopping basket carried a second letter addressed to the elder Mr. and Mrs. Rose, a missive enclosed bearing the same sweet and sad news.

Lenora pushed open the door to the mercantile. Mr. Aeschelman heard the tinkling bell and came through the brown curtains as he always did, greeting Lenora with a good morning before she reached the counter. His wide, friendly smile was as appealing in this prickly town as the lemonade Lenora had wished for weeks earlier. She returned the greeting and then, strangely, as she approached the counter, found herself reflexively sweeping her eyes over the displays around the store, searching for Deputy Davies, but she was the only shopper today. Feeling disappointed when she did not see his tall frame and warm eyes looking back at her, she walked toward the shop counter and set her reticule on it. *Of course he's not here. Deputy Davies is at Fort Laramie. What's wrong with you?*

Lenora pulled her shopping list from her reticule and handed it to Mr. Aeschelman. Then she asked to see Buffalo's one and only dress catalogue. As she suspected, after poring through pages of laced and beribboned women's foundations promising to pull in, push out, and plump up, she found nothing akin to a hard bustle. She resigned to write her mother and ask her to have one shipped to

339

her in the Territory. She returned the catalogue to
Mr. Aeschelman, thanked him, and told him she'd
return for her purchases in thirty minutes or so.
With her business complete at Aeschelman's,
Lenora wished she could hide there until this
dreadful shopping trip was finished, but she
couldn't. So feeling unsettled, and encouraging
herself out the door with a bit of chin-up-and-carry-
on, forthwith she set out for the milliner's. She
needed buckram for the bonnet to match her new
daffodil silk dress. Only Buffalo's hat maker carried
hat-making supplies.

She was relieved to see the street empty, the
few shoppers busying themselves inside shady
Main Street shops. When she was about a block
from the milliner's and roughly across the street
from Belles', she heard a man yelling angrily from
that direction. She turned to see what the ruckus
was just in time to see a large man stumble raggedly
out the door of the saloon, the result of an
encouraging shove by the barkeep. In a flash of
recognition, Lenora realized who the man clinging
to the post was, though she couldn't remember his
name. It was the man who had tried to heave Sam
Wright onto his horse many months ago in this
same spot. Lenora stared a few seconds, expecting
to see his little friend come flying out the saloon
door behind him. Pea-Pod Pendergrass Deputy
Davies had called him. The little man's name was
easier to remember than the big man's. Lenora
waited, but the little man did not appear.

Suddenly the large man was looking straight at her. Horrified to have made eye contact with the obviously drunk ranch hand, she turned then, clutched her shopping basket to her body, and continued down the boardwalk, heels clicking loudly as she went.

"Mrs. Rose!" yelled the large man, grinning lasciviously and waving one hand at her. "Wait! I'll eshcort you home."

Escort her home? How did he know her name? Lenora did not remember ever having made the man's acquaintance, but Buffalo was a small town, only a settlement really. Perhaps the man had been introduced to James in the course of business and knew her by association? Curious, she slowed down long enough to glance backwards. The man was dressed like all the ranch hands about Buffalo, though his hat had taken a tumble onto the dusty street outside Belles' place. His hair was in need of a cut, slick with dirt and sweat, and stood up ridiculously on one side, shoved skyward when his hat flew off. And like all the others, he was tanned and ruddy from hours in the sun. But unlike all the others, this ranch hand was following her down Main Street, leering and swaying and calling to her. And he knew her name.

"Wait, Mrs. Rose!"

Lenora kept walking at an even pace, refusing to add to the brouhaha by sprinting in public. She felt self-conscious for sure, and was growing increasingly annoyed at the molester, but she was

341

not panicked. It was, after all, broad daylight. She wished only that he'd give up and shut up before someone stepped out of a shop and observed the lout's insistence on speaking to her.

But the man was too stupid or too drunk to respond reasonably to a brush-off. He continued to call her name, ever louder it seemed, as he followed her down the street, keeping pace about twenty feet behind, close enough that Lenora could hear his heavy boots slogging along the boardwalk. His demanding tone was more unnerving that his footsteps. Each time she heard him call her name she recoiled at the cloak of intimacy inherent in the use. She thought of turning around and shushing him but quashed the idea. Acknowledging him might encourage him. Neither did she want to be seen speaking to him.

While she held her back and shoulders primly, her mind chug chugged like a steam engine, gears turning round and round as she tried to figure out how this obnoxious drunk knew her. Then it dawned on her that that the current flavor of gossip around town might make her an attractive morsel to men of base desires. Indeed, all the men in and around Buffalo, base or no, surely knew by now about the missing rancher, the wife he left behind who was with child, her association with the very eligible and very attentive deputy, and how that deputy had been whisked away to Fort Laramie on "emergency" duty. Horrified, Lenora realized with heart-stopping chagrin that the drunk man—and who knows how many other men—must think of her as nothing more than a common strumpet. Buffalo was a military town, after all, established to serve all the peculiar needs of the lonely men who lived and worked just minutes away. Lenora was reasoning through all this when the man's voice turned ugly, edged with contempt.

"Wait, bitch!"

Bitch? Feeling publicly unmasked and frantic at his angry tone, Lenora glanced right and left, abandoning all worry about being seen. Right now she would accept assistance from any male citizen of Buffalo of any stripe. But all of Main Street was empty.

Where was a good clump of ogling soldiers when a girl needed rescuing?

With the desire for self-preservation crowding out all conscious thought, she could only react. She cast about for a door, any door, to seek safety behind. In her fevered state even a barber's den would suffice. She saw a door handle and rushed to grab it. She flung herself through the doorway in such a panic she didn't have time or inclination to read the sign on the window to the right of the door that identified the sheriff's office.

Chapter Twenty-Four

The only sound in the two spartan rooms that comprised Buffalo's law enforcement office was Lenora's ragged breathing as she leaned against the door a few seconds to pull the reins on her runaway heart. She was hugely relieved to see an empty chair at Sheriff Morris' desk. But out of self-preservation, she stared several seconds to assure herself he was really absent, that her eyes weren't tricking her.

Once she was satisfied she was alone, her glance moved naturally to the other desk where Deputy Davies usually sat. She was surprised at the hollow ache she felt at the sight of his unoccupied chair and empty hat rack. As she worked to calm her breathing and with the faint smell of old coffee in her nostrils, she tried to visualize him sitting there, smiling in his warm and welcoming way. If he were here now, she rehearsed in her mind, he would stand politely to greet her as he usually did. He would bring her a chair and treat her with quiet respect. Unlike that skunky Sheriff Morris, Deputy Davies would listen sincerely to what she had to say and try to help.

Oh my. Am I falling in love with Deputy Davies? And what if he never returns to Buffalo? Now there was a disturbing thought, a quiet angst that shaded Lenora's mind like a silent gray cloud that floats slowly across the noonday sky, creating gloom where a moment ago there was happiness and light. What if he falls in with some girl he knew before he left Fort Laramie? He said he had lived there since he was eighteen. He must know many eligible young ladies. The settlement at Fort Laramie was older and bigger than the settlement at Buffalo. Chances are, she mused, he would return to the familiar and comfortable delights of home and decide that Buffalo had nothing to hold him.

But there wasn't time to weigh the merit of this revelation about her changing feelings for Deputy Davies. Likely Sheriff Morris was lunching at the Occidental and would turn the knob on the office door at any time. She must not dawdle. Determined to avoid another testy encounter with the crusty sheriff, Lenora walked to the window and scanned as much of Main Street as she could from her limited vantage point. The drunken ranch hand had continued on his way, likely discouraged when Lenora took refuge in the sheriff's office.

345

Wherever he was, he was gone now. She opened the office door and left, leaving it unlocked just as she had found it. Feeling lonely and lost and like she were drifting in a vast ocean with neither mast nor sail, she set out for the milliner's.

#

"Lenora, I didn't expect to see you here," said Mrs. Nolan, turning from the sales counter at the sound of Lenora's entrance.

Ellen Doherty was showing Mrs. Nolan a velvet winter bonnet, its long, silky blue ribbons draping fluidly down the front of the polished counter. Mrs. Doherty's face fell and her mouth became a straight line at the sight of Lenora. She shut the door behind her and, passing open shelves of elaborately decorated women's hats to her right and men's headgear to her left, approached the two women. She had seen the shock and then the mild disdain on the shopkeeper's face. On her own face Lenora wore a practiced mask of calm.

"Ellen, you know Lenora," said Mrs. Nolan.

Lenora noted that Etta's tone was a little breezier than usual.

"Mrs. Rose," said Mrs. Doherty with the slightest nod of her head.

Lenora was glad for this polite crumb of civility, though she knew that the milliner had tossed it her way only out of deference to Etta.

"Good afternoon, Mrs. Doherty," replied Lenora with a stiff smile.

"You done with your shopping already?"

346

asked Mrs. Nolan.

"No, I forgot that I needed buckram. And I'm waiting for Mr. Aeschelman to put my order together."

"I'll get it," said Mrs. Doherty. And without further ado, the bespectacled shopkeeper in the starched white shirtwaist left the counter to rummage among her boxes of notions for the stiffener Lenora needed for her new hat.

Lenora was mortified. Mrs. Doherty would use any excuse to get away from her, as if Lenora had brought head lice to this little party. She burned with unfounded shame. It was all so unfair.

Nonplussed, Mrs. Nolan ignored the shopkeeper's judgmental response and fingered the blue velvet hat. She lifted it from the counter and placed it on her head.

"What do you think?" Mrs. Nolan smiled wide.

"It makes you look twenty years younger," said Lenora.

"Good. Then I'll buy one in every color," said Mrs. Nolan with a straight face. Lenora smiled but did not laugh.

In short order Lenora and Mrs. Nolan had their buckram and new blue velvet hat, respectively, and were walking through the jingling doorway of Aeschelman's. As they approached the counter Lenora saw that Mr. Aeschelman had gathered her purchases into a bundle secured with paper and string, which he had set on the counter.

"Thank you Mr. Aeschelman," she said, reaching for the bundle. "How much do I owe you?"

"Lenora, you forgot your letters," interrupted Mrs. Nolan, glancing at the basket on Lenora's arm.

"Oh, so I did," she said, handing them to Mr. Aeschelman.

"Faustus forget too," said the proprietor, tapping his head as if to wake himself up. With his hand he signaled them to wait a moment. He walked to the end of the counter, rummaged around underneath, and returned with an envelope, which he handed to Lenora. "Fort Laramie," he said, pointing to the return address. And then he winked.

Lenora stood still as a fence post, staring at Mr. Aeschelman, trying to take in what had just transpired. So, his English was poor but his imagination was rich indeed. Swell.

"Thank you, Mr. Aeschelman." Lenora paid for her purchases and they left.

After Mrs. Nolan had checked on her house in town and found everything in order, the ladies continued to Olathe's for the wagon and the Morgans. Mr. Olathe's cool reception didn't surprise Lenora this time, though. She paid him for his services but didn't bother to favor him with a smile as she had done in the past, before James went missing and before the forces of Hell were unleashed on her. It was pointless to pretend that her reputation in Buffalo was any whiter than a soiled dish rag, especially if others wouldn't pretend as well.

"Lenora, you sit and I'll drive," said Mrs. Nolan as she stood by the wagon.

"You think you can handle them?" Lenora looked doubtfully toward the Morgans.

Mrs. Nolan made a shooing motion with her hand, urging Lenora to climb aboard. "Of course I can handle them. I handle Malcolm, and when he was alive, I handled Arthur. You just have to keep a firm grip on 'em is all."

"If your husband could hear you now!" said Lenora, laughing. She obediently hiked herself up onto the wagon bench.

Mrs. Nolan handed her cane to Lenora and then hoisted herself awkwardly onto the wagon. Lenora handed her the reins. In no time they were beyond the tall doors of the livery stable, had passed the last false storefront of Buffalo, and were alone on the prairie, headed toward Lenora's ranch.

"Now, let's hear what your deputy has to say," said Mrs. Nolan.

Lenora screwed up her face and gave the older woman an I-know-what-you're-trying-to-do look. "I should have known that's why you wanted to drive."

Mrs. Nolan only smiled.

Lenora reached into her basket and pulled out Luke's letter. She tore open one end of the envelope, pulled out the single page of cream paper, unfolded it, and began to read silently. "Oh no," she said after several seconds.

349

"What is it?"

"Deputy Davies says he's not coming back to Buffalo until after September. That's past the six-month deadline!"

"What's keeping him?"

"Sheriff Clarke needs him to stay on. He says I should speak to Judge Stillman myself."

"Yes. And what else?"

"Let me see here." Except for the jangling of the traces and the clop of the horses' hooves, all was quiet in the wagon while Lenora quickly read through the front and back of Luke's letter. Warm rays of late summer sunshine meant that the women could ride comfortably on the open buckboard without cloak or shawl. Nary a cloud dotted the wide blue sky above them as they rode in companionable silence, Mrs. Nolan guiding the horses while Lenora bent over Luke's letter.

At last Lenora stopped reading, folded the page in thirds, and slipped it back into the envelope. Then she took the envelope and folded it in half and shoved it to the bottom of her reticule, as if burying something rotten to stem the stench. She pulled the drawstrings tight and sat silently gazing out onto the prairie.

Mrs. Nolan watched all this with patient interest. Finally she said, "Is everything alright, Lenora?"

"I'm doomed."

"What do you mean, 'doomed'?"

"I mean it's all over. I've lost the ranch. Good

as gone. I'm returning to New York penniless, with child, and alone. There is not a scrap of hope left to me."

"Lenora," said Mrs. Nolan, turning to her bench mate, "I don't understand your sour thinking."

"That wily Sheriff Morris, he's thick with Judge Stillman. I'm sure of it."

"And what of that? You think Judge Stillman won't rule fairly on your behalf?"

"Not for Buffalo's notorious fallen woman, that Jezebel of Jezebels. God only knows what Judge Stillman has heard about me," she said, shaking her head. *And about my condition.*

"What an imagination you have."

Lenora grimaced and looked away. She didn't care to argue with dear Etta.

"Well, if it's as gloomy as you say, then I suppose it would be futile for the deputy to speak to Judge Stillman as well. He's an actor in this drama too, you know."

"But Deputy Davies is a law enforcement officer. Judge Stillman would listen to another representative of the law. Especially another man."

"Maybe, maybe not."

"Oh Etta, why doesn't He just strike me dead?" Lenora wailed. She bent over her lap, her head in her hands.

"And have you miss your appointment to petition Judge Stillman? I think not."

Lenora bolted upright. "You don't really think

I'm going to speak to him on my own behalf, do you?"

"I don't think it. I know it. I'm not going to let you lose your ranch merely because you're afraid to speak up. That would be poor stewardship."

"But I can't!" More wailing.

"Don't be a goose. Of course you can."

"How? Like this?" Lenora clasped one hand to her growing belly. "Everyone thinks the baby is Deputy Davies!"

"And that is untrue, or so you told me ...?"

Lenora turned then to look Mrs. Nolan in the eyes. "Etta, this is James' baby. Our baby."

"I believe you," said Mrs. Nolan, nodding her head in confirmation. "Then why can't you march right into Judge Stillman's office and tell the whole story about James' disappearance if it's true?"

Now there was a good question. Was the truth good enough? When James and Lenora had embarked on their great adventure years before, their sheer confidence in the rightness of what they were doing combined with the mutual bravado of youth had kept them afloat in rising waters. Untested confidence alone was their strength, confidence enough to endure every hardship, fight every foe, overcome every obstacle that threatened to steal away their dream.

But what had happened to the self-assured woman Lenora had once been? She hardly knew herself anymore. The thought of standing before Judge Stillman, in a motherly way yet alone, recounting her specious story of James' brash foray into the dark of night for no good reason, how his horse was found tied to a tree on the banks of the North-East Creek, and how his body had never been found, it all sounded so, so ... unbelievable. Lenora slumped lower on the buckboard bench. She didn't have the will to swim upstream anymore.

"This goose is going to be plucked," she said. "And you know what happens before the plucking." Lenora drew a hand across her throat. "Whack."

Mrs. Nolan laughed out loud. "So young to be so negative," she sputtered, still laughing.

"Other than the baby," said Lenora, patting her tummy, "I can't think of anything good that's happened to me in six months." Her countenance was as gloomy as her speech.

"That remains to be discovered."

The ladies rode in silence a while, becalmed by the gentle song of the rolling prairie, a soft breeze stroking their faces. In the distance low hills were beginning to cast bluish-purple shadows on their eastern flanks, blurring the outline of the trees. The lengthening shadows stirred a dark memory for Lenora.

"Etta, I was chased down Main Street by a drunkard while you were at Ellen's."

"Really? What happened?"

Lenora was reluctant to give voice to her memory of the run-in with the obnoxious ranch hand, but keeping the disturbing images of the day hidden inside her seemed to strengthen their dark power. She told the entire story to Mrs. Nolan, leaving off that particularly distasteful term the man had used to describe her. It upset Lenora to bring the word to her lips.

"That was Buck Jennings or my name isn't Marietta Applegate Nolan," said Mrs. Nolan with a flourish.

"Yes, that is the man! Deputy Davies pointed him out to me one day," said Lenora, remembering.

"The only good thing I can say about that despicable ranch hand," said Mrs. Nolan, giving the reins a little snap to encourage the Morgans, "is that he regularly blesses the people of Buffalo."

Lenora turned a puzzled face to her friend.

"With his absence," Mrs. Nolan continued. "Being an itinerant, he's away from Buffalo much of the time. Did you inform Sheriff Morris?"

Lenora paused, her first thought straying to Deputy Davies' empty desk and how she had lingered shamelessly in the sheriff's office, daydreaming about the handsome deputy and missing his tender attentions. She blushed at the memory.

"I took refuge in his office but he wasn't in, so I left."

"I'll talk to Malcolm as soon as I can. Get him to work with Sheriff Morris on running that man out of town for good."

"Thank you, Etta."

Chapter Twenty-Five

Four weeks later

The sun was a wavy red ball sinking slowly into an inky purple sky when Luke rode up to the hitching post in front of the Buffalo sheriff's office. He pulled on the reins to halt his horse, stiff but grateful that the numbing hours on the trail from Fort Laramie had finally come to a saddle-sore end. It was cold too. Autumn's chill crept early over the darkening landscape. Luke wanted only to leave a short note for Cyrus, alerting him of his unscheduled arrival, get a hot meal at the Occidental, and fall into his bed at Mrs. Byrne's as quickly as humanly possible. Every muscle in his body ached for sleep. September twentieth had come and gone. James Rose had been missing more than six months. By now Mrs. Rose had made her petition to Judge Stillman, and Luke had not been around to speak for her. He felt frustrated by impotence. He hadn't found James Rose's body. He hadn't helped his widow keep title to her ranch. He wondered if Judge Stillman had ruled in her favor or if he had already completed the paperwork to have her homestead transferred to the government. Luke winced, remembering how she had asked him to help her. He had promised to assist, but in the end he had not helped her at all. He wasn't even sure if his letter to Judge Stillman had ever arrived at the man's office. The justice of the court had never responded.

Luke wondered as he dismounted and tied his horse, just as he had wondered the two hundred and twenty lonely miles from Fort Laramie to Buffalo. Wondered why his awkward attempt at proposing to the man's widow had been met with tears. That hurt the most, wounded his pride to the point that he had seriously considered staying on permanently in Laramie. But a Davies didn't give up that easily. Only a coward ran and hid at the first rebuff. Luke liked to think he was made of tougher stuff. Still, he wondered what kind of reception Mrs. Rose would give him now that he had returned too late to be of any worldly assistance. With a heart heavy with longing for what could have been, he wondered if he would have been a different, cleverer sort of man when it came to women if only he had grown up with a ma to teach him the secrets of these mysterious beings.

And, more to the moment, he wondered if he would lose his job for insisting on returning to Buffalo before his work was finished at Laramie. The only thing Luke was sure of right now was the warm, wiggly puppy inside his coat front that was excitedly licking his neck and jaw. He had purchased the pesky mutt, a black-and-brown cutie with big trusting eyes, at Laramie for Mrs. Rose. Luke pressed one hand to his chest, directly over the excited pup, to restrain his slobbery affections while he gazed up and down the shadowy hulks that lined Main Street.

He was glad to be back in Buffalo. Beautiful Buffalo, where his heart was. Then, as he stepped onto the boardwalk, he heard someone shout his name.

"Deputy Davies! Deputy Davies!"

Luke looked in the direction of the shouting and saw Octavius Dunn walking determinedly toward him, his hand on the shoulder of a very unhappy little boy. It was his son, the same boy who had come to Luke's office carrying James Rose's pocket watch. Octavius stopped shouting when he saw Luke look in his direction.

"Deputy Davies," said the elder Dunn as he drew closer, "we didn't think you'd be back in town for months."

"Plans changed," said Luke, offering no explanation and too tired for small talk anyway. "What can I do for you?" Luke glanced at the boy and was disturbed to see tears brimming in his eyes.

The child looked terrified and then incredulous as his eyes grew wide at the bumping and shoving inside Luke's coat.

"I'm glad I saw you," said Octavius. "My daughter Lucille came by my shop yesterday afternoon to tell me a story."

"She tattled!" said the younger Dunn.

"Hush, Harold!" said the father, shaking the boy's shoulder slightly for emphasis. "You're in enough trouble as it is." Then he turned back to Luke. "I'm afraid my son has not been entirely truthful about the item he brought to you several months ago. That gold watch, I mean."

At the mention of the watch, the boy started to cry. He wiped his eyes with the back of his hand and sniffled. The words had an entirely different effect on Luke. The fog of tiredness that had clouded his brain cleared instantly. He studied the boy.

"This time Harold is ready to tell the whole truth, aren't you, Harold?"

The boy hesitated, his body trembling.

"Look up at the deputy, son," commanded the father.

Harold turned a wet face to Luke. Luke was anxious to hear what he had to say, but he felt awful for the boy. He looked utterly miserable. Luke remembered feeling exactly like that more than once over the course of years, although usually his mortification was associated with hijinks he had exercised on his hapless brothers. Other than keep quiet when he should have spoken, to date he'd done nothing wicked that involved a gold watch and a dead man, but time would tell.

"I didn't find the watch on the church steps," Harold said, his voice hardly above a whisper. He stared at Luke's coat. A furry little head popped up and two black eyes stared back at Harold.

The boy had Luke's undivided attention.

"Tell the deputy where you found it," said Octavius, prodding the reluctant miscreant.

There was a long, pregnant pause.

"I found it ... I found it ..."

Octavius tightened his grip on the boy's shoulder.

The boy got the message. "I found it in the cemetery," he said all at once.

"And what were you doing in the cemetery?" said Octavius.

Another long pause. "Shooting rocks at head stones," said the frightened child. His voice cracked as he spoke and he started to cry again.

"And why didn't you tell the deputy the truth, Harold?"

The boy's chest heaved.

"Look at the deputy, Harold."

The boy looked up at Luke. "Because I didn't want you to find the owner."

Luke squatted then, still cradling the puppy in his coat, to look at the boy face to face. "Where in the cemetery, son? Where exactly did you find it?"

"On the ground."

359

"Harold, the deputy wants the truth." Octavius grabbed the child by the chin and forced him to look up into his face. "I'll double your whipping if you don't tell Deputy Davies exactly where you found that watch."

"That is the truth, pa. I found it on the ground. I saw the gold chain sticking out by that German lady's grave, and I pulled it, and up came the watch."

Luke hardly heard the child. He had stopped listening. While Octavius handed his son a handkerchief, Luke stood and turned, stroking the puppy through his corduroy coat and gazing silently toward the eastern edge of Buffalo, where Main Street ended and the short ride to the church began.

Chapter Twenty-Six

"Mrs. Rose, looky," Ben Slocomb said, his arm gesturing west.

Lenora clutched the wire handle of the egg basket at her side and shaded her eyes with her free hand, looking westward to the Big Horn Mountains. Two men on horseback, possibly more—it was hard to tell from the distance and the angle—were riding toward her ranch. The early morning sun shed dazzling white light over the frosty prairie, making the riders appear more shimmery than distinct.

"They don't look like they're in a hurry. Probably not Indians," said Ben, shading his eyes too and squinting.

"No," agreed Lenora, her eyes trained on the riders. "I'm going to fetch James' rifle, his Colt too, just the same."

"Bring the rifle out to me, Mrs. Rose. You

stay in the house with the Colt."

Lenora nodded and walked quickly toward
the house. In less than a minute she returned with
her Sharps and a leather pouch of ammunition,
both of which she thrust into Ben's hands. She
lingered a moment longer to scrutinize the riding
party, but the horsemen were still too far away to
make out.

"Best get inside now. I'll talk to 'em for
you, Miz Rose."

Lenora thanked Ben and hurried to the
house. She felt uncomfortable leaving one so
young as Ben outside, alone, to meet the
strangers. But it wouldn't do to endanger her
unborn child. Once inside she started to bolt the
front door then thought better of it. Ben might
need to get inside quickly to defend himself. She
moved to the bedroom window, still gripping the
Colt, watching the dark blot to the west slowly
become larger and more distinct, though she still
could not identify the riders.

As she gazed across the prairie at the
horsemen, a thought seeped like ice water into
her mind, chilling her to the bottom of her soul.
She'd stood at this same window more than six
months ago, watching horsemen approach her
property bearing the worst news of her life. As
the memory washed over her, strangely, no tears
threatened. Instead, a squeezing sensation bore
down on her chest and she felt sick to her
stomach. She gripped the window sill to keep

from collapsing onto the floor.

Still clinging to the window sill for support, she saw Ben walk around the corner of the house, evidently having decided it was best to take the lead and walk out to greet the visitors. As she watched Ben approach them—she could see now that there were four riders—one of the forward men dismounted, handed his reins to another rider, and started walking toward Ben. When she saw Ben reach out and shake the man's hand, some of the tension drained from her. Ben talked with the tall man but she did not recognize him. After a few minutes Ben took the reins of the man's horse and began to lead it away, the three other riders following. The tall man started on foot toward the house.

Feeling more at ease but full of wonder, Lenora sat down on the edge of the bed to ease her roiling stomach. When the sickness passed she got up again, looked into the mirror above the dresser and smoothed her hair, and then removed her big work apron. She placed the Colt back in her underwear drawer where she had taken to storing it since James disappeared. She was covering up the gun with lacy underthings when she heard a loud rap rap rap in the front room.

#

"Deputy Davies," said Lenora as she opened the door, its hinge creaking from the cold. "I am so surprised to see you. We thought you would be delayed indefinitely at Fort Laramie."

"Ma'am," said Luke, touching the tip of his hat. "I had business to take care of here in Buffalo."

"Yes," said Lenora, absently, incredulous that Deputy Davies was actually standing on her front porch. Somewhere in the back forty of her mind she realized that Ben and the others were nowhere in sight. She perceived, as if she were outside herself watching this scene instead of participating in it, that something very dramatic was about to take place.

Luke paused, looking somber, eyes filled with pain. After an awkward second he spoke. "We found your husband's body, Mrs. Rose. Could you please come out? To the porch?"

Lenora nodded mutely. She shut the door, walked to the bedroom and picked up the gray woolen shawl that she had thrown on the bed in her haste to retrieve James' Colt. She wrapped it around her shoulders and returned to the front room. She opened the front door feeling as though she were moving through a dream. Luke stood politely by, waiting for her to seat herself on the backless bench. Once she was seated he sat down beside her. He removed his hat and held it, his elbows on his knees. He was sitting so close that Lenora could smell the woodsy smoke of evening campfires that clung to his thick corduroy coat and brown pants. She had foreseen this moment a thousand times in her dark imaginings. Now that it was here, she was beset by an otherworldly calm, though her physical senses were sharpened by the knowledge of his nearness. All was still. The ice blue chambray skirting of her dress flowed around the bench like a frozen waterfall.

"Someone murdered your husband, Mrs. Rose," Luke began, turning to Lenora and looking into her eyes. "We found his body buried in Christian Ebenezer's cemetery. He had been shot through the head. Based on the condition of the body, we figure he was killed the night he left or very near that time. Whoever did it hid his body in Aleida Aeschelmen's grave."

"She died only two weeks before he went missing." Lenora's voice was barely audible, as if she spoke from someplace deep inside herself.

"Someone took advantage of the ground being broken up, the grave being new and all. Yesterday me and Cyrus, Reverend Thomas, and Octavius Dunn, we started digging. His body was lying on top of her casket. No one could have known just by looking that there were two bodies buried in there."

"How can you be certain it was my husband?"

"Cyrus and Reverend Thomas recognized the clothes, boots too. And this." Luke reached into his pocket. When he pulled out his hand again he opened his palm. In the center was a small gold ring.

Lenora reached out and took it. She looked at the ring a few seconds, closed her hand around it, and let both hands fall to her lap softly, defeated. After a few seconds of tense silence, she seemed to come back to the moment. She turned to Luke.

"If there was no evidence to see at the cemetery, how did you know to dig there?"

Luke's head fell then, his gaze turning from her face to his knees. Slowly he put a hand into his coat pocket and pulled out the gold watch. With his other hand he took one of hers and placed the watch in it, closing his hand over hers and holding it gently. Then he looked into her wondering eyes.

"Mrs. Rose, I have to ask you to forgive me. Octavius Dunn's little boy found this watch two months ago. He brought it to the office. Told me he found it at the church. Cyrus and I looked all over the church grounds for anything that might lead us to the body. We found nothing, but that's no excuse for not bringing you this before now."

"I don't understand."

Luke swallowed. "I figured you'd be awfully upset to see this. It bothered me to think you were still grieving over him. I shouldn't have kept it back."

Lenora pulled her hand away from his and lifted the watch near her chest, turning it over in her hand. She opened it, ran her fingers along the smooth round edge of the glass face. After a few seconds she shut it with a click and turned back to Luke.

"I wish you had shown me this before now, Deputy Davies," she said softly. "His grandfather gave it to him. He was his grandfather's namesake, you know. He was closer to his grandfather than his own father. If I'd known you had this, I would have known with certainty that my husband was dead. James would never have parted with it." There was no anger in her tone, only poignant regret.

Luke shut his eyes and sighed. "I've been very selfish. I am very sorry," he repeated. "This has cost both of us, but mostly you."

Lenora put her hand on top of his. "I forgive you," she said, and then she removed her hand.

Luke nodded a thank-you. They sat in heavy silence a minute, then Luke spoke again. "Yesterday when I rode into town, Dunn met me with his boy. The kid lied about the exact location of the watch because he didn't want us to find the owner. He wanted to keep what he'd found. Earlier he had told me he found it on the church steps. I learned only late yesterday that he found it in the cemetery by Aleida Aeschelman's grave. That's when I figured out where to start digging."

"I see."

A horse neighed from the direction of the

barn, reminding Lenora that Luke had ridden from town with three others. "The other men— who came with you?"

"Cyrus, Octavius, and Reverend Thomas. They're tending to their horses while they wait for me. I told them I wanted to give you the news myself."

"Thank you, Deputy Davies. I appreciate your concern for my feelings."

They sat a while longer in silence, only the occasional rooster's crowing or cow's mooing from the barn interrupting their thoughts. Lenora was surprised at how well she was taking this news. But then, for so long all evidence, or at least what little she had, pointed to this, that James was dead. In a way, Deputy Davies' news was almost a relief, as if today, for the first time in months, she could stop holding her breath.

In the next moment Lenora idly wondered what the men were doing to occupy themselves. Even Ben was intentionally staying out of sight. By now, she surmised, he should be finished with morning chores and mounting his horse to return to his parents' place. Then, in the long silence, after a while she began to wonder why Deputy Davies seemed so absorbed in his thoughts, as if he hadn't said all he meant to say and was reluctant to speak. She decided to break the tension.

"Do you have any idea who killed him?"

"No. I have only pieces of the puzzle.

What's more, after seeing where his body was hidden, I've changed my mind about Sam Wright."

"Oh?"

"He's too sick and frail to get a body from the North-East Creek to the church site, then buried. Someone else may have helped him. I can't be sure."

"You think there are two people involved?" Lenora cast about in her mind what such a scenario could mean. She came up blank.

"Either that or Sam had nothing to do with it."

"But why? Why kill my husband?"

"That question will be answered once we find the killer. Cyrus thinks I'm out of my tree, but I've suspected from the first that the killer is the same person who's been bothering you around here." Luke ran his hands through his hair and looked around the yard, sweeping his eyes as though searching for some missed clue. "You told me the trespasser first came around the Sunday night after your husband disappeared, but you didn't come to town with the news till the next day. I've a mind to believe that the person or persons who killed your husband felt safe coming after you because he knew your husband was out of the way—that he was already dead. No one else knew you were alone."

"But that problem stopped when you locked up Sam."

369

"Someone could be using that fact for his own purposes."

Then, with no preamble, Luke reached for Lenora's hand again. His hand was large and warm, his touch gentle and affectionate as he covered hers. But when he spoke his tone was urgent, laced with intense feeling.

"Mrs. Rose, I once told you that any man would be proud to be the father of your child. I've been thinking since then that maybe I was not plain enough in my speaking."

Lenora's eyes grew wide.

"Your child needs a father, and you'd have fewer problems if you had a husband around. I ask you to let me be that man." Luke took his other hand and placed it under hers. With both of his big hands cupped around her small one, he waited.

Lenora looked down at his hands and then up again, into his face, her eyes soft with affection. She saw love and deep longing, causing a wellspring of sharp, mixed emotions to bubble up inside her. She knew she felt grateful for Deputy Davies' help, and clearly he was fond of her, but did she love him?

"I will consider your offer, Deputy Davies."

"It's Luke."

"Luke," she said. Then she smiled a small, guarded smile.

Luke removed his hands from hers and leaned back a little on the bench. "How did it go with Judge Stillman?"

"It didn't. He was delayed at Fort Douglas. I went to town with Mrs. Nolan to speak to him on the day he was supposed to conduct hearings at Fort McKinney, but he didn't appear. All that angst for nought," she said, shaking her head in remembrance.

"It doesn't matter, anyway. Before God and man, this property is yours now. The government can't take it."

"Almost mine, that is true," though it gave Lenora less comfort than she would have thought, considering the news of her husband she'd just received.

"Speaking of Mrs. Nolan," said Luke, standing to his feet and putting on his hat, "Where is she?"

"In town." Lenora stood then too, facing him.

Something dark flashed in Luke's eyes. "Since when?"

"Yesterday afternoon. I've been doing so well lately that I suggested she take a few days at home. Visit with her son. She didn't argue. Malcolm came for her before supper."

"Lenora," he said, using her given name for the first time. It tasted like a poem in his mouth. "You shouldn't be out here alone. It's not safe."

"You are right. I shouldn't be alone. I shouldn't be a widow, either."

Luke sighed gustily. "I want you to come

371

back to town with us, stay at the Occidental, at least until Mrs. Nolan can accompany you back here."

"I will not leave my ranch." Lenora's tone was controlled, but her mouth tightened into an I'd-like-to-see-you-try-and-make-me straight line.

Luke put his hands on his hips and frowned. "Why? Why do you insist on staying out here alone when there are Indians and cattle rustlers and, if your story is to be believed, trespassers in the night? Everyone who cares about you has tried to talk to you into moving into town but you won't listen. Common sense tells you a woman in your condition needs to be around other people."

Lenora took a step back, abruptly breaking the new aura of intimacy they had enjoyed only moments earlier. "If my story is to be believed? You suggest that I speak less than the truth?"

"I don't suggest anything. Sleeping with a rifle doesn't make a woman safe. You need a man around here."

Lenora bristled. "Deputy Davies," she said, "you made me believe that the notorious criminal you recently incarcerated, your malevolent scoundrel Sam Wright, was the main threat to my well-being. So why shouldn't I send Mrs. Nolan to town for a few days? And besides," she said, her chin tipped in defiance, "I am an independent woman. I do what I think is in the best interests of myself and my child and my ranch without consulting anyone. Now that the evidence is firmly established that my husband is deceased, there is no man on earth that I must seek permission from before I so much as wiggle a big toe."

Luke stared at her blazing eyes. "This independent man is going back to Buffalo," he said, borrowing her argument. "Mrs. Nolan will be here with you by morning."

Lenora opened her mouth to protest, but Luke had already turned his back to her and with long, angry strides, headed for the barn.

Chapter Twenty-Seven

Fully spent from an emotionally draining day, Lenora slid into the oversized tin bathing tub, the warm water covering her softly protruding midsection. A bigger fire than usual hissed in the wood stove, a fire she had assembled to warm the kitchen for a long, Saturday night soak. There was enough oil in the hurricane lamp for one luxurious hour, though the bath water would likely be intolerably cool before the oil ran out, hence the extra wood in the stove. All she needed now was a fizzy bath bomb to scent the water, and tonight's experience would be like the old days in New York. She made a mental note to order a box from Aeschelman's next time she went to town.

She relaxed in the warmth, hands resting fondly on her rounded belly, mulling Luke's proposal. Who would have thought? In the space of a day—no, an hour—James' death had been

374

confirmed and another man had asked for her hand.
Mrs. Nolan was right. A person's circumstances
could change drastically in a single day. Lenora's
had. But to her favor?

It was too much too fast. Did she *love* him?
She certainly was fond of him. Luke was strong,
reliable, and attentive, and obviously he cared for
her. And he was handsome, with broad, manly
shoulders and honest eyes. But, Lenora sniffed, he
was also one more man in her life who presumed
the liberty of telling her what to do. It seemed that
western men were as afflicted with the masculinity
disease as eastern ones. Never mind her superior
education, her good family, her ownership of a fine
ranch *that she hadn't lost* or even all the practical,
ranchlike things she'd learned to do since she had
moved to Wyoming Territory, like make jam and
hold a rifle. To these obdurate men she would
always be a delicate female in need of protection.

Lenora glanced down at her swollen belly
thoughtfully, hoping the reality of impending
motherhood would inspire some poignant bubble of
motherly wisdom to rise to the surface of her mind
and guide her. But in the dim cast of the oil lamp
and wavy refraction of the bath water, the hard
round lump that impeded her movement more every
day inspired only a bone-deep sense of fatigue.

"Should I marry him, *mon petit bonbon?*" she
said, patting her rounded belly, "Would you like
Mr. Luke for a papa? I do think I'm falling in love
with him, sweet one."

She sighed deeply. The warm water felt soooo good. With the coziness of the nearby wood stove and the crackle of the fireplace in the front room creating a sleepy backdrop to the drama that played across her mind, it was not long before exhaustion overtook her. In fifteen minutes she was fast asleep, her hands still protectively around her belly, cradling her little bonbon.

#

Lenora awoke in confusion. She blinked and shook her head, trying to clear her mind. As she glanced around the darkness in an effort to comprehend where she was and why she was sitting in cold water, it dawned on her: she was still in the tub and the oil had run out in the lamp. How long had she been sleeping? It felt past midnight. Shivering and feeling foolish, she clumsily pushed herself into a standing position and, feet still in the tub, reached for the towel she'd left on a nearby kitchen chair. As her hand touched the rough cotton, she heard someone step onto the front porch. She froze, her fingertips dripping motionless on the towel, goose bumps covering every inch of wet skin. The intruder took a few more steps, and then she heard the sound of the door latch being pulled. Every muscle in her body went rigid with cold, heart-stopping fear.

Before she could think of what to do, she heard the sound of someone running and then a violent thud as the runner bounded onto the porch.

"Stop it right there, Jennings!" a man shouted. "It's aimed at your head!"

Jennings? Lenora began to shake involuntarily as she heard the sickening thud of a body being slammed against her front door.

"Where'd you hide the body?" a man shouted. *Luke?*

Then a hard, muffled *whump* as someone's head was rammed against the door. In a panic, Lenora threw the towel around her naked body and ran to the bedroom, dripping and cold, to get her handgun. She should have dashed for the rifle over the door, but her first instinct was to run away from the noise, not toward it. From the front of the house she heard angry shouting.

"Where? Where is it?"

Lenora was certain now. Luke was on her porch with another man, surely Buck Jennings.

"What are you talking about?" snarled Jennings.

"You know who I'm talking about," said Luke with equal venom. "You tell me where you hid Rose's body or I'll blow a hole in your head bigger than that bragging maw of yours. Now tell me!"

Another unnerving *whump* against the unyielding plank door. Lenora's entire body shook with raw terror, a core deep shaking that was heightened by the cold. But the nearness of the two men made her keenly aware of her nakedness, superseding her fear of the violence on the porch. She jerked open a drawer and felt around for a

377

CRAZY *Woman* CREEK

nightgown. When her fingers recognized soft flannel she yanked it, threw it over her head, grunting and pulling awkwardly against the cotton that dragged against her wet skin. Feeling less vulnerable now that she was covered, she opened her underwear drawer and grappled in the dark for the Colt. Once her fingers felt the cold, hard muzzle, she picked it up and walked hesitantly to the door of her bedroom. But even with the gun in her hand, she was too petrified to step beyond the door frame into the front room.

Her breathing was fast and furious as she listened in terror, the scene playing out on the porch etched like acid on her mind. She could feel the tension building outside as palpably as the cold wood floor beneath her feet. She held the Colt with two wobbly hands, aiming at the door. From the porch she heard the click of a trigger followed by a long, strained silence.

"There's a lower place in Hell reserved for creatures like you."

Lenora imagined Luke's face up close as he growled at Jennings.

"You jackass," said Jennings.

In the next instant Lenora heard the tell-tale sound of a man hawking in his throat, then an ugly splooth as someone—she imagined it was Jennings—used spittle to provoke. She waited for an explosion of male outrage, but none came.

"I may be a jackass," said Luke, "but I'm a jackass with a gun, and it's aimed at your neck. I'd blow your brains out, but there's no use shooting where there's no target." A skull slammed against the door a third time. "Where's his body?" Luke was shouting now.

Another taut silence. Lenora involuntarily tensed her chest muscles so hard that her diaphragm ached. Finally she heard Jennings speak, all bravado drained from his voice. He sounded pinched, as though Luke had gripped his throat and was squeezing his airway.

"He's buried in that German woman's grave. Next to the church."

"Down! Get down!"

Luke sounded positively wild to Lenora, and in a second she heard Jennings slump to the porch floor.

"Lenora," shouted Luke. "Can you hear me?"

"Yes?" Her voice sounded like a kitten's mew, she was shaking so badly.

"Stay where you are until I tell you what to do."

"I will."

He needn't have worried. Lenora was still frozen to the entrance of her bedroom. She heard shuffling, muffled thuds, and obscene curses, the particularly obscene ones belched by Jennings. Several times Luke told him to shut up. After what seemed like a very long time, the disturbing rustling noises stopped.

"Lenora, you can open the door now," said Luke, his breathing ragged.

Lenora pulled the latch and slowly cracked the door, half crazed with fear that this was all a nightmare and that some evildoer pretending to be Luke waited to pounce on the other side of the door. But once she saw him looking down at her, she flung open the door and rushed toward him, still holding the Colt, now aimed straight at Luke's midsection. His eyes got wide and in a swift, practiced movement, for the second time in a matter of months he lunged for her gun and grabbed it from her.

In one breathless moment his arms were around her, holding her tightly to his hard chest. He was damp with sweat despite the frigid night air, but to Lenora he was safety. He was home. He held her for a long while, stroking her hair, neither one speaking, until at last she stopped trembling. Finally he released his hold and pulled her away from him, just far enough to gaze down into her eyes. Seeing the tears streaking her face, he reached into a pocket, drew out a hanky, and handed it to her.

Lenora wiped her face with the hanky and started to speak, but Luke put his finger to his lips and tilted his head to urge her into the house. As she moved toward the door, Lenora glanced at Buck Jennings. Luke had tied him up like a hog going to market, but his hands and feet were roped firmly behind his body instead of in front. He was gagged, and he looked very uncomfortable. He looked mad, too. Jennings glared at Lenora, a look of pure evil that sent shivers up her spine. She started shaking all over again.

Once inside the house, Luke touched Lenora's elbow, guiding her toward the fireplace in the front room where a bank of hot embers threw an intimate red glow over the two of them.

"You alright?" he whispered, gripping both of her shoulders.

"I'm fine," she lied. "What happened?"

He didn't answer. Instead he pulled her to him and bent his head and kissed her, a long, deep kiss, pressing his body to hers firmly but gently, sparking such intense desire in her she felt excited and frightened all at once. She could feel the power of his longing, and it made her knees go weak. She put her arms around his waist and melted into him. Finally he broke away, but he held her firmly, his hands bracing her upper arms.

"I'll explain everything tomorrow. Right now I need two blankets. One for me and one for the snake," said Luke, jerking his head toward the porch. "We'll stay here until daylight, and then I have to get him to town. I'll need your wagon. I'll return it later tomorrow."

"Alright," said Lenora, nodding obediently.

She left him by the fire while she fetched two blankets from the bedroom. He took them and left. An hour later Lenora was still so wound up she could not sleep. She tip-toed to the front room and peered through the window. In the silver-blue shadows of night she saw Luke's blanket-draped silhouette. He sat upright on the bench, eyes open, cold moonlight glinting on the gun in his lap. Buck Jennings lay still and shapeless on the porch floor under the other blanket.

When she awoke the next morning they were gone.

Chapter Twenty-Eight

Lenora was standing in her kitchen peeling potatoes for supper when she heard the sound of horses and a wagon rolling into the yard. She wiped her hands on her apron and then hung it on a hook. Luke had said he would return her wagon today, so she was ready for company. She wore the dress he said he liked so much, her striped white-and-pink gown with the dainty pink flowers. But now it was altered where she had let out the tucks in front to make room for her expanding girth.

Lenora knew Luke would unhitch her horses and secure the wagon before he knocked on her door. She waited a while in the house, allowing him time to set everything in order. By the time he emerged from the barn she was waiting for him on the porch, wrapped in her emerald-green cloak. The sky was heavy and still, a thick, unbroken blanket of gray that stretched as far as the eye could see, a sure sign of impending snowfall.

Luke saw her waiting as he emerged from the barn. He smiled. "Let's walk. We'll be warmer that way," he said. He extended his hand to her, and with her warm hand in his cool one together they began walking toward the open prairie. "I promised you an explanation," he started.

"Indeed. I'd like to know how it was that both you and Buck Jennings were on my property last night. I have enough troubles," she said, glancing down at her rounded belly hidden beneath her cloak. But she smiled as she spoke, making light of the situation.

"I'm sorry you had to be there for the worst of it," said Luke. "My whole point in coming back last night was to keep you out of it.

"After I left here with Cyrus and the others, I decided to pay a visit to the Slocombs. I needed to talk to Ben. So I left the others and turned my horse toward their place. Mrs. Slocomb invited me to stay to dinner. Seeing that it was late and I was hungry, I stayed."

They reached the end of the cleared portion of land around the house. They slowed their steps as they began to make their way through tall dry wheatgrass, which rustled pleasantly as they walked.

"Once I was back on my horse and headed for town, I had a real bad feeling, uneasy like. It was the strongest sense of unease I've ever known, like a voice in my head that wouldn't quit until I turned my horse back toward your place."

Lenora's face grew ashen, remembering the evil in Buck Jennings' eyes. "You waited in the barn, didn't you?"

"I did." Luke stopped walking and turned to face Lenora. "I kept thinking about the coincidences, how you were never bothered by a trespasser whenever Mrs. Nolan was with you, how someone started creeping around your property before the news of your husband's disappearance had made its way around town. And then it all made sense. Jennings is gone from the Buffalo area much of the time. And he's the meanest son of a—" Luke paused abruptly. "Forgive me, Lenora, but that snake has been holding a grudge against your husband and everything he owns, including you, for a long time."

Lenora looked puzzled. "What do you mean?"

"After I turned Jennings over to the provost marshal at Fort McKinney, we finally got what we needed from him." Luke took both of Lenora's hands in hers. His eyes darkened and he looked very serious. "The night your husband disappeared, he was mighty mad, wasn't he?"

Lenora cast her eyes to the ground in shame. Luke didn't insist on a response.

"According to Jennings, James found him wandering somewhere on your property. We figure your husband mistook Jennings for a cattle rustler.

Jennings was so drunk he didn't even know where he was."

Lenora nodded sadly in acknowledgment.

"That's the only part of his story I have no trouble believing. Jennings says your husband insulted his mother and they started wrangling. He claims he shot your husband in self-defense."

Lenora looked up again. "James was unarmed."

"He says your husband went for his throat."

"Everyone knows my husband was small of stature, especially compared to Mr. Jennings."

"I know. I helped dig up his body."

Lenora shut her eyes at the mention of her husband's decayed remains.

"I'm sorry to bring it up again," said Luke.

"That's alright. Some things must be said."

"As for the body, I have plans to come back tomorrow and take you to town to make arrangements," Luke said.

Lenora only nodded. Speaking of the body was too difficult.

"Let's keep walking," said Luke. "It's cold."

A large flock of geese approached then, forming a sharp V in the northern sky. The cacophony caused Luke and Lenora to look up. They walked slowly, watching with casual interest as the honking party flapped its way to the next watery feeding spot.

"I don't understand why he had such a grudge against me," Lenora said, thinking aloud.

"Jennings had nothing against you, or Ulysses for that matter. But whatever happened out by the creek that night made him powerful angry, and he isn't the type to bury the hatchet, not even when it comes to a dead man. He went after you and Ulysses because you belonged to James Rose. I'm surprised you didn't wake up one morning to find your barn burned to the ground."

"After all this time?"

"I told you Jennings is a mean one. And from everything I've heard around town," he paused, "your husband had a temper to match Jennings'."

Lenora nodded soberly. There was no use trying to deny James' proclivity to anger.

"It was just bad luck that Buffalo's two angriest men, one blind drunk, crossed paths in the night with no witnesses around. And Lenora," Luke said, "Jennings is dishonorable as well. His intentions toward you were of the basest sort."

Lenora's eyes grew wide with understanding. What if Luke hadn't spent half the night waiting in her barn? She swallowed. "But my dog?"

"That's just stupidity in boots. Either he killed Ulysses because his barking thwarted his evil plans toward you, or he took his anger out on Ulysses just for the hell of it. I first thought of Jennings when I saw the carnage in the barn loft, though I didn't have enough clues then to see the whole picture."

"Luke, would you really have shot him last night if he hadn't given you the information you wanted?"

"Did you think I would?" He gave her a sidelong glance.

She paused to think before answering. "Yes."

"Jennings thought so, too, though fortunately for us, he hadn't yet heard that we'd dug up the body, or he might not have implicated himself."

They walked along, holding hands in silence a while longer, enjoying the quiet intimacy of empty prairie. Then Lenora remembered Sam Wright.

"Does this mean you'll set Sam free?"

"Don't know. I don't think he had anything to do with your husband's murder. But I suspect he knew that Jennings was involved. I questioned Sam again this morning before I left town. He said that Jennings had spouted off in the past about your husband. Apparently James was less than polite when Jennings came asking for work."

"I didn't know that Mr. Jennings had ever approached James about a job."

Luke nodded. "I got the feeling this morning that Sam was in sympathy with Jennings. He didn't seem surprised, either, when I told him that Jennings had been arrested. Sam's crime is that he didn't tell us what he knew."

"I see."

"Lenora," said Luke, stopping to face her again. He took both of her hands in his own and pulled them to his chest, warming them. They stood intimately close, all around them the stillness of the open prairie the only witness to this moment. A large, lone snowflake fell from the sky, landing on

Luke's shoulder. His eyes were intense, almost pleading when he looked into hers. "You told me you would consider my request. I know it was a long night and you've had little time to think about it, but you aren't going to send me back to Fort Laramie wondering where I stand with you, are you?"

Before Lenora could answer, several more lacy snowflakes, so large they seemed like feathers, fell from the sky. She removed one hand from his and gently cupped it around his face. His cheek was ruddy with cold but his eyes were warm and sparkling with affection. "I will marry you, Luke." And then she added, softly, "I love you."

"I love you, Lenora."

He kissed her then, his soft lips pressed against hers with tender feeling. That same sense of headiness Lenora had felt in front of her fireplace in the night washed over her, leaving her breathless. When she opened her eyes, snowflakes were falling thicker and faster, wetting her hair. She hardly noticed.

"I'll need thirty days of mourning," she said, pulling away from him a little. He kept his arms around her waist, shielding her a little from the cold.

"I understand. I can wait, but it won't be easy," and he kissed her again.

Just then the puppy woke up and began to wiggle. Luke put his hand into his coat and brought up the furry bundle, cradling him with one hand on the outside of his coat.

"He's for you."

"Oh, he's beautiful!" she said, stroking his tiny head with two fingers. The puppy yawned and stared wide-eyed at Lenora.

"I bought him at Laramie. He's not your Ulysses, but he could learn to be a good companion."

"Thank you. I love him already," she said. Then, "Luke, would you care if I wore daffodil silk for the wedding?"

Luke raised his eyebrows. "Daffodil?"

"It's a brilliant sort of yellow."

"Is that what independent women wear to get hitched these days?"

Lenora laughed. "I wouldn't know. An independent woman is not a slave to fashion." Then more soberly she said, "When must you return to Fort Laramie?"

"Never."

"Pardon me?" Lenora's face screwed up into a question mark.

Luke reached into his coat pocket and pulled out a folded piece of paper, holding it out before her. "This was waiting for me at Fort McKinney when I brought Jennings in this morning," he said. "Sheriff Clarke hired my brother Matt to replace me."

Lenora's mouth fell open in surprise. "How did you manage that?"

"I told Matt he should apply for the job. That other fellow Clarke hired injured himself someplace between Collins and Laramie. It'll be a while before he's good for anything."

"That's very sad."

"Sort of. Made Matt happy enough. He couldn't wait to get deputized."

"Why?"

"I told him about all the beautiful women who throw themselves at a badge."

About the Author

Ginny Welch was raised in Santa Clara, California, where she earned a Bachelor's in English. She married and moved to northern California where she earned a Master's in communications at California State University, Chico and where she was first paid for her writing: $25 for a two-page magazine article on how to get a permanent job through temporary work. Since those early days she has worked as a newspaper (foods and politics) writer, book editor, proposal writer and editor, and freelancer—moving around the United States as she followed her husband's job transfers. She has four grown children and now resides in Virginia. *Crazy Woman Creek* is her second novel.

Virginiahullwelch.com

Please leave a review on Amazon:

Click Here to Review Crazy Woman Creek

Other Books by Virginia Hull Welch

The Lesson, inspirational romantic comedy based on a true story
What to Do When the Blessings Stop, nonfiction
The Hiss from Hell Only Women Hear, nonfiction, coming winter 2018

I love hearing from my readers. You can contact me at:
Virginia Hull Welch - Author - Home

www.ingramcontent.com/pod-product-compliance
Lightning Source LLC
Chambersburg PA
CBHW031418240626
47154CB00001B/98